# The Last Dreamweaver

## THE DREAMER SAGA, BOOK ONE

E.M. LUCAS

GOLDEN THREAD PUBLISHING

# Contents

# Acknowledgements

Writing a book is never a solitary journey, and I have so many people to thank for their support along the way.

To my incredible beta readers—Dean, Holly, Alix, Lakin, and Jessica—your feedback and insights helped shape this story into what it is today.

To my editor, Fay, thank you for your sharp eye and thoughtful guidance, which made this book stronger in every way.

To Dean and everyone at OSW, your creativity and support mean the world to me.

To Gray, whose beautiful maps brought this world to life—thank you for your artistry and dedication.

To my mother, who has always told me I can do anything—your belief in me has been a foundation of my confidence and perseverance.

And to my wife, Cayci—your unwavering support, your belief in me, and your gentle nudges to finish this book mean more than I can ever say. Thank you for being my constant.

*For Evie and Maddie—may your dreams become reality.*

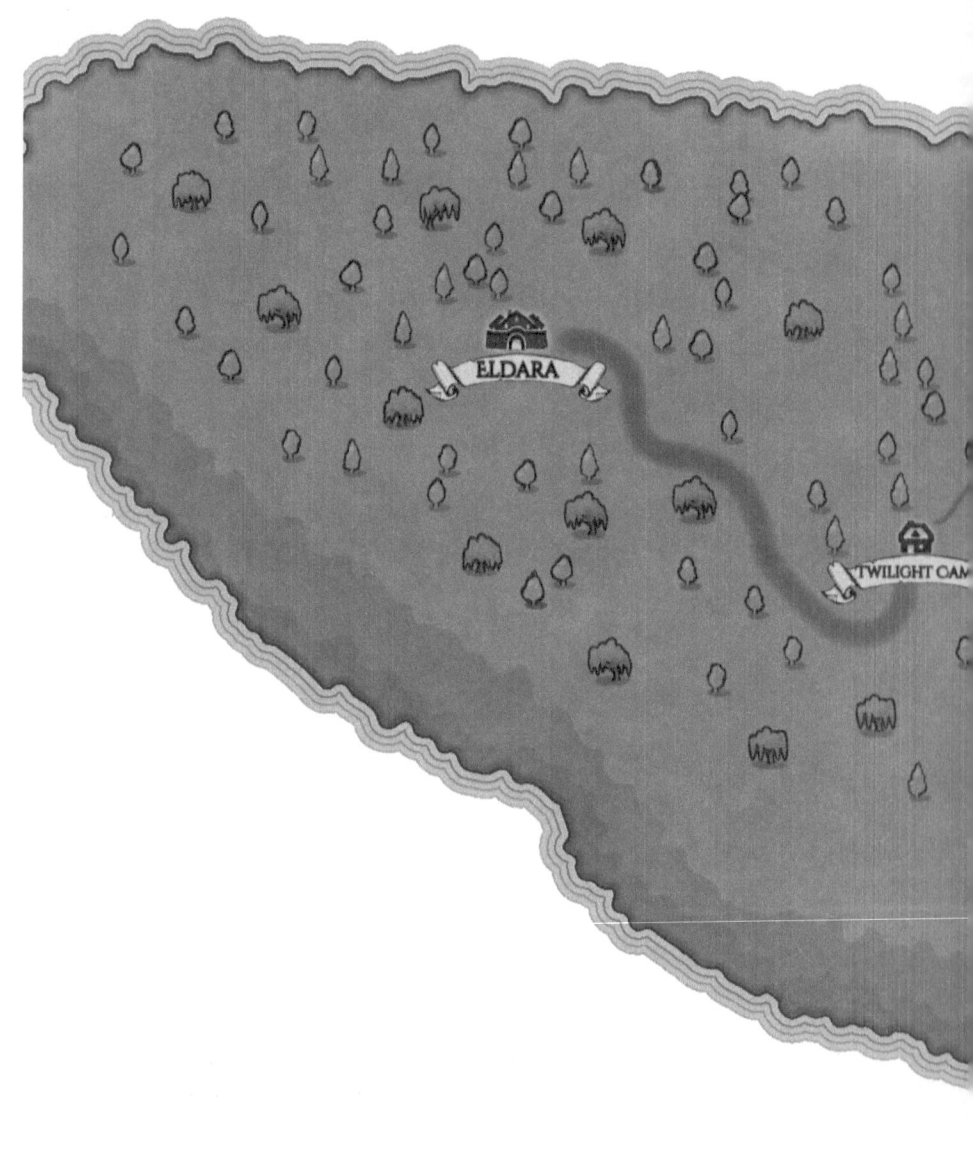

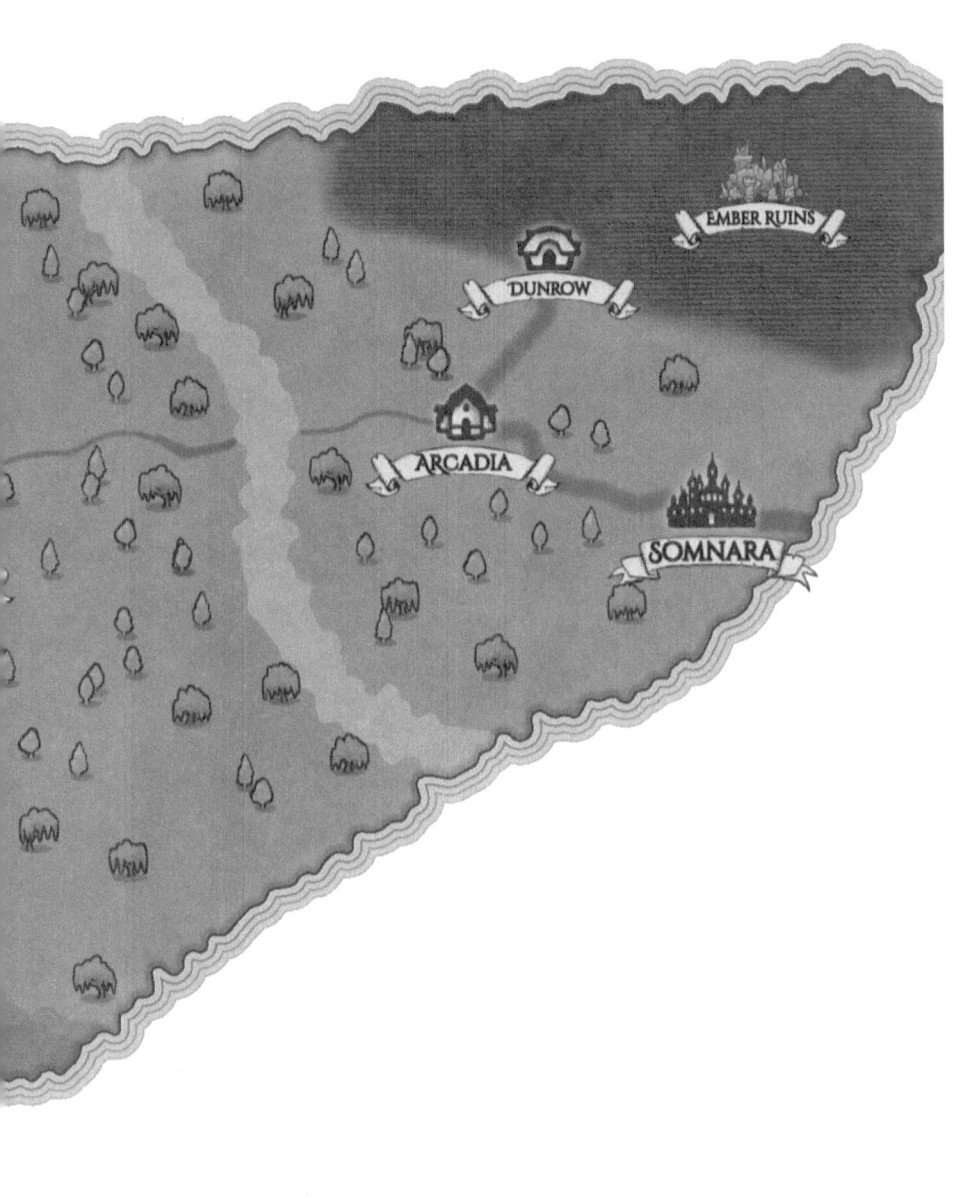

# Dreamweaver

A strange light pierced Liora's dreams, yanking her awake. Her cottage bedroom glowed with unnatural light filtering through gnarled branches. The pulsing radiance cast shadows on her quilt, too bright for moonlight, too golden for dawn.

She sat up dizzy, fighting sleep's fog. The light beckoned with an energy that raised her arm hair. She strained to distinguish whispers from rustling leaves as the glow intensified.

Leaves and twigs snapped under her bare feet as she left her cottage. Her heart pounded with each step into the forest. Though logic urged retreat, something deeper drew her into the darkness.

The light transformed into something vaster, more significant. Liora looked up through the canopy, her breath catching.

The twin moons of Somnus hung suspended in the star-strewn sky, their silvery faces sliding into perfect alignment with the sun. As they merged, an otherworldly twilight descended over the forest. The air itself seemed to thicken, heavy with possibility and ancient magic that made Liora's skin tingle. An Eclipse of Dreams - but that was impossible. The celestial event only occurred once a century.

Power thrummed through the earth beneath her feet, rising up through her bones like lightning seeking ground. The stone's glow intensified in response, its light now almost blinding. Liora's head spun as unfamiliar sensations crashed over her - the dreams of every sleeping creature in the forest suddenly pressing against her consciousness.

The whispers grew louder, more insistent. They were no longer formless sounds but words, though in a language Liora didn't recognize. Her heart hammered as the Eclipse's shadow deepened, transforming the familiar woods into something alien and dangerous. Whatever was happening, she knew with bone-deep certainty that nothing would be the same after this night.

The familiar paths she'd walked since childhood seemed transformed. Mist curled around the bases of ancient oaks like ghostly fingers, while the golden light painted everything in otherworldly hues. The trees themselves appeared to shift and sway, though no wind stirred their branches. Had she stumbled into one of her dreams? The boundary between reality and fantasy felt paper-thin.

Her feet carried her deeper into the transformed woods, drawn by an inexorable force she couldn't name. The familiar scent of pine and loam twisted into something sharper, more metallic - like the air before a storm but threaded through with notes of honey and smoke.

Bark scraped against her palm as she steadied herself against a gnarled oak. The texture felt wrong - too smooth in places, too rough in others, as if the tree itself was reshaping beneath her touch. A chorus of night birds erupted overhead, their calls distorted into something that sounded almost like laughter. Or was it crying? The distinction blurred as the Eclipse's power continued to build.

Dead leaves crackled beneath her bare feet, but the sensation rippled up through her body like waves on a pond. Each step sent shivers of awareness through her nerves, as if the forest floor had become a living thing responding to her presence. The rich earth smell grew stronger, earthy and ancient, carrying hints of decay and rebirth that made her head spin.

The whispering voices wove between the trees, accompanied by sounds that shouldn't exist in nature - crystal chimes, distant drums, the singing of steel on steel. Liora's skin prickled as cool mist wrapped around her ankles, its touch both gentle and invasive. The moisture carried traces of something sweet and forbidden, like overripe fruit on the edge of fermentation.

A branch snapped somewhere in the darkness, the sound sharp as breaking bones. Liora spun toward it, her heart hammering against her ribs. The golden light pulsed in response to her fear, casting wild shadows that danced and twisted like living things. More sounds emerged from the darkness - rustling movements, scratching claws, and underneath it all, a deep thrumming that seemed to emanate from the earth itself. The forest was awakening to something ancient and powerful, and she stood at its heart.

Through a gap in the foliage, something caught her eye - weathered stone rising from the forest floor like a forgotten sentinel. As she drew closer, her breath caught. Intricate symbols covered its base, their edges worn smooth by centuries of rain and wind. The markings flickered between molten gold and deep amber, responding to her presence in a way that sent chills down her spine. The stone's power reached for her, ancient and insistent, waiting to be awakened.

Liora's fingers trembled as she reached toward the ancient stone. The markings pulsed brighter with each inch she closed between them, like a living heartbeat responding to her presence. Her skin tingled with anticipation, every nerve ending alive and singing with an energy she couldn't explain.

The stone's surface felt warm beneath Liora's fingertips, like sunlight trapped in rock. Power surged through the contact point, racing up her arm and spreading through her chest in a wave that stole her breath. The symbols carved into the stone blazed brighter, their light seeming to sink into her skin and flow through her veins.

The ground beneath her feet no longer felt solid. Liora's body hummed with energy that made her feel both weightless and impossibly heavy, as if gravity itself couldn't decide what to do with her. Her heart thundered against her ribs in an erratic rhythm that matched the pulsing of the stone's light. Was this what drowning felt like? She gasped for air that tasted of lightning and starlight.

Pain lanced through her head as more visions crashed over her - a desolate landscape of ash, armies clashing beneath a blood-red sky, figures wielding dream-stuff like weapons. The magic burning through her veins felt ancient and wild, untamed power that threatened to tear her apart from the inside. Her fingers refused to release the stone despite her desperate attempts to pull away.

Dark spots danced at the edges of her vision as the power continued to build. The whispers grew to a deafening roar, and Liora's skin felt like it might burst into flames at any moment. Something was changing inside her, fundamental pieces of who she was being unmade and reformed by this ancient magic. The Eclipse's light seemed to pierce straight through her now, turning her bones to glass and her blood to liquid fire.

The connection hooked deep into her chest, as though invisible threads were weaving themselves between her heart and the ancient stone. The symbols carved into its surface burned brighter, their meaning hovering just beyond her grasp. Power thrummed through the connection, raw and ancient, calling to something that had slumbered within her all along.

Golden light erupted from beneath her palm, so brilliant it turned the night to day. The forest held its breath as the power built to a crescendo, reality bending around her like a bow drawn too tight. Through it all, one truth blazed in her mind with crystal clarity - this was no accident. The stone had been waiting for her, and her alone.

The power surged beyond her control, no longer a gentle current but a crushing wave that threatened to sweep her consciousness away. Liora's legs buckled as golden light poured from the stone, through her arm, and into her chest. The forest spun around her, trees blurring into streaks of shadow and starlight.

The connection between her and the stone stretched like a thread pulled too tight. Her fingers refused to release their grip even as the world tilted and warped. The whispers in her mind crescendoed into a roar, fragments of ancient voices crying out in languages she'd never heard. Was this how it ended - consumed by whatever power she'd awakened?

Darkness swallowed Liora as her knees hit the forest floor. The golden light from the stone pulsed through her veins, each beat revealing flashes - visions, memories, and everything in between. Her muscles seized as the visions crashed over her like waves in a storm.

A grand city of gleaming spires stretched before her - Somnara, though she'd never seen it before. The buildings warped and twisted as dark tendrils of corrupted dream-magic wound through the streets. At its heart stood a figure wreathed in shadow, his crown of twisted metal reflecting the blood-red sky. His presence sent ice through her veins even in this vision-state.

Bodies lay scattered across a battlefield, their dreams forever silenced. Among them stood familiar faces she had yet to meet - a silver-haired man with kind eyes, a young rebel with a crooked smile, others whose names hovered just beyond reach. Their fates intertwined with hers in a tapestry of destiny she couldn't yet comprehend. The scene shifted, showing her these same people gathered around a campfire, their faces illuminated by hope despite the darkness pressing in.

The twin moons aligned once more, their light painting the world in shades of twilight. Power surged through the air as reality itself began to fray at the edges. She saw herself standing before the dark figure, raw magic crackling between them as the fate of Somnus hung in the balance. But was she strong enough to face him? The doubt tasted bitter on her tongue even as the vision faded.

The forest floor beneath her feet dissolved into mist, leaving her floating in a void filled with dancing symbols and echoing voices. The stone's markings burned themselves into her mind, each one carrying weight and meaning she couldn't grasp. Through the chaos, a single word repeated itself, growing clearer with each echo: Dreamweaver.

Her body felt impossibly light, then crushingly heavy. The void collapsed inward, compressing time and space until nothing remained but darkness and the thundering of her own heartbeat. Liora tried to scream but found no air in her lungs, no way to voice the terror clawing at her throat as everything she knew unraveled around her.

Cold air shocked her system as her eyes flew open, lungs heaving desperately. Her quilt lay twisted around her legs, damp with sweat. Moonlight filtered through her window - ordinary, silver moonlight, not the golden radiance that had filled her vision moments before. But the phantom sensation of power still hummed beneath her skin, and when she pressed her trembling hand to her chest, her heart raced with the memory of ancient stone and whispered prophecies.

***

The cottage floorboards creaked as Liora paced, the dream's power still thrumming through her. Sunlight caught dust motes stirred by her movement while her fingers traced patterns, leaving trails of fading golden sparks.

The smell of fresh bread from the village bakery drifted through her open window, a reminder that life continued as normal despite the unsettling visions that haunted her. She needed to head to the mill soon - Bennet would be waiting. But the weight of the dream pressed against her chest, making even simple tasks feel monumental.

Her hands shook while braiding her hair, recalling how golden energy had always sparked at her fingers in quiet moments - tiny flashes when she laughed, warmth in her palms while tending Gemini's herbs. Simple magic, easily controlled, nothing like the raw power from her dream.

Bennet's warnings echoed in her mind as she gathered her work apron. "Keep it hidden," he'd always said, his weathered face creased with concern. "There are those who wouldn't understand." She'd learned to suppress the magic, to contain the warmth that threatened to escape her hands in moments of intensity. But after her dream, that restraint felt fragile.

Golden sparks crackled between her fingers as she tied her apron. The rough cotton anchored her to reality while memories of the dream tugged at her - that forest stone's whispers and the dark power flowing through her veins felt nothing like her usual small magics.

The walk to the mill loomed impossibly far. Each step toward Bennet and the safe routine of daily life felt treacherous. The power humming beneath her skin might burst free at any moment. Her fists clenched white-knuckled, fighting to contain the threatening golden light.

Through her window, she watched the village stirring - merchants preparing, children playing, the blacksmith at work. These people had sheltered her despite strange happenings. The thought of endangering them made her sick with worry.

The path to the mill gave no solace. As Liora walked, her mind fixated on the ancient stone's symbols. Each step intensified the energy under her skin, as if the dream had roused something permanent.

A crow's cry jolted her from her thoughts. It circled above, its shadow dancing like an omen. More crows joined, their wings dark against the pale sky. Their unusual flocking unsettled her. The energy sparked beneath her skin, threatening gold light from her fingers. She buried her hands in her apron, walking faster. The mill loomed ahead, but stood eerily quiet - no smoke, no turning wheel.

At least she could tell Gemini. Her friend listened without judgment when hiding became too much. Unlike Bennet's caution, Gemini saw beauty in Liora's gift, even if they didn't understand it.

The mill's rhythm normally steadied her racing thoughts. But today that comfort rang hollow. Golden energy sparked at her fingers as she reached for the door, making her snatch back her hand. Villagers bustled past, caught up in their morning routines. None of them noticed her hesitation, or the way she had to take three deep breaths before attempting to grab the handle again. Their normality felt like a mockery of the chaos churning inside her.

The door swung open before she could reach for it again, revealing Bennet's concerned face. "You're late," he said softly, then paused as he caught sight of her expression. His eyes flickered to her trembling hands, where tiny sparks still danced between her fingers.

Liora quickly shoved her hands into her apron pockets, but not before a nearby child pointed and asked his mother about the "pretty lights." The woman hurried her son along without a second glance, but panic clawed at Liora's throat. She'd never lost control like this in public before. The dream had changed something fundamental within her, and she wasn't sure she could keep it hidden anymore.

Bennet ushered her inside, his calloused hand gentle on her shoulder. The familiar scent of flour and wood smoke clung to his worn work clothes, a comforting constant in her increasingly chaotic world. His silver-streaked hair caught the morning light filtering through the mill's high windows, reminding her how the years had etched deeper lines around his eyes.

Those eyes studied her now with the same patience he'd shown when teaching her to work the mill's complicated machinery. No judgment, just quiet concern that made her throat tight with emotion. He'd been more than just her employer these past years - he'd become the father she'd never had.

His weathered face carried stories in every crease and scar, tales of hard work and harder winters that he'd share during quiet evenings by the hearth. The slight limp in his left leg spoke of an old injury he rarely discussed, though she'd noticed it worsened in cold weather.

His hands never stopped moving as he watched her, measuring grain with the unconscious precision of decades of practice. Those hands had guided hers through countless tasks, had steadied her when she stumbled, had offered comfort when nightmares plagued her sleep. Now they moved with deliberate care, as if he feared sudden movements might startle her.

"The dreams are getting worse." Bennet's words weren't a question. He shifted his weight, favoring his good leg as he moved closer. "Tell me what you saw this time."

The stone's pulsing light flashed through her mind, and golden energy crackled between her fingers in response. A nearby sack of grain toppled, spilling its contents across the wooden floor. Liora jumped back, heart pounding as the evidence of her lack of control spread at her feet.

"There was a stone in the forest." The words tumbled out as she dropped to her knees, desperately trying to gather the spilled grain. "It glowed when I touched it. And now I can't..." Her voice cracked as another spark leapt from her fingertips, scattering more grain across the floorboards.

Bennet knelt and gripped her hands. A jolt passed through her, but the energy remained trapped. "The day I hoped would never come," he whispered, staring past the mill walls. His words sank into her chest - he'd known about this all along.

Boot steps echoed on the wooden porch outside, heavy and purposeful. The sound yanked Liora's attention to the door, her heart stuttering as metal clinked against metal. Bennet's fingers dug into her hands, a silent warning to stay still, to keep the power contained. But the golden light continued to build beneath her skin, responding to her rising panic as the footsteps drew closer.

The door creaked open as Kai, a young bard who did work for Bennet, entered. Bennet's grip on Liora's hands tightened for a moment before he released them, rising to his feet with a barely concealed wince.

"The west wheel's giving us trouble again," Bennet announced, his voice shifting to the no-nonsense tone he used for mill business. "Best we see to it before more grain goes to waste." His eyes met Liora's, carrying an unspoken message - their conversation wasn't over, just delayed.

Liora's fingers still tingled as she followed him through the maze of machinery, the familiar paths now feeling treacherous. Every metal surface seemed to hum with potential energy, calling to the power coursing through her veins.

The broken wheel loomed before them, its massive wooden spokes cracked and splintered. The damage looked worse than usual, with deep fissures running through the aged wood. Flour dust hung thick in the air around it, catching the morning light in ethereal swirls.

Bennet circled the wheel, his experienced eye cataloging each point of damage. "We'll need to replace these three spokes at least," he muttered, running calloused fingers along a particularly nasty split. "The binding's shot too."

Water dripped steadily from the wheel's paddles, each drop echoing in the sudden quiet as the main machinery ground to a halt. The silence pressed against Liora's ears, making the crackle of energy beneath her skin seem deafening in comparison.

"Hand me that mallet," Bennet instructed, pointing to the workbench. Liora reached for it, then yanked her hand back as golden sparks danced across the metal head. The mallet clattered to the floor, its fall echoing through the mill.

Kai stepped forward smoothly, scooping up the tool and passing it to Bennet. His amber eyes flickered between Liora and the scattered sparks fading against the floorboards, but he said nothing.

Liora pressed her trembling hands against her apron, fighting for control as Bennet began removing the damaged spokes. Each strike of the mallet sent vibrations through the floor that seemed to resonate with the energy building inside her.

The wheel groaned as Bennet worked, ancient wood protesting its dismantling. A particularly loud crack made Liora jump, and for a heart-stopping moment, golden light flared around her hands like a beacon. She quickly shoved them behind her back, but not before catching Kai's startled expression.

The wooden floorboards creaked as Kai lingered, his gaze fixed on Liora's hands. Bennet cleared his throat, straightening to his full height despite the twinge in his bad leg. "Kai, fetch some fresh timber from the storehouse. We'll need it for the new spokes." His tone left no room for argument.

A moment of tension stretched between them before Kai nodded, backing toward the door. His footsteps faded into the mill's ambient creaks and groans, leaving behind a heavy silence punctuated only by the steady drip of water from the broken wheel.

"Liora." Bennet's voice softened as he stepped closer, mindful of the golden sparks still dancing around her fingers. "There are those who understand what's happening to you. People who can help." His weathered hand reached for her shoulder but stopped short as the energy flared brighter. "I'll send word today. Just try to stay calm until-"

Without warning, the mill's familiar sounds grew distant, replaced by a high-pitched ringing that seemed to vibrate through Liora's bones. Reality slipped away as the golden energy surged outward. Liora felt herself falling into a void beyond time and space. Bennet's voice faded beneath the rush in her ears as darkness took her.

# Eldara's Mill

The world tilted and blurred around Liora. Reality fractured, shards of consciousness spinning into a void that pulled her deeper, deeper into the recesses of her mind. Colors bled and reformed into twisted shapes, her thoughts scattering like leaves in a storm as the dreamscape claimed her.

The familiar cobblestones of Eldara's village square materialized beneath her feet, but wrong - so wrong. Shadows writhed between the buildings like living things, devouring the warmth she associated with home. The market stalls stood empty and decaying, their cheerful awnings now tattered ribbons that whispered against rotting wood. Even the air felt thick, coating her lungs with the taste of ash and despair.

Row upon row of villagers stood frozen in the square, their vacant eyes reflecting nothing but emptiness. These were faces she knew - the baker who always saved her a sweet roll, the weaver who taught her to mend her own clothes, children who should have been playing chase between market stalls. Now they might as well have been carved from stone, puppets waiting for their master's strings. Their silence screamed louder than any cry for help.

The shadows coalesced, darkness gathering like spilled ink until it took shape. A man emerged as if birthed from the night itself, his cloak rippling with captured dreams and stolen hopes. Dark energy crackled at his fingers as he moved through the villagers, conducting his lifeless orchestra. His power snaked out in midnight tendrils, seizing throats and minds.

Power radiated from him in waves that made the air shimmer and distort, bending reality to his will. Dreams - not the gentle kind that brought comfort in the night, but twisted nightmares that fed on fear - danced at his command. As he turned toward her, his eyes blazed with recognition and cruel intent, and Liora felt the weight of his attention like ice spreading through her veins.

"Such potential, wasted on someone so weak." His voice slithered through the air, each word dripping with contempt. "You will either be my puppet or the one to bring this village to their knees. The choice, dear Dreamweaver, is yours."

Heat built beneath Liora's skin as power surged through her veins. She reached for it, trying to direct it, to shape it into something that could help. But the magic refused to bend to her will. It burst from her in wild, uncontrolled pulses that sent shockwaves through the square.

A blast of raw energy shattered the nearest market stall, sending splinters flying. Another surge cracked the cobblestones, golden light splitting the ground like lightning. The baker's shop erupted in flames as her power lashed out again, the fire spreading faster than natural flames should.

The magic pulsed again, stronger this time, and Liora watched in horror as the village well exploded, raining debris and water across the square. Screams finally broke through the unnatural silence as villagers fled the destruction - her destruction. The man's laughter echoed off the buildings, a sound of pure satisfaction at watching her powers tear apart everything she loved.

The shadow stretched across the cobblestones, growing impossibly large as he advanced. His presence pressed against her mind, a cold weight that threatened to freeze her thoughts. The dreamscape wavered at the edges, buildings and market stalls blurring like a painting left in the rain.

His laughter cut through the chaos, a sound that promised pain and subjugation. The shadow of his cloak reached for her with grasping tendrils, and Liora felt ice spread through her veins. Each attempt to fight back only fed his power, her own magic turning traitor in her hands. The darkness crept closer, threatening to swallow her whole.

Terror clawed at her throat as she watched her wild magic tear through another building, the structure crumbling like a house of cards. Was this her destiny - to destroy everything she tried to protect? The dark man's presence pressed closer, his shadow now a towering wall of darkness that blocked out what little light remained. Her power pulsed again, raw and untamed, and she heard the screams of those caught in its path.

The screams of her people pierced through the chaos, each cry driving daggers into Liora's heart. Through the swirling darkness, she glimpsed Bennet clutching his arm where her wild magic had struck him, his kind eyes now filled with pain and betrayal. The sight sent her stumbling backward, golden energy crackling uselessly at her fingertips.

More faces emerged from the shadows - the baker's children writhing on the ground, their small bodies wracked with the aftermath of her power. The weaver pressed against a crumbling wall, blood trickling from where debris had struck her temple. Each person she'd tried to save now bore the marks of her failure, their suffering a testament to her inadequacy.

The villagers' accusations cut deeper than any physical wound. "You were supposed to protect us," they cried, their voices a chorus of disappointment and fear. A young girl - one who'd once brought Liora flowers - cowered behind her mother, tears streaming down her soot-stained face. The trust in those innocent eyes had been replaced by terror, and something in Liora's chest shattered at the sight.

Golden light continued to pour from her hands despite her desperate attempts to contain it. Each surge brought fresh waves of destruction, fresh cries of pain from those she loved most. Through it all, the shadow's laughter echoed like thunder.

Liora jerked upright, gasping for air as the dream's tendrils released their hold. Her cheeks felt wet, and the lingering screams of villagers echoed in her mind. The mill's familiar creaks and groans anchored her back to reality, but her hands still crackled with residual energy, golden sparks dancing between her trembling fingers.

"Easy there, lass." Bennet's weathered hand settled on her shoulder, steady and warm against the cold fear that gripped her. His touch should have been comforting, but all she could see was him clutching his wounded arm, eyes filled with betrayal.

The magic surged beneath her skin, a tide she couldn't control. It pushed against her restraint, demanding release. Pressure built in her chest, behind her eyes, at her fingertips - everywhere at once. Golden light pulsed through her veins, visible beneath her skin like lightning trapped in glass.

"I can't-" The words caught in her throat as another wave of power rolled through her. The nearest workbench rattled, tools sliding across its surface. Flour dust swirled in impossible patterns, catching the morning light like stars fallen to earth. "Something's wrong. It's too much."

Bennet's grip tightened on her shoulder, but Liora barely felt it. The magic demanded freedom, screaming through her blood like a storm seeking release. Her vision blurred with golden light, and the air around her began to shimmer and twist. This wasn't like her usual loss of control - this was something else entirely, something bigger, darker, more dangerous. And it was about to break free.

***

The magic erupted from Liora like a dam breaking, golden light exploding outward in a devastating wave. The force knocked Bennet backward, his grip torn from her shoulder as he slammed into the far wall. Flour dust ignited in the air, creating brilliant sparks that danced and swirled in a deadly constellation around her. The room filled with an otherworldly hum that set her teeth on edge and made her bones vibrate.

Support beams groaned overhead as her power lashed out, seeking escape through any means possible. The ancient wood, weathered by decades of use, couldn't withstand the onslaught. Splinters rained down as cracks spider-webbed across the ceiling. The familiar scent of sawdust mixed with the sharp, electric tang of untamed magic that poured from her in endless waves.

Tools flew from their hooks, clattering against walls and embedding themselves in wooden posts. A millstone teetered on its mounting, the grinding surface glowing with reflected golden light. Liora tried to pull the power back, to cage it once more within her chest, but it slipped through her mental grasp like water through desperate fingers. Each attempt to control it only seemed to feed the maelstrom.

The mill's structure buckled under the assault, decades-old joints separating with sharp cracks that echoed like gunshots. Debris whirled through the air in a deadly dance - broken boards, shattered glass, and twisted metal all caught in the vortex of her unleashed power. The window frames burst outward, showering the ground below with lethal shards. Through the gaps, morning light streamed in, transformed into sickly golden beams by the energy still pouring from her body.

A support beam snapped overhead with a sound like breaking bones. The roof sagged inward, and Liora's power responded by intensifying, as if sensing the threat to her life. Golden tendrils of energy wrapped around floating debris, transforming simple wood and metal into deadly projectiles that ricocheted off walls and floor. The mill's death throes had become a chaos of splintering wood, shattering glass, and wild magic that threatened to tear the building apart from within.

Liora's gaze darted around the collapsing mill, her heart thundering against her ribs. Shards of wood and metal hung suspended in the air around her, caught in the golden storm of her magic. The familiar walls that had sheltered her for years now threatened to become her tomb. A haunting whisper in her mind wondered if this was how it would end - buried beneath the rubble of her own making.

"No!" The word tore from her throat, raw and desperate. Her outstretched hands trembled as she tried to push back against the chaos. The magic responded with a violent surge, sending another shock wave through the building. Beams groaned overhead, and the remaining windows exploded outward in a shower of glass and splintered wood.

Through the swirling debris, Bennet's figure caught her eye. He pressed himself against the far wall, face pale beneath a coating of flour dust. Their eyes met across the maelstrom, and the fear in his expression cut deeper than any falling beam could. He dove to the side as a section of the roof caved in, rolling behind a stack of grain sacks just as timber crashed where he'd stood moments before.

The impact shook the entire structure. Support beams twisted and snapped like kindling, sending cascades of debris raining down. Golden energy crackled along the falling pieces, transforming them into deadly projectiles that ricocheted off walls and floor. The mill's death throes had become a deadly dance of splintering wood and wild magic that threatened to tear the building apart from within.

Liora stood in the epicenter of destruction, her shoulders shaking with each ragged breath. Shafts of morning light cut through the settling dust, illuminating the devastation around her - splintered beams, crumbling walls, and the precious mill stones cracked beyond repair. Tears carved paths through the flour dust coating her cheeks, each drop carrying the weight of her failure.

Her legs gave out, and she sank to her knees among the wreckage. Golden sparks still danced at her fingertips, mocking her with their beauty even as they reminded her of the chaos they'd unleashed. The remnants of her power hummed beneath her skin like a trapped storm seeking release.

"I... I didn't mean to. It just... happened. I can't control it!" The words tumbled out between sobs, her voice cracking under the strain of contained hysteria. Flour dust swirled around her trembling form, catching the light like fallen stars.

Bennet strode through the debris toward her, his boots crunching glass and wood. Even after the chaos she'd caused, he approached with his usual confidence. His dust-streaked, cut face showed only worry.

"It's not the end of the world, Liora. Mistakes happen, but running won't help."

Her hands curled into fists against the wooden floor, fighting a wave of shame as his gentle wisdom collided with her self-loathing. Destruction surrounded her - broken beams and shattered windows proved how dangerous she was. Golden energy flickered between her fingers, an unwanted reminder that this power lurked inside her, waiting.

Liora's fingers traced the jagged edge of a broken support beam, each splinter a reminder of the destruction she'd caused. The rough wood caught at her skin, but the physical pain felt distant compared to the ache spreading through her chest. All around her, the mill - her sanctuary - lay in ruins because she couldn't contain the power burning inside her.

Through the broken roof, sunlight illuminated her failures: shattered millstones that had served generations, twisted metal gears frozen forever, and Bennet's scattered tools strewn across the floor. Her gaze caught on a small wooden flower she'd carved into one of the posts years ago - now split down the middle, the petals torn apart.

"I should leave." The words scraped past her throat, raw and bitter. "Before I destroy something else. Before I hurt-" She couldn't finish the sentence, her eyes darting to Bennet. The cuts on his face might be shallow, but they could have been so much worse. Next time, her lack of control might not leave anyone standing.

A sob caught in her throat as she stepped backward, nearly stumbling over a fallen beam. The urge to run clashed with her desperate need to stay, to somehow make things right. But the evidence of her destructive nature surrounded her, and each breath drew in the dust of her failures.

Liora stumbled through the wreckage, her boots catching on splintered wood and twisted metal. The destruction followed her like a shadow, each step revealing another piece of her childhood transformed into debris. Golden sparks still danced at her fingertips, refusing to fade even as she fought to suppress them.

A sharp pain shot through her palm, and Liora looked down to find her nails had broken skin. Blood welled up in tiny crescents where she'd clenched her fists too tight, trying to cage the power that refused to be contained.

At the threshold of what remained of the door, Liora paused. Bennet's presence behind her felt like a physical weight, his silence heavier than any words of comfort he might offer. The broken mill wheel lay before her, half-buried in rubble, its ancient wood split clean through. Water still trickled over its splintered surface, each drop catching the light like tears.

The wheel had turned for generations, grinding grain to feed the village, marking the steady rhythm of life in Eldara. Now it lay shattered, just like her illusions of normalcy.

***

Liora trudged through the village, each step heavier than the last. Her heart pounded in her chest. Smoke still tinged her clothes from the fire at the mill, and the scent stung her nostrils with every breath. She pressed a hand against her side, where the edge of a wooden beam had scraped her skin, leaving a searing line of pain.

As she approached the small cottage that Gemini Estelle called home, nestled at the village's edge, Liora hesitated. She didn't want to be here—not like this, not as another burden on Gemini's endless compassion.

The door of the cottage creaked open, and there stood Gemini, her soft eyes widening with concern. "Liora! What happened?" Gemini hurried forward, her gentle hands immediately inspecting the scrapes and burns.

Liora tried to step back, embarrassed and ashamed. "I... I lost control again. The mill—it's in ruins because of me."

Gemini's eyes softened, and she shook her head, guiding Liora inside. "Come on, let's get you cleaned up first." Her tone was soothing, the voice of a healer who had seen more pain than one could bear yet chose to offer solace rather than despair.

The inside of the cottage was a sanctuary, filled with the scent of herbs and the soft hum of nature's enchantment. Drying flowers and bundles of sage hung from the ceiling, and vials of healing tinctures lined the shelves. A gentle fire crackled in the hearth, casting a warm, orange glow over the room.

"Sit here," Gemini instructed, guiding Liora to a wooden chair by the fire. She quickly gathered clean cloths and a bowl of water, her movements efficient yet tender.

As Gemini knelt to clean Liora's wounds, her touch was like the sun warming frozen earth. Liora couldn't help but feel a lump form in her throat. She scanned her friend's face for signs of frustration or judgment but found only unwavering care.

"I didn't mean to," Liora whispered, her voice cracking. "One moment, I was just trying to help fix the mill... and the next, everything was on fire. I don't understand what's happened to me. What if I hurt someone, Gem?"

Gemini's hands paused in their work, her brow furrowing. "I thought you had your powers under better control. What changed?"

The fire crackled, sending shadows dancing across the walls. Liora's fingers twisted in her lap as the memory of the dream flooded back. "There was this stone in the forest. It called to me in my sleep. When I touched it..." She shuddered. "It glowed with this strange light, like nothing I've ever seen. And now my powers are... different. Stronger. Harder to control."

"A glowing stone?" Gemini reached for a jar of healing salve, her movements deliberate as she processed this information.

Liora closed her eyes, trying to recall the details through the haze of memory. "And there was something else - in the dream, I saw an eclipse. The moons aligned perfectly with the sun, and everything felt... charged. Like the air before a lightning strike."

Setting down the jar with a soft clink, Gemini's expression shifted to one of concern. "That's interesting you mention an eclipse. A traveler passed through yesterday, speaking of signs in the sky. He said the Eclipse of Dreams is coming."

The words hit Liora like a physical blow. "The Eclipse of Dreams? But that's just a legend, isn't it?"

"Ten days," Gemini whispered, her voice barely audible above the crackling fire. "The first one in a hundred years. The traveler said Draven is hosting a festival in Somnara for it."

Liora's breath caught in her throat at the mention of Emperor Draven's name. Stories of his cruelty had reached even their remote village - whispered tales of dissidents vanishing in the night, of entire communities stripped of their will through dark magic. The thought of him hosting a festival seemed wrong, like poison masked as honey.

Her fingers traced the edge of the chair, remembering the stories Bennet used to tell. How Draven had risen to power through manipulation and fear, twisting the ancient magic of dreams into something corrupt. The Emperor's influence had spread like a shadow across

Somnus, turning what was once a realm of wonder into a land of carefully measured words and downcast eyes.

Liora's eyes welled up at the thought of the Emperor, and she reached out to grasp Gemini's hands. The physical connection grounded her, making the chaos of her mind feel momentarily bearable.

They sat in comfortable silence for a while, the crackling fire providing a soothing backdrop as Gemini continued to tend to Liora's injuries. The steady rhythm of her friend's presence acted as a salve for more than just her physical wounds; it touched the fractures of her spirit with a tenderness that only true friendship could provide. For in the presence of such unwavering love and support, even the darkest fears began to lose their power.

# Anchored in the Storm

T he flame danced as Liora's fingers skimmed the dresser, throwing shadows on the wall. Dried flowers dangled by her window, their petals evoking memories of meadow days. The golden sparks that had ravaged the mill still tingled under her skin, but darkness dampened their power. For now.

Her collection of river stones - smooth and cool to touch - clinked together as she gathered them from her pockets. The day's work had stained them with dust and debris from the mill's collapse. Each one bore a different pattern, unique swirls that had caught her eye during countless walks along the riverbank. She arranged them on her windowsill, a ritual that usually brought comfort but tonight only reminded her of the ancient stone from her dreams, pulsing with that strange, beckoning light.

The floorboards creaked under her feet as she crossed to her bed, where a worn quilt lay rumpled from her restless sleep the night before. Bennet said it was her mother's, each patch telling a story of their life. The memories woven into its fabric felt like accusations now.

A gust of wind rattled the window pane, making the candle flame dance wildly. Liora's hand shot out instinctively to steady it, but golden light sparked between her fingers unbidden. The flame surged, growing unnaturally bright for a heartbeat before she snatched her hand back, her heart pounding. Even here, in this sanctuary of child-hood memories, her power refused to lie dormant.

Her reflection caught her eye in the small mirror above her dresser - a gift from Bennet on her sixteenth birthday. Shadows played across her face, deepening the worry lines that hadn't been there months ago. The girl who stared back looked haunted, her eyes holding secrets she'd rather forget. Behind her, the dried flowers swayed in another breeze, their shadows painting shifting patterns across the walls like the mysterious inscriptions from the stone in the forest.

The quilt's familiar weight settled around Liora as she perched on the edge of her bed. The broken mill wheel flashed through her mind - the splintering wood, Bennet's narrowed eyes, the surge of power she couldn't contain. Her fingers twisted in the fabric, catching on a loose thread from where the stitching had come undone. Like her control. Like everything else.

Golden sparks danced at the corners of her vision, remnants of power that refused to fade. The same power that had nearly crushed Bennet beneath falling timber. Each time she closed her eyes, she saw it again - the wheel splitting apart, the support beams groaning, the look of concern etched across his weathered face. What if next time she couldn't stop it? What if next time someone got hurt?

Sleep pulled at her consciousness like a current, threatening to drag her under into dreams she couldn't control. What terrors waited in her dreams tonight? The cloaked figure from her nightmares seemed to lurk in every corner, ready to drag her down into darkness the moment she surrendered to sleep. Her power stirred restlessly beneath her skin, responding to her fear.

She lay back against the rough cotton of her pillow, pulling the quilt tight around her shoulders like armor. As exhaustion finally began to win out over anxiety, Liora squeezed her eyes shut and prayed to whatever gods might be listening that tonight, just for once, her dreams would grant her peace.

The world dissolved around Liora, colors bleeding into shadows as reality twisted and warped. The familiar comfort of her bedroom melted away, replaced by the village square - but wrong, distorted, like a reflection in troubled waters. Moonlight filtered through clouds that shouldn't exist, casting sickly shadows that writhed and danced of their own accord.

Villagers stood frozen in grotesque tableaus throughout the square. Martha, the baker's wife, remained suspended mid-stride, her basket of morning bread tipped at an impossible angle. Old Willem hunched over his cane, jaw slack and eyes glazed with an emptiness that made Liora's stomach turn. Even the children stood like painted dolls, their usual laughter replaced by an unnatural silence.

Dark tendrils of dream magic slithered between the villagers' feet, weaving patterns that pulsed with malevolent purpose. The magic felt wrong - corrupted and twisted, nothing like the golden warmth that sometimes sparked from Liora's own fingers. This power reeked of control and domination, of dreams perverted into nightmares.

A figure materialized from the shadows, tall and imposing in flowing robes that seemed woven from darkness itself. It was the dark man from before, but somewhere in her heart Liora knew he had a name. Draven. Emperor Draven.

His presence sent ice through Liora's veins, freezing her in place as surely as if he'd cast his spell upon her too. Power radiated from him in waves that made the air itself shiver.

"Your fear makes you weak," Draven's voice echoed, though his hood remained still.

Liora tried to step forward, to reach out, to do something - anything - but her body refused to obey. The golden spark of her power fluttered weakly within her chest, a candle flame against an ocean of shadow. Martha's empty eyes stared through her, accusing in their blankness.

"I can't let this happen," Liora whispered, her voice breaking. "But how do I stop it if I am the one causing it?" The words tasted like ash in her mouth as golden light began to seep from her skin, responding to her distress. But instead of helping, it seemed to feed the darkness, making the shadows grow deeper.

***

The village square twisted and warped around Liora, reality bending like molten glass. Shadows stretched and writhed beneath her feet, their edges razor-sharp against the sickly moonlight. Her heart thundered against her ribs as the dream pulled her deeper, each breath coming shorter than the last.

Thick, oily air pressed against her skin, coating her lungs with each desperate gasp. The oppressive weight of Draven bore down, crushing hope beneath its terrible presence. Golden sparks flickered at her fingertips, weak protests against the overwhelming darkness.

The villagers stood like abandoned marionettes throughout the square. Martha's eyes stared unseeing past Liora, her basket of bread frozen mid-spill, the loaves suspended in air that had become thick as honey. Old Willem's joints creaked with unnatural angles, his beloved cane now a prop in this twisted theater.

"Their dreams sustain me." Draven's voice rolled across the square like thunder, each word dripping with malice. His dark robes rippled without wind, shadows coalescing around his towering form. "You will as well. It is inevitable."

Bile rose in Liora's throat as rage and terror warred within her chest. Her power surged in response, golden light pulsing beneath her skin. But the magic felt wrong, tainted by her fear, threatening to spiral beyond her control just as it had at the mill.

Draven's hands wove intricate patterns through the air, trailing ribbons of corrupted dream magic. The darkness responded to his touch, twisting into cruel shapes that wrapped around the villagers' throats like nooses. Each gesture was precise, calculated - a maestro conducting a symphony of nightmares.

The air crackled with opposing energies as Liora's golden light clashed against Draven's shadows. Reality fractured along the seams where light met dark, sending splinters of broken dreams raining down around them. Each shard reflected a different horror - herself lost to power, the village in ruins, everyone she loved trapped in eternal nightmare.

"Watch closely," Draven commanded, his hood turning toward her. "See how easily dreams become chains." His fingers clenched into a fist, and the villagers jerked like puppets, their bodies contorting in ways that made Liora's stomach lurch.

Martha's mouth opened in a silent scream as dark tendrils burrowed into her chest. Old Willem collapsed to his knees, but his eyes remained blank, unseeing. The children's faces twisted into masks of terror, yet no sound escaped their lips.

Golden light erupted from Liora's palms unbidden, her power responding to her desperate need to help. But instead of breaking Draven's hold, the light seemed to feed the shadows, making them grow stronger, darker, hungrier. His laughter echoed through the square as Liora's worst fears began to manifest - her power wasn't saving anyone, it was making everything worse.

The golden light pulsed harder beneath her skin, responding to her growing anger. These were her people. Her village. Her home. The power that had terrified her for so long now demanded release, fueled by the need to protect those she loved. Before doubt could take hold, Liora thrust her hands toward the nearest villager.

Light exploded from her palms in blinding streams, far stronger than she'd intended. The golden energy wrapped around Martha first, burning away the shadow-tendrils like morning sun melting frost. But the power didn't stop. It kept flowing, building, spreading beyond her control. The magic pulled at something deep inside her, threatening to tear her apart.

More villagers began to stir, awareness flickering in their eyes as her power broke Draven's hold. But the golden light was changing, taking on a wild, feral quality that made the air crackle and spark. Cracks appeared in the cobblestones beneath her feet, spreading outward like lightning strikes frozen in stone. Fear clawed at her throat - this was exactly what she'd dreaded, exactly why she'd hidden her powers for so long.

The magic surged again, stronger than before, ripping free of her desperate attempts to contain it. Golden waves pulsed outward in devastating rings, shattering windows and sending debris flying. Through the chaos, Draven's laughter grew louder, more triumphant. Her worst fear was coming true - in trying to save everyone, she was becoming the very danger she'd fought so hard to prevent.

Golden energy ricocheted off cobblestones in wild, untamed arcs. The force knocked Martha backwards, her basket splintering against a wall. Old Willem stumbled, his cane clattering across the square as more villagers fell victim to her desperate attempts to help. Each burst of power sent new waves of destruction rippling through the village, transforming her rescue attempt into a catastrophe.

"Such raw potential, yet so utterly wasted." Draven's voice cut through the chaos like a blade into her chest, each syllable confirming her deepest fears - she wasn't their savior, she was their doom.

The magic continued to pour from her hands in violent surges, beyond any semblance of control. Where her power touched the villagers, it shattered Draven's hold for mere moments before his shadows swooped in, dragging them deeper into his influence. Their faces contorted with fresh anguish as his grip tightened, punishment for her failed intervention.

Her heart slammed against her ribs, each beat a desperate protest against the walls of despair closing in around her. The village square warped and twisted, reality bending under the weight of colliding magics. Shadows writhed beneath her feet as golden light continued to burst from her palms in devastating pulses. Just as darkness threatened to swallow her whole-

∗∗∗

Golden light still sparked from Liora's fingertips as she bolted upright, her heart hammering against her ribs. The phantom screams of villagers echoed in her mind, their faces twisted in terror from her uncontrolled magic. Her hands trembled as she pressed them against the rough wool blanket, willing the residual power to fade before it could manifest in the waking world.

Pale sunlight crept through the weathered shutters, casting long shadows across her small bedroom. The familiar sight of her collection of dried wildflowers should have been comforting. Instead, the morning rays transformed innocent shadows into reaching tendrils that reminded her too much of Draven's corrupted magic.

The lingering images from her nightmare crystallized with brutal clarity. Her powers hadn't saved anyone - they'd only amplified the chaos, turning her desperate attempt to help into a wave of destruction. The golden light that burst from her hands had shattered windows, splintered wood, and thrown the villagers she'd tried to protect like scattered leaves in a storm. Her shoulders hunched as fresh guilt pressed down on her chest. What if these dreams weren't just night terrors, but glimpses of what she might become?

Sharp pain shot through her palms. Liora unclenched her fists to find crescent-shaped marks where her nails had once again dug into flesh. The small wounds grounded her in reality, yet even now, she felt the magic stirring beneath her skin, responding to her distress like a wild animal sensing weakness.

The floorboards creaked outside her door - probably Bennet starting his too-early routine at the mill. Liora forced her breathing to slow, pushing the power back down into that dark place she kept it locked away. She couldn't let him see her like this, couldn't risk him realizing just how close to the surface her powers lurked. The memory of yesterday's disaster at the mill was warning enough of what happened when she lost control.

Golden sparks danced across Liora's vision as she pushed herself upright, desperate to shake off the nightmare's grip. The magic surged without warning, crackling through her veins like lightning. A wave of energy burst from her body, slamming into the wooden chair by her bed. The force knocked it backwards, sending it crashing into her dresser. The impact echoed through her small room like a thunder-clap. Her collection of dried wildflowers scattered across the floor, petals crushed beneath the fallen furniture.

Liora lunged forward, arms outstretched as if she could somehow catch the cascade of falling items. Another pulse of power rippled from her fingertips, this time catching her bedside table. The ceramic water pitcher atop it wobbled, then shattered against the floor. Water spread across the wooden planks, soaking the scattered flower petals and turning them into a soggy mess.

The magic wouldn't stop. It coursed through her body in waves, each pulse threatening to destroy something else. Her hands shook as she pressed them against her chest, trying to contain the power threat-ening to burst free. But fighting it only seemed to make it stronger, like trying to dam a river with twigs.

Footsteps thundered up the stairs - Bennet, coming to investigate the noise. Liora's heart seized. She couldn't let him see her like this, couldn't risk him discovering just how dangerous she truly was. The magic pulsed again, stronger this time, and the morning light catching the golden sparks transformed her small bedroom into a chaos of dancing shadows and destructive energy.

The door burst open, wood cracking against stone as Bennet rushed inside. His weathered face fell as he took in the destruction - shattered pottery, scattered flowers, and the golden light still dancing around Liora's trembling form. The magic surged again, sending another wave of energy rippling through the room. A shelf of books teetered pre-cariously on the wall.

"Stay back!" Liora thrust her hands out, trying to warn him away, but the gesture only released another pulse of power. The force knocked Bennet back a step, his broad shoulders hitting the door-frame. Pain and guilt twisted in her chest as she watched him stumble. Even trying to protect him only put him in more danger.

The magic crackled through her veins like lightning, each heartbeat bringing a fresh wave of destructive energy. Golden sparks showered from her fingertips, setting tiny fires in the scattered debris of her belongings.

"I... I didn't mean to. It just... happened. I can't control it anymore." The words caught in her throat as another surge of power rippled outward. The remaining glass in her window cracked, spider-web patterns spreading across its surface. Her hands shook as she pressed them against her chest, trying to contain the wild energy threatening to break free.

The floorboards groaned beneath her feet as the magic pulsed again. Dust and splinters rained down from the ceiling beams, filling the air with a haze that caught the morning light. Through it all, Bennet stood his ground, his presence both comforting and terrifying. If she couldn't get this power under control, he'd be the next thing she destroyed.

Through the settling dust and golden sparks, Bennet inched forward, his weathered hands raised in a calming gesture. His eyes darted between Liora's trembling form and the destruction surrounding them, assessing not just the physical damage but the emotional toll etched across her face. The floorboards creaked beneath his careful steps, each one measured and deliberate.

"You don't have to be afraid of yourself, Liora." His voice carried the same steady warmth he used when teaching her to repair the mill's mechanisms. " But you can't run from what's happening to you. This... gift of yours needs a path."

"It's not a gift." The words tore from her throat, raw and bitter. Golden light pulsed from her hands in response to her rising emotions, sending another shower of sparks cascading across the room. "It's a curse. I don't know how to make it stop."

Liora's shoulders hunched as she tried to make herself smaller, to contain the chaos threatening to break free. But the magic refused to be caged, sparking between her fingers like lightning searching for ground. The destruction around her room stood as testament to her failure to control it.

Golden sparks danced across Liora's vision as Bennet edged closer, his boots crunching over shattered glass. Her heart thundered against her ribs, each beat sending fresh pulses of power crackling through her veins.

"Stay back," she pleaded, but Bennet kept moving forward with the same steady determination he showed when facing down storms that threatened the mill. The magic surged in response to her fear, sending another wave of energy rippling through the room.

The floorboards groaned beneath his feet as he closed the distance between them. Liora pressed herself against the wall, hands trembling as she tried to contain the wild energy threatening to break free. Another shelf buckled, sending books cascading to the floor.

"I've watched you grow up, Li." His voice carried the same gentle tone he used when teaching her to repair complex machinery. "You've never been the type to hurt anyone on purpose. That hasn't changed just because you have this gift."

Fresh tears spilled down her cheeks as she gestured at the destruction surrounding them. "Look what I did to my room. To my flowers. To the mill yesterday. Everything I touch is falling apart."

Bennet knelt beside the remains of her water pitcher, carefully gathering the splintered pieces. His weathered hands moved with surprising gentleness as he collected the fragments. "Things break. We fix them. That's what we do."

The magic pulsed again, but weaker now, responding to the familiar rhythm of his words. Liora's shoulders slumped as exhaustion began creeping in, replacing the wild energy with bone-deep weariness.

"What if I can't fix this?" The question came out barely above a whisper as she stared at her hands, still sparking with golden light. "What if I'm broken?"

Bennet closed the final distance between them, his calloused hand coming to rest on her shoulder. The touch should have triggered another surge of power, but instead, it felt like an anchor in a storm. "You're not broken, Li. You're just becoming who you were meant to be."

# The Festival

Liora's boots crunched against the gravel path as she wound her way through Eldara's morning bustle. The familiar sight of the village square, with its weathered cobblestones and bright flower boxes, felt different now - tainted by the whispers that followed in her wake.

The bakery's warm scent of fresh bread drifted across the square, but even Maya, the baker who'd slipped her sweet rolls since childhood, turned away when their eyes met. The morning sun cast long shadows across the ground, and Liora noticed how people stepped around them, as if her very shadow might harbor dangerous magic.

Market stalls that normally buzzed with cheerful haggling fell silent as she passed. Mothers pulled their children closer, and old Willem actually crossed to the other side of the street, his usual friendly wave conspicuously absent. The weight of their fear pressed against her chest, making each step harder than the last.

The broken mill loomed ahead, its mighty wheel still and silent against the morning sky. The sound of hammering and sawing drifted down, punctuated by voices calling back and forth. Among them, she recognized Kai's clear tenor rising above the rest in a work song that made the other workers laugh.

Bennet stood in the thick of it, his sleeve rolled up as he directed the repairs. His weathered face creased with a smile when he spotted her, and unlike the others, he didn't hesitate to wave her closer. A few workers shifted uneasily, their tools falling silent.

Kai's song trailed off as she approached, but his amber eyes held no fear - only curiosity as he studied her. He adjusted his colorful scarf and offered a slight bow that somehow managed to be both theatrical and genuine. "The lady of the morning arrives," he announced, earning a few nervous chuckles from the workers.

The tension eased slightly as Bennet stepped forward, enfolding her in a warm embrace that smelled of sawdust and sunshine. His strong arms tightened around her, and she felt his breath against her ear as he whispered, "I have a messenger ready to ride. After the festival tonight, they'll take my message to someone who can help you."

Liora's heart skipped a beat at his words, but before she could respond, he pulled back with a broader smile. "Come to help with repairs?" he asked loudly enough for the others to hear. His eyes held a warning - play along, say nothing of their whispered exchange.

The other workers had already turned back to their tasks, though Kai lingered nearby, absently strumming his lute as he watched their interaction with undisguised interest. His presence made Liora nervous - had he overheard Bennet's whispered message?

A crash from above sent everyone scrambling as a support beam slipped. Liora instinctively reached out, golden light flickering at her fingertips before she could stop it. The workers froze, tools suspended mid-motion, as they stared at her glowing hands with undisguised fear.

Liora clenched her fists, extinguishing the telltale glow as quickly as it had appeared. The support beam crashed to the ground, sending splinters flying. Workers scrambled backward, their tools abandoned in their haste to put distance between themselves and her magic.

Only Kai remained where he stood, his amber eyes fixed on her hands with an intensity that made her skin prickle. His fingers had stilled on the lute strings, but his expression held fascination rather than fear. She turned away from his scrutiny, focusing instead on Bennet's steady presence beside her.

"Everyone back to work," Bennet called out, his voice carrying the authority of years spent managing the mill. The workers hesitated, exchanging uneasy glances before slowly returning to their tasks. Their movements were stiff, deliberate, as if they expected another burst of magic at any moment.

The morning sun caught the flame tattoo on Kai's neck as he stepped closer, his voice pitched low enough that only Liora and Bennet could hear. "That's quite a gift you're hiding there." His casual tone belied the sharp intelligence in his gaze.

Bennet's hand settled on Liora's shoulder, steady and reassuring. "Perhaps this isn't the best time for questions, young bard." The warning in his voice was clear, though Kai seemed unfazed by it.

A whisper of wind stirred the sawdust at their feet, carrying with it the scent of approaching rain. Liora's fingers tingled with residual power, and she fought the urge to check if they were still glowing. The last thing she needed was another display of uncontrolled magic.

"The festival preparations won't wait for fair weather," Bennet announced, deliberately changing the subject. He gestured toward the village square, where colorful banners were already being strung between buildings. "Liora, why don't you help with the decorations? I believe Gemini was asking for you earlier."

Relief flooded through her at the excuse to escape, but Kai's voice stopped her before she could turn away. "I'll be performing tonight," he said, his fingers resuming their idle strumming. "Perhaps you'll share a dance? I know some songs that speak of golden light and hidden power."

The threat - or was it an offer? - hung in the air between them. Liora forced herself to meet his gaze, searching for any sign of malice behind his easy smile. Finding none made her even more uneasy.

Thunder rolled in the distance as she finally stepped away, leaving Bennet to manage the repairs and Kai's knowing looks behind. But she could feel the bard's eyes following her across the square, and she wondered if he would keep her secret - or if he had secrets of his own.

***

Rafe Delacroix threaded through the morning crowd in Eldara's marketplace, catching fragments of hushed conversations about golden light and strange occurrences at the mill. His jaw clenched at the way they spoke of the girl - as if she were some curiosity to be dissected rather than a person drowning in powers she never asked for.

The weight of his sword pressed against his hip as he moved, a constant reminder of the battles that had shaped him into the warrior he'd become. Each whispered word about the Dreamweaver, Liora was her name, stirred memories of his own losses to Draven's forces, feeding the familiar burn of vengeance in his chest.

The leather strap of his shoulder guard bit into his skin as he adjusted it, a familiar comfort against the growing unease in his gut. More villagers huddled near the well, their heads bent together in conspiratorial whispers. A child pointed toward the scorched corner of Liora's home, only to have his hand quickly pulled down by his mother. The scene twisted something inside Rafe's chest. He'd witnessed enough witch hunts in other villages to recognize the early signs.

Through the morning mist, he caught glimpses of fresh protective symbols carved into doorframes - crude, hasty things. The irony wasn't lost on him. The very power they feared might be the only thing standing between them and Draven's forces, should they ever reach this far into the borderlands.

Through gaps between villagers, he spotted Liora standing alone at the stone well. Rafe's breath caught in his throat. The morning sun painted Liora in shades of gold, catching the auburn highlights in her dark hair as she stood by the well. His steps faltered, the familiar weight of his sword forgotten as he watched her delicate fingers trace patterns on the weathered stone.

Her face held a quiet strength beneath its beauty - high cheekbones touched with color from the cool morning air, full lips pressed together in concentration. But it was her eyes that drew him in - deep brown with flecks of amber, holding shadows and light in equal measure. They spoke of secrets, of battles fought alone in the dark hours when no one else was watching.

The simple dress she wore couldn't hide the grace in her movements, the fluid way she shifted her weight as she drew water from the well. Even that mundane task held an otherworldly quality, as if she existed somehow apart from the ordinary world around her. The whispers of the villagers faded to background noise as Rafe studied the curve of her neck, the way her shoulders squared against invisible burdens.

A protective instinct surged through him, foreign and fierce. The villagers' fear suddenly felt personal - an affront to something precious and rare. He wanted to shield her from their suspicious glances, their crude protective symbols and whispered accusations. The desire to step between her and their judgment caught him off guard with its intensity.

Heat crept up his neck as she turned, those remarkable eyes meeting his across the marketplace. His hand tightened on his sword hilt, seeking anchor against the pull of her gaze. Power radiated from her in subtle waves, like heat from summer-warmed stone, but it wasn't fear that made his heart hammer against his ribs. Something deeper called to him, something that made his carefully maintained control feel as fragile as morning frost.

The crowd shifted between them as market-goers haggled over fresh bread and early spring vegetables. Rafe caught glimpses of golden light flickering around Liora's fingers as she clenched them into fists, fighting for control even now.

Before he could close the distance, Liora vanished into a gap in the crowd, leaving only the echo of her presence and the fading warmth of uncontrolled magic in the air. Rafe's chest tightened with frustration and concern - she shouldn't have to face this alone.

Movement caught his eye - a lean bard lounging against a market stall, flame tattoo stark against his neck, watching the scene unfold with too-keen interest. Something about the man's calculating gaze set Rafe's combat instincts humming with warning.

The bard's fingers drummed against his instrument in a rhythm that seemed to pulse in time with the residual magic hanging in the air. Rafe had seen that look before, in the eyes of those who sought to use others' power for their own gain.

Torn between pursuing the girl and confronting the bard, Rafe's hand flexed near his weapon. The morning sun caught the flame tattoo on Kai's neck, and something about its design tugged at Rafe's memory - a symbol he'd seen in darker places, worn by those who traded in secrets and souls.

A raven's harsh cry split the morning air, drawing his gaze to the eastern horizon. Dark clouds gathered there, promising a storm. Or perhaps something worse. He couldn't wait any longer. The last Dreamweaver needed to understand what was coming, whether she wanted to or not. Too many had died while he played it safe. He wouldn't add Eldara to that list.

The Eclipse was coming. Whether Liora knew it or not, she would have to be ready to accept her destiny.

***

The lantern light danced across Liora's skin as she lingered in the shadows at the edge of the village square. Her hands trembled, and she tucked them into the folds of her dress, fighting the telltale tingling that threatened to spark into something dangerous. The festive glow caught the worn carvings on the nearby buildings, ancient symbols that seemed to mock her attempts at control.

Laughter erupted from a cluster of villagers near the center of the square, where Elena spun in circles with her new husband. The couple's joy radiated outward, infectious enough that even the grumpiest elders tapped their feet to the fiddle's cheerful tune. But the music grated against Liora's nerves, each note a reminder of how separate she felt from their carefree celebration.

The smell of roasted chestnuts and mulled cider wafted past, carried on a breeze that set the lanterns swaying. Their shifting patterns reminded her too much of the way magic moved beneath her skin - unpredictable, wild, waiting to break free. A child darted past, nearly brushing against her skirts, and Liora pressed herself further into the shadows of the baker's awning.

Bennet's words from earlier echoed in her mind as she watched the revelry. "You can't hide forever," he'd said, his eyes full of that knowing concern that made her chest ache. But what choice did she have, when every laugh and song threatened to crack her careful control? The burn marks in her bedroom this morning were proof enough of what happened when she let her guard down.

The armed stranger's face flickered through Liora's mind - sharp jawline, intense dark eyes that had locked onto hers at the well. Her magic stirred beneath her skin, responding to the memory in a way that made her breath catch. She pressed her palms flat against the rough wood of the baker's awning, trying to ground herself.

The fiddle's melody shifted to something slower, drawing Liora's attention back to the dancers. Through the crowd, she caught a glimpse of the stranger. The lantern light caught the sharp angles of his face, casting shadows that emphasized his strong jawline and the slight stubble darkening his chin.

His black hair fell in careless waves, a few strands dipping toward eyes that reminded her of rich earth after rain. The kind of eyes that seemed to see straight through pretense, past the careful walls she'd built. A scar traced his left eyebrow, disappearing into his hairline - a mark that spoke of battles and close calls, adding danger to his already magnetic presence.

The leather vest he wore hugged broad shoulders, moving with fluid grace as he navigated between clusters of villagers. His weapons belt rode low on lean hips, the metal fittings catching golden glints from the festival lights. The way he moved reminded her of a predator - not the frenzied rush of a wolf, but the controlled power of a mountain cat, each step precise and measured.

The way his hand had rested on his sword hilt should have fright-ened her. Instead, she'd found herself studying the scarred knuck-les, wondering what stories they could tell. Dangerous thoughts. She couldn't afford to be distracted, not when her control was already so fragile.

A child's shriek of laughter jerked her attention back to the festival. The sound pierced through her like a needle, making her magic surge. Golden light threatened to spill from her fingertips. She curled them into fists, nails biting into her palms.

But her thoughts drifted back to him anyway. The stranger had watched her draw water, his gaze steady even when she'd fumbled the bucket. No fear in those eyes, no judgment - just something else, something that made her stomach flutter in a way that had nothing to do with magic.

Liora's heart hammered against her ribs. She shouldn't be thinking about the curve of his mouth or the way his dark hair had fallen across his forehead. Shouldn't be remembering how time seemed to slow when their eyes met. She was already dangerous enough without adding these feelings to the mix.

The magic beneath her skin pulsed in time with her quickening heartbeat. Was this how it started? First the dreams, then the loss of control, and now this pull toward a complete stranger? She couldn't trust her own reactions anymore.

Another burst of laughter drew her attention to Elena and her new husband. They moved together as if they'd been dancing all their lives, perfectly in sync. Liora's chest tightened. She could never risk that kind of closeness, not with her powers growing more unstable by the day.

Yet she couldn't shake the memory of how the stranger's expression had softened when she'd met his gaze. As if he'd recognized something in her. As if he'd known her, somehow. Ridiculous thoughts, she told herself. Dangerous ones.

A familiar touch jolted her from her brooding. Gemini's fingers wrapped around her wrist, warm and insistent, her friend's face flushed from dancing. "Come on! We have to dance!" The healer's enthusiasm sparkled in her eyes, matching the festive ribbons woven through her dark curls.

The tingling in Liora's hands intensified. "I'm trying... but something feels off. I can't shake the feeling that something's coming, something bad."

"You worry too much!" Gemini rolled her eyes, tugging Liora toward the circle of dancers. "Just enjoy tonight; we need moments like this to remember why we live." The healer's determination radiated from her in waves, as unstoppable as spring rain.

Liora let herself be pulled forward, even as her heart hammered against her ribs. The stranger's eyes tracked her movement through the crowd, and magic stirred beneath her skin in response. Dream energy sparked between her fingers, invisible to all but her - a reminder that no matter how much she yearned to lose herself in the celebration, danger lurked just beneath the surface of her control.

The fiddle's melody wrapped around Liora like a warm embrace, pulling her toward the heart of the celebration despite her reservations. Her feet moved of their own accord, each step matching the rhythm that pulsed through the square. The magic inside her stirred in response, but for once it didn't feel like a threat - instead, it danced with the music, a gentle harmony rather than the usual discordant clash.

Couples spun past in blurs of color and laughter, their joy painting the air with threads of golden dream energy that only she could see. Old Willem, who usually hunched over his cane complaining about his aches, now clapped and stomped with the vigor of a man half his age. Even stern-faced Martha twirled with abandon, her usual frown replaced by a smile that erased decades from her weathered face. The sight tugged at something deep in Liora's chest, a longing she usually kept buried beneath layers of fear and control.

Her eyes drifted shut, and for a heartbeat, she allowed herself to simply exist within the music. The violin's sweet notes wove through her consciousness, almost drowning out the whispers of her night-mares. But darkness lingered at the edges of her awareness - the cloaked figure from her dreams, the feeling of magic spiraling out of control, the terror of harming those she loved. The memories pressed against her mind like shadows creeping across the festival's warm glow.

The music came to a crescendo, and Gemini's grip on her wrist tightened, anchoring her to the present moment. But Liora couldn't shake the feeling that this night balanced on a knife's edge, with joy on one side and catastrophe on the other. The tingling in her fingers in-tensified, and she fought to keep the magic contained as more villagers pressed in around her, unknowingly dancing at the edge of a precipice.

The magic beneath Liora's skin surged without warning, setting her nerve endings ablaze. Her heart thundered against her ribs as the air around her crackled with an energy that had nothing to do with the festival's joy. The golden threads of dream energy that had danced with the music moments ago twisted into dark, writhing shadows. Something was coming - something that made her powers recoil in recognition.

Gemini's fingers slipped from her wrist as the healer was swept away by the continuing dance. Liora stepped forward, drawn by an instinct she didn't understand. The tingling in her hands intensified until she could barely keep the power contained. Just a little closer, she thought. Just a little closer and maybe she could understand what her magic was trying to tell her.

The crash came like thunder, shattering the night. Wood splintered and metal screamed as the festival arch at the square's entrance collapsed. Screams replaced music, and the dancers scattered like leaves in a storm. The golden glow of celebration transformed into chaos in the space of a heartbeat.

Liora stumbled backward, her magic exploding outward in response to her fear. Dream energy crackled visibly around her fingers now, impossible to hide. Through the panicked crowd, she caught a glimpse of dark-armored figures pouring into the square.

This was it. Her nightmare made real.

# Liora's Nightmare

**D**ark shapes burst through the smoke, their weapons glowing with corrupted dream magic. Liora's heart hammered against her ribs as villagers scattered in every direction. Old Willem stumbled, his cane clattering across the cobblestones. Martha's earlier smile twisted into a mask of terror as she pulled children behind her, shepherding them toward safety.

The magic inside Liora writhed and surged, responding to the chaos around her. Her fingers sparked with golden light she couldn't contain, drawing dangerous attention from Draven's soldiers. Their hollow eyes fixed on her through the thickening smoke, and their weapons hummed with an answering darkness that made her skin crawl. Was this what her nightmares had warned her about?

A fresh blast shook the courtyard, sending caustic fumes searing through Liora's chest. Through streaming eyes, she spotted Bennet trying to help fallen villagers to their feet. A soldier advanced on him, weapon raised. The sight sent a jolt of protective fury through her body, and her magic responded before she could stop it. Golden energy burst from her hands, knocking the soldier back - but also shattering every lantern in a ten-foot radius, plunging that section of the square into darkness.

The smoke twisted into unnatural shapes, coiling around ankles and wrists like serpents made of shadow. Liora's stomach lurched as she recognized the magic at work. Villagers caught in the smoke's grip went rigid, their eyes glazing over as if trapped in a waking nightmare. Their screams cut off mid-cry, replaced by an eerie silence that chilled her more than any noise could have.

Through the chaos, she spotted the armed stranger fighting Draven's men with deadly skill. Their eyes locked across the mayhem, sharing a moment of recognition before another wave of soldiers surged into the square, swallowing him into the storm of smoke and shadow.

The horrible familiarity of it all froze her in place, exactly like her nightmares.

"We have to move! Stay close to me!" Gemini's fingers dug into Liora's arm, her friend's touch anchoring her to reality. Sweat beaded on Gemini's forehead, her usual calm replaced by raw fear.

"I-I can't just..." The words caught in Liora's throat as golden light sparked between her trembling fingers. Power welled up within her, pulsing in sync with her thundering heartbeat, begging to break free. One of the warriors spun at the luminescence, his vacant gaze finding her through the haze. The tainted force radiating from his blade sent chills down her spine.

Her muscles tensed, ready to run - but then she saw Bennet stumble as he tried to help another villager. The sight of him vulnerable, in danger, cut through her paralysis. The magic thrumming beneath her skin wasn't just a curse to fear. It could protect. It had to.

Her grip tightened around Gemini's palm for a brief moment before releasing it. Terror still flooded her veins, yet another emotion surged within - an overwhelming urge to shield those she called her own. Energy crackled at her fingertips as she moved ahead, placing her body as a barrier between the oncoming warriors and the escaping townspeople. Though she caught glimpses of the unknown man's blade slicing through more assailants, she willed her attention to remain on the danger directly in front of her.

A child's scream cut through the chaos - Ana had broken free from her brother's grip, running straight toward the approaching soldiers. Without thinking, Liora lunged forward. The magic inside her exploded outward in a wave of golden light, far more powerful than anything she'd ever produced before. It knocked the closest soldier back, but also shattered every window in the square. Glass rained down as screams filled the air, and Liora's heart stopped. Had she just made things worse?

"Use your magic, Liora! We need you to fight!" Gemini's voice cut through the chaos like a blade, sharp with desperation but edged with something else - faith. Her friend stood amid the destruction, hands raised as she tried to shield a group of children. Their eyes met across the smoke-filled square, and Liora saw none of the fear or doubt that plagued her own heart. Only trust.

***

The choking fumes seared Rafe's chest while he muscled past the terrified throng. His blade weighed down his arm but brought comfort in its well-worn handle - an unwelcome echo of countless such evenings.

Shrieks cut through the celebration melodies still drifting from discarded instruments, weaving an eerie symphony with the disorder.

Two of Draven's soldiers materialized from the smoke ahead, their dark armor gleaming in the scattered lantern light. The first barely had time to raise his weapon before Rafe's blade found the gap beneath his arm. The second managed a wild swing that Rafe ducked, responding with a precise thrust through the throat.

His gaze jumped from corpse to corpse, his chest tightening whenever he spotted raven tresses. He repeated the silent prayer with every thundering pulse: she wasn't among them. She couldn't be. A youngster's wail pulled his focus toward the street's edge. As the haze parted momentarily, he detected motion beside the bread merchant's storefront - a recognizable figure assisting another to stand. His lungs seized at the sight. It was her.

The distance between them felt endless. Each step forward met resistance as fleeing villagers pushed past him in blind panic. The smoke thickened, threatening to obscure his view of her again. No. He wouldn't lose sight of her.

A blast of corrupted dream magic sailed past his head, close enough that he felt its cold caress. The soldier who cast it emerged from the smoke, already preparing another attack. Rafe didn't hesitate. His blade found home between the man's ribs before the spell could form.

The soldier's body hadn't hit the ground before Rafe was moving again. Three more of Draven's men blocked his path to Liora. Their armor marked them as elite guards - hand-picked for their cruelty. Good. He had some cruelty of his own to repay.

"Looking for the Dreamweaver?" The middle guard's sneer was audible even through his helmet. "Emperor Draven sends his regards." The words hit Rafe like a physical blow. They knew about Liora. They'd come specifically for her.

Blood roared in Rafe's ears as he raised his sword. The guards spread out, confident in their numbers. Their mistake. The first soldier fell before he could raise his weapon.

The second managed to loose a blast of corrupted magic that Rafe barely dodged. The cold of it brushed his cheek as he rolled, coming up inside the soldier's guard. His sword found the gap between helmet and armor. Two down.

The third soldier turned to run, perhaps hoping to alert others. Rafe's thrown dagger caught him in the back of the knee. He didn't waste time finishing him off - Liora's voice had come from the direction of the old granary, and it was already ablaze.

A burning beam crashed down from the baker's shop, sending sparks spiraling into the night sky. The heat seared his skin as he vaulted over it, his boots crunching on broken glass and splintered wood. Where was she?

More screams erupted to his left - not hers, but close. Rafe sprinted toward the sound, shouldering past a group of terrified villagers. His chest tightened at their faces, so familiar in their fear. Just like the others. Just like every village Draven had destroyed while Rafe watched, helpless. Memories flooded back - survivors' vacant stares, burning homes, that awful silence after.

Liora's voice cut through the chaos again, closer now. "Help! Someone please!" The desperation in her tone sent ice through Rafe's veins. He exploded from behind the cart, blade already swinging.

Rafe sprinted toward the burning building, his heart hammering against his ribs. The hair on the back of his neck stood up, as a blade whistled past his ear, having jerked backward just in time. Quickly, he recognized the bard's familiar face twisted in a snarl.

The warmth he'd displayed before had vanished, replaced by cold calculation that made Rafe's stomach turn. Of course - the songs, the stories, the way the bard, named Kai as he'd found out earlier, had wormed his way into village life. It all made sense now.

"Should've known." Rafe parried another strike, steel ringing against steel. "Draven's gotten clever, sending a bard to do his dirty work."

Kai's amber eyes flashed in the firelight as he pressed forward with surprising skill. "You rebels are all the same - so caught up in your righteous cause that you miss what's right in front of you." His blade danced through the smoke, forcing Rafe to give ground. "Three months I've been here, watching, waiting. And no one suspected a thing."

The realization hit Rafe harder than Kai's next blow. Three months - exactly the time frame when they'd first got word of a potential dreamweaver. "You've been reporting on her." His voice came out as a growl as he launched a vicious counterattack. "Every slip of power, every nightmare. You've been feeding it all back to him."

A blast of corrupted dream magic erupted from Kai's free hand, catching Rafe off guard. He rolled away, but not before the cold magic scraped across his shoulder, leaving numbness in its wake. So the bard had more than one trick up his sleeve. "I believe in survival," Kai shot back, pressing his advantage. "Something you rebels never learned."

The numbness spread down Rafe's arm, making his sword feel like lead. He switched hands, falling back on years of training with both sides. "We survive by standing together," he gritted out, deflecting another spell with his blade. "Not by betraying each other to tyrants."

Kai's next attack came high, but Rafe read the feint in his eyes. He dropped low instead, sweeping Kai's legs from under him. The bard crashed down hard, his blade skittering away across the cobblestones. "You don't understand," Kai gasped as Rafe's sword pressed against his throat. "The Eclipse is coming. Nothing can stop Draven now."

"The Eclipse?" Rafe leaned closer, his voice barely above a whisper. "Tell me what you know." But even as the words left his mouth, he saw the shift in Kai's expression. The bard's hand twitched toward a hidden knife in his boot.

Steel whispered against flesh. One clean stroke - that's all it took. Kai's eyes widened in surprise, then dimmed as his life drained onto the cobblestones. The flame tattoo on his neck seemed to flicker one last time in the firelight before going still.

Blood dripped from Rafe's blade as he straightened, his jaw clenched tight. Another death. Another necessary evil in this endless war. But the mention of the Eclipse gnawed at him. What was Draven planning?

Liora's scream pierced through his dark thoughts, closer now than before. Rafe wiped his blade clean on Kai's elaborate vest, leaving a crimson streak across the intricate patterns. No time for regrets. He had to reach her before Draven's forces did. The granary's flames cast long shadows as he sprinted toward her voice, leaving the bard's body cooling in the street.

***

Dark mist coiled around villagers' ankles as they stumbled backward, their screams piercing the festival air. Draven's soldiers advanced in perfect formation, their armor gleaming under the festival lanterns. The soldiers' hands glowed with corrupted dream magic that snaked out to capture fleeing villagers, turning their eyes vacant and hollow.

A young boy tripped and fell near Liora, his small frame shaking as a soldier's shadow loomed over him. The soldier's magic crackled, ready to strike. Memories of Liora's nightmares flashed through her mind

- the same vacant stares, the same helpless victims. But this wasn't a dream. This was real, and that child needed help.

Energy surged through Liora's veins as the soldier reached for the boy. Power built within her like a storm. As the soldier's hand lowered, time slowed, her heart hammering. She questioned her control, feared making things worse, but the boy's frightened whimper silenced her doubts. She had to act.

Dream energy sparked at her fingertips, different from before. Not the wild, destructive force that had destroyed the mill, but something controlled—almost gentle. The power responded to her will, waiting rather than rushing out unchecked.

Golden light burst from Liora's outstretched hands, rippling through the air like sunlight on water. The warm energy flooded her veins, building from a gentle hum to a crackling current that made her skin tingle. For one perfect moment, the magic felt natural, like an extension of her will rather than the wild force she'd always feared.

The soldier's dark magic recoiled from her light, his hand jerking back from the boy's face. Power continued to surge through Liora, each pulse growing stronger than the last. The familiar whispers of doubt crept in as the magic swelled beyond her initial control. Was it too much? Her fingers trembled as she tried to direct the flow.

Heat blazed along her arms, no longer the gentle warmth from before but an inferno threatening to break free. The golden light intensified, casting harsh shadows across the square. This wasn't like the mill - this was raw power responding to her desperation.

The magic surged past her control with each pulse, sweat forming as she fought to contain it. The energy transformed from protective to volatile, crackling wildly. Behind her, Gemini gasped and gripped her shoulder in warning.

The magic exploded outward in a violent surge, ripping through the air like a tidal wave of golden light. The shockwave flung the nearest villagers backward like ragdolls. Festival stalls and decorations shattered, lanterns exploding into shards of burning glass.

Screams erupted as bodies hit the ground. The boy lay crumpled by a cart, blood dripping from his nose. Gemini's grip vanished as the blast threw her backward. The air warped and shimmered, a dome of distorted reality pulsing from Liora's hands. She fought to stop the flow, but the magic had grown wild, feeding on her panic and strengthening with each attempt to contain it.

Blood trickled from her nose as the magic tore at her body. Through the chaos, she glimpsed motionless forms across the square. How many had she hurt? The question burned as fiercely as the magic in her veins.

The energy wave faded, revealing devastation like her darkest nightmares. Smoke curled from scorched earth while residual power crackled through the air. Her gaze landed on Gemini's crumpled form near an overturned cart. Blood matted her friend's dark hair, and her chest rose and fell in shallow, uneven breaths. The sight sent ice through Liora's veins. She'd done this. In trying to save one child, she'd hurt dozens - including the person who believed in her most.

A soft whimper drew her attention to the boy she'd tried to save. He huddled against a wall, blood trickling from his nose, eyes wide with terror - not at the soldiers, but at her. The truth hit harder than any physical blow: her nightmares hadn't shown her what Draven might do to the village. They'd shown her what she would do herself.

Liora stumbled backward. Her boots crunched over shattered glass and splintered wood, each step carrying her further from the devastation she'd caused. The tingling in her hands refused to fade, a constant reminder of the power that had torn through the festival square.

Around her, survivors aided the wounded. A mother held her sobbing child, eyeing Liora with fear. Two men grimly hoisted an unconscious elder onto a makeshift stretcher. Near the fountain, now cracked and dry, someone had draped a cloth over a still form. Liora's heart clenched - had she killed someone?

"I tried to help," she whispered, the words tasting like ash in her mouth. Her gaze drifted to Gemini, who lay motionless except for the shallow rise and fall of her chest. The same friend who'd believed in her, encouraged her. The same friend she'd nearly killed with her reckless attempt at heroism.

Blood dripped from Liora's nose onto her trembling hands, mixing with tears she hadn't realized were falling. The magic still hummed beneath her skin, eager to respond to her turmoil. But she forced it down, locked it away like a rabid animal. Better to never use it again than risk another disaster like this.

Liora stumbled toward Gemini's still form, each step weighted with guilt and desperation. The crunch of broken glass under her boots echoed the shattering in her chest. Her friend's face was too pale, dark hair matted with blood where she'd struck the cart.

The soldiers' boots thundered against the cobblestones, drawing closer in measured steps that promised retribution. Liora collapsed to her knees beside Gemini, reaching out with trembling fingers to check for a pulse. It fluttered beneath her touch - weak but present. The relief crashed through her like a wave, even as shadows from the advancing soldiers fell across them both.

Magic stirred in her chest again, a desperate animal clawing for release. But Liora forced it down, choking back the power that had already caused so much destruction. The square lay in ruins around her, testament to what happened when she tried to be a hero. She wouldn't risk hurting anyone else - not Gemini, not the villagers, not even herself.

Dark energy crackled through the air as the soldiers raised their hands. Liora bent over Gemini's body, trying to shield her friend from whatever came next. Maybe this was what she deserved.

Agony erupted at the base of her skull, sharp and sudden. Stars burst behind her eyes as cobblestones rushed up to meet her. The festival lanterns above spun into ribbons of amber and gold, bleeding together like watercolors in rain. Through the encroaching darkness, Gemini's crumpled form wavered in her vision. A plea formed on Liora's lips - keep her safe, protect her where I failed - but blackness claimed her before the words could escape.

# Smoke and Ash

Pain lanced through Liora's skull as consciousness returned, each throb matching the distant crackle of flames. The taste of smoke coated her tongue. Her fingers brushed rough-hewn floorboards, so different from the festival square's cobblestones where she'd fallen.

Shadows danced across unfamiliar walls as she pushed herself to sitting, her muscles screaming in protest. This wasn't her home - wasn't anywhere in the village she recognized. A small window revealed flickers of orange light painting the night sky, and beneath the smoke she caught the sharp scent of herbs hanging from the rafters.

The festival square flashed through her mind - the destruction she'd caused, Gemini's still form. Bile rose in her throat. The magic stirred again, responding to her panic, but she forced it down. Never again. The cost was too high.

A bowl clattered somewhere in the darkness. Liora's heart jumped as she spun toward the sound, ignoring the way the room tilted. Through the gloom, shelves lined with jars and bottles took shape. A healer's hut? But who had brought her here, and why? The soldiers should have taken her to Draven's fortress, not hidden her away.

Voices approached from outside - hushed but urgent. Liora's fingers closed around a fallen broom handle, the wood smooth and solid against her palm. She might have sworn off her magic, but she wouldn't go down without a fight. The door's hinges creaked. Shadows stretched across the threshold. Her grip tightened as footsteps entered the hut.

Relief flooded through Liora as Gemini's familiar form emerged from the shadows, though guilt twisted her stomach at the sight of bandages wrapping her friend's arm. The wound she'd caused with her uncontrolled magic. Yet here Gemini was, moving with practiced grace as she gathered supplies from the shelves, her steps measured despite her injury.

The sharp scent of medicinal herbs filled the air as Gemini crushed leaves into a paste, her movements precise and focused. She worked in comfortable silence, the way she always did when treating injuries. Only the slight tremor in her hands betrayed any sign of pain or fatigue.

"I thought I'd lost you back there," Gemini murmured, finally breaking the silence as she pressed a cool compress to Liora's forehead. "But you're tougher than you look." Her touch was gentle, careful - so different from the chaos Liora's own hands had unleashed. The implied forgiveness in her friend's care made Liora's chest tighten.

Warmth spread from the compress, easing the throbbing in Liora's head. She wanted to apologize, to explain, but the words stuck in her throat. Instead, she watched as Gemini methodically cleaned and dressed her other injuries, each tender touch a reminder of a friendship she didn't deserve. Not after what she'd done.

A crash echoed from outside, making them both jump. Gemini's hand found Liora's in the darkness, squeezing once - a silent promise of support. More voices approached the hut, closer now. Different from before. Liora tensed, but Gemini's grip remained steady, anchoring her as fresh fear threatened to overwhelm them both.

A shadow darkened the window, and Liora's breath caught. Through the warped glass, a man's silhouette stood guard, his sword catching orange glints from the distant fires. Blood dripped from the blade's edge, each drop marking time like a crimson heartbeat.

Gemini's fingers tightened around Liora's wrist as the man turned. His dark hair fell across his face as he turned, catching the firelight in ways that reminded her of ravens' wings. Scars marked his exposed forearms - testament to fights she could only imagine. One particularly savage mark curved from wrist to elbow, still pink and new.

Those eyes found hers now - deep brown touched with amber, like autumn leaves in twilight. They held none of the fear or disgust she'd come to expect from others. Instead, she saw understanding there, and something else that made her chest tighten. Recognition, perhaps. The look of someone else who carried their own demons.

His presence should have frightened her - this dangerous man who moved like a shadow and killed with such efficiency. Yet something in the way he positioned himself between the door and where she sat with Gemini suggested protection rather than threat. Like a wolf guarding its pack. The thought sent an unexpected warmth through her chest, even as guilt gnawed at her for putting him in this position. For putting any of them in danger.

"They're still looking for you." His voice was low, rough with smoke and battle. "Draven's men don't stop until they're certain the Dreamweaver is dead." The title sent ice through Liora's veins. How did this stranger know what she was, when she had only heard the word a day ago? The man - the same one who'd approached her at the well earlier - shifted his weight, sword rising slightly as voices echoed from the burning village.

"Bennet?" Her voice cracked, brittle as autumn leaves. Gemini's face twisted away, unable to meet her gaze. A shadow crossed the stranger's weathered features, his mouth carving downward into granite.

His words emerged with deliberate precision. "Should the Dreamweaver get away, Draven's men will seize villagers as prisoners. They're shackling and hauling off anyone they suspect has ties to you. They got Bennet first, but the old man gave them hell first."

The stranger's sword caught another orange flicker as he turned fully toward Liora, his features sharp in the dim light. Blood stained his sleeve, but his movements remained fluid, controlled. The set of his jaw spoke of someone who'd seen too much death, yet his dark eyes held an intensity that made her pulse quicken.

"I'm Rafe Delacroix," he said, voice low and urgent as boots crunched past the hut. "I've led them away for now, but we don't have much time. They'll be back, and they'll destroy everything in their path to find you." His words carried the weight of experience.

The air grew thick as Rafe's next words hit like physical blows. "Draven's hunting anyone with Dreamweaver blood. You're the last one - he's killed the rest." Gemini's hand found Liora's shoulder, steadying her as the room tilted. All those years of strange dreams, of power she couldn't control - they weren't a curse or an accident. They were her heritage, her birthright.

Heavy footsteps approached again, closer this time. Rafe melted back into the shadows, but his words hung in the air between them. The last Dreamweaver. The weight of those words pressed down on Liora's shoulders as she stared at her trembling hands, remembering the destruction they'd caused mere hours ago.

"I'm not what you think I am, I'm no hero." The words scratched her throat, bitter as ashes. "You saw what happened out there. People got hurt because of me." Her fingers brushed against the worn fabric of her sleeve, focusing on its texture rather than the weight of expectation pressing down on her shoulders.

Gemini's bandaged arm caught the flickering light, a silent accusation that made Liora's stomach twist. The image of Bennet being dragged away flashed through her mind, followed by the screams of villagers caught in her uncontrolled blast. Power like that needed to be contained, not unleashed. She'd spent years burying it for a reason.

Gemini's fingers found Liora's trembling hand in the darkness, warm and steady despite the bandages that wrapped her injured arm. The touch anchored Liora, pulling her back from the edge of panic as boots crunched through leaves outside the hut.

"Remember when we were kids?" Gemini's voice dropped to barely a whisper, yet carried the strength of sunlight breaking through storm clouds. "You always wanted to protect everyone - even that mangy cat that kept stealing fish from the market." Her fingertip swept gentle loops across Liora's skin, using the same soothing motion she employed to calm distressed villagers.

The memory sparked something in Liora's chest - not the destructive power that had exploded in the village square, but a gentler warmth. That scraggly cat had turned into the best mouser in Eldara, once someone gave it a chance. Gemini's knowing smile suggested she was thinking the same thing.

"Maybe this is our chance to make a difference, Li." Gemini leaned closer, her eyes reflecting the distant flames yet holding nothing but certainty. "I'll be with you, no matter what path you choose." The promise settled around Liora's shoulders like a familiar blanket, pushing back the chill of fear that had taken root.

Blood still stained Gemini's bandages, evidence of Liora's lack of control, yet here her friend sat - wounded but unwavering, offering support instead of blame. Rafe's boots scraped against the wooden floor as he moved closer, the sound breaking through the tense silence. Shadows from the burning village danced across his face, highlighting the intensity in his dark eyes as they fixed on Liora. His sword lowered slightly, but the warrior's tension never left his frame.

"I've seen what Draven does to villages like this," he said, voice rough with smoke and memory. "The people he takes never come back the same - if they come back at all." His gaze flickered to the window where fresh screams pierced the night, then back to Liora with renewed urgency. "But you have power. Real power. Join us, and we'll help you learn to use it. To control it."

The word 'control' sent a shiver down Liora's spine as her magic stirred in response, a restless energy that had always felt more like chaos than power. Yet something in Rafe's tone - the raw conviction behind his words - made her pause. His belief in her potential felt different from Bennet's gentle encouragement or Gemini's steadfast support. It carried the weight of someone who'd seen both darkness and light, and still chose to fight.

"Draven needs to be stopped," Rafe continued, taking another step closer. The firelight caught old scars on his hands, testament to battles fought and survived. "And you could be the key. Not just to saving Eldara, but all of Somnus." His words hung in the air between them, heavy with possibility and threat. Through the window, flames painted the sky in shades of amber and crimson, a brutal reminder of what failure would cost.

More boots crunched through leaves outside, closer now. Rafe's hand tightened on his sword hilt as his gaze met Liora's one final time. The question burned between them, demanding an answer - would she run from her power forever, or finally face what she was meant to become?

"...I can't."

***

Rafe's fingers tightened around the hilt of his sword as Liora's shoulders tensed, her back turned to him in silent refusal. The familiar weight of failure settled in his chest. Another village lost.

Blood dripped from a gash above his eye, each drop a reminder of tonight's chaos. The metallic scent mixed with smoke and ash - Draven's calling card. His mind flashed to Northhaven, to Silverbrook, to a dozen other villages reduced to cinders. Always the same pattern. Always arriving too late to do more than count the dead.

The healer, Gemini, caught his eye from where she crouched beside Liora. Her steady gaze held understanding, maybe even alliance. But it wasn't enough. They needed Liora's power, raw and untamed as it was. He'd seen what she could do during the attack - that burst of energy that had scattered Draven's soldiers like leaves in a storm. Untrained, yes. Dangerous, perhaps. But also exactly what the rebellion desperately needed.

His own first days with the rebellion ghosted through his mind - the doubt, the fear of failing those who counted on him. General Varden's patience as he learned to channel his rage into purpose. Now here he stood, trying to offer that same guidance to someone else. The irony wasn't lost on him.

A floorboard creaked beneath his boot as he shifted his weight, and Liora flinched at the sound. Her fear was a tangible thing, filling the small space between them. The same fear he'd seen in countless faces before Draven's forces swept through. But this time had to be different. This time, he couldn't afford to fail. The last Dreamweaver couldn't be allowed to slip through their fingers - not when so much hung in the balance.

The blanket settled around Liora's shoulders, Gemini's touch gentle as she tucked the edges close. Rafe's grip loosened on his sword hilt, the raw tension in his muscles easing at the quiet tenderness of the scene before him. Here, in this cramped hut with danger prowling outside, these two women had carved out a moment of peace.

Their whispered words drifted to him in fragments. Comfort. Reassurance. The kind of bond that went deeper than friendship. The way Gemini's hand lingered on Liora's arm reminded him of his sister, lost in the flames of Draven's rage. That same fierce protectiveness blazed in Gemini's eyes now as she positioned herself between Liora and the door - between Liora and him.

A knot formed in his throat. The last Dreamweaver wasn't just some weapon to be claimed for the rebellion. She was a person, someone's anchor in a world torn apart by Draven's tyranny. The weight of her power might rest heavy on her shoulders, but the weight of Gemini's unwavering loyalty seemed to steady her.

Their hushed conversation continued, heads bent close together. Gemini dabbed at a cut on Liora's temple while murmuring something that brought a fleeting smile to Liora's face. When was the last time anyone in the rebellion had shown that kind of care? They'd all grown so focused on survival, on the next battle, the next strategy. This simple act of kindness felt like a reminder of what they were actually fighting for.

Blood trickled down his cheek, and Rafe swiped it away with his sleeve. The night's chaos still echoed in his ears - screams, clashing steel, the crackle of flames. But here, watching Gemini tend to Liora with such gentle determination, a new understanding clicked into place. Forcing Liora to choose between her power and her connections would only drive her further away. Perhaps the path forward wasn't about severing bonds, but strengthening them.

Ash and blood painted the night air, the scents mixing into a familiar cocktail that churned his stomach. How many villages had he seen burn? The memories rose unbidden - Northhaven's chapel bells melting in the inferno, Silverbrook's wells running red. Each failure etched deeper into his bones than any battle scar. The sword at his hip felt heavier with each lost soul he couldn't protect.

A flash of movement caught his eye - just an owl taking flight, its wings silent against the star-scattered sky. But the tension remained, thrumming through his veins like a plucked bowstring. Somewhere in that darkness, Draven's men searched, their torches bobbing like fallen stars through the trees. They'd followed his false trail north, but they'd double back soon enough. They always did.

Liora shifted behind him, a soft sound of pain escaping her lips as Gemini worked. The sound twisted something in his chest, raw and urgent. She was different from the others - not just another villager to evacuate or another soldier to train. The power that had erupted from her during the attack had been wild, untamed, but beneath that chaos lay something pure. Something that could turn the tide of this endless war, if only she'd trust herself enough to try.

The night pressed closer, and a faint shimmer caught Rafe's eye. Golden light danced across Liora's fingertips as she fell into a troubled sleep, her power leaking through despite her desperate attempts to contain it. The glow pulsed in rhythm with her breathing, casting ethereal shadows on the hut's weathered walls.

He'd seen magic before - the dark shadows Draven's soldiers wielded, the silver-tinged magic of Nero Thorne, the weak echoes in ancient ruins. But this... this was different. Pure. Untainted. Like watching starlight take form. His chest tightened as memories of old tales surfaced - stories of Dreamweavers who could reshape reality itself, their powers flowing as natural as breathing. Was this what those legends had looked like, before Draven twisted everything?

After a few hours of tense quiet, dawn's pale fingers crept through the hut's window, and Rafe shifted his weight, wincing as his muscles protested the long night's vigil. The golden light still danced across Liora's sleeping form, catching in her dark hair like trapped starlight. Her face had softened in sleep, the fear and tension melting away to reveal someone younger, more vulnerable than the power she wielded suggested.

A strand of hair fell across her face, and his fingers itched to brush it away. He'd seen her strength during the attack - raw, untamed energy that could reshape reality itself. But here, curled on her side with one hand tucked beneath her cheek, she looked almost peaceful. The contradiction twisted something in his chest, a feeling he couldn't afford to examine too closely.

The dawn light painted shadows beneath her lashes, highlighting the curve of her cheek and the small scar near her temple - a reminder of tonight's chaos. His mind flashed to the moment she'd stepped between a soldier and a child, power blazing in her eyes. That fierce protectiveness, even at the cost of exposing herself, had stirred something in him he thought long buried beneath years of battle and loss.

Liora murmured something in her sleep, her fingers twitching as golden sparks danced between them. The display reminded him of festival lights, of times before Draven's shadow fell across their lands. When was the last time he'd allowed himself to notice such beauty? The war had stripped away so much, leaving only strategy and survival. Yet watching her now, he felt an echo of that lost wonder.

A cool breeze swept through the hut's window, carrying the scent of smoke and dawn-wet leaves. Liora shivered, and before he could stop himself, Rafe found himself removing his leather coat. The material was worn, marked with patches and battle scars, but still warm. He draped it over her sleeping form, careful not to wake her. As he withdrew his hand, her fingers brushed his - just for a moment - sending an unexpected jolt through his battle-hardened defenses. Rafe retreated to his post by the door, trying to ignore how right his coat looked wrapped around her shoulders.

A bird called from somewhere in the forest - a morning dove's soft coo breaking the silence. Normal sounds returning meant they'd truly gone. Rafe's shoulders eased as he cataloged their next steps: they'd need supplies, weapons, a safe route to the rebellion's camp. The weight of responsibility settled back into place, comfortable as his sword belt.

The growing light revealed fresh tracks in the mud outside - boot prints leading north toward the mountain pass. Good. His false trail had worked better than expected. But they couldn't count on that luck lasting long. Rafe shifted his weight, floorboards creaking beneath him as he turned from the window. Dawn's arrival meant decisions could no longer wait. The time had come to wake Liora and Gemini, to see if the night's horrors had changed their minds about joining the fight.

# Hope

The sulfuric fumes scorched Liora's windpipe as she stood in Eldara's ruined square. Shards of glass crunched beneath her feet, remnants of windows shattered during last night's attack. A child's doll lay abandoned nearby, its dress singed and dirty - a stark reminder of how close they'd come to losing everything.

Her fingers trembled as she traced the scorched pattern on a nearby wall, the twisted spiral of energy unmistakably from her own magic. Not from Draven's forces, but from her desperate attempt to help. Old man Turner limped past, arm bandaged where her wild surge had thrown him against the bakery wall. He wouldn't meet her eyes.

The morning sun cast long shadows through the haze, highlighting the destruction in harsh relief. Where festive lanterns had hung just hours ago, now only burned rope ends dangled. The cheerful music replaced by quiet sobs and the scrape of rubble being cleared. Her home - everything she'd known - lay broken around her, and her own power had helped break it.

Rafe's words about the rebellion echoed in her mind as she watched Gemini tend to Mrs. Bradford's burns. The healer's movements were stiff, favoring her right side where Liora's magic had struck her. Yet Gemini still worked tirelessly, offering comfort along with her remedies. The sight of her friend's resilience twisted something deep in Liora's chest.

A child's cry pierced the morning quiet as little Sara stumbled over debris. Without thinking, Liora reached out to steady her - but the girl flinched away, eyes wide with fear. The same fear Liora had seen in so many faces during the attack, when her powers had exploded outward. Sara's mother hurried over, scooping up her daughter and hurrying away without a word. The silence that followed felt heavier than the smoke still hanging in the air.

The elderly woman's arm trembled as Liora helped her over a fallen beam. Mrs. Blackwood - who'd given Liora sweets as a child - now kept her gaze fixed ahead, lips pressed into a thin line. Her weathered hand gripped Gemini's arm instead of Liora's, even though Gemini winced with each step.

Broken glass and splintered wood crunched under their feet as they picked their way through what remained of the market square. The bakery's roof had partially collapsed, and the scent of burned bread mingled with the acrid smoke still hanging in the air. A cat darted past, fur singed, fleeing from shadows that no longer held threats.

"Here we are, Mrs. Blackwood." Gemini's voice carried a gentleness Liora envied as they helped the old woman settle onto an overturned cart. The healer immediately began checking the burn on Mrs. Blackwood's leg - a burn Liora recognized from her own magical surge, not from Draven's forces. Her stomach clenched.

Other villagers gathered nearby, speaking in hushed whispers that died whenever Liora glanced their way. She caught fragments - "dangerous" and "shouldn't stay" - before they turned their backs. These were people who'd known her since childhood, who'd celebrated her birthdays and consoled her losses. Now they looked at her as if she were one of Draven's soldiers.

A child's ball rolled to a stop at Liora's feet. She bent to pick it up, but its owner - little Tommy from two houses down - scrambled backward when she tried to return it. His mother appeared, snatching him up without a word and hurrying away. The ball lay forgotten in the dirt as Liora's hand fell to her side, each whisper and fearful glance driving home what she'd become to them: a danger to be avoided, a threat in their midst.

Gemini's fingers moved with practiced grace as she dabbed at a child's bloodied knee. The little girl's sobs had quieted to hiccups, soothed by the healer's gentle touch and soft humming. A bruise darkened the child's temple - another mark from the chaos Liora's magic had caused.

Through the haze of smoke, Liora caught Gemini's meaningful glance toward old Willem, who sat slumped against a broken cart. His weathered face was blank, eyes fixed on nothing as he clutched a singed family portrait. The glass had shattered, leaving tiny cuts across his palms that he didn't seem to notice.

Her feet felt leaden as she crossed the rubble-strewn ground. Each step brought fresh waves of guilt as she passed the scorch marks her power had left. Willem didn't look up as she lowered herself beside him, her hand hovering uncertainly before settling on his trembling shoulder.

"I'm... I'm sorry," Liora whispered, her voice catching. "I tried to help, but..." She swallowed hard, watching another group of villagers hurry past, their fearful glances cutting deep. "I don't know if I belong here anymore."

Willem's fingers tightened on the portrait frame, a splinter of glass drawing a fresh bead of blood. He didn't pull away from her touch, but his silence spoke volumes. In the distance, more voices called for help, and Gemini's quiet reassurances to the child drifted over on the smoke-laden breeze. The morning sun climbed higher, casting harsh light on all they'd lost - and all Liora had failed to protect.

Whispers slithered through the morning air like smoke. "Did you see what she did?" "What if she brings more of them here?" The words pierced deeper than the glass shards littering the ground. Liora's hands curled into fists at her sides, power tingling beneath her skin - unwanted, uncontrollable.

A group of villagers clearing debris stopped their work as she passed, their conversation dying like a snuffed flame. Young Joey, who'd always begged her to tell stories during harvest, ducked behind his father. The man's arm curved protectively around his son, eyes hard as he watched her approach. The distance between them stretched wider than the physical steps separating them - a chasm carved by fear.

The baker's wife hustled her children inside as Liora neared their damaged shop, the door slamming with finality. Through the cracked window, small faces peered out before being pulled away from view. These same children had danced around her at the festival, begging for treats and stories. Now they hid as if she were one of Draven's soldiers come to steal their dreams.

Power thrummed beneath Liora's skin, responding to her rising distress. A nearby lantern post creaked, its metal twisting slightly before she forced the magic down. But the damage was done - more villagers scattered, leaving her alone in a widening circle of empty space. The message was clear: she didn't belong here anymore. Perhaps she never had.

***

Gemini's robes rustled against broken cobblestones as she made her way toward Liora, each step sending fresh waves of pain through her injured leg. She watched her friend standing alone amid the destruction, shoulders hunched as if bearing the weight of the entire village's fear. The morning light caught the unshed tears in Liora's eyes, and Gemini's heart ached at the sight.

"Li," she called softly, noting how Liora's hands trembled at her sides. The air around them hummed with residual energy, making the hair on Gemini's arms stand on end. Yet she pressed forward, ignoring the warning glances from nearby villagers who scrambled to clear her path.

Blood seeped through the makeshift bandage on her thigh as she closed the distance between them. The pain barely registered compared to the anguish etched across Liora's face. Gemini had seen that look before - in the eyes of wounded animals, cornered and desperate. One wrong move could send her friend fleeing into the forest, perhaps never to return.

A child's cry pierced the morning air, and Liora flinched as if struck. The power emanating from her intensified, causing nearby debris to shift and scatter. But Gemini didn't retreat. Instead, she reached out, her fingers brushing Liora's arm with the same gentle touch she used to calm her most frightened patients.

"You're not alone in this," Gemini whispered, her voice steady despite the tremor in her injured leg. The words hung between them as more villagers hurried past, their fearful murmurs carrying on the smoke-laden breeze. Liora's gaze remained fixed on the ground, but her shoulders relaxed slightly at Gemini's touch, the dangerous energy around them beginning to subside.

Gemini steadied herself against a fallen beam, her leg protesting as she lowered herself beside Liora. The dawn breeze wafted with the bitter stench of ash and terror, but she focused on her friend's ragged breathing. The residual magic in the air made her skin prickle, but she refused to let it deter her.

A gentle squeeze of Liora's shoulder drew a shuddering breath from her friend. Through their years together, Gemini had learned to read the subtle shifts in Liora's expression - the downward tilt of her chin, the way her fingers twisted in her lap. The guilt radiating from her now was almost tangible, heavier than the smoke that still clung to their clothes.

Blood trickled down Gemini's leg as she shifted closer, but she pushed the discomfort aside. The wound could wait. The villagers' whispers grew louder, and she caught fragments of their fears - "dangerous," "uncontrolled," "just like the stories." Each word seemed to strike Liora like a physical blow, and the air around them crackled with untamed energy.

"None of us knew what was coming, Liora." The words fell soft and steady from Gemini's lips, a counterpoint to the chaos around them. "You did what you could, and you did it with a heart full of courage. Don't forget that." Her fingers remained steady on Liora's shoulder, anchoring her friend as another wave of power rippled through the air.

She'd witnessed Liora's kindness too many times to let fear guide her now - seen her friend weave flower crowns for crying children and spend hours helping the elderly with their daily tasks. That gentle soul hadn't vanished with the emergence of her powers; it had simply found a new way to protect those she loved.

"Remember when I first started healing?" Her voice cut through the heavy silence between them. "That old man with the broken arm - I was so afraid I'd make it worse. My hands shook so badly, I could barely tie the bandage." The memory drew a flicker of recognition across Liora's face, her shoulders losing some of their rigid tension.

She leaned closer, ignoring the warning throb from her wound. "I'm scared too, Liora. None of us knows what's ahead... but if we let fear hold us back, we're only helping Draven do what he wants. Together, we can learn, we can grow. You don't have to carry this alone." The words emerged steady despite the tremor in her leg, each syllable weighted with shared understanding.

"I tried, but... look at what happened." Liora's voice cracked, her gaze fixed on the scorched ground where her magic had left its mark. "I don't know if I'm even capable of protecting anyone. Maybe... maybe I'm just dangerous." The words fell between them like stones, heavy with the weight of unspoken fears.

"Look at me," Gemini urged, her voice soft but firm. When Liora's gaze remained fixed on the ground, she reached out and cupped her friend's chin, gently turning her face until their eyes met. The raw fear she saw there made her heart ache, but she refused to let it deter her. "Yesterday, when those soldiers attacked, you didn't run. You stood your ground. That's not the action of someone dangerous - that's the mark of a protector."

Through the haze of smoke and morning light, she caught glimpses of villagers watching them, their whispers carrying on the breeze. A subtle shift in Liora's expression caught Gemini's attention - a slight straightening of her shoulders, a flicker of something other than fear in her eyes. The change was small, barely noticeable to anyone who didn't know her as well as Gemini did, but it was there.

Hope, fragile as a butterfly's wing, but present nonetheless.

***

Through the haze of morning smoke, Liora watched as figures emerged from the tree line. Rafe led the small group, his determined stride carrying him across the debris-strewn ground. Behind him walked a woman with sharp features and calculating eyes. Three other rebels followed, their movements precise and purposeful as they fanned out among the villagers.

The newcomers didn't hesitate to help. They lifted fallen beams, cleared pathways through the rubble, and spoke quiet words of comfort to shell-shocked survivors. Their presence seemed to breathe new life into the weary villagers, who had been working since dawn to salvage what they could from the destruction.

The woman's voice cut through the morning air as she organized the efforts, directing rebels and villagers alike with calm authority. "We'll need to shore up that wall before it collapses. Marcus, Elena - see to the wounded in the town hall." Her efficiency brought order to the chaos, transforming random acts of assistance into coordinated relief.

Rafe made his way toward Liora and Gemini, his eyes taking in the devastation around them. The set of his jaw spoke of familiar pain, as if he'd seen scenes like this before. His hand rested on the pommel of his sword - not threatening, but ready.

"The damage could have been worse," Rafe said as he reached them, his voice low and steady. "I've seen what happens when Draven's forces have free rein. You slowed them down, gave people time to escape."

Liora's throat tightened at his words. The memory of her magic bursting forth, wild and untamed, flashed through her mind. But before she could voice her doubt, another crash echoed from the village center.

The rebels moved as one unit, rushing toward the sound. A section of the baker's roof had finally given way, threatening to trap those inside. Without hesitation, Rafe's people formed a chain, passing buckets and moving debris while the woman coordinated their efforts.

"Jayne Finnegan," Rafe said quietly. "She's the finest spy you'll ever meet, and one hell of a rebel."

Their seamless cooperation sparked something in Liora's chest - a flutter of possibility. These weren't just fighters; they were protectors, working together to save what could be saved and help those who needed it most.

The morning sun broke through the smoke, casting long shadows across the village square as more villagers emerged to join the rebels' efforts. In that moment, watching strangers and neighbors work side by side, Liora felt the weight of isolation lift ever so slightly from her shoulders.

The morning breeze carried ash through the air as Rafe knelt beside Liora and Gemini.

"We've been searching for you, Liora." Rafe said, his voice dropping to barely above a whisper. "The rebellion needs a Dreamweaver. Without one, we can't hope to match Draven's power." His gaze drifted to the horizon where smoke still rose from the village's eastern quarter. "When his forces return - and they will return - they'll finish what they started. Bennet, the others they took... they won't survive long in Draven's custody."

Liora's hands trembled at the mention of Bennet's name. The vision she'd had of him being dragged away, fighting against the soldiers' grip until dream magic subdued him, burned fresh in her mind.

"You have a strength within you that could save countless lives," Rafe continued, his eyes meeting Liora's with an intensity that made her want to look away. "Join us, and together, we can bring an end to Draven's tyranny." The earnestness in his voice carried no trace of doubt, no hint of the fear that churned in Liora's stomach at the thought of wielding her powers again.

In the distance, Jayne directed more rebels to secure a crumbling wall, her commands mixing with the sounds of shifting debris and muffled sobs from the villagers who'd lost everything. The choice Rafe offered felt impossible - risk causing more destruction with her untamed powers, or watch as Draven's forces returned to claim what remained of her home.

The morning light cast harsh shadows across Rafe's face, highlighting scars Liora hadn't noticed before - remnants of battles fought and survived.

"I was younger than you when they came," he said, his voice dropping low enough that only Liora and Gemini could hear. "My sister had just started showing signs of dream magic. Nothing like your power, but enough to draw their attention." His grip tightened on the sword hilt, knuckles whitening. "They took her first. Then my parents, when they tried to stop them. I watched our village burn from the forest where my mother had hidden me."

The weight of his words hung in the smoke-filled air. Around them, the sounds of reconstruction continued - wood scraping against stone, voices calling out for supplies, the occasional crash of unstable debris giving way. But in their small circle, time seemed to slow, wrapped in the gravity of Rafe's confession.

"Every village I couldn't save, every family torn apart - they fuel this fight," Rafe continued, meeting Liora's gaze with an intensity that made her breath catch. "Draven thinks fear will keep us in line.

But fear?" A bitter smile crossed his face. "Fear's what drove me to learn how to fight back. To gather others who refused to bow to his tyranny."

The crash of falling timber from a nearby building punctuated his words. Jayne's voice rang out, directing rebels to secure the structure. Rafe rose in one fluid motion, his hand extending toward Liora. "We all have to make sacrifices," he said, his voice carrying the weight of years of loss and determination. "But together, we can make them count. Your power could be the difference between watching more villages burn and finally stopping Draven's reign of terror."

Gemini shifted her weight, the movement causing her to wince from her bandaged arm. Yet her eyes held a fierce determination as she gazed at the destruction around them. The morning light caught the tear tracks on her cheeks, but her voice remained steady.

"We can't just watch this happen to other villages," she said, turning to face Liora. Her uninjured hand reached out, fingers brushing against Liora's trembling ones. "Your power - it's not a curse. It's a chance to stop all this." The conviction in her voice cut through the haze of smoke and doubt.

"If there's even a chance we can save one person from experiencing this-" Gemini gestured at the devastation around them, her eyes lingering on a child being comforted by one of the rebels "-then we have to try." She squeezed Liora's hand, the pressure gentle but insistent. "I'll be right beside you, every step of the way."

A crash echoed from somewhere in the village, followed by shouts for help. Gemini was already turning toward the sound, her healer's instincts taking over despite her own wounds. But before moving away, she caught Liora's gaze one final time. "We've spent our whole lives helping others in small ways. Maybe it's time we did something bigger."

Rafe's outstretched hand remained steady, patient, but the memory of Gemini's bandaged arm twisted like a knife in her gut.

Her gaze drifted to the villagers working alongside the rebels, their movements synchronized in purpose despite their differences. A child's laughter pierced the morning air as Jayne lifted him onto her shoulders to reach a stuck shutter. The sound struck something deep within Liora - a reminder of all that could be lost. All that she could destroy if her powers spun out of control again.

"I can't," she whispered, the words catching in her throat like smoke. Her hands clenched at her sides, fighting against the tingling sensation that had become all too familiar. Even now, her power stirred beneath her skin, a reminder of its wild and untamed nature. "I'll only make things worse. I'm not... I'm not what you think I am."

A shadow passed over Rafe's face, but before he could respond, shouts erupted from the village center. Another wall was giving way, and this time the crashes seemed closer, more urgent. Delacroix rushed toward the sound, leaving Liora alone with her refusal hanging in the ash-filled air, the echo of his faith in her ringing hollow against her fears.

# Leaving Eldara

T he rebels' whispers cut through the morning air like knives. Liora caught fragments of their hushed conversations - "dangerous," "liability," "unstable" - each word striking deeper than the last. Her fingers trembled as she pressed them against her palms, trying to suppress the familiar tingling that threatened to surface.

Jayne stepped forward, her boots crunching over scattered debris as she approached Rafe. The woman's calculating gaze swept over Liora before settling on her fellow rebel. "We've lost too many already, Delacroix." Her voice carried across the ruined square, clear and cutting. "She can't control her magic. How do we know she won't destroy more than Draven's forces? One wrong move, and we're all at risk."

Rafe's jaw tightened, but before he could speak, another rebel called out. "I saw what happened during the attack. She nearly brought down half the square trying to help." The words carried an accusation that hung heavy in the smoke-filled air. "Our mission is to protect lives, not put them at greater risk."

The magic prickled beneath Liora's palms, echoing the fierce ache that constricted her heart. Her gaze tracked Jayne's subtle movement toward her weapon - a warning rather than an attack. That small action revealed everything: they viewed her as a danger to be contained, not a comrade to embrace. As dawn's misty rays filtered through the air, she noticed Gemini's worried look, but her companion's support did little to protect her from the barrier of suspicion rising to encircle her.

Movement drew her attention as another villager limped past, supported by two others. Their gazes slid past her as if she were invisible - or perhaps something worse. Something dangerous. The distance between her and the others stretched wider, a physical manifestation of the gulf her powers had created.

Gemini surged forward, placing herself between Liora and Jayne with shoulders squared. "You speak of danger, but what about opportunity? What about hope?" Her voice cut through the morning air, steady and clear as a bell. "I've known Liora my entire life. She has more courage and compassion in her heart than most show in a lifetime. The power within her isn't a curse - it's a gift waiting to be understood."

Jayne's laugh held no warmth. "A gift? Such naive words from a village girl who's never seen what real power can do." Her fingers drummed against her sword hilt as her gaze swept over the gathered rebels. "I've watched Draven flay the skin from children while their parents screamed. Seen him turn entire villages to ash with corrupted dream magic. He doesn't just kill those who oppose him- he breaks them, piece by piece, until death feels like mercy."

The morning shadows seemed to deepen as Jayne's words painted pictures of horror across the ruined square. "The last Dreamweaving hopeful I buried - a boy no older than sixteen - died believing he could make a difference. Draven kept him alive for weeks, twisting his dreams until the boy couldn't tell reality from nightmare. When we found him, he was nothing but a shell, begging us to end it."

A heavy silence fell over the group as Jayne turned her attention back to Liora. "You're right to want no part in this fight. The path you're considering - it only ends one way. I've dug too many graves, marked too many cairns with names of those who thought they could stand against him. Your fear isn't weakness, girl. It's wisdom."

Rafe's footsteps echoed across the ruined square as he moved between Jayne and Gemini. His presence seemed to fill the space, commanding attention without demanding it.

"I've seen what fear does to people," Rafe said, his voice carrying to every person, rebel and villager alike, in the square. His gaze swept over them all, lingering on those who bore fresh wounds from the attack. "It tears us apart faster than any of Draven's weapons. We stand here pointing fingers while he burns another village, breaks another family."

The tingling in Liora's hands subsided as Rafe turned to face her directly. His dark eyes held none of the accusation she'd seen in the others. Instead, she found something that made her heart skip - understanding. The same understanding she'd glimpsed when he'd pulled her to safety during the attack.

"You want control, Liora. I see it in every move you make, every time you clench your fists against your power." Rafe's words drew murmurs from the rebels, but he continued, his voice steady. "That desire for control - that's not weakness. It's exactly what we need. Someone who understands the weight of power, who wants to use it right rather than just use it."

Jayne's boots scraped against broken stone as she shifted her stance. The sound pulled Liora's attention back to the precarious balance of the moment - one wrong move could still shatter this fragile offer of acceptance. But as Rafe stood there, bridging the gap between her and the rebels, Liora felt something she hadn't expected: hope, small and sharp as a splinter, working its way into her heart.

The morning shadows stretched across the ruined square as the rebels dispersed, their boots crunching over scattered debris. Liora watched them go, her gaze lingering on Jayne's retreating form. The woman's words about broken dreamweavers and unmarked graves still echoed in her mind, but they mingled now with Rafe's steady defense and Gemini's unwavering faith.

A breeze stirred the ashes at her feet, wafting the bitter scent of burning and something else - possibility. The tingling in her hands had subsided to a gentle warmth, no longer feeling like a threat about to explode. She flexed her fingers, studying the way sunlight played across her palms. These same hands that had caused so much destruction - could they really become tools of protection instead?

Gemini's presence beside her radiated strength, a silent reminder that she wasn't alone in this choice. If Gemini believed in her this strongly, if Rafe saw potential where others saw danger - maybe they weren't wrong. Maybe there was more to her power than the chaos she'd always feared.

Her feet carried her forward before her mind fully registered the decision. Each step across the broken square felt like crossing a threshold. Rafe turned at her approach, his dark eyes catching the morning light.

"I want to join the rebellion," Liora said, the words falling from her lips like stones into still water. Her hands trembled, but she forced them steady at her sides. "I want to become a Dreamweaver." The title felt foreign on her tongue, weighted with both promise and responsibility. Behind her, she heard Gemini's sharp intake of breath, and ahead, something flickered in Rafe's expression - surprise, perhaps, or satisfaction. But beneath the fear still coursing through her veins, a small flame of determination had taken root. Whether it would grow into strength or consume her, only time would tell.

\*\*\*

Rafe hefted another sack of dried meat onto the cart, his muscles burning from the repeated motion, but they needed to move before Draven's soldiers returned. The destruction of Eldara still haunted him - another village he'd failed to protect.

"She's not ready." Jayne Finnegan's voice cut through the silence as she secured water skins to the wagon's side. Her fingers worked the knots with practiced efficiency, but her jaw remained tight with concern. "Taking her to Twilight now... we might as well paint a target on all our backs."

"And what would you have me do?" Rafe's voice came out sharper than intended. He dropped another bag into the cart with more force than necessary, sending a cloud of dust into the air. "Leave her here for Draven's men to find? Watch him use her to enslave everyone while we hide in the shadows?"

Jayne's hands stilled on the ropes. "You saw what happened during the attack. Her power... it's unstable. Dangerous." She met his gaze, unwavering. "The path you're setting her on leads to death, Rafe. Maybe all of ours."

"Every path leads to death under Draven's rule." Rafe ran a hand through his hair, frustration building in his chest. "At least this way, we have a chance. She's different than the rest. They were all just kids who were born with the gift. Liora has it in her blood. Her mother was a Dreamweaver, she worked with Thorne. This girl's all we have. She's the last Dreamweaver, Jayne. The last one."

"And what about the healer?" Jayne's voice softened slightly, changing the subject. "Gemini. She's not built for this life. The road to Twilight isn't kind to gentle souls."

Rafe's thoughts drifted to Gemini's unwavering loyalty to Liora, the way she'd stood her ground even as chaos erupted around them. "She made her choice. They both did. Besides, we need a healer, and she's got more spine than most soldiers I've met."

"That's what worries me." Jayne secured the final knot with a sharp tug. "The ones with spine are usually the first to break. When they do, it's never clean."

A twig snapped in the darkness beyond their small camp, and Rafe's hand instinctively went to his sword. He shared a quick glance with Jayne, who had already drawn her dagger. The weight of their conversation hung in the air, unfinished but pressing.

"We move at first light," Rafe muttered, scanning the treeline. "Whether you think they're ready or not, we're out of time and out of options." He could only pray he wasn't leading them all to their deaths.

***

Liora's fingers traced the weathered grain of Eldara's gate, memorizing every groove and splinter. The wood felt warm beneath her touch, as if holding onto yesterday's flames. Behind her, boots crunched on gravel as the rebels prepared to move out, but she couldn't tear her gaze from the village that had been her entire world until now.

Smoke still curled above the distant rooftops, dancing against the morning sky like ghostly fingers. The miller's wheel lay broken, its steady rhythm silenced. How many mornings had she walked this path, listening to its creaking song? The thought of never hearing it again twisted something deep in her chest.

Her pack weighed heavy on her shoulders, filled with the fragments of her old life - a spare dress, the smooth river stone Bennet had given her on her sixteenth birthday. Each item felt like an anchor, trying to hold her in place even as her feet prepared to carry her away.

Gemini's hand brushed her arm, gentle but insistent. Her friend's presence steadied her, though Liora caught the slight tremor in Gemini's fingers, betraying her own uncertainty. They were both leaving everything they'd known, stepping into a world where magic and rebellion replaced the simple rhythms of village life.

The sound of Rafe checking weapons with his rebels drifted over, reminding her that time was slipping away. Was she ready for this? The power thrumming beneath her skin answered with a restless pulse, neither a yes nor a no. Her hand fell from the gate, fingers curling into a fist. The life she'd known, the safety of predictable days - all of it had burned away in last night's flames. There was no going back.

Gemini's hand found Liora's shoulder, her touch carrying the warmth of countless shared moments in Eldara's quieter days. The weight of her friend's palm seemed to anchor Liora, keeping her from drowning in the tide of doubt that threatened to pull her under.

"This isn't goodbye," Gemini murmured, her voice steady despite the ash that still clung to her clothes. "It's just... until we return. Stronger and ready to help." Her words held no trace of the uncertainty that had clouded her eyes during the attack, replaced now by a quiet determination that Liora had always admired.

Jayne called out a warning - they needed to move before Draven's soldiers returned. But Gemini didn't rush her, didn't pull away. Instead, she squeezed Liora's shoulder gently, the gesture speaking volumes about years of friendship and trust. It reminded Liora of the times Gemini had tended her wounds after failed attempts at controlling her power, never once flinching away in fear.

The rising sun caught in Gemini's hair, highlighting streaks of gold among the dirt and soot. For a moment, Liora saw her friend as others might - not just a village healer, but someone whose quiet strength could help reshape the world. Perhaps that same strength lived in her too, waiting to be uncovered.

Rafe's boots scuffed against the ground as he approached, his shadow stretching long in the morning light. The hard lines of his face softened as he caught Liora's gaze lingering on the village gates.

"I remember the last time I looked back," he said, his voice rough with memory. "My village burned for three days. Draven's men made sure nothing remained but ash and broken promises."

Liora's fingers clutched tighter around the smooth river stone in her pocket.

"The tavern was destroyed," he murmured with longing. "All my mother and father's hard work. The flames danced in every windowpane around the marketplace, transforming our town into an endless reflection of devastation."

"I couldn't save them then," Rafe said, his hand resting on the hilt of his sword. "But every village we protect now, every person we free from Draven's control - it honors what was lost." His eyes met hers, carrying both pain and purpose.

"We fight not because it's easy," Rafe continued, his voice dropping lower, "but because we must. Because if we don't, who will?" The question hung in the air between them, heavy with truth.

Liora pulled the river stone from her pocket, running her thumb over its worn surface. Bennet had told her it came from the deepest part of the river, where the current ran strong and true. Like her power, he'd said - if only she'd let it flow.

"I hope I'm strong enough for that," she whispered, more to the stone than to her companions. "For all of this." The words felt small against the vastness of what lay ahead.

"You are," Rafe answered, and something in his tone made her look up. His eyes held none of the doubt she'd seen in the other rebels' faces, only a quiet certainty that seemed to reach past her fears.

The sun climbed higher, casting long shadows through the gate's wooden slats. Behind them, Jayne called out final preparations, her voice carrying the edge of urgency that had become familiar since the attack. Liora tucked the stone back into her pocket, feeling its coolness press against her palm like a promise.

Liora's boots scraped against the worn path as she took that first step away from Eldara. The setting sun painted the sky in shades of amber and blood, casting long shadows that seemed to reach for her like grasping fingers. Each step felt heavier than the last, as if invisible threads were trying to pull her back to the only home she'd ever known.

Gemini's steady presence beside her anchored her to the moment, their shoulders occasionally brushing as they fell into step together. The familiar scent of her friend's herb-stained clothes mixed with the smoke that still clung to their hair, creating a bitter reminder of why they had to leave. Ahead, Rafe and Jayne moved with the fluid grace of experienced fighters, their eyes constantly scanning the treeline for threats.

The crunch of gravel beneath their feet seemed to echo with finality. Liora's hand found the river stone in her pocket again, its smooth surface warming against her skin. The power within her stirred restlessly, as if responding to her turmoil. She forced her fingers to relax their grip, remembering how that same power had torn through the festival grounds just hours ago.

A cool evening breeze carried the distant sound of the mill's broken wheel, its damaged frame creaking a mournful farewell. Liora's throat tightened as she glanced back one final time. The village looked smaller now, its familiar shapes blurred by distance and gathering dusk. The sight burned itself into her memory - the crooked chimney of Bennet's house, the flowering vines that still clung to the tavern's walls, the weathered fence posts that marked the boundary of her childhood world.

The image wavered as tears threatened to spill, but Liora blinked them back fiercely. This wasn't an ending, she told herself, even as her heart ached with each step that carried her further from home. This was a beginning - though of what, she wasn't yet sure. The power humming beneath her skin seemed to pulse in agreement, pushing her forward into the gathering darkness where Rafe and Jayne's silhouettes led the way toward an uncertain future.

# Freezing Night

The wooded trail wavered in Liora's vision while weariness seeped through her limbs. She watched her companions trudge onward - Gemini marching with forced purpose that concealed her exhaustion, Rafe maintaining his guard with rigid posture, and Jayne moving with the practiced precision of someone long accustomed to flight. Their elongated shadows twisted into unsettling forms on the debris-covered earth, and every footfall drew them further into the unknown.

Jayne's raised hand brought them to a halt. "We'll camp here for the night." The words hung in the cooling air, and Liora's stomach knotted. The thought of sleeping, of surrendering to dreams that might spiral beyond her control, sent a chill down her spine. Her fingers found the river stone in her pocket, its smooth surface offering little comfort against the growing darkness.

"I don't think-" The words died in her throat as a whistling sound cut through the air. Dream-infused arrows burst against nearby trees, releasing clouds of shimmering mist that twisted reality into nightmare shapes. A soldier's cry of recognition - "It's Delacroix!" - shattered the forest's silence.

The world tilted sideways as the dream magic took hold. Trees stretched and warped like melting wax, their branches reaching down with grasping fingers. Rafe's blade sang as he deflected another arrow, but the corrupted magic had already begun its work. Through the haze, Liora saw Gemini stumble, caught in the disorienting effect of the spell.

The forest floor rippled beneath Liora's feet like the surface of a disturbed pond. Her power stirred in response to the chaos, pushing against her control as Draven's soldiers emerged from the twisted shadows. Their weapons gleamed with an unnatural light that left trailing afterimages in the air, and the sound of their approach seemed to come from everywhere at once. The magic within her surged, demanding release, even as fear threatened to freeze her in place.

The clash of steel against steel filled the warped forest as Rafe met the first soldier with savage precision. His blade found gaps in armor that Liora hadn't even noticed, each strike drawing sprays of crimson that seemed to hang suspended in the dream-twisted air. Jayne moved like a shadow among the trees, her daggers finding throats before her targets could cry out.

Liora's heart hammered against her ribs as she watched another soldier crumple, his face frozen in permanent surprise at Rafe's brutality. This wasn't the controlled sparring she'd glimpsed in the village square - this was survival, raw and merciless. The soldier's blood spread across the forest floor, dark and real against the surreal landscape.

More arrows whistled through the air, their dream-magic payloads bursting against tree trunks and spreading confusion like poison. A soldier screamed as Jayne's blade found his kidney, the sound cutting off in a wet gurgle that made Liora's stomach turn. The forest itself seemed to pulse with each death, reality bending further out of shape.

Through the chaos, Gemini's voice reached her, steady despite the madness surrounding them. "Liora, we need you! Your power - use it to protect us!" Her friend ducked beneath a soldier's wild swing, narrowly avoiding the blade's edge.

The magic within Liora surged in response to Gemini's words, pressing against her control like a dam about to burst. Images of the village festival flashed through her mind - the chaos, the destruction she'd caused. Her hands trembled as another soldier fell to Rafe's sword, his dying breath carrying a curse.

The forest warped again, trees bending at impossible angles as more soldiers emerged from the shadows. Rafe's blade was a blur of motion, but even he couldn't hold back the tide forever. Blood dripped from a cut above his eye, and his movements had begun to slow.

Jayne appeared beside Liora, her voice sharp with urgency. "If you're going to do something, do it now!" She spun away to meet another attacker, her daggers finding home in the soldier's throat. The brutality of it all threatened to overwhelm Liora's senses.

A soldier's blade swept toward Gemini's unprotected back, and something inside Liora finally snapped. Golden light exploded outward from her hands, and the dream-twisted forest seemed to hold its breath, waiting to see what she would do next.

The golden light twisted and writhed like a living thing, responding more to Liora's panic than her intent. It surged through the warped forest in waves, catching soldiers mid-stride as they charged. Their bodies froze, muscles locked in grotesque poses as the magic took hold, eyes wide with terror.

Horror gripped Liora's chest as she saw the light reaching for her companions. Rafe's sword arm slowed, his movements becoming

sluggish as though he fought through honey. The magic didn't dis-
criminate between friend and foe, feeding off her fear rather than her
purpose.

Jayne stumbled, fighting against the creeping paralysis that threatened to lock her joints. Her daggers slipped from nerveless fingers,
clattering against roots that writhed beneath her feet. The sound
echoed wrongly in the dream-twisted air, stretching and distorting like
everything else.

Rafe's eyes met hers across the battlefield, filled with a mix of awe
and growing fear as the paralysis crept up his legs. He tried to speak,
but his words came out slurred and distant. The sight of him struggling against her magic sent fresh waves of panic through Liora's chest.

Tears blurred Liora's vision as she watched Jayne sink to her knees,
fighting the paralysis with every breath. The seasoned fighter's face
showed no judgment, only grim determination as she struggled against
the effects of Liora's magic. That acceptance somehow made it worse.

Through the golden haze, Liora caught glimpses of the frozen
soldiers, their faces locked in expressions of terror and rage. Some
had toppled completely, lying like discarded dolls on the forest floor.
Others remained upright, perfect statues of violence interrupted.

The magic finally began to ebb, leaving Liora trembling and
drained. As the golden light faded, her companions slowly regained
their mobility, but Draven's soldiers were still frozen. With a grin,
Jayne retrieved her daggers and plunged them into a soldier's gut.

Blood sprayed across fallen leaves as Rafe's blade found another
frozen soldier's throat. His movements were still sluggish from the
lingering effects of Liora's magic, but determination drove his sword
through paralyzed flesh. The wet sounds of execution filled the twisted
forest as the rebels dispatched their helpless enemies.

Liora pressed her forehead against the cold earth, trying to block out the sounds of death she'd enabled. Her shoulders shook with each muffled thud of bodies hitting the ground. The magic had receded, leaving her hollow and sick, but its golden afterimage still burned behind her eyes - a reminder of how quickly her power had turned against friend and foe alike.

Jayne moved through the carnage with mechanical precision, her daggers ending lives with quick, efficient strokes. Her face remained impassive as she worked, but her hands trembled slightly - whether from the aftermath of paralysis or something else, Liora couldn't tell. The seasoned fighter paused only once, meeting Liora's gaze with an unreadable expression before moving to her next target.

A soldier's dying gurgle cut through the air, followed by Rafe's labored breathing as he yanked his blade free. The sound drove fresh waves of nausea through Liora's stomach. She'd made this slaughter possible - had turned living, breathing people into helpless statues for the rebels to cut down. The fact that they were enemies didn't ease the weight of responsibility crushing her chest.

Jayne's calloused hands gripped Liora's shoulders, hauling her up from the blood-stained earth. Liora's legs trembled, threatening to give out, but Gemini slipped an arm around her waist before she could fall. The healer's touch steadied her, even as the metallic scent of death clung to their clothes.

"We need to move. More patrols will come to investigate." Jayne's eyes scanned the twisted trees, her daggers already cleaned and sheathed. She nodded to Gemini. "Keep her on her feet. We can't afford to slow down."

The forest floor shifted beneath their feet as they picked their way through the aftermath of battle. Dream magic still lingered in the air, making the shadows dance and writhe at the edges of Liora's vision.

Each step carried them further from the carnage, but the weight of what she'd done pressed down on her shoulders like a physical thing.

Gemini's fingers squeezed Liora's arm as fresh tears spilled down her cheeks. "You did better this time," she whispered, her voice steady despite their hurried pace. "The magic responded to your need to protect us. That's why we're all still walking."

The words pierced through Liora's fog of guilt. She remembered the golden light surging outward, how it had slowed but not stopped her companions. The paralysis had been temporary for them, while Draven's soldiers had remained frozen until the end. Perhaps there was a measure of control in that, even if it didn't feel like enough.

***

The forest blurred past as Rafe led the group through the night to the morning, his boots crushing fallen leaves with each determined stride. His sword arm tingled - an aftereffect of Liora's magic that sent shivers down his spine. Behind him, labored breathing and stumbling footsteps told him the others were struggling to keep pace.

The raw energy still crackled in the air, making his skin prickle like static before a storm. He'd felt power like this only once before - when Draven had decimated his village. But where Draven's magic had reeked of corruption and control, Liora's burst forth pure and wild, like a spring storm breaking winter's grip.

Rafe glanced back at her, noting how she clung to Gemini's arm, both women looking pale and shaken. The guilt etched across Liora's face made his chest tighten. She hadn't meant to unleash such force - that much was clear. But the fact that she could, untrained and afraid... what might she become with proper guidance?

His fingers flexed around his sword hilt, muscle memory from countless battles keeping him alert despite the lingering numbness. Two of his rebels, Marcus and Elena, stumbled against each other, their movements still jerky and uncoordinated from the magical back-lash. He needed to find them shelter soon, somewhere they could recover their strength.

The memory of Liora's power exploding outward replayed in his mind - that brilliant surge of light that had knocked them all back, friend and foe alike. For a moment, he'd seen genuine fear in the eyes of Draven's soldiers. They'd fled not from his blade, but from her raw potential.

Sweat trickled down Rafe's back despite the cool forest air. This changed everything. If Liora could harness that power, control it... they might actually stand a chance against Draven. But first, they had to keep her alive long enough to learn - and convince her to embrace what she clearly feared.

Through the canopy above, sunlight filtered down in broken shafts, reminding him they no longer had the cover of night. They needed to make better time, but his people were exhausted. Elena had started limping, and Marcus looked ready to collapse. Even Gemini, steady as she'd been through everything, showed signs of strain.

The weight of responsibility pressed down on Rafe's shoulders. He'd promised to protect Liora, to help her understand her powers. Now, watching his team struggle in the aftermath of those same pow-ers, doubt crept in. Was he leading them toward salvation or destruc-tion? The answer might determine the fate of not just their rebellion, but all of Somnus.

Rafe's jaw clenched as Marcus stepped forward, the man's face twisted in a sneer that set Rafe's teeth on edge. The morning light caught the fresh burn marks on Marcus's sleeve - evidence of Liora's uncontrolled power from earlier.

"We're supposed to trust our lives to someone who can't even control her own magic?" Marcus's words cut through the forest clearing like a blade. "I've seen what happens when power goes wrong. My sister died because of wild magic like that." His eyes fixed on Liora with an accusation that made Rafe's hand instinctively tighten on his sword hilt.

The memory of his own first encounter with untamed magic flashed through Rafe's mind - the screams, the chaos, the aftermath. But this was different. Liora wasn't Draven, and her power, though raw, held none of the emperor's malice. Still, Marcus's words had struck a nerve with the other rebels. Elena shifted uncomfortably, and even steadfast Gemini's expression tightened with concern.

The tension crackled between them like lightning about to strike. Marcus's hand drifted toward his dagger, and Rafe recognized the fear driving his actions - the same fear that had driven so many to turn against those with power. But before either man could move, a branch snapped in the distance, and birds erupted from the canopy in a panicked flurry. Draven's patrols were getting closer.

"We all started somewhere," Rafe's voice cut through the tense silence, his eyes scanning the faces of his team. "Elena couldn't hold a sword without dropping it her first week. Marcus, you threw up after your first battle." He let that sink in, noting how Marcus's grip on his dagger loosened slightly. "And me? I got my entire squad captured because I rushed in without thinking. Every one of us made mistakes while learning our place in this fight."

A quiet scoff drew his attention to Jayne, who leaned against a weathered oak tree, her calculating eyes fixed on Liora. The spy's usual mask of indifference had slipped, revealing something that might have been respect. "The kid's got moxie," Jayne declared, her tone carrying the weight of someone who didn't give praise lightly. "Did you see how she stood her ground when those soldiers came at us? Most untrained recruits would've run."

The unexpected support from Jayne - who trusted about as easily as a wounded wolf - lifted some of the weight from Rafe's shoulders. Yet he couldn't ignore the way Elena still kept her distance from Liora, or how Marcus's jaw remained clenched tight enough to crack teeth. The fear ran deep, and one moment of chaos had awakened old terrors in his people.

Another branch snapped in the distance, closer this time, and Rafe's hand returned to his sword. They'd lingered too long, letting fear and doubt slow them down while Draven's soldiers drew ever nearer. He caught Liora's eye, seeing her appreciation for standing up for her. Gemini leaned in whisper something to Liora, and the girl had just the fainted pull of a grin.

As they all turned to move on, Rafe watched a quiet exchange between the two women, noting how Gemini's presence seemed to settle something in Liora's stance. The healer had a way about her - a steadiness that acted like a balm on raw nerves. Even now, as Gemini's gentle words carried across the clearing, the tension in Liora's shoulders began to ease.

The sound of pursuit had faded, but Rafe kept his guard up, fingers never straying far from his sword hilt. He'd seen too many ambushes to trust the forest's seeming peace. Still, this moment of respite gave him time to study their newest recruits. Gemini's quiet strength complemented Liora's raw power in ways he hadn't anticipated. Where Liora burned like lightning, Gemini flowed like a steady stream, wearing down resistance through persistence rather than force.

Jayne's earlier objections echoed in his mind. "A healer will slow us down," she'd argued, her practical nature showing through. "And if she gets captured, they'll use her to draw out the Dreamweaver." But watching Gemini now, the way she grounded Liora with just a touch and a few soft words, Rafe knew he'd made the right call. They needed more than just fighters in this rebellion. They needed healers for the soul as much as the body, as Nero liked to say.

The thought of Nero Thorne made Rafe's jaw clench. The old Custodian's methods were effective, but harsh - like tempering steel through fire. Without someone like Gemini to balance that intensity, Liora might break under the pressure. He'd seen it happen before, watched promising recruits crumble when pushed too hard, too fast.

Marcus stumbled again, a groan escaping his lips before he could catch it. The sound made Rafe's shoulders tense - any noise could give away their position. But the exhaustion in that sound was unmistakable. They'd been pushing hard since dawn, and even Rafe's trained fighters were reaching their limits.

"We need to rest." Jayne's quiet voice carried the weight of command, though she posed it as a suggestion. She'd fallen into step beside him, close enough that he caught the slight tremor in her usually steady hands. "They're dead on their feet, and you know we can't fight like this."

The strategic part of Rafe's mind rebelled against stopping - they weren't far enough from Eldara, weren't safe enough yet. But watching Elena stumble for the third time, seeing how Liora leaned heavily on Gemini despite her attempts to hide her exhaustion, he knew Jayne was right. The growing darkness would cover their tracks, but it would also make travel more treacherous.

"First watch is mine," Rafe announced, scanning the deepening shadows for a defensible position. His hand hadn't left his sword hilt since they'd fled the village, and the muscles in his arm ached from the constant tension. But he'd learned long ago that exhaustion was preferable to death, and he wouldn't risk their safety by letting someone else take first watch - not when his nerves still hummed with the lingering effects of Liora's power, keeping him almost painfully alert.

***

The camp rustled with activity around Liora, rebels setting up a defensive perimeter for the night. Their furtive glances in her direction stung more than her aching muscles. One man openly shifted away as she passed, his hand tightening on his weapon. The gesture sent a fresh wave of shame through her chest.

Her bedroll lay at the edge of camp, positioned beneath a gnarled oak. Gemini had insisted on setting it up while Liora helped gather firewood, though her friend's kindness only amplified her guilt.

Sleep pulled at her consciousness like a current, despite her fear of what dreams might come. The forest canopy swayed overhead, branches casting shifting shadows across her face. Each time her eyes drifted shut, flashes of the ambush blazed behind her eyelids - the surge of uncontrolled power, the rebels diving for cover, Rafe's expression of mingled concern and disappointment.

A twig snapped nearby and Liora's eyes flew open, her heart racing. But it was only Rafe, making his rounds of the camp's perimeter. Their gazes met briefly before she turned away, unable to bear the weight of his scrutiny. As exhaustion finally claimed her, one last thought drifted through her mind: Would she ever learn to control what lurked inside her, or would she remain a danger to everyone who tried to help?

The nightmare seized Liora with cold, spectral fingers. Inky darkness pressed against her skin as she thrashed against invisible bonds. Tendrils of shadow coiled around her wrists and ankles, holding her suspended in a void where even her screams died before reaching her lips.

A pale light cut through the murk, drawing her gaze like a moth to flame. A stone hung suspended before her, its crystalline surface rippling with currents of golden energy. Each pulse sent waves of power washing over her, and the shadows recoiled from its radiance. Ancient symbols etched across its surface flickered and danced, whispering secrets in a language that tugged at the edges of her consciousness.

The stone's light intensified, burning away the darkness until Liora floated in a sea of golden mist. Her bonds dissolved, leaving her free but still trapped within the dream's grip. Energy reached for her like searching fingers, and where it touched, her skin tingled with familiar power - the same force that had erupted from her during the attack on Eldara.

Images flashed through the golden haze - faces contorted in fear, buildings crumbling, dreams twisting into nightmares. Each vision stabbed at her heart, showing the destruction her untamed power could unleash. Yet beneath the horror, a deeper truth pulsed within the stone's light: these were not just warnings, but possibilities. Choices yet unmade.

The stone's glow penetrated deeper, past her skin and into her very essence. It resonated with something inside her, awakening an awareness she'd tried to suppress. Her power answered the stone's call, rising up unbidden. Golden light blazed from her palms, matching the stone's rhythm. The force of it tore a gasp from her throat as reality began to fracture around her, dreams and nightmares bleeding through the cracks.

Liora's hand moved toward the glowing stone as if pulled by an invisible thread. Her fingers trembled inches from its crystalline surface, power already crackling through the air between them like static before a storm. The rational part of her mind screamed to pull back, but something deeper, more primal, urged her forward until her fingertips brushed the cold, smooth face of the stone.

Raw energy exploded through her body, flooding every nerve with liquid fire. The sensation ripped a gasp from her throat as golden light blazed from her skin, turning the darkness to day. Power sang through her veins, intoxicating and terrifying all at once - more than she'd ever felt, more than she could possibly contain. Her heart thundered against her ribs as the force built within her, seeking release.

A scream built in her throat as the energy reached a fever pitch. Was this what waited for her if she embraced her power? Not protection or salvation, but only ruin? The stone pulsed in response to her fear, sending another wave of force crashing through her body. Ancient symbols blazed across its surface, their meaning hovering just beyond her grasp even as they seemed to whisper of destiny and doom.

The golden light exploded outward in a final surge that shattered what remained of the dreamscape. As darkness rushed in to fill the void, Liora caught one last glimpse of the devastation she'd caused - a blasted wasteland where nothing lived or grew.

The vision shattered like glass, leaving Liora gasping in the darkness. Her heart slammed against her ribs as she bolted upright, fingers clawing at the bedroll. Golden afterimages danced behind her eyes - the stone's pulsing light, ancient symbols that seemed to whisper destiny. The power that had coursed through her moments ago left only phantom tingles in its wake, but the memory of that raw energy still made her tremble.

Around her, the camp remained untouched. No withered trees, no blasted earth, no destruction radiating outward from where she lay. The other rebels slept peacefully, their forms barely visible in the pre-dawn gloom. Only the racing of her pulse and the cold sweat on her skin testified to the vision's reality. That stone - it had felt so real, so familiar. Like something half-remembered from a forgotten life.

A prickling sensation at the base of her neck drew her attention to the camp's edge. Rafe stood in the shadows of a gnarled oak, his posture tense as he watched her. The concern in his expression made her stomach twist. Had he seen her thrashing in her sleep? Witnessed some inadvertent display of power? The thought sent fresh anxiety coursing through her veins.

His gaze burned into her, full of questions she couldn't - wouldn't - answer. Liora forced her breathing to slow and settled back onto her bedroll, turning away from his scrutiny. She pulled the blanket up to her chin, feigning sleep even as her mind raced. The stone's golden light still pulsed behind her closed eyelids, a beacon calling her toward some unknown destiny.

Each breath came easier as she focused on keeping her body still, projecting an illusion of peaceful slumber. But sleep remained impossibly distant as questions tumbled through her thoughts. What was that stone? Why did it feel so significant? And most troubling of all - had the vision shown her power's true nature, or merely her deepest fears given form?

# Twilight

General Kael Varden's fingers traced the mountain paths leading to Draven's stronghold, each route a possible avenue for victory—or devastating defeat. The candlelight caught the silver threading in his commander's insignia, a reminder of past glories now tarnished by his defection. Strange how quickly allegiances could shift, like sand beneath a soldier's feet.

A sharp rap at his door interrupted his brooding. "Enter," he called, not bothering to look up from the map. The sound of boots on wooden planks told him it was another of Draven's former soldiers—they always walked with that particular rigid stride. The messenger delivered his report: the girl with the untamed powers had arrived. Kael dismissed him with a wave, his mind already churning with possibilities.

Power radiated from her, raw and untamed—he'd felt it even from across the camp. It reminded him of Draven's might, before corruption had twisted it into something darker. His jaw clenched at the memory of serving under that tyrant, of watching dream magic perverted into a tool of oppression. But perhaps this girl, this Liora, could be shaped into something more useful.

The candle guttered as a draft swept through the room, casting wild shadows across the map. Kael's hand instinctively moved to the region marking Eldara, where Draven's forces had just attacked. The timing was perfect—chaos always created opportunity. And if he played this right, he might finally grasp the influence he deserved.

A cold smile tugged at his lips as he plotted his next move. The rebels were so eager to trust, so desperate for allies that they never questioned a defector's true motives. His fingers drummed against the table as he considered his options. The girl would need guidance, support—things he could provide while steering her toward his own ends. Let Nero Thorne teach her control; Kael would teach her ambition, whether she realized it or not.

Kael's fingers froze on the map as his pendant slipped free, its silver surface catching the candlelight. The worn family crest—a falcon clutching a sword—stared back at him, each scratch and dent a chapter of his past. His throat tightened at the sight.

Memories flooded back unbidden. The proud smile on his father's face when he'd first earned his commander's rank. The weight of responsibility as he'd led his first campaign, his men looking to him with unwavering trust. The metallic taste of victory after each successful strategy played out exactly as he'd planned.

The pendant felt heavier now, laden with the ghosts of decisions he couldn't unmake. He remembered the exact moment everything changed—standing in Draven's war room, watching as the Emperor ordered the execution of an entire village for harboring a single rebel. Kael's hand had stayed steady as he'd saluted, even as his stomach churned.

His fingers traced the falcon's outline, remembering how his family name had once stood for protection, not betrayal. The Varden legacy stretched back generations, each member serving with distinction in Somnus's military. Now here he sat, plotting against both sides, the pendant a mockery of everything he'd once held dear.

The candlelight flickered, casting dancing shadows across the maps spread before him. Each route he'd marked represented another piece in his elaborate game—one that would either restore his family's honor or destroy what little remained of it. The thought of Liora's raw power made his pulse quicken with possibility.

His hand closed around the pendant, feeling its familiar edges dig into his palm. The metal warmed against his skin as he recalled his mother's words when she'd given it to him: "Power without purpose is nothing but destruction waiting to happen." He wondered what she would think of his purpose now.

The sound of marching feet outside his tent pulled him back to the present. The rebel camp was preparing for night watch, their dedication almost admirable. Almost. Kael had seen how quickly dedication could turn to desperation, and desperation to betrayal. He'd orchestrated enough of both to recognize the signs.

He tucked the pendant back beneath his tunic, its weight settling against his chest like an accusation. The map before him showed clear paths to victory, but victory for whom? The question nagged at him as he marked another potential route with his quill.

Kael pushed away from the map-strewn table, his boots scraping against the wooden floor as unwanted memories threatened to surface. The pendant's weight against his chest felt like an anchor, dragging him back to moments he'd rather forget. His fingers brushed the cold metal before dropping away, as if burned.

Through the tent's thin walls, he heard the rebels training—their determination evident in each clash of steel and bark of command. They trusted him now, relied on his tactical expertise to guide their strikes against Draven's forces. The irony wasn't lost on him. Every strategy he provided drew from years of serving the very tyrant they fought against. Their suspicious glances hadn't escaped his notice, particularly from those who remembered facing him across battle-fields not so long ago.

The tent flap rustled, and Kael's posture straightened instinctively. A rebel lieutenant entered, bringing reports of Draven's latest movements. Kael accepted the scrolls with a measured nod, maintaining the careful mask of the devoted defector. Yet beneath that facade, his mind raced with calculations. Each piece of intelligence was another card in his hand, and he was playing a game far more complex than simple rebellion.

A commotion outside drew his attention—the girl, Liora. Raw energy crackled through the air, making the hairs on his neck rise. Such potential, such force... waiting to be shaped by the right hand. His fingers drummed against the table as he watched through the tent's gap. Whether that hand would be the rebellion's or Draven's remained to be seen. For now, he would wait, observe, and plan. After all, true power lay not in choosing sides, but in knowing when to change them.

***

The healers swarmed around them like concerned moths, their white robes fluttering in the evening breeze as they guided the wounded rebels through the hidden entrance of the Twilight Camp. Liora hesitated at the threshold, her eyes drinking in the sight before her. The camp sprawled through a natural hollow in the forest, sheltered by ancient trees whose branches wove together overhead like protective fingers.

Lanterns hung from ropes strung between the trees, casting pools of warm light that pushed back against the encroaching darkness. Their glow revealed a collection of mismatched tents in various states of repair, some patched with different colored fabrics that somehow made them more charming rather than shabby. The largest tent dominated the center of the camp, its peak rising above the others like a watchful guardian.

The scent of herbs and healing balms mingled with woodsmoke from cooking fires, creating an oddly comforting atmosphere despite the circumstances that had brought them here. Somewhere in the distance, someone strummed a guitar, its melancholy notes floating on the evening air like fallen leaves.

People moved through the spaces between tents with purpose, their shadows dancing against canvas walls. Some carried supplies, others tended to the wounded, and still others huddled in small groups, their heads bent together in urgent conversation. The camp hummed with an energy that spoke of both determination and barely contained chaos.

A group of children darted past, their laughter a stark contrast to the gravity of the situation. They weaved between the tents, playing some game that involved touching certain trees in a specific order. Their presence made the camp feel more like a village than a rebel hideout, though the armed guards at strategic points served as stark reminders of reality.

Steam rose from a large pot hanging over one of the cooking fires, carrying the promising aroma of stew. Several rebels gathered around it, holding out bowls with eager expressions. Their faces bore the same mix of exhaustion and hope that Liora had seen in her traveling companions.

The healers' tent buzzed with activity as more wounded were brought in. Through its partially open flap, Liora caught glimpses of organized chaos - neat rows of cots, shelves lined with bottles and bandages, and efficient movements of those tending to the injured. The sounds of pain and comfort drifted out in equal measure.

Near the edge of camp, a makeshift training area had been set up. Even now, as evening settled in, a few rebels practiced with wooden swords or rehearsed hand-to-hand combat moves.

The camp felt like a world unto itself, existing in some liminal space between reality and dream. As another group of healers hurried past, their white robes now stained with blood, Liora realized that this hidden refuge represented both sanctuary and sacrifice - a place where hope and hardship walked hand in hand through the gathering dusk.

Rafe led them past the healers' tent, waving off their concerned glances. "You two need food more than bandages right now." His hand brushed the small of Liora's back, guiding her toward the large central tent. The touch sent an unexpected warmth through her tired muscles.

"The common room's where everyone gathers," he explained, pushing aside the heavy canvas flap. "Strategy meetings, meals, whatever brings people together. Sometimes just to remember we're not alone in this fight." His voice carried a weight that made Liora wonder how many battles he'd seen, how many friends he'd lost.

The tent's interior opened up like a cavern. Lanterns hung from crossbeams, casting pools of golden light over scattered tables and benches. The earthy scent of wood smoke mingled with something herbal - tea, perhaps, or healing tonics.

As they stepped inside, conversations died mid-sentence. Dozens of faces turned toward them, expressions ranging from curiosity to outright suspicion. Liora felt the weight of their stares like physical pressure against her skin. The silence grew thick enough to choke on.

A mug clattered against a table somewhere in the back, the sound sharp as breaking glass in the stillness. Liora's fingers twitched, dream energy crackling just beneath her skin in response to the tension. Gemini's hand found hers, squeezing gently - a reminder that she wasn't facing this alone.

The stew steamed in front of Liora, its rich aroma a stark contrast to the cold stares drilling into her back. She focused on the wooden spoon in her hand, watching ripples form as her trembling fingers disturbed the surface. Beside her, Gemini's steady presence offered what little comfort it could against the weight of so many suspicious eyes.

The bread Gemini tore and shared between them tasted like ash in Liora's mouth. Each bite stuck in her throat, requiring conscious effort to swallow past the knot of tension. A child pointed at her from across the room before being hurriedly shushed by its mother.

Rafe's voice cut through the murmurs as he addressed someone behind them. "She's here because we need her." His tone carried an edge of steel that seemed to dare anyone to challenge him. The whispers didn't stop, but they grew more subdued, slinking into darker corners of the tent. Liora kept her eyes fixed on her bowl, unsure whether to feel grateful for his defense or mortified by the attention it drew.

Liora watched Rafe's shoulders tense as he positioned himself between her and the staring rebels. The muscles in his back rippled beneath his worn shirt, and her cheeks warmed at the way his stance radiated protective strength. Her spoon clinked against the bowl as she forced herself to take another bite of stew.

The whispers continued to drift around them like poisoned smoke. A flash of dream energy sparked between her fingers, and she clenched her hand into a fist, willing it away. How could Rafe stand so confidently beside someone who could lose control at any moment?

His dark hair fell across his forehead as he turned to check on her, and their eyes met briefly before she looked away. The concern in his gaze made her stomach flutter, but she couldn't shake the memory of how he'd frozen when her powers had exploded in the forest. Even he, for all his brave words, feared what lurked beneath her skin.

Another rebel brushed too close to their table, and Liora's magic surged in response to her anxiety. The lantern above them flickered, casting dancing shadows across Rafe's face. The sharp planes of his jaw tightened as he noticed, though he tried to hide it.

She watched him scan the room with practiced efficiency, noting exits and potential threats. His movements held the fluid grace of a fighter, beautiful and deadly. But would those quick reflexes ever be turned against her if she lost control again?

The stew grew cold in front of her as she struggled to eat, hyperaware of both Rafe's proximity and the distance he maintained. Not enough to be obvious to others, but she felt it - that careful space between them, just wide enough to react if necessary.

His sword hand never strayed far from his weapon, and Liora couldn't stop wondering if that habit had developed before or after he'd witnessed her powers firsthand. The thought sent another tremor through her fingers, and she gripped her spoon tighter to hide it.

A child's cry from outside made her jump, and golden light sparked visibly between her fingers. Rafe's hand twitched toward his sword before he caught himself. The motion, small as it was, felt like a blade between her ribs.

Heat crept up her neck as she noticed his arms again, corded with muscle from years of fighting. Fighting against threats to his people - was that what she'd become? The way he'd looked at her in the forest, eyes wide with shock as her power had frozen their companions, haunted her thoughts.

More rebels filtered into the tent, and Liora felt their stares like physical pressure against her skin. Rafe shifted his weight, angling his body to shield her from the worst of their attention. The protective gesture made her heart ache even as she wondered how long it would be before he realized she was too dangerous to defend.

***

Liora watched Gemini's back disappear into the crowd around the food tent, her friend's absence leaving a hollow space at the rough-hewn table. The whispers seemed louder now, pressing in from all sides without Gemini's steadying presence to hold them at bay.

Her fingers traced absent patterns on the wooden surface, tiny sparks of golden light following in their wake. Back in Eldara, the mill's steady rhythm had helped quiet these moments of restless energy. Here in the rebel camp, every pulse of dream magic felt like another crack in her careful control.

The faces around her blurred together, yet each sidelong glance burned like a brand. A child's laughter cut through the din - bright and clear until its mother noticed Liora and hurried them away. The golden light beneath her skin flickered in response, and she pressed her palms flat against the table, willing the power back down.

The night air carried hints of autumn's approach, a crisp edge that made her think of harvest festivals and simpler days. Days before she'd known what lived inside her, before she'd watched her home burn. Before she'd learned that being the last Dreamweaver meant carrying the weight of so many fearful stares.

A shadow fell across the table, different from the constant shift of bodies around the food tent. The movement caught in her peripheral vision, subtle but deliberate, pulling her from thoughts of home and harvest. Liora's hands stilled against the wooden surface as the dream energy inside her responded to the presence, coiling like a spring ready to release.

Liora's shoulders tensed as the shadow stretched longer across the table. The man's presence carried a weight that seemed to push the whispers back, creating a pocket of stillness in the busy camp.

He moved with the fluid grace of a predator, each step measured and precise as he circled to face her. Silver threaded through his dark hair, and scars marked the weathered planes of his face. But it was his eyes that held her - deep wells of knowing that seemed to see straight through her carefully constructed walls.

The bench creaked as he sat across from her, his movements deliberate and unhurried. Others in the camp gave their table a wide berth now, their fearful glances taking on a different quality - respect mingled with wariness. The man's calm seemed to ripple outward, settling over their corner of the camp like a heavy blanket.

Power radiated from him in controlled waves, so different from her own wild surges. The golden light beneath her skin responded, reaching toward his silver energy, so very different, like a flower turning toward the sun. Liora fought the urge to pull away, to hide this unconscious reaction.

His silence stretched between them, assessment clear in his steady gaze. Questions burned on her tongue - who was he, what did he want, how did he control the power that seemed to bend reality around him?

But something in his posture suggested patience, as if he was waiting for her to find her own answers in the quiet he'd created.

Rafe materialized from the shadows between the food tents, his presence breaking the heavy silence. The flickering lamplight caught the fresh scrapes on his jaw, evidence of the morning's skirmish. His eyes darted between Liora and the silver-haired stranger, a mix of respect and caution in his stance.

"Liora, this is Nero Thorne." Rafe's voice carried an undercurrent of reverence that seemed at odds with his usual demeanor. "Before Draven's rise, he served as Custodian of the Veil - one of the last guardians of dream magic's secrets. There's no one alive who knows more about what you can do."

The golden light beneath Liora's skin pulsed stronger at Rafe's words, as if recognizing the weight of Nero's title. Her fingers quivered despite her attempts to steady them.

"When Draven's forces swept through the temples, burning everything they could find about dream magic, Nero was there. He saved what others couldn't - or wouldn't."

"Scrolls that dated back to the first Dreamweavers, artifacts that could channel dream energy in ways we've forgotten - Nero protected them all." Rafe's voice dropped lower, tension threading through his words. "He watched his fellow Custodians fall trying to defend our history, but he knew the knowledge had to survive. That someday someone like you would need it."

The golden light pulsed stronger at Rafe's words, and Liora curled her fingers into fists beneath the table. Her power recognized something in Nero that she couldn't yet understand, reaching toward him like a compass finding true north. The sensation frightened her almost as much as the uncontrolled surges that had destroyed her home.

"Three days he spent in the burning archives," Rafe continued, his eyes never leaving Nero's face. "Three days while Draven's men hunted through the halls, searching for anyone who dared preserve the old ways. He emerged with a library's worth of knowledge hidden away - knowledge that might help you understand what you are, Liora. What you could become."

"It's an honor to meet you, Master Thorne." The words felt small in her throat, inadequate against the weight of all he represented.

Nero's gaze held steady, seeming to look past her uncertain expression to something deeper. "The honor is mine, Liora." His voice carried the weight of ancient tomes and forgotten wisdom, distant yet somehow anchoring. The air between them hummed with untapped potential, like the moment before lightning strikes. "Though I have known you since you were born."

"H-how?" The question caught in her throat, barely a whisper. The wooden table beneath her hands began to smoke again as her control slipped, power responding to the turmoil inside her.

"A story for another time." His voice carried the same weight as before, but something softened around his eyes. "When you're ready to hear it. For now, there are more pressing matters." He gestured to the smoking table, where the wood had begun to char beneath her fingertips.

The dream energy inside her coiled tighter at his deflection, responding to her frustration. Questions burned on her tongue - about her mother, about the temples, about everything he might know of who she was meant to be. But his steady gaze held a promise of answers to come, if she could find the patience to wait for them.

Around them, the busy camp seemed to fade into shadow, leaving only this moment of connection between student and teacher, past and future.

Rafe shifted his weight, breaking the spell that had settled over their corner of the camp. But Nero's eyes never left Liora's face, and she felt the weight of unspoken expectations pressing down on her shoulders. The dream energy inside her coiled tighter, responding to a call she wasn't sure she was ready to answer.

The firelight caught in Nero's eyes as he leaned forward, his presence commanding attention without raising his voice. "Control is more than just holding back power, Liora. It's choosing how—and why—you wield it." The dream energy beneath Liora's skin responded to his words, pulsing in time with her heartbeat.

"Every surge, every spark - they're not mistakes to be feared, but messages to be understood."

The weight of his words settled over her like a heavy cloak. Part of her wanted to run, to hide from the responsibility his presence represented. But a deeper part recognized the truth in what he offered - a chance to understand the power that had haunted her dreams and destroyed her home. Her fingers tingled with residual energy, leaving fresh scorch marks on the wooden table.

Rafe's hand found her shoulder, warm and steady. "You're in good hands, Liora. Nero's teachings will be the key to your growth and our success against Draven." The contact grounded her, drawing her back from the edge of overwhelming possibility that Nero's words had opened before her.

"Tomorrow, before dawn," Nero said, "we'll begin with the fundamentals of mental discipline. Without a foundation of control, even the simplest dream can turn into a nightmare."

The night air grew heavier as he spoke, charged with the potential of what tomorrow might bring. Liora's fingers traced the scorched wood beneath them, evidence of her lack of control. Each mark felt like a reminder of Eldara, of homes burning and people fleeing from her uncontrolled power.

"The path ahead won't be easy," Nero's eyes held hers, seeing past her careful mask to the fear that lurked beneath. "But every Dreamweaver before you has walked it. Including your mother."

"My mother?" Liora whispered.

"Another time," Nero reminded.

Around them, the camp had grown quieter, though whether from respect for Nero or fear of her power, Liora couldn't tell. The dream energy inside her hummed with anticipation, responding to something in Nero's presence that promised understanding - and perhaps, finally, control. Her chest tightened with equal parts determination and dread as she nodded, accepting the weight of what tomorrow would bring.

# *Lyra Solari*

Rafe's boots crunched against fallen leaves as he guided them through the winding paths between tents and makeshift shelters. The rebel camp sprawled through the forest like a living thing, structures blending into the natural landscape. His hand brushed the hilt of his sword with each step, eyes scanning the shadows between trees.

"How could he have known her?" Liora's voice dropped to barely above a whisper as she followed close behind Gemini. Gemini's hand found Liora's arm in the darkness, steadying her as they navigated around a jutting tree root. The healer's touch carried its usual calming influence, but questions still churned in Liora's mind, making the golden light flicker beneath her skin.

The canvas walls of their assigned quarters came into view, the fabric worn but sturdy against the night wind. Rafe paused at the entrance, his expression softening as he caught the tail end of their conversation.

"Here's your shelter for as long as you're here." Rafe's voice carried an edge of amusement as he gestured to the sparse interior. A few bedrolls lay scattered across the packed earth, alongside a trunk that had seen better days.

Heat crept up Liora's neck as Rafe's gaze darted between her and Gemini, his lips quirking into a knowing smile. "Don't worry, I'll make sure no one disturbs you two." The implication in his tone made her stomach flip.

"Oh, we're not—" The words tangled on Liora's tongue as she tried to correct his assumption. Gemini's quiet laugh beside her only made the situation more awkward as golden sparks danced across her fingertips, betraying her embarrassment.

The crunch of heavy boots against gravel made Liora's spine stiffen. A tall figure emerged from between two tents, his polished insignia catching the moonlight. The way he moved reminded her of a predator - graceful but dangerous.

Rafe straightened, his hand snapping up in a crisp salute. "General Varden." The warmth that had softened his features moments ago vanished behind a mask of military discipline. "I was just showing our new recruits to their quarters."

"At ease, Delacroix." General Kael Varden's voice carried the cultured accent of someone from a large city. His gaze swept over Liora and Gemini, lingering a beat too long on Liora's hands where the dream energy still pulsed beneath her skin.

"General, may I present Liora and Gemini Estelle from Eldara." Rafe's tone remained carefully neutral, but Liora caught the slight tension in his jaw.

Something flickered behind Kael's eyes - hunger maybe, or calculation. His smile didn't reach those eyes as he extended his hand to Liora.

"A pleasure to meet you both. We've heard... interesting things about your abilities."

The dream energy coiled tighter in Liora's chest as she accepted his handshake. His grip was firm, almost crushing, and cold despite the warm night air. Every instinct screamed at her to pull away.

"Thank you for the welcome, General." Liora kept her voice steady even as unease crawled up her spine. There was something familiar about him that she couldn't place - something that echoed in her nightmares.

Kael's attention shifted to Gemini, but Liora noticed how his gaze kept darting back to her, measuring and assessing. Like a merchant appraising valuable goods. Or a hunter sizing up prey.

"I look forward to seeing your progress in training." His words carried an edge that made Liora's skin crawl. "Time is growing short before the Eclipse."

The general melted back into the shadows between tents, but his presence lingered like a bad taste in Liora's mouth. She caught Rafe watching her, his expression unreadable in the darkness. The dream energy thrummed through her veins, responding to the warning bells clanging in her mind.

***

Rafe's boots crunched against the frost-covered ground as he and Jayne patrolled the perimeter of Twilight Camp. The air bit at his exposed skin, but he welcomed the chill - anything to keep his mind off the chaos of the past few days.

"So," Jayne said, breaking their comfortable silence. "How do you feel about our new Dreamweaver?" Her tone carried that dangerous edge of curiosity that always spelled trouble.

Rafe kept his eyes forward, scanning the tree line. "She's different from the others we've found. More powerful, more..." He searched for the right word. "Beautiful."

A knowing laugh escaped Jayne's lips. "That's not what I meant, and you know it." She stepped over a fallen log, her movements fluid despite the uneven terrain. "Don't think I've not seen how you look at her."

Heat crept up Rafe's neck, and he was grateful for the dim light. "I look at her the same way I look at any potential ally." The lie felt bitter on his tongue.

"Right." Jayne's voice dripped with sarcasm. She bumped his shoulder playfully. "Face it, Delacroix, you're sweet on her."

"It's not like that. She needs protection, especially now."

"And what about Gemini?" Jayne's question cut through his defenses like a well-aimed blade. "Have you considered how she might feel about your... protective instincts?"

Rafe's mind drifted back to that moment outside their tent, the way Liora had stumbled over her words, cheeks flushed as she insisted they were just friends - it had stirred something in his chest he wasn't ready to examine.

"They're not..." He cleared his throat, adjusting his sword belt. "Li made it clear they're just close friends. Both of them did, actually." The memory of Gemini's knowing smile haunted him.

Jayne kicked a stone along the path, her boots scuffing against the frozen earth. "Have you seen the way Gemini moves? Like some kind of forest spirit, all grace and..." She caught herself, a rare blush coloring her cheeks in the dim light.

The slip wasn't lost on Rafe, but he filed it away for later ammu-
nition. Right now, his thoughts were too tangled in golden magic and
frightened eyes to focus on teasing his friend.

"Be careful, Delacroix." Jayne's voice had lost its playful edge. "That
girl isn't here to warm your bed or heal your broken heart. She's here
because Draven wants her dead, and we need her alive."

"You're reading too much into it," he muttered, but the words felt
hollow even to his own ears.

His mind betrayed him, conjuring images of Liora's soft curves, the
way her hair caught the firelight, how her lips parted slightly when she
concentrated. Heat pooled in his belly at the thought of teaching her a
different kind of control, of showing her pleasure instead of pain. He
pushed the thoughts away, ashamed of his own weakness.

"She needs to focus on mastering her powers," Jayne pressed, her
voice cutting through his inappropriate musings. "One mistake, one
moment of lost control, and we all pay the price. You've seen what
happens when she loses focus."

The memory of golden light exploding outward, of soldiers frozen
in twisted poses, flashed through Rafe's mind. Of Rafe's own body
being frozen. Yet even that display of raw power hadn't diminished his
attraction - if anything, it had intensified it.

"Li's stronger than you give her credit for," he managed, trying to
keep his voice steady.

Jayne's sharp gaze cut through the darkness. "Li? Since when are
you on nickname terms with our Dreamweaver?"

Heat crept up Rafe's neck again. He'd picked up the nickname
from Gemini without realizing it, hearing it whispered in gentle tones
in quiet moments. The way it rolled off his tongue felt natural, intimate - dangerous.

"Heard Gemini call her that," he muttered, adjusting his sword belt again. The familiar weight of steel offered little comfort against Jayne's knowing stare. His fingers traced the worn leather, remembering how Liora's hand had brushed against it earlier that day when she'd stumbled into him.

Jayne's boots stopped their rhythmic crunch against the frozen ground. Her silence spoke volumes, and Rafe could feel her piecing together all the little moments he'd tried to hide - the lingering glances, the way he positioned himself between Liora and potential threats, how his voice softened when speaking to her.

"You're in deeper than I thought, Delacroix." Jayne's words carried a mix of concern and something else - understanding, perhaps?

"She's not some fragile flower that needs sheltering."

Jayne turned to face him fully. "No, she's a weapon, Rafe. One that could turn the tide of this war. And weapons don't need lovers - they need handlers."

The crude assessment made his blood boil, but a treacherous part of his mind whispered that she might be right. His eyes drifted toward the camp where he knew Liora slept beside Gemini, probably tossing and turning as nightmares plagued her dreams.

Jayne's words echoed in his head: weapons don't need lovers. Maybe she was right. Maybe these feelings, this growing attraction that threatened to consume him, needed to be buried deep alongside all his other regrets. But as he resumed his patrol, Rafe couldn't shake the image of Liora's smile, or the way his heart raced every time she said his name.

\*\*\*

The mist curled around Liora's ankles like ghostly fingers, each tendril glowing with an otherworldly luminescence. Above her, stars scattered across the twilight sky formed patterns she'd never seen before, their light somehow closer and more intimate than in the waking world.

Her feet carried her forward through the ethereal landscape, each step disturbing the pearlescent fog that carpeted the ground. The dreamscape stretched endlessly in every direction, its boundaries blurred and shifting like watercolors bleeding into one another.

The silence pressed against her ears, so different from the constant whispers and doubts that had followed her through the rebel camp. Here, even her own heartbeat seemed muted, as if the very air absorbed sound itself. The feeling was familiar yet foreign, like a half-remembered lullaby.

A soft pulse of light caught her attention, drawing her gaze to the horizon. The glow pulsated with a gentle rhythm that matched her heartbeat, calling to something deep within her core. Her feet turned toward it before her mind made the conscious decision to move.

Each step brought the light closer, its warm radiance cutting through the ethereal fog. The mist thinned as she approached, revealing hints of solid ground beneath her feet. Crystalline formations jutted from the earth, their faceted surfaces reflecting and refracting the mysterious light until the air itself seemed to shimmer with countless tiny stars.

Liora's breath caught in her throat as the source of the glow became clearer. It hovered just above the ground, a sphere of pure light that pulsed with the same golden warmth she'd felt in her own attempts to control her power. But unlike her chaotic bursts of energy, this light held a steady, controlled brilliance.

The air grew thicker with dream energy as she drew closer, making her skin tingle and her hair stand on end. Power hummed through the space between her and the light, different from anything she'd experienced in her training with Nero. This felt older, more primal.

Her hand lifted of its own accord, reaching toward the glowing sphere. The dream energy surrounding it responded to her presence, sending out tendrils of light that danced around her fingers like curious spirits. Something whispered at the edge of her consciousness, a voice just beyond her understanding, speaking words that seemed to resonate with her very soul.

To Liora's surprise, a figure began to emerge from the mist. A woman, silver hair flowing like liquid moonlight around her shoulders. Dream energy pulsed through the air, making the mist swirl and dance around her feet as she moved with otherworldly grace toward Liora.

Liora's breath caught in her throat as the woman's presence washed over her, bringing with it a sense of peace she hadn't felt since before the attack on Eldara. The chaos that had been churning inside her since joining the rebellion seemed to quiet, if only for a moment.

"Liora, child of dreams." The woman's voice carried like wind chimes in a gentle breeze, each word resonating with ancient power. "I am Lyra Solari, a keeper of what has been hidden and what will be revealed. You feel unmoored, yet here, you are closest to yourself."

The crystalline formations around them caught Lyra's ethereal light, splitting it into countless rainbow fragments that danced across the misty ground. Each reflection seemed to pulse with its own rhythm, creating a symphony of light that matched the beating of Liora's heart.

Questions tumbled from Liora's lips before she could stop them. "I don't understand... why am I here? Who are you?" The words felt clumsy compared to Lyra's melodic speech, but the burning need to understand overwhelmed her self-consciousness.

Lyra's movements were fluid as she closed the distance between them, her silver robes rippling like water. The air grew thick with dream energy, making Liora's skin tingle with recognition of power far more controlled than her own chaotic bursts.

"I am but a guide, dear one." Lyra's eyes held wisdom, yet sparkled with an almost playful light. "You are on the path to a power greater than yourself, but it must be forged with wisdom, not haste. I can help you see what lies beneath the surface."

The mist began to shift around them, taking on shapes and colors that seemed to respond to Lyra's presence. Images flickered through the fog - too faint to recognize.

Dream energy curled around Liora's fingers unbidden, responding to her heightened emotions. But instead of the usual fear that accompanied her power's manifestation, she felt a strange sense of rightness, as if something long dormant was finally awakening.

The mist twisted and coalesced at Lyra's command, transforming into shimmering scenes that hung in the air like liquid paintings. A river curved through mountains, its waters neither raging nor still, but flowing with perfect rhythm. The sight stirred something deep within Liora's chest, a recognition of harmony she hadn't known she was missing.

"Power without purpose is like a river without banks," Lyra's voice flowed through the space between them. "It destroys what it might have nourished." The mist shifted again, showing trees growing in perfect balance with their surroundings, neither overshadowing nor yielding to their neighbors. Liora watched as seasons cycled through the vision, each change flowing naturally into the next.

Energy tingled along Liora's skin as she absorbed the meaning behind Lyra's demonstration. This wasn't about forcing her power into
submission or holding it back until it burst free. It was about finding
the natural flow, like water finding its path downhill.

The question tumbled from Liora's lips before she could stop it, her
voice trembling with a mixture of wonder and fear that had become
all too familiar. "So... I can control it?"

Lyra's presence wrapped around her like a warm embrace, steady
and reassuring in a way that made the chaos inside her quiet. The
silver-haired woman's smile sparkled with a warmth that eased the
knot of tension in Liora's chest.

"In time, with patience and self-awareness," Lyra's melodic voice
floated through the crystalline air. "You must first understand yourself
before you can harness the magic within." The dream energy pulsed in
response to her words, creating ripples through the mist that seemed
to echo their truth.

Something shifted inside Liora at those words, like a key turning in
a lock she hadn't known existed. The persistent fear that had haunted
her since the disaster at Eldara began to transform into something else
- a small spark of determination that grew stronger with each beat of
her heart.

Lyra's form started to fade like starlight at dawn, her silver hair
dissolving into the swirling mist. But the warmth of her presence
lingered, leaving behind a clarity that cut through Liora's doubts like
a blade through silk. The dream energy around her felt different now
- less like a wild storm and more like a river waiting to be directed.

Liora's eyes snapped open, her heart still thrumming with the lingering energy of the dream. The canvas of her tent filtered the dawn
light, casting everything in a muted blue glow that reminded her of
the dreamscape's ethereal mist. Beside her, Gemini's steady breathing

provided an anchor to reality, grounding her as the last wisps of her encounter with Lyra Solari settled into her memory like leaves drifting to rest on still water.

The dream energy that usually crackled beneath her skin felt different now - not the wild, untamed force that threatened to burst free, but something more akin to a river waiting to find its course. Liora lifted her hand, watching as tiny sparks of golden light danced between her fingers, responding to her thoughts rather than her fears. The control felt natural, as if Lyra's lesson had unlocked something that had always been there, waiting to be discovered.

A soft rustling beside her drew her attention as Gemini stirred, mumbling something about breakfast. The familiar sound brought a smile to Liora's lips, but it couldn't dispel the profound sense of change that had taken root in her chest. Lyra's words echoed in her mind: "Power without purpose is like a river without banks." The truth of it resonated through her entire being, making her previous attempts at controlling her abilities seem like trying to catch smoke with bare hands.

Her fingers curled around the rough blanket as determination settled into her bones. Today's training with Nero would be different than her previous brushes with power - she could feel it in the steady thrum of energy flowing through her veins. The chaos that had marked her previous attempts at control seemed distant now, replaced by a clarity that felt as natural as breathing. Lyra's presence in the dream might have faded like morning mist, but the understanding she had sparked remained, a compass pointing toward a path Liora hadn't known she was seeking.

# Master Nero Thorne

Golden morning light filtered through the canopy, dappling Liora's skin as she followed Nero deeper into the forest. The dream energy beneath her skin pulsed in time with her footsteps, responding to the ancient power that seemed to radiate from this secluded grove. Pine needles cushioned each step, releasing their sharp scent into the crisp morning air.

Liora's breath caught as Nero crouched beside a fallen log, his weathered fingers tracing patterns in the morning dew that sparkled on the bark. The forest hummed around them, alive with birdsong and rustling leaves.

"Watch," Nero whispered. The droplets of dew lifted from the bark, dancing in the air like tiny stars. "This is what some would call natural magic. The essence of life itself, flowing through every living thing."

The display mesmerized Liora, but beneath her skin, that familiar golden energy churned and sparked, wanting to break free. It felt nothing like the gentle dance of water droplets before her.

"What you carry within you is different." Nero's voice took on a grave tone. "Dream magic shapes reality itself. It springs not from the physical world, but from the realm of possibility - from hopes, fears, and the spaces between what is and what could be."

A tendril of golden light escaped Liora's fingertips, weaving through the air like smoke. The dew drops shattered, falling back to the earth as her power brushed against them. Her chest tightened with familiar shame.

"Natural magic requires harmony with the world around you." Nero gestured to the forest. "But dream magic..." He paused, studying her face. "Dream magic demands harmony with yourself first."

The words struck something deep within Liora. Every disaster, every loss of control - had they stemmed from her own internal chaos? The golden light flickered and died as uncertainty gripped her.

"The power you hold can reshape dreams, bend reality, create what has never been." Nero's eyes held a mixture of wonder and warning. "But it is wild, untethered to the natural order. That's why control has been so difficult."

A distant crow took flight, wings beating against the morning air. Liora watched it soar, remembering how her power had torn through the festival, through the mill - through everything she'd tried to protect. "How do I stop it from destroying everything I touch?"

"You don't stop it." Nero stood, brushing dirt from his robes. "You learn to dream with purpose." His hand reached out, silver light suddenly dancing between his fingers - different from her dream magic, yet controlled, purposeful. "And I will show you how."

"Your power feeds on emotion," Nero's voice carried the weight of experience as he turned to face her. His weathered hands gestured to a worn meditation stone at the center of the clearing. "But emotion without control becomes chaos. Sit."

The stone's rough surface pressed into Liora's legs as she settled into position. Her power thrummed beneath her skin, a caged bird beating against its confines, desperate for release. She forced her breathing to slow, matching Nero's steady rhythm.

"Close your eyes," Nero's voice floated through the morning air. "Feel the boundary between what is real and what exists in dreams." His words seemed to ripple through her consciousness, drawing her attention to something she'd never noticed before - a gossamer-thin membrane separating reality from... something else.

Golden light danced behind Liora's closed eyelids as her awareness brushed against that boundary. It felt like touching spider silk - delicate yet stronger than steel, humming with ancient power. Her breath caught as she realized she could feel it responding to her touch.

"The Veil exists everywhere, always." Nero's voice seemed to come from both beside her and within her mind. "Most cannot perceive it, let alone cross it. But you, Liora - you were born with the ability to walk between worlds."

The membrane pulsed beneath her mental touch, sending shivers down her spine. Images flickered through her mind - fragments of dreams, wisps of possibility, echoes of fears and hopes that didn't belong to her. Her power reached for them instinctively.

"Careful," Nero cautioned as golden light began to leak from her fingertips. "The dreamscape is vast and treacherous. Like an ocean, it can pull you under if you're not prepared." The light retreated, but Liora could still feel the dreams calling to her, tempting her to reach further.

Sweat beaded on her forehead as she struggled to maintain her focus. The boundary between worlds seemed to thin, becoming transparent as glass. Through it, she glimpsed swirling colors and shifting shapes - the raw stuff of dreams waiting to be shaped.

"Your gift allows you to draw power from dreams themselves," Nero explained. "To weave reality from possibility. But dreams are not meant to exist in our world unchanged. They must be filtered, focused, given purpose."

The golden energy within her surged in response to his words, pressing against her skin like summer lightning waiting to strike. Liora felt her control slipping as the power responded to her excitement, to her fear, to every emotion that flickered through her heart.

"Breathe," Nero commanded, his hand settling on her shoulder. The touch anchored her, drawing her back from the edge of that vast dream-ocean. "This is only the beginning. Learning to pierce the Veil is simple - learning to do so safely, with purpose and control, that is the true challenge ahead."

"Inside every person exists the power of dreams," Nero's voice carried on the breeze, whispering between the ancient trees. "It shapes their hopes, their fears, their very understanding of the world. But there are those who see this power not as something to protect, but as something to control."

The word formed on Liora's lips before she could stop it, bitter as ashes: "Draven."

"Yes, very much Draven." Nero's expression darkened like storm clouds gathering on the horizon. His fingers closed into a fist, extinguishing the silver light. "He believes that by controlling dreams, he can control reality itself. That by bending the will of dreamers, he can reshape the world according to his desires."

The mere mention of Draven's name sent ice through Liora's veins, and something darker stirred within her chest. The golden dream energy twisted, responding to her fear, her anger, her shame. Shadows leaked from her fingertips, coalescing into a form that made her stomach clench.

The wraith rose before her, a mirror of her darkest thoughts given shape. Its form shifted like smoke, sometimes resembling the destruction she'd caused at the mill, other times taking on the faces of those she'd hurt. Liora's breath caught in her throat as she recognized Gemini's features twisted in pain.

"That," Nero said softly, "is what we call a wraith - that which we have not accepted within ourselves." His voice remained steady, but Liora noticed how his hand had moved to the hilt of his blade. "Every person carries them, these specters built from shame, guilt, and fear."

The wraith's edges rippled, responding to Nero's words. Liora felt its connection to her, like a thread of darkness stretching between them. Its presence made the golden dream energy within her recoil, yet she couldn't look away from the manifestation of her own darkness.

Marcus's sharp intake of breath drew her attention. He stood at the edge of the clearing, his face a mask of barely contained horror as he watched the wraith take shape. The distrust in his eyes cut deeper than any blade - he'd been right about her all along.

The wraith sensed her spike of emotion. Before Liora could react, it lashed out with a blast of shadow-tinged energy that tore through the clearing. Marcus dove behind a tree, but not before Liora saw the confirmation of his fears written across his face.

Guilt surged through her chest as the blast dissipated, leaving scorched earth in its wake. The wraith fed on the emotion, growing larger, more substantial. Its form settled into a twisted version of herself, golden eyes now black as pitch.

"Control it," Nero commanded, but Liora felt frozen, trapped between her power and her fear. The wraith's presence pressed against her mind, whispering of every failure, every moment of lost control, every person she'd hurt.

Nero's voice cut through her panic. "Protect him, Liora! Dreams can shield as well as harm - show Marcus what your power truly means!"

Marcus's fear pierced through her spiral of guilt and shame. His wide eyes met hers across the clearing, and something shifted inside her. The golden energy thrumming beneath her skin responded to a new purpose, no longer fighting against her but flowing with her intent.

Light burst from her outstretched hands, coalescing into translucent shields that sprang up around Marcus. The wraith's next attack splashed harmlessly against their surface, its darkness unable to penetrate the barrier born of her desire to protect.

More constructs emerged from the dream energy as Liora's imagination took flight. Golden spears materialized in the air, their tips sharp with purpose rather than malice. They flew at the wraith, not to destroy but to contain, to push back against the darkness that had escaped her control.

The wraith howled, its form rippling as it tried to evade her weapons. But these weren't born from fear or guilt - they carried the weight of choice, of conscious intent. Each impact forced the creature back, its edges beginning to blur and fade.

Liora felt something unlock within her chest as she watched her constructs dance through the air. This was what her power could be - not a force of destruction, but a shield against the darkness. The golden energy sang through her veins, no longer fighting to break free but working in harmony with her will.

The wraith's features - her features - began to soften as understanding dawned. This shadow wasn't something to be destroyed or banished. It was a part of her, born from her fears and failures. Fighting it had only made it stronger.

Instead of forcing it away, Liora opened herself to the darkness it represented. She acknowledged the guilt, the shame, the fear of loss of control. The wraith's movements slowed as she accepted these parts of herself, its form growing transparent.

A space opened within her heart, not a prison but a sanctuary for these darker aspects of herself. The wraith drifted toward it, drawn by acceptance rather than forced by combat. Its edges dissolved into mist as it settled into place, no longer fighting but becoming part of her whole self.

The golden shields around Marcus remained, steady and strong, as the last wisps of the wraith faded away. Liora met his gaze again, and this time she saw something new in his expression - not fear, but the first glimmer of understanding.

The golden shields dissolved into mist, leaving Liora's skin tingling with residual power. Her heart still raced, but for the first time since her magic had awakened, the energy beneath her skin felt... settled. Like a wild horse that had finally accepted its rider.

"Well done." Nero's weathered face broke into a smile as he approached. The silver light still danced between his fingers, but it seemed dimmer now compared to the golden glow that lingered in the air. "You've taken your first true step on the path of a Dreamweaver."

The word struck Liora differently now. Before, it had felt like a burden, a title that carried too much weight. But after what she'd just experienced - the way her power had responded to her will rather than her fear - maybe being a Dreamweaver wasn't about controlling dreams. Maybe it was about understanding them.

Nero gestured toward a narrow path that wound deeper into the forest, where the morning light barely penetrated the thick canopy. "Walk with me." His voice carried an undercurrent of urgency that made Liora's newfound calm waver. "There is much more you need to understand about your gift - and about why Draven fears it so much."

Liora cast one last glance at Marcus, who still stood frozen by the tree. The fear in his eyes had been replaced by something else - confusion, perhaps, or curiosity. But she couldn't focus on that now.

***

The dream energy still pulsed beneath Liora's skin as she followed Nero to the edge of the training grounds. Sunset painted the sky in deep purples and golds, casting long shadows through the trees.

Her boots crunched over fallen leaves as they entered a small clearing. Here, the trees formed a natural circle, their branches weaving together overhead like guardians of an ancient sanctuary. The space hummed with an energy that made her skin tingle - whether from latent dream magic or her own anticipation, she couldn't tell.

Nero moved with practiced grace through the clearing, his weathered coat catching the dwindling sunlight. As he turned to face her, something caught Liora's eye - a flash of silver thread against the dark fabric of his coat's interior. The emblem there, though faded with age, still held traces of its former glory: a crescent moon and star, intertwined in an eternal dance.

"That emblem - I've seen it before, in one of Bennet's books."

Nero's fingers traced the worn symbol, his weathered face softening with memory. "The Mark of the Veil. The Custodians of the Veil were the guardians of dream magic, before Draven twisted everything we stood for." His voice carried the weight of years.

Shadows deepened across his features as he spoke of his past. "I dedicated my life to preserving the old ways, even though I could never truly wield the power myself." A bitter smile crossed his face. "Imagine spending decades studying something you can't touch."

Wind whispered through the clearing, stirring fallen leaves around their feet. Nero's hands moved through the air, demonstrating his silver natural energy. "For some us, natural magic was all we had. We were born without the gift you have, that... others had. We could study it, understand it, but we would never be as powerful as a Dreamweaver. Please don't mistake my whisper for a shout, Liora."

The morning light caught his eyes as he watched Liora attempt the same motion, her untrained power creating waves of golden energy that made the leaves dance. "I resented those born with the gift, once. Thought it unfair that some could channel such power while others merely watched from the shadows."

His voice grew heavy with regret. "That bitterness blinded me. When Draven's forces came, I hesitated. That moment of weakness cost us everything." The emblem seemed to dim as clouds passed overhead, matching his darkening mood.

Nero's gaze fixed on Liora with renewed intensity. "But now, teaching you - helping you understand your power - perhaps I can make amends for my failure." His hands steadied as he adjusted her meditative stance.

"I swore to protect dream magic and failed," Nero continued, watching as golden light swirled around Liora's fingers. "But you, Liora—you might be our last hope to make things right."

The forest seemed to hold its breath as Nero's words hung in the air. Liora's fingers trembled, golden light still dancing between them as she processed what he'd said. Her heart ached with questions she'd never dared to ask.

Liora watched the silver wisps curling around Nero's fingertips, so different from her own golden light. The energy felt familiar yet strange, like a melody played in a different key. Her power thrummed beneath her skin, responding to the display.

"Dream magic flows from here," Nero pressed a hand to his chest, "and here." His fingers touched his temple. "It's why no two Dreamweavers manifest their powers the same way. Your mother - she could step into others' dreams as easily as walking through an open door. Her gift came from her deep empathy, her desire to understand and heal."

The mention of her mother made Liora's concentration slip. The golden light between her fingers flared, casting wild shadows across the clearing. The energy that had flowed so naturally moments ago twisted into knots in her chest. Her hands dropped to her sides.

"My mother? Tell me about her." The words tumbled out before she could stop them, carried on a breath that felt too tight in her lungs. The forest's whispers faded to silence, as if nature itself leaned in to listen.

Nero's eyes found hers, searching. "What do you remember of her?" His voice held a gentleness she hadn't heard before, like he was handling something fragile.

The memories slipped through her mind like water through cupped hands - a flash of warm brown eyes, the echo of a laugh, the ghost of fingers brushing through her hair. "Just... fragments. From when I was very small." Her throat tightened. "Bennet never spoke much about her. Only that she was an amazing woman."

"Bennet spoke true." Nero's fingers traced the silver emblem on his coat again, his gaze distant. "She was a Dreamweaver - perhaps the finest I've ever known." His eyes refocused on Liora, sharp with an emotion she couldn't name. "But her full story... that will have to wait for another time." The shadows had lengthened across the clearing, and something in his tone suggested more shadows lurked behind his words.

Liora's fingers traced patterns in the golden light still dancing around her hands, trying to process Nero's words about her mother. But he was already moving on, his voice taking on the rhythmic cadence of a storyteller sharing ancient wisdom.

"In the beginning, the world brimmed with raw magic," Nero's hands wove silver threads through the air, creating shimmering images that danced in the fading light. "The first Dreamweavers walked among mortals who wielded power as casually as breathing. But they saw the devastation wrought by those drunk on their own strength - entire cities reduced to ash, mountains crumbled to dust, rivers turned to blood."

The images shifted, showing shadowy figures raising their hands to the sky. Liora's breath caught as a silvery barrier materialized in the vision, separating two distinct realms. "The Dreamweavers created the Veil," Nero continued, "a barrier between our world and the source of magic, dreams. Only those born with the gift of dreams could pierce it, along with the Custodians they chose to guard its secrets."

"But that's not right." The words burst from Liora's chest before she could stop them, her golden light flaring with emotion. "How can anyone decide who deserves magic and who doesn't? The actions of a few shouldn't condemn everyone else."

Nero's expression hardened, the silver light vanishing from his hands. "You speak from a place of privilege, young one. You were born with this gift - you never had to watch others abuse power beyond their understanding." His voice carried the weight of centuries of witnessed destruction. "Sometimes walls exist not to imprison, but to protect."

Leaves stirred around them as Nero's expression darkened. "But power draws the hungry, the ambitious. Draven's ancestors saw the

Dreamweavers as a weapon, a means to control not just dreams but the very fabric of reality itself." His silver light flickered and died, leaving only Liora's golden glow illuminating the clearing.

The branches overhead creaked as a chill wind swept through. "They began hunting them, claiming their abilities for themselves through dark rituals and forbidden magic."

Liora's power surged with her rising emotions, casting wild shadows across Nero's face as he continued. "Those who survived went into hiding. The knowledge was scattered, preserved in fragments by those of us who could no longer wield true dream magic."

The golden light between her fingers pulsed like a heartbeat as understanding dawned. Her gift wasn't just power - it was legacy, responsibility, the echo of those first Dreamweavers who had sought to bridge worlds rather than dominate them.

"Master Thorne?" Her voice wavered slightly. "I keep hearing whispers about the Eclipse of Dreams. I heard legends of it as a kid, but what exactly is it?" The question had burned in her mind since discussing it with Gemini before the festival. A lifetime ago.

Nero's shoulders tensed, almost imperceptibly. "The Eclipse of Dreams is both our greatest opportunity and our greatest threat. It occurs once every century, when the twin moons align perfectly with the sun."

Liora watched as he traced a pattern in the air, dream energy following his fingertips to create a miniature celestial display. The tiny moons circled each other, their silver light reflecting off his weathered features. "During the Eclipse, the barriers between reality and dreams blur, making even the smallest spark of power potentially catastrophic."

"Is that why Draven-" Liora started, but Nero's sharp nod cut her off.

"He's waiting for it. The Eclipse would amplify his control over the Ark of Dreams beyond anything we've seen. If he succeeds in harnessing that power..." Nero's words trailed off, the miniature moons flickering out as his hand dropped to his side.

"How long?" she managed to ask, her throat tight. "How long until the Eclipse?"

"Six days," Nero replied, his eyes meeting hers with an intensity that made her want to look away. "So little time to master what others spend years learning. I wish it didn't have to be this way."

The dream energy coiled tighter in Liora's chest as she processed Nero's words about the Eclipse. Her fingers twisted in the worn fabric of her sleeve, a nervous habit she'd never quite broken. "The Ark of Dreams - what is that? I've never heard of it."

Liora's heart quickened as Nero's expression darkened, the last rays of sunlight casting deep shadows across his face.

"The Ark was born of pride and fear," Nero's voice carried an edge she'd never heard before. "The ancient rulers of Somnus couldn't bear the thought that only Dreamweavers could wield such power. They corrupted some of our own, promising them glory and riches to help create an artifact that would grant them access to the dreamscape."

"They accomplished their goal," Nero went on. "Though the cost proved devastating. Somnus became isolated from everything beyond its borders, yet that paled in comparison to what followed. The Ark demands endless sustenance - stealing away both sweet reveries and dark terrors, aspirations and dreads - harvested from unsuspecting souls to maintain its strength."

Liora's stomach churned as understanding dawned. "That's what Draven's been doing to the people? Using their dreams to power the Ark?" The words tasted bitter on her tongue.

Nero nodded grimly. "Every being under Draven's control feeds the Ark with their hopes, their fears, their very essence. It's a perversion of what the Veilstone was meant to be - a bridge between dreams and reality, not a prison for stolen memories."

"The Veilstone?" Liora's heart skipped as the word sparked something deep within her, like a half-remembered lullaby. The dream energy hummed in response, reaching toward the mere mention of it.

Nero's eyes softened as he studied her reaction. "Unlike the Ark, which steals and corrupts dream energy, the Veilstone amplifies what already exists within a true Dreamweaver. It doesn't take - it enhances, guides, protects. But it requires a pure heart and unwavering purpose to wield."

A shiver ran down Liora's spine as Nero continued, "The Veilstone lies hidden, waiting for a Dreamweaver worthy of its power. It calls to them, speaking through dreams and visions until they're ready to claim it."

"The Eclipse changes everything," Nero's voice dropped lower, as if the very trees might be listening. "If one holds the Veilstone during the alignment, they will have power beyond imagination. In Draven's hands, it would mean eternal darkness. But in yours-"

The sound of approaching footsteps drew their attention. Derek emerged from the shadows, his expression grim. "Master Thorne, you're needed at the war council. General Varden has news from the eastern border."

Nero rose smoothly, though Liora caught the slight stiffness in his movements that betrayed his age. "We'll continue this discussion tomorrow, Liora. Trust your instincts, but question your desires."

As Nero followed Derek back toward the camp, Liora remained seated on the log, watching their forms disappear into the darkness.

The dream energy within her stirred restlessly, like water disturbed by an unseen current.

A distant owl called through the night, its cry echoing off the surrounding hills. But beneath that natural sound, Liora thought she heard something else - a faint humming, just beyond the edge of perception, calling to the power that flowed through her veins.

# Too Much, Too Soon

G emini watched her friend push food around her plate, the stew growing cold as Liora's thoughts seemed to drift elsewhere. The dining area felt eerily empty without the usual bustle of rebels, most of them attending a secret council called by General Varden.

"I just don't understand why Nero keeps so many secrets," Liora muttered, her spoon creating ripples in the untouched broth. "He knew my mother, Gem. He knew what I was, what I could become, and he never came for me."

A protective instinct flared in Gemini's chest as she reached across the rough wooden table, her fingers brushing Liora's wrist. "Sometimes people keep secrets to protect others," she offered, though the words felt hollow even to her own ears.

"Just... be careful, Li. Sometimes people who seem the most transparent have the most to hide."

"You don't trust him?" Liora's brow furrowed, and Gemini felt a familiar ache—the need to protect her friend warring with the desire to support her independence.

"I trust that you're smart enough to make your own judgments," Gemini said carefully, stirring her own stew. "I just worry. Everything's happening so fast, and-"

A sudden commotion from the direction of the council chambers cut through their conversation, and both women turned toward the sound of raised voices.

Rebels poured into the dining hall, their faces drawn with a mix of concern and agitation. The raised voices had died down, but tension lingered in the air like smoke after a fire. She caught snippets of whispered conversations—something about Arcadia, whatever that is, the Veilstone and increased patrols.

Rafe appeared through the crowd, his usual confident stride masking what she recognized as nervous energy. He dropped onto the bench beside Liora, flashing that signature grin that never quite reached his eyes. "What's for dinner—more of Cookie's famous mystery stew?"

The forced lightness in his tone set off warning bells in Gemini's mind. She'd spent enough time mending wounds to recognize when someone was hiding pain—emotional or physical. "How did the council meeting go?"

His smile faltered, shoulders dropping slightly as he glanced between them. The dining hall's ambient noise seemed to fade away as he leaned forward, voice dropping. Something in his demeanor reminded her of patients right before delivering bad news to their families.

"I—" Rafe started, then stopped as General Varden strode past their table, his cold gaze lingering a moment too long on Liora. Gemini's protective instincts flared as she watched Rafe's jaw tighten, his knuckles whitening around the edge of the table. Whatever had happened in that meeting, it wasn't good news for any of them.

"The General's planning something big," Rafe muttered, his eyes darting to ensure no one else was within earshot. "A mission that could win us the war—or get us all killed." The way his hand tightened around his untouched mug made Gemini's stomach clench.

"You ever hear of Arcadia? The village known for its outrageous harvest festivals," Rafe's fingers traced invisible patterns on the wooden table. "Now? The people there might as well be ghosts. They work the fields like clockwork, no light in their eyes, no recognition when you call their names. Draven's turned them into living puppets."

The image of entire families trapped in such a state made Gemini's fingers curl into fists beneath the table. She'd seen the aftermath of physical wounds, had mended countless broken bones and torn flesh, but this—this was a violation of the soul itself. Her gaze drifted to Liora, whose face had drained of color.

"Children too," Rafe continued, his voice dropping to barely above a whisper. "Saw a little girl tending the chickens. She didn't even flinch when she stepped on a thorn, just kept moving like nothing happened. That's what Draven's dream magic does—strips away everything that makes them human."

She reached for Liora's trembling hand under the table, offering what comfort she could as Rafe's words painted an ever-darkening picture of what awaited them all if they failed.

"Varden thinks if we can break Draven's hold there, we'll gain more than just allies," Rafe continued, his voice taking on an edge that reminded Gemini of a blade being sharpened. "Arcadia has the people and supplies to arm our forces, and its position..." He traced an invisible map on the wooden table surface, his finger stopping at what she assumed represented the village's location.

A chill ran down Gemini's spine as she watched Liora absorb this information, her friend's face a mix of determination and barely concealed fear. The healers' training in her recognized the signs of someone steeling themselves for pain, and she wanted nothing more than to shield Liora from whatever dangerous path Varden was about to set them on. But the way Rafe's gaze kept drifting to the General's retreating back suggested this mission wasn't just about strategy—there was something else, something he wasn't telling them.

Gemini's heart raced as she watched Liora's fingers tighten around her spoon. The metal bent slightly under the pressure, dream magic crackling beneath her friend's skin.

"Master Thorne was at the council, wasn't he?" Liora's voice trembled. "Why would they need him there?" The confusion in her tone made her sound younger, more vulnerable than the powerful Dreamweaver everyone expected her to be.

Rafe's frown deepened as he leaned back, running a hand through his disheveled hair. "They needed his assessment of your abilities, Liora. The council wanted to know if you were..." He paused, guilt flickering across his features. "If you were ready to take part in the mission."

"What?" The word burst from both women simultaneously. Gemini's protective instincts flared. "She's barely had time to learn control," Gemini protested, even as Liora shook her head frantically, whispering, "I'm not ready. I can't—I'll hurt someone again."

"It's not up for debate." Rafe's voice carried a finality that made Gemini's blood run cold. "Master Thorne gave his approval. You'll be part of the team going to Arcadia, Liora. The briefing will be tomorrow. We've only got four days until the Eclipse." The words hung in the air like a death sentence, and Gemini watched helplessly as the last bit of color drained from her friend's face.

Gemini tensed as Jayne approached their table, balancing two bowls of steaming stew. The spy's calculated movements and sharp eyes missed nothing, taking in the group's taut expressions.

Gemini shifted in her seat as Jayne slid onto the bench across from them, the spy's movements carrying a lethal grace that drew her gaze. Something about the way Jayne's dark hair fell across her face, partially obscuring those keen eyes, made Gemini's breath catch. The feeling startled her – where had that come from?

"I take it you told them?" Jayne settled beside Rafe, sliding one bowl toward him. Heat crept up Gemini's neck as she watched Jayne's fingers wrap around her spoon, noting the calluses that spoke of years handling weapons. The contradiction between Jayne's deadly skills and her current domestic task stirred something unexpected in Gemini's chest. She forced her attention back to her cooling stew, but her eyes kept drifting to Jayne's hands, imagining how they might feel-

"Please," Liora's voice cracked, her fingers finding Gemini's under the table. "I need to know what I'm walking into. What exactly does Varden expect me to do?" She squeezed Liora's hand, turning to Jayne with determination burning in her throat.

"I'm coming with her." Gemini didn't phrase it as a question, but Jayne's slight nod eased some of the tension in her shoulders. The spy's eyes softened fractionally - perhaps recognizing the fierce protectiveness that drove Gemini's demand. But when Liora opened her mouth to press for details, Jayne's expression hardened again.

"The fewer people who know the full plan, the better," Rafe cut in, his hand moving to rest on his sword hilt - a gesture Gemini had noticed he made when uncomfortable.

Gemini watched as Liora pushed back from the table, her stew forgotten. The dining hall's shadows seemed to deepen around her friend, dream magic crackling beneath her skin like lightning before a storm.

"I should go," Liora whispered, her voice barely audible over the murmur of conversations around them. The defeat in her tone made Gemini's heart ache. This wasn't the determined friend who'd stood against Draven's forces in Eldara, but a scared young woman being pushed too far, too fast. Dream magic sparked between Liora's fingers as she gripped the edge of the table, leaving tiny scorch marks in the worn wood.

Rafe reached out as if to stop her, but Gemini caught his wrist, shaking her head slightly. She recognized the wild look in Liora's eyes - the same expression she'd worn after the mill collapsed, when her powers had spiraled beyond her control. Pushing her now would only make things worse. The fear of harming others had always been Liora's deepest wound, and Varden's mission threatened to tear it wide open again.

As Liora fled the dining hall, magic trailing in her wake like invisible tears, Gemini felt torn between following her friend and staying to gather more information about the mission that could get them all killed. The choice was taken from her as she heard a hard intake of breath as Rafe got up to walk after her.

The weight of responsibility pressed down on her shoulders as she watched him follow Liora into the darkness, knowing that no amount of healing skills could mend the kind of wounds this path was inflicting on her friend's spirit.

***

The gravel crunched under Liora's boots as she strode toward her tent, her heart hammering against her ribs. Mission. The word echoed in her mind, carrying equal measures of terror and exhilaration. Her fingers tingled with untamed energy, and she clenched them into fists to keep the power contained.

Footsteps approached from behind - quick, determined steps she'd begun to recognize. She quickened her pace, not ready to face anyone, especially not him. Not when her emotions threatened to spiral out of control.

"Liora, wait." Rafe's voice carried across the evening air, closer than she'd realized. The concern in his tone made her chest tighten.

She slowed but didn't stop, her tent just yards away. The canvas flapped in the breeze, beckoning her toward its promise of solitude. A branch snapped behind her as Rafe closed the distance.

"Please." His hand caught her shoulder, gentle but firm. The warmth of his touch sent an unexpected shiver down her spine, and she forced herself to turn around.

Rafe's dark eyes searched her face, his usual confidence replaced by something softer, more vulnerable. "I'm sorry. This isn't how I wanted any of this to happen."

Liora's throat constricted. She wanted to speak, to tell him it wasn't his fault, but the words wouldn't come. Instead, she stared at the scar along his jaw, unable to meet his gaze.

"We shouldn't have pushed you into this so quickly." His hand dropped from her shoulder, leaving a ghost of warmth behind. "But I've seen what you're capable of, Li. You're stronger than you know."

The nickname caught her off guard. Something in her chest cracked, and she felt her powers surge in response, making the air around them shimmer like heat waves over summer grass.

Rafe noticed - of course he noticed - but he didn't step back. Instead, he stayed right where he was, his presence steady and unwavering as the magic danced between them, neither afraid nor impressed, just... there. Understanding.

She took a shaky breath, trying to center herself the way Nero taught her, but Rafe's presence made it difficult to focus. His steady gaze held neither judgment nor fear - just a quiet confidence that made her wonder if he saw something in her that she couldn't see in herself.

The moonlight caught the edge of his scar, throwing it into sharp relief against his skin. How many battles had he fought? How many times had he faced down death with that same steady resolve?

The magic slowly ebbed from Liora's fingertips, leaving behind an emptiness that felt worse than the loss of control. She flexed her hands, remembering the destruction she'd caused in Eldara. The screams. The flames. The look in Gemini's eyes when she'd nearly... No. She couldn't think about that now.

"You won't be alone out there," Rafe said, breaking into her spiral of dark thoughts. His voice carried the weight of experience, of countless first missions and the warriors who'd survived them - or hadn't. "I won't leave you, I promise." The words hung between them, heavy with meaning that went beyond mere reassurance. Something shifted in the air, subtle but unmistakable, like the moment before a storm breaks.

Liora shook her head, taking a step back. "You can't promise that. No one can." Her voice cracked on the last word, and the magic stirred again, making the air thick with potential.

"Watch me." Rafe's expression softened, and he reached out, hesitating for a moment before his fingers brushed her arm. The touch grounded her, drawing her focus away from the chaos building inside.

The conviction in his voice made her chest ache. How could he be so sure? She opened her mouth to argue, to remind him of all the ways her powers could destroy everything around her, but the words died in her throat as his hand slid down to catch hers.

Warmth spread from where their fingers touched, and for a moment, the magic inside her settled. Not disappearing, but calming, like waves after a storm. Liora stared at their joined hands, wondering if he could feel the current of power that still hummed beneath her skin.

"I know you're scared," Rafe said, his thumb tracing a small circle on her wrist. "But fear doesn't make you weak, Li. It makes you human." The nickname again, spoken with such casual familiarity that it threatened to break down the walls she'd built around herself.

Liora's heart thundered against her ribs as she stared at their joined hands. His thumb traced another circle on her wrist, and she felt her powers respond, not with their usual chaotic surge but with something gentler, like ripples on a still pond.

The evening air wrapped around them, carrying the scent of pine and woodsmoke from the nearby fires. Shadows danced across Rafe's face, softening the hard lines of battle-worn features. His dark eyes held hers, and the intensity of his gaze made her breath catch in her throat.

"You don't have to carry this alone," he murmured, taking a half-step closer. The space between them crackled with unspoken words and possibilities. Her powers hummed beneath her skin, responding to the quickening of her pulse, but for once, she wasn't afraid of losing control.

Rafe's free hand came up to brush a strand of hair from her face, his touch feather-light against her cheek. The scar along his jaw caught the moonlight as he leaned closer, and Liora found herself wondering how it would feel beneath her fingertips.

The magic inside her swirled and danced, but instead of the usual chaos, it felt like a song - wild and beautiful and somehow right. She swayed toward him, drawn by something stronger than gravity. His breath ghosted across her lips, warm and alive and real.

Time seemed to slow, stretching like honey in the summer sun. The sounds of the camp faded away until all she could hear was the rhythm of their breathing and the whisper of wind through canvas. Rafe's hand slid from her cheek to the nape of her neck, gentle but sure.

Her eyes fluttered closed as the distance between them shrank to nothing. She could feel the warmth of his lips, not quite touching hers but close enough to send electricity dancing down her spine. The magic inside her sang louder, harmonizing with the thundering of her heart.

"Liora!"

The sound of her name shattered the moment like glass. Liora jerked back, her powers swirling in confused eddies as Gemini's voice carried across the evening air. The loss of Rafe's touch left her skin tingling, magic sparking beneath the surface like static before a storm.

Rafe stepped away, his expression unreadable in the deepening shadows. His hand lingered for a heartbeat longer before dropping to his side. "I should check the perimeter." The words came out rough, catching in his throat like gravel.

Liora watched him disappear into the darkness between the tents, his footsteps fading until she couldn't distinguish them from the evening sounds of the camp. Her powers churned inside her, matching the turmoil in her chest. What had almost happened? What would have happened if Gemini hadn't...?

"Li?" Gemini's voice was closer now, tinged with concern and something else - hesitation, maybe guilt. Her friend's familiar presence helped ground the magic that still danced beneath Liora's skin, though it couldn't quite settle the racing of her heart.

"I'm sorry," Gemini said, reaching for Liora's hand. "I didn't mean to interrupt, but..." She trailed off, biting her lower lip. The firelight from nearby tents caught the worry in her eyes.

Liora shook her head, trying to clear it. "Nothing to interrupt." The lie felt hollow even as she spoke it. Her powers flickered in protest, making the canvas walls of nearby tents shiver.

"Li." Gemini's voice took on that tone she used when calling out obvious untruths. "I saw how he looked at you. How you looked at him." She squeezed Liora's hand. "But we barely know him. Any of them. And with everything that's happened..."

The unfinished sentence hung between them, heavy with memories of Eldara, of betrayal and loss. Liora's chest tightened as images flashed through her mind - flames consuming homes, screams piercing the night, trust turning to ash in her mouth.

"I know," Liora said, but her powers surged again, betraying her uncertainty. The air around them thickened with potential energy, making Gemini's hair float slightly as if caught in an invisible breeze.

Gemini pulled her into a tight hug, ignoring the crackling magic that danced between them. "Just be careful," she whispered against Liora's hair. The words carried the weight of shared history, of nights spent crying over losses too deep for words, of promises made in the dark when the world seemed to be falling apart.

# The General's Burden

K ael's boots clicked against the worn cobblestones as he strode
through Somnara's Market District, the morning bustle doing
little to mask the underlying tension that permeated the air. The
familiar weight of his general's insignia pressed against his chest - a
reminder of what he'd given up, and what he might yet reclaim.

Merchants cowered as he passed, their eyes downcast in a way that
stirred both satisfaction and disgust within him. Even here, his repu-
tation preceded him. The smell of fresh bread and spices wafting from
the stalls did nothing to mask the stench of fear that clung to every
corner of Draven's capital.

The Whispering Fountain caught his attention, its waters dancing
with an ethereal grace that belied its true nature. How many times
had he stood here as Draven's general, watching citizens whisper their
deepest desires only to have them twisted into weapons against them?
The memory left a bitter taste in his mouth.

Above him, the Emperor's Palace dominated the skyline, its
spires reaching toward the heavens like accusatory fingers. Kael's jaw

clenched as he remembered the opulent halls where he'd once commanded respect, where strategy and power had been his closest companions. Now, those same halls housed the man he'd betrayed - though
whether that betrayal was his defection to the rebels or his current
thoughts of returning to Draven's fold, he couldn't quite decide.

The Arcane Tower loomed to his left, its shadow falling across his
path like an omen. Scholars in their robes hurried past, their arms
laden with scrolls and artifacts. They knew better than to meet his
gaze.

A patrol of Draven's guards marched past, their armor gleaming
in the morning light. Kael kept his face carefully neutral, though his
hand instinctively tightened on his sword hilt. They didn't recognize
him - his appearance had changed enough since his defection - but
the familiar rhythm of their steps stirred something in him. Pride?
Longing? He pushed the thought aside.

The Fortress of Woe rose before him, its dark walls a testament
to Draven's power. How many prisoners had he personally escorted
through those gates? How many rebels had he watched break under
interrogation? The memory should have filled him with shame, but
instead, he felt a troubling sense of nostalgia.

Street performers danced near the market square, their movements
careful and controlled - entertainment approved by Draven's regime.
Kael watched a young girl twirl with practiced precision, her smile
never quite reaching her eyes. This was what the city had become: a
perfectly choreographed display of submission.

A bell tolled from the Emperor's Palace, its deep resonance washing
over the city like a wave of authority. Citizens paused in their activities,
heads bowing instinctively at the sound. Kael caught himself doing the
same and straightened with a scowl. He needed to return to the rebel
camp before his presence was noticed, but something about Somnara's

oppressive grandeur called to him, whispering promises of power that grew harder to resist with each passing day.

The air grew thicker with each step deeper into the palace, laden with the residual energy of Draven's dream magic. Kael's skin prickled as he passed beneath towering archways, their shadows seeming to reach for him with ghostly fingers. Two guards flanked him, their movements mechanical and eyes glazed - clear signs of Draven's influence.

The grand corridor opened into the throne room, and Kael's breath caught despite himself. Massive dreamcatchers hung from the vaulted ceiling, their crystalline cores pulsing with captured nightmares. The artifacts swayed without wind, creating dancing shadows that made the marble floor appear to ripple beneath his feet.

Dark tapestries adorned the walls, depicting scenes of conquest that seemed to move when viewed from the corner of one's eye. Kael recognized some battles he'd led himself, though the artistry painted him as more monster than man. Perhaps that hadn't been so far from the truth.

Draven's throne dominated the far wall, carved from what appeared to be solid obsidian but gleamed with an inner light that made Kael's eyes water. The Emperor's personal dreamcatcher loomed behind it, larger than the others and thrumming with barely contained power. Its presence made the air feel electric, charged with potential and threat.

Incense burned in brass braziers, the sweet smoke carrying undertones of something metallic that reminded Kael of battlefields. He wondered how many dreams had been harvested to create that particular scent, how many minds had been twisted to fuel Draven's displays of power.

The guards' boots clicked against the floor in perfect unison, the sound echoing off the high ceiling in a rhythm that felt deliberately designed to unsettle. Kael kept his own stride measured, refusing to let his discomfort show. He'd played this game before, though never from such a precarious position.

A servant scurried past, eyes fixed firmly on the floor as she tended to one of the braziers. Her movements were precise, almost mechanical - another puppet dancing on Draven's strings. Kael remembered when he'd found such control admirable rather than disturbing. Now, he wasn't sure which reaction troubled him more.

The throne room's grandeur spoke of power absolute and uncontested, every detail carefully crafted to inspire awe and fear in equal measure. Kael felt both emotions warring within him, along with a third he didn't want to name: hunger. This was what real power looked like, not the scrappy resistance he'd allied himself with.

Torchlight caught the edge of his vision, drawing his attention to a new tapestry being hung - this one depicting the fall of Eldara. The artistry was exquisite, the terror captured in the villagers' faces almost lifelike. Kael's hand tightened on his sword hilt as he recognized Liora in the scene, her power painted as wild and destructive. He wondered if Draven knew just how accurate that portrayal might prove to be.

Kael's boots echoed against the marble floor as he approached Draven's throne, each step a battle between muscle memory and survival instinct. The familiar path stretched before him - how many times had he walked it as a loyal general? The weight of the rebel insignia beneath his coat burned against his chest like a brand of shame.

Draven's shadow stretched across the floor, a dark tendril that seemed to reach for Kael's feet. The emperor's presence pressed down on him with physical force, dream magic crackling in the air between them. Had the throne always been this high, or was it his newfound position as a traitor that made Draven tower over him like an avenging god?

The dreamcatchers above swayed without wind, their crystalline cores pulsing in rhythm with Kael's quickening heartbeat. Each one held countless nightmares - some he'd helped collect during his time as general. A flash of memory struck him: a child's scream as her dreams were harvested, his own hand steady on his sword hilt as he watched. The memory should have disgusted him. Instead, it filled him with a complicated longing.

The throne's obsidian surface caught the torchlight, reflecting Draven's face in fractured patterns that made him appear more demon than man. His eyes fixed on Kael with predatory intensity, tracking each movement as though cataloging weaknesses. Those same eyes had once looked upon him with approval, even pride. The loss of that regard shouldn't have stung as much as it did.

Draven's fingers drummed against the throne's armrest, each tap sending ripples of dark energy through the air. Kael fought to keep his posture straight, remembering how those same hands had once bestowed honors upon him. The Emperor's face had changed since their last meeting - sharper, more angular, as though the dream magic he wielded had begun carving away his humanity piece by piece.

The crown sat heavy on his brow, its black metal seeming to absorb the light rather than reflect it. Had it always looked so much like a cage? Or was that just another trick of perspective, now that Kael stood on the other side of loyalty?

Those eyes - Kael remembered when they'd been merely brown, unremarkable even. Now they shimmered with an inner darkness, pupils expanded until only a thin ring of color remained. Dream magic had changed them, as it changed everything it touched.

A network of dark veins spread across Draven's exposed skin, pulsing in time with the dreamcatchers overhead. They traced patterns that seemed almost deliberate, like a map of conquered territories etched into his flesh. His hands, once steady with a sword, now moved with an unnaturally fluid grace that spoke of power barely contained. Every gesture carried weight, as though the very air bent to his will.

Draven's smile spread across his face like a crack in marble, revealing teeth that gleamed too white against his shadowed features. The expression held no warmth - it never had, Kael realized, though he'd once convinced himself otherwise. Silver threads shot through Draven's dark hair, not signs of age but markers of power, each one representing a dream consumed or a mind broken to his will. The sight stirred something in Kael's chest: not fear, but a hungry recognition of what real power looked like when worn as a crown.

Kael's throat tightened as Draven's voice echoed through the throne room. The familiar tone - smooth as silk yet sharp as a blade - stirred memories of countless war councils and victories shared. His hand instinctively moved to touch his general's insignia before he caught himself.

"General Varden, how good of you to join me. I trust you have information of value?" The emperor's words dripped with honeyed venom. Kael forced his features into the mask of composure he'd worn countless times in this very chamber, though his pulse quickened beneath his collar.

"The girl grows stronger each day," Kael said, the half-truth bitter on his tongue. "But her control remains... questionable." The words felt like betrayal - to whom, he wasn't quite sure anymore. The dreamcatchers above swayed in response to his inner turmoil, their crystalline cores pulsing with captured nightmares that seemed to mock his indecision.

"You're aware, of course, that this rebellion is a futile endeavor. Betrayal is a dangerous game, Kael." Draven's smile never wavered, but his eyes hardened like frost on a battlefield. The unspoken threat wrapped around Kael's throat like a noose, familiar and almost welcome in its clarity. This, at least, was honest - unlike the rebels' lofty ideals of freedom and justice.

The words slithered through Kael's mind like poison, each syllable rekindling memories of power that made his fingers itch. His general's insignia burned against his chest, a reminder of glory days when his commands shaped the fate of armies. The rebels' faces flashed through his thoughts - Liora's raw potential, Rafe's unwavering loyalty - but they blurred against the stark reality of Draven's might surrounding him.

His throat constricted around unspoken words as the emperor's shadow stretched between them like a bridge across his divided soul. The throne room's oppressive grandeur pressed down on him, each breath weighted with the cost of his choices. He'd convinced himself the rebellion offered redemption, but standing here, that notion felt as substantial as morning mist against Draven's solid promises of power.

Draven's presence scraped against his mind like a whetstone, sharpening thoughts he'd tried to bury. How many times had he watched the rebels struggle with their limited resources, their desperate strategies? The memory of their latest raid, Wormwood, burned fresh in his mind - the chaos, the casualties, all for a handful of supplies that wouldn't last a week.

The air crackled as Draven leaned forward, his whispered words cutting through Kael's defenses like a blade through silk. "Why settle for scraps when you could command the feast? The rebellion clings to hope, but hope is a fool's game. I offer you certainty." The promise hung between them, heavy as a headsman's axe, and Kael felt his carefully constructed loyalties begin to crumble beneath its weight.

Kael's fingers traced the outline of his pendant through his coat, each ridge and valley a reminder of past glories. The metal felt warm against his chest, almost burning - or was that the heat of shame rising beneath his skin? Draven's words echoed in the vast chamber, each syllable striking true against the cracks in his conviction.

"Think, Kael. A position of power, security... all within your grasp. Or exile, forever a fugitive." Draven's voice cut through his thoughts like a blade through silk, each word precise and deadly. The emperor's shadow stretched between them, a dark bridge across the chasm of his betrayal, offering a path back to everything he'd surrendered.

His hand twitched toward his sword hilt, an old habit seeking comfort in familiar steel. The blade had tasted blood for both sides now; which cause did it truly serve? Kael's hand fell from his sword hilt, the familiar weight of command settling back onto his shoulders like an old cloak.

Perhaps this was the wiser path. How many lives could he save from within the empire's ranks? A general's word carried weight, could soften harsh orders, redirect troops away from civilian targets. The rebellion would fail regardless - he'd seen enough battles to recognize a losing strategy. At least this way, he might shield some from the worst of the coming storm.

The throne room's shadows seemed to wrap around him like embracing arms, welcoming him back to the fold. His fingers brushed against the rebel insignia beneath his coat, and for the first time since his defection, the metal felt cold, foreign. Draven's smile widened fractionally, recognition flickering in those calculating eyes. The air between them hummed with possibility, with power waiting to be reclaimed. After all, what was betrayal compared to survival? What was principle against pragmatism?

"Join me and we can reshape Somnus. Together." Draven's voice carried the same silken persuasion Kael had used on the young Dreamweaver. The emperor's shadow stretched between them, a dark bridge across years of shared victories and calculated cruelties. The familiar pull of power tugged at Kael's core, impossible to ignore.

He'd told Liora that embracing her full potential meant accepting the darkness within - had he believed those words, or merely echoed Draven's philosophy? The line between manipulation and truth blurred like smoke in his mind.

The throne room's oppressive grandeur pressed closer, dream magic crackling in currents that made his skin prickle with remembered power. Each breath drew him deeper into Draven's web, and Kael wondered if Liora had felt this same inexorable pull when he'd spoken of unleashing her true strength. The parallels twisted in his gut like a knife, but the pain felt almost welcome - a reminder that he'd always been more monster than mentor.

Kael's voice caught in his throat, barely louder than a breath. "It might be the only way..." The words hung in the air like smoke, more confession than conversation. His fingers traced the rebel insignia one last time before letting his hand fall away. The metal felt cold now, dead against his chest - like the ideals it represented.

Draven's satisfied smile spread across his face like frost across a window, and Kael felt the last threads of resistance snap within him. The emperor's shadow stretched between them, no longer a divide but a bridge back to everything he'd surrendered. Power hummed in the air, dream magic crackling with potential - or perhaps warning.

The distinction hardly mattered anymore.

***

The iron door creaked open, and Kael's boots echoed against stone as he descended into the dungeon beneath Draven's fortress. The stench of fear and desperation clung to the walls, a familiar companion from his days as Draven's general. His fingers traced the hilt of his sword - not that he'd need it with this old miller.

Bennet sat slumped against the wall, his weathered face bruised but defiant. The sight stirred something in Kael's chest, a memory of his own father's stubbornness. He pushed it aside. Sentiment had no place here, not when power hung in the balance.

"The girl," Kael said, crouching before Bennet. "Tell me how she came to you." His voice carried the practiced edge of authority, honed through years of command. The other villagers huddled in their cells, watching with wide eyes.

Bennet's laugh came out as a wheeze. "I know you. You were the one hunting her mother, weren't you? Another of Draven's dogs, hunting children." The words stung more than they should have, but they came with dim recognition.

The torch on the wall cast dancing shadows across Bennet's face as Kael leaned closer. "I'm offering you a chance, old man. Tell me what I need to know, and perhaps your fellow villagers won't suffer for your stubbornness." The threat hung heavy in the damp air.

"You wanted to kill her because she could have stopped Draven," Bennet spat, blood staining his teeth. "But she gave her life to protect her child. Scared and alone. And now here you are. What kind of monster are you now?" His eyes bore into Kael's, and for a moment, the general saw himself reflected in that gaze - not the powerful figure he aspired to be, but something darker.

Kael's boot connected with Bennet's ribs, drawing a sharp gasp. "When did Liora's powers first manifest? How long have you been harboring her?" The questions came rapid-fire, each punctuated by another kick. The villagers' whimpers filled the cell.

Through the pain, Bennet smiled. "She'll stop you, you know. Draven. All of you. The power you're so desperate to control? It was given to her freely. She'll use it to protect, not destroy. That's the difference between her and men like Draven."

Rage flared in Kael's chest. He grabbed Bennet by the throat, slamming him against the wall. "Protection is an illusion," he snarled. "Power is the only truth in this world. And soon, she'll understand that as well as I do."

The door above creaked open again, and footsteps approached. Kael released Bennet, who slumped to the floor, still wearing that knowing smile. The general straightened his uniform, composing himself. He had what he needed - confirmation that Liora's lineage was as he thought.

He would soon leave for Twilight. He had a rebellion to conduct, after all.

# Tangled Emotions

G olden light filtered through the canopy, casting dappled shadows across Liora's hands as she followed Nero through the misty forest clearing. Her thoughts drifted to last night—to Rafe's calloused fingers brushing against hers, to the surge of magic that had sparked between them, to the way his breath had lingered on her lips before Gemini's interruption.

The memory sent a flutter through her chest, and with it, wisps of dream energy curled around her fingers unbidden. Liora clenched her fists, trying to suppress the magic before it could manifest.

"Your power responds to that which moves you deeply," Nero's voice cut through her reverie. He stood beside an ancient oak, his silver-streaked hair catching the morning light. "Whether it be fear, anger, or..." His knowing look made heat rise to her cheeks.

"I wasn't—" Liora started, but the golden threads of energy betrayed her, dancing more vigorously around her hands.

"The heart cannot lie, young one." Nero's eyes crinkled with something between amusement and concern. "Just as the moon pulls at the tides, your emotions guide your power. Fighting against them only creates more turbulence."

Liora released a frustrated breath, watching as the magical threads scattered like startled fireflies. "But how can I protect anyone if I can't even control my own feelings?"

"Control is not about suppression." Nero gestured to a fallen log covered in moss. "It's about understanding. The same passion that causes destruction can also fuel protection—it depends on how you channel it."

The weight of his words settled over her as she perched on the log, remembering how her magic had exploded during the festival, how it had hurt Gemini. Yet there had also been moments—brief flashes—when that same power had shielded others.

"Your mother struggled with similar questions," Nero added softly, and Liora's head snapped up. He refused to fully speak of her mother, so each mention felt like uncovering a precious stone. "She learned, as you will, that mastery over one's emotions comes not through force, but through patience and acceptance."

"Now," he continued, lowering himself onto a stone across from her, "close your eyes. Let your mind drift to what you're feeling in this moment—all of it, without judgment. The uncertainty, the hope, the fear, even the..." he paused meaningfully, "...affection."

Heat crept up Liora's neck as she closed her eyes, hyper-aware of Nero's scrutiny. The golden threads of magic pulsed beneath her skin, responding to each flutter of emotion that crossed her mind.

"Let the feelings flow through you," Nero's voice guided, steady and sure. "Like water over stones, they shape you but need not control you."

Rafe's face swam into her thoughts—his determined eyes, the way his hand had trembled against hers. The magic surged, and this time

Liora didn't fight it. Golden light bloomed around her, casting dancing shadows through her closed eyelids.

"Good," Nero murmured. "Now think of the festival. Of what
happened when fear took hold."

The memory slammed into her like a physical blow. Screams echoed
in her mind, and the golden light twisted, darkening at the edges.
Gemini's pained face flashed before her, and Liora's hands began to
shake.

"Stay with it," Nero commanded. "Notice how the energy shifts
with each emotion. Fear constricts, while love expands. Neither is
inherently good nor evil—they simply are."

Liora forced herself to breathe through the chaos of feelings. The
magic responded, settling into a steady pulse that matched her heartbeat. When she opened her eyes, the clearing was filled with a soft,
ambient glow.

"The same power that wounded your friend also saved lives that
night," Nero reminded her. "The difference lay not in the magic itself,
but in your relationship to it."

Understanding dawned like the first rays of sunrise. "It's not about
controlling the power," Liora whispered, watching the golden light
dance between her fingers. "It's about accepting it as part of myself."

"Precisely." Nero's approval warmed her more than she expected. "But remember, young one—your gift reaches beyond your own
heart. Each person you encounter carries their own storms of emotion."

"To be a true Dreamweaver means more than balancing your own
feelings," he said, his eyes taking on that distant look that meant he
was seeing beyond the present moment. "You must learn to navigate
the tempests of others' hearts as well."

Liora frowned, her golden magic dimming as confusion clouded her thoughts. "What do you mean, navigate others' hearts?" The words felt clumsy on her tongue, weighted with implications she couldn't quite grasp.

Nero's eyes softened as he leaned forward, his weathered hands gesturing to the space between them. "Your power extends beyond your own mind, Liora. Like finding shelter in a storm, you can enter the thoughts and dreams of others—see what they see, feel what they feel."

The very idea sent a shiver down her spine. "That's... that's possible?" Her voice came out barely above a whisper, the golden threads of magic responding to her mix of wonder and apprehension.

"More than possible. It is part of who you are." Nero straightened, his expression growing solemn. "If you wish, I can show you. My mind is open to you—my dreams, my memories. Though remember," his voice took on an edge of warning, "memories are delicate things, easily bruised by a Dreamweaver's touch."

Liora hesitated, the magic swirling around her fingers like curious birds. But Nero's steady gaze gave her courage, and she reached out with her power, letting it brush against the edges of his consciousness.

The world tilted. Suddenly, she stood in a grand hall of marble and crystal, watching a younger Nero practice intricate patterns of silver light. The memory carried an undertone of dedication, of countless hours spent perfecting each movement.

The scene shifted, fragmenting like light through a prism. A woman with familiar eyes—her mother's eyes—stood before Nero, her voice urgent but indistinct. Shame and regret crashed through the memory like a tidal wave, threatening to sweep Liora away with its intensity.

More images flashed past: a battlefield strewn with bodies, a midnight escape through rain-slicked streets with a little girl, a promise made and broken. Each memory carried its own weight of emotion, its own story waiting to be uncovered.

Liora reached deeper into Nero's memories, letting her magic brush against them like fingers through water. The scenes shifted and changed with each touch - a kaleidoscope of moments both joyful and painful. Her power responded instinctively, golden threads weaving through the fabric of his thoughts.

"Feel how they respond to your presence," Nero's voice echoed, both in her mind and in the physical world. "Notice how you can shape them, change their flow." The memories bent like light through crystal, reshaping themselves at her slightest touch.

A chill ran down her spine as she realized the implications. These weren't just images - they were pieces of Nero's life, his most intimate experiences laid bare before her. With just a thought, she could alter them, erase them, or create new ones entirely.

"This is the power Draven wields through the Ark of Dreams," Nero's tone hardened. "He uses it to dominate minds, to reshape memories until people forget who they truly are. The Ark amplifies this ability beyond measure, allowing him to control entire populations."

The golden threads of Liora's magic recoiled at the thought, withdrawing from Nero's memories like a startled animal. Her stomach churned as she imagined Draven wielding such power, turning people's own minds against them.

"The temptation to use this gift for personal gain will always be present," Nero continued, his eyes boring into hers. "Even with the best intentions, it's easy to justify small intrusions, minor alterations. But each violation leaves a scar on both the wielder and the victim."

Liora nodded, feeling the weight of responsibility settle over her shoulders. The power humming beneath her skin no longer felt like a gift, but rather a double-edged sword that could heal or harm with equal measure.

"Great vigilance is required," Nero stressed, leaning forward. "Every time you touch another's mind, you must remember that you hold their very essence in your hands. One careless moment, one selfish impulse, and you could shatter someone's entire world."

The warning rang true, yet Liora couldn't help but wonder what it would feel like to brush against Rafe's consciousness. Would his memories taste of steel and woodsmoke? Would she feel the heat of his determination, the depth of his loyalty? The golden threads of magic stirred at the thought, reaching out unconsciously.

Nero's knowing chuckle broke through her reverie. "Perhaps we should focus on mastering the basics before you go exploring young Delacroix's mind," he said, his eyes twinkling with amusement. "Though I suspect his thoughts already drift quite frequently in your direction."

Heat flooded Liora's cheeks as she ducked her head, unable to meet Nero's knowing gaze. The golden threads of magic danced more vigorously around her fingers, betraying the flutter in her chest at the mere mention of Rafe's name. She couldn't deny how her power responded to thoughts of him, how it yearned to reach out and touch his consciousness, to understand the depths behind those determined eyes.

"Your reaction to him is natural," Nero said, his voice gentler now. "As is the way your magic responds. Every Dreamweaver's power is shaped by their purpose, their driving force. Some find it in duty, others in revenge." He paused, studying her. "And some find it in love."

But Liora barely heard his words about purpose. Her mind had snagged on two others that sent ice through her veins: "final exercise." The golden light around her fingers flickered and dimmed, like candles in a sudden draft.

"You already sense it, don't you?" Nero asked, reading her expression. "Our time here grows short. The Eclipse approaches, and with it, Draven's plans advance. We cannot linger in the safety of Twilight much longer."

The morning light seemed to dim as Nero continued, "On the road, there will be no time for proper training. No safe space to explore your abilities." He gestured to the clearing around them. "This was your final lesson, Liora. The rest you must learn through experience."

Her hands trembled as the implications sank in. Final lesson. No more training. She wasn't ready. The golden threads of magic scattered like autumn leaves in a storm, reflecting her inner turmoil.

"But I've barely begun to understand," Liora protested, her voice catching. "I can't even control my power when I'm calm, let alone in battle. How am I supposed to—" She broke off, the weight of expectation crushing down on her chest.

Nero's expression remained maddeningly serene. "You have learned more than you realize. The foundation is laid—now you must build upon it."

But all Liora could think about was how she'd failed to protect her village, how she'd hurt Gemini, how every attempt to use her power seemed to end in disaster. The golden light had completely vanished now, leaving only the cold knot of dread in her stomach.

She stared at her empty hands, seeing not their present stillness but the destruction they could cause. Everyone was counting on her—Rafe, Gemini, the entire rebellion. And she was going to fail them all, just as she'd failed before. The certainty of it settled over her like a shroud, heavy and suffocating.

***

The makeshift dining area felt worlds away from the bustling camp beyond the ancient trees. Across from Gemini, Jayne Finnegan sat with perfect posture, her calculating eyes taking in every detail of their surroundings even as she spread soft cheese on a piece of crusty bread.

The aroma of herbs wafted up from the steaming tea pot between them, reminding Gemini of her garden back in Eldara. A pang of homesickness twisted in her chest, but she pushed it aside.

"It's these small moments that keep us going, isn't it?" Gemini picked up a bright red apple, turning it in her hands without taking a bite. "A shared meal, a bit of laughter... It's something to hold onto during these times." The words felt heavy on her tongue, weighted with everything left unsaid about the darkness pressing in around their little sanctuary.

Gemini's heart fluttered as Jayne leaned forward, reaching across the table. Her fingertips brushed Gemini's hand, ostensibly to grab another piece of bread, but the contact lingered a heartbeat too long. The spy's touch sent electricity racing up Gemini's arm, and she found herself holding her breath.

Gemini swallowed hard, setting down the apple she'd been fidgeting with. Their eyes met across the table, and the world seemed to narrow to just this moment, just this space between them. The sounds of the camp faded away, replaced by the thundering of her own heart.

A twig snapped nearby, shattering the spell. Jayne withdrew her hand as if burned, her walls slamming back into place. But Gemini caught the slight tremor in her fingers as she reached for her tea, the barely perceptible flush on her cheeks. Something had shifted between them, subtle as a change in wind direction but just as significant.

"Liora's been training hard with Master Thorne, hasn't she? How is she handling all the pressure?" Jayne's eyes never left Gemini's face, all business once more, reading every micro-expression with the precision of a scholar studying ancient texts.

Gemini traced her fingertip along the rim of her teacup, watching the steam curl upward in delicate spirals. The way Jayne leaned forward, all calculated interest and sharp attention, set off warning bells. Those questions about Liora weren't as casual as they seemed.

"She's stronger than she seems," Gemini offered, keeping her voice light despite the tension coiling in her shoulders. "Master Thorne's really helping her understand her powers. It's a lot, but she's rising to the challenge." The words tasted like half-truths on her tongue - true enough to satisfy, yet carefully crafted to protect the vulnerability she'd witnessed in her friend's eyes after each training session.

A muscle twitched in Jayne's jaw, almost imperceptible in the dappled sunlight filtering through the leaves. The spy's fingers drummed once, twice against the wooden table before going still. That controlled stillness spoke volumes to Gemini - Jayne wanted more, needed more information for whatever web she was weaving within the rebellion's ranks.

The breeze carried the scent of pine and sword-steel from the training grounds, reminding Gemini of how far they'd come from Eldara's herb gardens and quiet afternoons. She lifted her chin, meeting Jayne's calculating gaze with the same steady strength she used when treating wounded rebels - gentle but unwavering. Let Jayne read what she would in that gaze; she'd find no weakness to exploit.

"It's good to hear she's progressing," Jayne said at last, but her eyes never left Gemini's face, searching for tells in every micro-expression.

"Her powers are indeed impressive... but also dangerous." Finnegan's fingers tightened around her teacup, "Have you noticed any instability? Anything that could... endanger others?"

"We all have our moments of doubt, don't we?" Gemini kept her voice steady, though her heart thundered against her ribs. The memory of Liora's face after training - exhausted, afraid, but determined - flashed through her mind. She wouldn't let anyone twist that vulnerability into a weapon. "Even the most seasoned warriors struggle with control sometimes."

A crow called overhead, its harsh cry splitting the tense silence between them. Jayne leaned forward, her posture relaxed but her eyes sharp as drawn steel. "That's precisely my concern. One moment of lost control from someone with her level of power..." She left the sentence hanging, heavy with implication.

"Strange, isn't it? How quick we are to fear power in the hands of allies, yet we're so willing to leave it unchecked in the hands of tyrants?" She met Jayne's gaze steadily, letting the words settle between them like stones in still water.

Jayne's lips thinned, the only sign that the barb had landed. "I'm not questioning her intentions, Gemini. But good intentions won't save us if-" A commotion from the training grounds cut through their conversation - shouts and the clash of steel against steel. Gemini rose from her seat, grateful for the interruption, but Jayne's words followed her like shadows as she turned toward the sound.

"Rafe's always been driven by his heart - it's what makes him such a compelling leader." Jayne's words carried a note of fondness, but her eyes remained cold and calculating. "But I've seen how he looks at her, Gemini. The way he hovers, how quick he is to defend her mistakes." The implication hung heavy in the air, and Gemini felt her chest tighten with protective instinct.

Gemini traced her fingers along the rough grain of the wooden table, memories of her father's gentle hands mixing healing poultices surfacing unbidden. "The heart shapes us all differently, doesn't it? Sometimes it leads us to heal, sometimes to fight. But it always leads us somewhere true."

A knowing glint flickered in Jayne's eyes as she leaned forward, her voice dropping to barely above a whisper. "And where did your heart lead you, Healer Estelle? That's quite a name to carry in these parts."

The weight of her family name settled heavy on Gemini's shoulders. She'd spent years deflecting questions about her lineage, protecting the precious fragments of her past like delicate herbs pressed between pages. But something in Jayne's steady gaze drew truth from her like water from a deep well.

"My father was a healer in Eldara," Gemini began, her voice soft but clear. "The kind who'd travel for days just to tend to a sick child, who'd give his last copper to buy medicines for those who couldn't afford them." The memory of his warm smile brought both comfort and an ache that never quite faded.

Her fingers curled around her cooling teacup as she continued. "My mother... she was different. An assassin from the Guild, wounded during a mission gone wrong." The words felt strange on her tongue, secrets long held now taking flight. "She stumbled into my father's cottage one stormy night, more dead than alive."

Heat crept up Gemini's neck as Jayne's eyebrows rose slightly. "He nursed her back to health, never asking questions about the daggers hidden in her boots or the poison vials sewn into her cloak. Just treated her wounds, told her stories while she healed, showed her that hands skilled at dealing death could learn to preserve life instead."

"They fell in love," Gemini said, a sad smile tugging at her lips. "The healer and the assassin. Mother left the Guild, learned to use her knowledge of poisons to craft antidotes instead. They built a life together, had me..." Her voice trailed off, the pain of what came after still raw even years later.

Jayne reached across the table, her calloused fingers brushing Gemini's wrist in an unexpectedly gentle gesture. "What happened to them?"

"They vanished when I was eight," Gemini whispered, fighting back the familiar sting of tears. "One morning they were there, teaching me about herbs and pressure points, and by nightfall..." She shook her head, unable to finish the thought.

The shadows had lengthened around their small table, and somewhere in the distance, a bird called out a mournful song. "I never learned what took them - whether it was the Guild claiming vengeance or something darker. But they taught me that love can transform us, shape us into something new. Even if it ends in pain, it's worth the risk."

Gemini watched as something shifted in Jayne's expression, the calculated mask softening around the edges.

"Perhaps you're right," Jayne murmured, her voice carrying an unfamiliar gentleness that made Gemini's heart flutter. "Sometimes the most dangerous thing isn't power itself, but our fear of it."

The afternoon light caught the flecks of gold in Jayne's eyes, and Gemini found herself leaning forward before she could stop herself. "What about you?" The words slipped out, soft but steady. "Finnegan - that's quite a name to carry as well."

A shadow passed over Jayne's face, something ancient and painful flickering behind her carefully constructed walls. Her hand stilled on the table, and for a moment, Gemini thought she glimpsed a scared child beneath the spy's armor.

"That's..." Jayne's voice caught, almost imperceptibly. "That's a story for another time, perhaps. When the shadows aren't quite so long." She pushed back from the table, the movement precise but lacking its usual fluid grace.

Gemini's heart clenched as she caught the telltale shimmer in Jayne's eyes before the spy turned away. Tears - actual tears - from the woman who prided herself on being untouchable. The sight struck Gemini like a physical blow.

The space Jayne left behind felt heavy with unspoken words and half-formed confessions. Gemini watched her retreating form, noting how her usually confident stride seemed slightly off-kilter, as if she was carrying an invisible weight.

The cooling tea before her had long since lost its comforting aroma, but Gemini couldn't bring herself to move. Her mind replayed every moment of their conversation, searching for hidden meanings in each carefully chosen word and lingering touch.

What had really happened here? The question echoed in her mind as she absently traced the rim of her teacup. Had this been another of Jayne's carefully orchestrated information-gathering sessions, or had something genuine broken through those well-maintained walls?

More importantly, what was this thing growing between them - this delicate, dangerous thing that made her pulse quicken and her thoughts scatter? Gemini pressed her palm against her chest, feeling her heartbeat's uneven rhythm, and wondered if she was walking into a trap of her own making.

# Liora's Mission

G olden light pulsed beneath Liora's skin as she entered the war tent, the magic responding to the tension thick in the air. Her steps faltered when she noticed the gathering - Rafe's reassuring presence near the entrance, Jayne's calculating gaze, and Nero's stoic form in the shadows. The others filtered in behind her: Gemini's gentle touch at her elbow, Derek's suspicious glare, and Marcus's barely concealed hostility.

General Varden's voice cut through the murmurs, commanding attention with its practiced authority. "The time has come to discuss the Veilstone." His eyes lingered on Liora, making her skin crawl with an unease she couldn't quite name.

The word 'Veilstone' resonated within her, stirring something in her dreams - or perhaps her memories. Liora's magic flickered in response, drawing concerned glances from those around her. She curled her fingers into her palms, willing the power to settle.

"The Custodians of the Veil weren't fools," Kael continued, spreading ancient maps across the wooden table. "They knew such power couldn't fall into the wrong hands. So they hid it where only a true Dreamweaver could find it." His gaze fixed on Liora again, heavy with expectation.

Heat crept up her neck as the others turned to stare. The weight of their attention pressed against her chest, making it harder to breathe. Nero stepped forward, his presence steadying as he spoke. "The location reveals itself only to those ready to bear its burden."

Rafe's voice cut through the tension. "And you think Liora's ready?" The doubt in his tone stung, even though she shared it herself. Her magic stirred restlessly, responding to her uncertainty.

"She must be," Kael replied, his fingers tracing paths on the weathered parchment. "The Eclipse approaches, and Draven grows stronger. Without the Veilstone, we stand no chance of victory."

Gemini moved closer to Liora, her proximity offering silent support. "And what happens if she's not ready?" her friend challenged, voice steady despite the tremor Liora could feel in her touch.

The magic beneath Liora's skin surged, golden light spilling from her fingertips unbidden. Maps rustled in a phantom wind as her power responded to her rising panic. She wasn't ready - couldn't be ready. Not when she could barely control the magic she already possessed.

Liora's heart hammered against her ribs as Kael's silence hung in the air. The golden light beneath her skin pulsed faster, matching her racing pulse. She forced her breathing to slow, remembering Nero's lessons about control, but her magic refused to settle.

"Delacroix and Master Thorne will lead the expedition," Kael announced, his calculating gaze sweeping across the gathered faces. "Their experience makes them best suited to guide you through enemy territory."

The word 'territory' sent a chill down Liora's spine. She'd never ventured far from Eldara before everything changed, and now they spoke of walking straight into Draven's domain. Her fingers found the river stone in her pocket, clutching it until the edges bit into her palm.

"The road to Somnara is treacherous," Rafe added, his voice steady but his shoulders tense. "But we have an advantage - they won't expect us to take such a direct route."

Liora's stomach twisted as she remembered the stories of travelers who'd disappeared along that road. Whispers of Draven's patrols, of entire villages falling under his dark influence. She caught Gemini's worried glance and tried to school her features into something less terrified.

"Your first objective will be Arcadia," Kael continued, pointing to a mark on the map. "The village has fallen under Draven's control, but its resources are vital to our cause. We'll need their supplies to prepare the rebellion for open war."

Images flashed through Liora's mind - the chaos at Eldara's festival, the screams, the destruction her own magic had caused. Would Arcadia be the same? Would she lose control again? The golden light flickered more intensely, drawing concerned looks from those nearest to her.

"The villagers there are under his thrall," Nero interjected, his eyes finding Liora's. "Your abilities as a Dreamweaver may be our only hope of freeing them without bloodshed."

Liora's fingers trembled as she traced the path to Somnara on the map, her magic casting dancing shadows across the parchment. The golden light beneath her skin pulsed with each thundering beat of her heart as Kael laid out their desperate gambit.

"Once Arcadia is freed," Kael's voice carried the weight of command, "we'll have the supplies needed to launch our assault on Somnara during the Eclipse." His eyes locked onto Liora's, dark and unflinching. "But without the Veilstone, none of it matters. The rebellion dies before it begins."

The magic surged through her veins, responding to the pressure crushing down on her chest. She couldn't breathe, couldn't think past the enormity of what they were asking. One mistake, one loss of control, and everything would crumble.

"After Arcadia is secured," Kael continued, his finger trailing across the map to a point deep in enemy territory, "your party will cross the Ashen Dunes, and seek out the Veilstone temple."

Gemini's hand found Liora's arm, steadying her as the golden light flickered wildly. "And what happens in this temple?" Her friend's voice carried the concern Liora couldn't voice past the tightness in her throat.

Nero stepped forward from the shadows, his presence both reassuring and terrifying. "The temple will test her," he said, his eyes finding Liora's with an intensity that made her magic spark. "It will determine if she is worthy of wielding the Veilstone's power."

The word 'worthy' echoed in Liora's mind, mocking her attempts at control as her power rippled through the tent. She'd never felt worthy of anything - not her magic, not their trust, not this impossible task they laid before her.

"And if she fails?" Rafe's question cut through the tension, sharp as a blade. His hand rested on his sword hilt, knuckles white with strain.

Nero's response fell like stones into still water. "She dies."

The word "dies" slammed into Liora like a physical blow. She stumbled back, bumping into Gemini who steadied her with gentle hands. The river stone in her pocket felt impossibly heavy, anchoring her to reality as panic clawed at her throat.

Nero's eyes found hers. "The temple's trials are unforgiving," he continued, his voice carrying the weight of ancient knowledge. "But death comes for us all if we fail to act."

Her fingers curled into fists as she fought for control, remembering his lessons about breathing, about intention. But how could she focus when he spoke so casually of her death? The magic responded to her fear, making the maps flutter and the tent poles creak ominously.

"The Eclipse approaches," Nero pressed on, unmoved by her obvious distress. "If Draven uses his Ark of Dreams during that convergence, he'll trap all of Somnus in an eternal nightmare." His words painted vivid images in Liora's mind - villages full of hollow-eyed people, their dreams twisted and controlled by Draven's dark magic.

The golden light beneath her skin pulsed faster as she remembered the festival, remembered how easily Draven's soldiers had dominated the minds of her neighbors. Would that be the fate of everyone she loved?

General Varden's voice cut through her spiraling thoughts. "Draw no attention," he instructed, his calculating gaze sweeping across their faces. "Use the cover of night and forest." His eyes lingered on Liora's still-glowing hands. "And control your... assets."

Heat crept up her neck at the implied criticism, but she forced herself to focus on steadying her breathing. The golden light dimmed slightly as she channeled Nero's teachings, though it refused to fade entirely. The magic hummed beneath her skin, a constant reminder of both her power and her vulnerability.

"Draven's forces are everywhere," Kael continued, his finger tracing paths between settlements on the map. "One mistake, one moment of carelessness, and all our hopes die with you." The weight of responsibility pressed down on Liora's chest, making it harder to breathe.

She could feel Rafe's concerned gaze, could sense Gemini's protective presence at her side. But neither of them could help her face
the trials that waited in that temple. Neither of them could ensure
she wouldn't fail and doom them all. Her magic flickered erratically,
matching the rhythm of her racing thoughts.

"This is our only chance," Varden's voice carried the finality of a
closing tomb. "You have four days. The fate of Somnus rests in your
hands, Dreamweaver." The title felt like a collar around her throat,
choking her with expectations she wasn't sure she could meet. The
golden light flared once more before she managed to wrestle it back
under control, leaving only the faintest glow beneath her skin - and
the crushing weight of an entire realm's destiny on her shoulders.

***

The torches along the stone walls cast dancing shadows as Liora followed the guard to General Varden's chambers. Her footsteps echoed
through the corridor, each one amplifying the unease churning in
her stomach. The guard's armor clinked with each step, a metallic
reminder of the military precision that governed the rebel camp -
precision she'd need for the mission ahead.

Golden wisps of dream energy curled around her fingers as her
mind wandered to the war council's words. The Veilstone, a beacon
of power that could turn the tide against Draven. But what happened
if she failed to claim it haunted her thoughts. Would she join them,
another failed hero in a long line of casualties?

Nero's training sessions flashed through her mind - the careful control, the measured breaths, the balance between power and restraint.
Her magic responded differently now, less wild, more focused. But

would it be enough? The Veilstone demanded more than just control - it required a strength she wasn't sure she possessed.

The guard stopped before Kael's door, and Liora's heart thundered against her ribs. Her magic pulsed in response, golden light seeping from her skin. This mission wasn't just about claiming an artifact - it was about survival. If she failed, if the stone rejected her, death would be a mercy compared to what awaited the rebellion. The darkness gathering at the edges of her vision whispered of futures best left unexplored.

Kael stood at his war table, maps and tactical markers scattered across its surface. He didn't look up as she entered, his fingers tracing battle lines with practiced precision. "Do you know why I summoned you here, Liora?"

The air felt thick with anticipation as he finally raised his gaze to meet hers. His eyes held an intensity that made her want to step back, but she held her ground. "Your potential far exceeds what Nero Thorne would have you believe. I've watched your training - seen how you restrain yourself, afraid of what might happen if you truly let go."

His words stirred something deep within her - a forbidden yearning for the raw power she kept locked away. "Think of what you could accomplish if you embraced your emotions instead of suppressing them. Anger, ambition, desire - these aren't weaknesses to be controlled, but strengths to be harnessed."

Images flashed through Liora's mind: herself standing before armies, dream magic flowing unrestricted through her veins. No more cowering, no more doubt. Just pure, unstoppable force. The vision was intoxicating.

"Some whisper about justice and balance," Kael continued, moving around the table toward her. "But what has balance achieved against

Draven's tyranny? Sometimes, power must be met with power. You could be that power, Liora."

Kael's boots scraped against the stone floor as he circled behind her. "The Veilstone isn't some trinket to be asked for politely. It must be dominated, controlled. Only then will its power truly be yours."

A chill ran down Liora's spine as his words settled over her. The golden wisps of her magic flickered, responding to her unease. This wasn't what Nero had taught her during their sessions in the forest clearing. His lessons spoke of harmony, of working with the flow of dream energy rather than forcing it to submit.

"If you approach it with hesitation, with doubt, it will reject you." Kael's voice carried the weight of certainty, but something in his tone set her teeth on edge. "You must be willing to seize what's rightfully yours."

The memory of Nero's gentle guidance floated through her mind. He'd shown her how claiming didn't mean taking - how power freely given was stronger than power seized by force. Her magic had responded differently then, flowing like water rather than crackling like lightning.

The torchlight caught Kael's face as he moved back into view, shadows dancing across his features. His eyes held an intensity that reminded her of Draven's soldiers during the attack on Eldara - that same hunger for control, that same belief that power meant dominance. Her magic pulsed beneath her skin, but not in response to his words. Instead, it seemed to recoil from them.

"Why hesitate, Liora?" Kael's voice dropped lower, more intimate. "I've seen what you can do. Let your emotions fuel you, and control will follow. Imagine what we could accomplish if you stopped holding back."

The torchlight caught the gleam in his eyes, and for a moment, Liora saw something that made her blood run cold - an echo of Draven's hunger for power, masked behind different words but equally consuming.

"You speak of power as if it's the only answer," she managed, her voice steadier than she felt. The torchlight caught the shadows under his cheekbones, making him look almost skeletal for a moment.

Kael's lips curved into what might have been a smile, but it didn't reach his eyes. He moved closer, each step deliberate as a stalking wolf. "Power is the only answer that matters in war, Liora. Or have you forgotten what happened to Eldara?"

The mention of her home village sent a spike of pain through her chest. Dream magic stirred beneath her skin, responding to the surge of emotion. A nearby candle flame flickered violently, its shadow dancing across the war table's scattered maps.

"I haven't forgotten," she said, taking a step back. "But unleashing destruction won't bring back what was lost. It won't protect anyone." Nero's teachings echoed in her mind - about balance, about purpose beyond revenge.

The general's expression hardened. "Protection? Is that what Nero's been filling your head with?" He swept his arm across the table, sending markers scattering. "While you practice restraint, Draven's forces grow stronger. Every day we wait, more villages are put to the torch, and their citizens enslaved. What horrors your precious Bennet is enduring will be only the beginning when the Emperor finds the rest of us."

Dream energy crackled in the air between them, responding to the tension. The torches dimmed and brightened in irregular pulses, casting strange patterns across Kael's face. His intensity reminded her of something - or someone - but the connection danced just beyond her grasp.

"Let me show you what real power can accomplish," he pressed, extending his hand. "Together, we could end this war before more innocent blood is spilled." His voice dropped to a whisper, honey-sweet and deadly. "Isn't that what you want?"

A memory flashed through Liora's mind - the chaos at Eldara, her powers spiraling out of control, the horror on people's faces. She remembered Gemini's unwavering support, Nero's patient guidance, and Rafe's quiet faith in her. Their faces grounded her against the intoxicating pull of Kael's offer.

The air grew thick with tension as she raised her chin, meeting his gaze directly. "You're right about one thing, General," she said, her voice low but firm. "I do want to end this war. But not like this. Not by becoming what we're fighting against."

Liora turned toward the door, her heart hammering against her ribs. The magic beneath her skin buzzed like angry wasps, responding to the turmoil churning inside her. Each step away from Kael felt like wading through mud, weighed down by the lingering echoes of his words.

Behind her, she heard the soft scrape of General Varden's boots on the floor as he followed her. His presence pressed against her back like a physical weight, making her spine stiffen.

Her fingers brushed the cold metal of the door handle when his voice cut through the silence. "Your mother made the same choice, you know." The words sliced through her like a blade of ice. "Chose restraint over power. Look where that got her."

Something dark and primal surged within Liora, making the torches flare brilliantly for a heartbeat. Her grip tightened on the handle until her knuckles turned white, but she forced herself to breathe - just as Nero had taught her. In and out. Control, not surrender.

Without turning back, she pushed open the door. The hinges groaned in protest, a sound that seemed to echo through the corridor beyond. As she stepped through, Kael's last words followed her like a shadow: "Look where that got her." The door closed behind her with a final, heavy thud.

# Clear Road

The fire crackled as Rafe settled beside Marcus. His muscles ached from the night's watch, but sleep felt distant with the departure for Arcadia in the morning.

"Did you hear about the Wormwood raid?" Marcus leaned forward, his voice barely above a whisper. "The General ordered no survivors. Said we couldn't risk word getting back to Draven." The flames reflected in Marcus's eyes, making them gleam with an unsettling intensity.

Rafe's jaw tightened. He'd seen the aftermath of that raid - the scorched earth, the silence where there should have been life. Kael had claimed strategic necessity, but the brutality felt excessive, even in war. "We're not executioners," Rafe muttered, more to himself than the others.

"It's not just that." Sara, one of their newer recruits, glanced over her shoulder before continuing. "The way he looks at Liora during training... like she's a weapon he wants to sharpen." Her words sent a chill down Rafe's spine that had nothing to do with the night air.

Memories of countless battles fought alongside Kael Varden flashed through Rafe's mind - the general's unwavering courage, his tactical brilliance that had saved their lives more times than he could count. But lately, that brilliance had taken on a darker edge, tinged with something that reminded him too much of Draven's calculating cruelty.

"Kael's methods... they're starting to feel a bit too much like Draven's," Marcus said, voicing the fear they'd all been dancing around. "Almost like he's enjoying it." The words hung heavy in the air, like smoke that refused to dissipate.

Rafe wanted to defend his old friend, to dismiss these concerns as paranoid whispers born of exhaustion and fear. But he couldn't shake the hungry gleam in Kael's eyes when discussing Liora's potential power. It was the same look he'd seen in Draven's eyes.

"We need to watch him," Sara insisted, her hand unconsciously tightening around her weapon. "Before he-" She cut off abruptly as footsteps approached their circle, and conversation shifted to mundane matters of watch rotations and supply runs.

But even as they discussed these routine tasks, Rafe's mind churned with growing unease. He'd sworn to protect Liora. If Kael Varden was indeed sliding toward darkness, that protection might need to extend to guarding her from their own general.

The night grew deeper, and one by one the others drifted away to their tents, leaving Rafe alone with his thoughts and the dying embers. No, he decided, General Kael Varden had been through too much with them to turn. But something felt... off. And in these dangerous times, that feeling couldn't be ignored. Movement caught his eye - a shadow passing between tents, tall and familiar. Kael, heading toward his quarters with purpose in his stride. Rafe rose silently, decision made. Tonight, he would follow.

Rafe slipped between the shadows of the tents, his footsteps silent against the packed earth. Ahead, Kael's figure moved with deliberate purpose, taking a path that led away from the main camp rather than toward his quarters. Something about the general's furtive movements set Rafe's instincts on edge.

The night air carried whispers of conversation, and Rafe pressed himself against a tree trunk as Kael paused near the edge of the camp. Two other figures emerged from the darkness - rebels Rafe didn't recognize. Their hushed tones carried an urgency that made his skin prickle.

Moonlight caught the glint of something metallic passing between hands. Rafe squinted, trying to make out what it was, but Kael's broad shoulders blocked his view. The general's voice, usually commanding and clear, had dropped to a whisper that barely carried on the breeze.

A twig snapped somewhere behind Rafe, and he froze. His heart hammered against his ribs as he waited to see if the sound had alerted the conspirators. Years of combat had honed his instincts, and right now every one of them screamed that he was witnessing something he wasn't meant to see.

The conversation ahead grew more heated, though still too quiet to make out the words. One of the unknown figures jabbed a finger toward the center of camp - toward where Liora slept. Rafe's muscles tensed, ready to spring into action if needed.

Kael's response was swift and sharp, his hand closing around the other man's wrist. Even from this distance, Rafe could see the threat in the general's posture. The stranger backed down immediately, nodding in apparent submission to whatever Kael had demanded.

A cloud passed over the moon, plunging the scene into deeper darkness. Rafe blinked, trying to adjust his vision, but when the light returned, the two strangers had vanished. Only Kael Varden remained, staring into the shadows with an expression Rafe had never seen before - something caught between triumph and apprehension.

The sound of approaching footsteps forced Rafe deeper into the shadows. A patrol was making its rounds, their torchlight threatening to expose his position. He held his breath, pressing himself flat against the rough bark as they passed.

When he looked back, Kael too had disappeared. Only the disturbed earth and trampled grass gave any indication of the meeting that had taken place. Rafe's mind raced with possibilities, none of them good. Whatever he'd just witnessed felt like the first thread pulling loose from a carefully woven tapestry.

Moving with careful precision, Rafe began making his way back toward the main camp. He needed to warn someone - Nero perhaps, or even Liora herself. But as he stepped into a patch of moonlight, a familiar voice froze him in place. "Interesting night for a walk, isn't it, Delacroix?"

Rafe's muscles tensed at Jayne's voice. He turned to face her, keeping his expression neutral despite the thundering of his heart. The moonlight caught the flame tattoo on her neck as she stepped closer, her amber eyes scanning the shadows behind him.

"Just getting some air," Rafe said, though the lie felt hollow on his tongue. He'd worked with Jayne long enough to know she rarely engaged in casual conversation, especially at this hour.

She circled him like a predator sizing up its prey, her boots silent against the packed earth. "You've noticed it too, haven't you? The change in him." Her voice dropped lower, barely above a whisper. "The way he looks at her during training."

"What are you suggesting?" He matched her quiet tone, aware of how sound carried in the night air.

"I'm suggesting that our dear general might not be as committed to our cause as he once was." Jayne stopped directly in front of him, close enough that he could see the tension in her jaw. "The raid on Wormwood wasn't necessary. Those people posed no real threat."

Rafe's hands clenched involuntarily. He'd tried to push those memories away - the scorched buildings, the silence where children's laughter should have been. "He said it was strategic necessity."

"And you believe that?" Jayne's eyes narrowed. "Or are you too loyal to your old friend to see what's right in front of you?" Her words cut deeper than she probably intended, striking at the doubt that had been growing in his own mind.

The sound of approaching footsteps made them both stiffen. Jayne melted back into the shadows with practiced ease, but her final whispered words lingered in the air: "There's something I'm missing, Rafe. Something to do with Liora, this whole mission. Something's coming, and I don't think we're going to like it."

Rafe stood alone in the clearing, his mind churning with possibilities. The secret meeting, Jayne's warnings, the growing darkness he'd sensed in Kael - it all pointed to something he didn't want to believe. But he couldn't ignore the evidence anymore, not when Liora's safety might be at stake.

***

The canvas walls of the tent rippled in the night breeze, casting strange shadows across Liora's face as she lay on her thin bedroll. Beside her, Gemini's steady breathing provided a rhythm to measure the endless minutes by. Sleep refused to come.

General Varden's words about her mother twisted through her thoughts like thorny vines. What did he know? The memories she had of her mother were fragments at best - a gentle hand brushing hair from her face, the scent of lavender, a laugh that seemed to make flowers bloom. Nothing of power or restraint or choices that led to destruction.

The dream magic stirred beneath her skin, responding to her turmoil. A small flame appeared above her palm, dancing and flickering with each unsteady breath. Liora watched it pulse, remembering how the torches had flared during her confrontation with Kael. The same power, but this tiny flame felt different - controlled, purposeful. Like Nero had taught her.

A log shifted in the dying fire outside, sending up a spray of sparks that glittered against the night sky. The sight reminded her of the festival lights in Eldara, before everything changed. The flame above her palm guttered and died as her throat tightened. She rolled onto her side, pulling the rough blanket tighter around her shoulders, but the memory of Kael's knowing smile followed her into the darkness.

The exhaustion of the day finally pulled Liora under, her consciousness slipping away like water through cupped hands. Even in sleep, tension lined her face as dreams and memories tangled together in her mind.

Mist swirled around her feet as she opened her eyes to find herself standing in a vast, ethereal space. The air itself seemed to pulse with an otherworldly rhythm, each beat sending ripples through the silvery fog that stretched endlessly in all directions.

The same stone from before hung suspended before her, its crystalline surface catching impossible light and fracturing it into a thousand glittering fragments. The Veilstone, she recognized somewhere deep within herself. Its glow called to something deep within her, a resonance that made her power stir and reach toward it like a flower seeking the sun.

The stone's glow suddenly flared, blinding in its intensity. Liora threw up her hands to shield her eyes, but the light pierced through her defenses, searing itself into her mind.

Her breath caught as images flooded her mind - Eldara burning, Draven's shadow stretching across Somnus, and something darker still lurking at the edges of her consciousness. The Veilstone's weight seemed to increase with each passing second, threatening to drag her down into the swirling mist below.

Cold sweat beaded on her forehead as she struggled to maintain a grip she didn't even know she had. The roots beneath the pedestal began to writhe, reaching up toward her with grasping tendrils. Each one seemed drawn to the stone's fading light, hungry for the power it contained.

A familiar voice cut through the whispers - a woman's, as if born from memory. Stronger, commanding. "Balance," it warned, the single word reverberating through Liora's bones. The Veilstone's glow steadied for a moment, then dimmed further.

The mist pressed closer, its silvery surface now shot through with veins of darkness. Liora's arms ached from the stone's weight, but something deeper than physical strength kept her fingers locked around its surface. The power within called to her own, a resonance that both terrified and enthralled her.

Shadows danced at the edge of her vision, taking shapes that seemed almost human before dissolving back into the mist. Each one reached toward her with ghostly hands, their touch leaving trails of ice across her skin. The Veilstone's light pulsed weaker still, barely visible now.

Her knees buckled as another wave of visions crashed through her mind - herself wielding powers beyond imagination, reshaping reality with a thought, becoming everything Draven feared. The stone grew colder, its surface now painful to touch, but still she held on.

The roots continued their relentless climb, wrapping around her legs with increasing urgency. Each tendril seemed to whisper with Kael Varden's voice, promising strength without restraint if she would just let go of her fears. The stone's light flickered once more, barely a spark now.

The roots tightened around Liora's ankles, thorns pressing against her skin as her panic rose. Each ragged breath seemed to make them grow faster, thicker, more menacing. The Veilstone's glow flickered wildly in response to her fear, casting erratic shadows through the misty dreamscape.

A soft silver light cut through the chaos, and the vines stilled their frenzied dance. Lyra Solari emerged from the ethereal fog, her presence bringing an inexplicable calm to the turbulent space. With a graceful wave of her hand, the thorny tendrils retreated, slithering back into the mist like chastised serpents.

"Your emotions shape this world, Liora," Lyra's voice carried the gentle authority of ancient wisdom. "Each fear, each doubt—they are part of you, and they give power to your magic. But without focus, they can turn against you." The silver-haired woman knelt beside Liora, her otherworldly glow casting back the encroaching shadows.

Liora's hands trembled as she pushed herself up, the Veilstone's weight still heavy in her mind. "I keep trying, but... I feel like I'm slipping. What if I lose control?" The words caught in her throat, thick with the fear that had plagued her since Eldara.

"Control does not mean absence of fear, nor the avoidance of pain," Lyra's fingers brushed Liora's temple, cool and soothing. "It means knowing yourself and embracing every part of who you are. Only then will your power become truly yours."

The mist swirled around them as Lyra guided Liora to her feet, positioning her hands palm-up. "Close your eyes," she instructed. "Feel the energy flowing through you—not as something separate, but as part of your own essence."

Warmth spread from Liora's center outward as she followed Lyra's guidance. The chaos of her thoughts began to settle, like leaves falling gently after a storm. The Veilstone's presence felt less overwhelming now, its power harmonizing with her own instead of threatening to consume it.

"Your magic responds to truth," Lyra's voice seemed to come from everywhere and nowhere. "Not the truth others would have you believe, but your own truth. What lies beneath the fear, Liora?"

The answer rose unbidden in Liora's mind—a desire to protect, to heal, to restore balance to a world thrown into chaos. As she acknowledged this truth, the dreamscape shifted. The thorny vines transformed into flowering branches, their blooms casting soft light into the surrounding mist.

The dream began to fade, but Lyra's presence lingered like starlight at dawn. "Remember," her voice echoed as consciousness pulled at Liora's mind, "I am more than a dream, and you are more than your fears." The Veilstone's glow pulsed once more, steady and sure, before dissolving into the approaching morning.

Liora jerked awake, her heart hammering against her ribs as the Veilstone's ethereal glow faded from her mind. The tent's canvas walls pressed close, yet she felt exposed - as if the dream had stripped away some vital defense. Her hands trembled, still feeling the stone's weight and warmth.

Sweat cooled on her skin as she pulled herself upright, careful not to wake Gemini sleeping nearby. The dream clung to her thoughts like cobwebs, refusing to dissolve into the usual morning haze. Each detail remained sharp - the writhing roots, the whispering shadows, and that voice... her mother's voice, speaking of balance.

The power that had surged through her in the dream still echoed in her veins, different from the chaotic bursts she'd struggled to control. This felt focused, purposeful. Like the tiny flame she'd conjured before sleep, but deeper somehow. Connected to something ancient and vast that waited just beyond her reach.

Pale dawn light filtered through the tent's walls, painting everything in shades of gray. Liora pressed her palms against her eyes, trying to sort through the tangle of emotions the dream had left behind. Fear wrestled with determination, doubt with understanding. Lyra Solari had shown her both warning and promise - power enough to reshape worlds, but only if she could first reshape herself.

A guard called the morning watch outside, making Liora start. She lowered her hands to find them steady now, though her pulse still raced beneath her skin. Something had shifted during the night, leaving her changed in ways she couldn't yet name. The dream's message burned in her mind: mastery meant more than control - it meant acceptance of both light and shadow, strength and restraint, power and purpose.

***

Rafe pushed the bowl of steaming porridge across the rough-hewn table, his dark eyes fixed on Liora's trembling hands. The morning air hung thick with unspoken words and the lingering scent of woodsmoke from the camp's cooking fires.

"You look like you've seen a ghost," he murmured, sliding onto the bench opposite her. His own breakfast lay untouched, steam rising in lazy spirals that matched the circles under his eyes.

Liora stared into the bowl, watching the surface ripple with each tremor of her fingers. The dream's remnants still clung to her thoughts like morning mist, making it hard to focus on the here and now. "Maybe I have," she whispered, more to herself than to him.

Rafe's hand twitched toward hers but stopped short, hovering over the weathered wood between them. "The nightmares again?" His voice carried an edge of understanding that cut deeper than pity ever could.

The porridge burned her tongue as she forced herself to eat, buying time before answering. Around them, the camp stirred to life, but their corner remained isolated - the calm before the storm.

"Different this time," Liora managed between careful bites. "It fel t... real. Like someone was trying to show me something important." She glanced up to find Rafe watching her with an intensity that made her chest tight.

His jaw clenched, a muscle jumping beneath the skin. "What did you see?" The words hung between them like smoke, heavy with implications neither dared voice aloud.

Liora's spoon clattered against the bowl as memories of the dream flooded back. The ethereal woman with silver hair, the stars that seemed to dance at her command, the whispered promises of hidden knowledge. Her throat tightened as she tried to put the vision into words.

"There was a woman," she began, her voice barely above a whisper, yet unwilling to name Lyra Solari. "She spoke about... about what lies beneath the surface." It felt strange on her tongue, carrying weight she didn't fully understand.

"She said I was on a path," Liora continued, forcing the words past her uncertainty. "That there was power greater than myself, but it needed wisdom." The morning sun caught the steam rising from their bowls, creating ghostly shapes that reminded her of the dream's swirling mist.

Rafe's expression darkened further. "Master Thorne needs to hear about this." He glanced over his shoulder, scanning the growing crowd of rebels for their mentor's familiar figure. "If someone is appearing to your in your dreams, it could mean-"

Rafe's words faded into the morning air, his brow furrowing as he studied Liora's face. The camp's bustle seemed to fade around them, leaving only the quiet space between heartbeats.

Sunlight caught the dark strands of his hair as he leaned forward, his shoulders tensing. "About the other night," he started, his voice dropping lower. "I shouldn't have-"

"Don't." Liora's pulse quickened at the memory - the warmth of his body, the way his fingers had brushed her cheek, the breath of space between them before reality crashed back in. "You don't need to apologize for that."

His eyes widened, surprise flickering across his features before settling into something softer, more vulnerable. The wooden bench creaked as he shifted his weight, clearly wrestling with what to say next.

Heat crept up Liora's neck as the moment stretched between them. The morning's dream suddenly felt distant, replaced by the vivid memory of almost-possibilities and unspoken words.

The porridge sat forgotten between them, steam no longer rising from the cooling bowls. Around them, the camp continued its morning routine, oblivious to the weight of things left unsaid at their table.

Liora's hands pressed flat against the rough wood as she pushed herself up from the bench. The movement broke whatever spell had settled over their quiet corner, sending reality rushing back in with the sound of clashing practice swords and shouted orders from the training grounds.

Rafe's mouth opened as if to speak, but no words came. His dark eyes followed her movement, carrying an intensity that made her chest ache with things she couldn't afford to feel.

Jayne's boots crunched against the frost-covered ground as she approached their table, her expression grim in the morning light. "We need to move," she announced, cutting through the tension between Liora and Rafe. "If we want to reach Arcadia by afternoon, we leave now."

The warmth of the moment shattered like ice. Liora's chest tightened at the mention of Arcadia - a name that carried the weight of captured souls and broken promises. Her magic stirred beneath her skin, responding to the spike of anxiety that shot through her.

"The scouts confirmed the road is clear," Jayne continued, her eyes darting between them. A knowing look crossed her face, but she pressed on. "We'll need to cross the river before the patrols change. Master Thorne is waiting."

# Arcadia

Liora's hands trembled as she peered through the dense foliage at Arcadia. The village stretched before them like a painting drained of color, its inhabitants moving with mechanical precision through their daily routines. Her stomach churned at the sight of Draven's soldiers patrolling the perimeter, their dark uniforms stark against the pale buildings.

Their trek had proven remarkably smooth. The water crossing went without incident, and they'd encountered barely any guards to dodge along the way. Though Marcus voiced suspicions about the unusual ease of their progress, Rafe advised him to simply accept such good fortune when it came.

The afternoon sun cast long shadows across the rebels' hiding spot, and Liora counted seven guards making their rounds. Each villager they passed didn't even flinch, their eyes glazed and movements puppet-like. The display of Draven's control over them made her skin crawl.

Rafe's whistle cut through her spiraling thoughts. He gestured for the rebels to gather, his expression grim as he unrolled a crude map of Arcadia on a fallen log. The parchment crinkled under his fingers as he traced their planned route. A crouched Nero's eyes scanned the area as he spoke.

"We move at dusk," Rafe said, his voice barely above a whisper. He assigned positions with practiced efficiency - Marcus and Derek to take out the western guards, Jayne and Nero to secure their escape route, and others to various tactical positions. When he turned to Liora, his eyes softened. "You'll provide magical cover as we approach. Keep us hidden, nothing more."

Relief flooded through her at the simplicity of her task. Just concealment - no combat, no direct confrontation. She could handle that, couldn't she? The memory of her last training session, where she'd accidentally shattered three practice targets, nagged at her conscience.

"Are we sure about this?" Marcus's voice cut through the group's murmured acknowledgments. "One slip in her control and we're all exposed. Master Thorne should be in charge of cover." His words carried the weight of others' unspoken doubts, and Liora felt their stares like physical pressure on her shoulders.

Heat crept up Liora's neck as the group's attention shifted to Nero. He stood from his crouched position, brushing dirt from his weathered coat with deliberate care.

"You misunderstand the nature of her and my magic, Marcus." Nero's quiet voice carried an edge of steel. "My abilities cannot affect the minds of others, they're suited for perception and guidance - useful for training, but limited in scope. What we need is raw power, shaped with precision." His eyes met Liora's. "Which is exactly what she possesses."

The dream energy humming beneath Liora's skin responded to his words, sending tingles down her arms. She curled her fingers into fists, willing the power to stay contained as Nero continued.

"I can wield a blade as well as any of you, and that's where I'll be of most use." He rested a hand on the sword at his hip. "But maintaining a veil over our entire group while we traverse open ground? That requires something far beyond my capabilities." The weight of his gaze settled on Marcus. "We either trust her, or we abandon the mission. There is no middle ground."

Marcus's jaw clenched, but he offered no further argument. Rafe seized the moment of silence to resume outlining their approach, though Liora barely heard him over the thundering of her heart. Trust. Such a simple word, yet it felt like chains around her chest, binding her to an expectation she wasn't sure she could meet.

A commotion from the village drew their attention - a changing of the guard. As Draven's soldiers rotated positions, Liora watched their mechanical movements and tried to steady her breathing. In a few hours, everything would depend on her control. The thought sent another tremor through her hands, and she quickly hid them in the folds of her cloak before anyone could notice.

Jayne approached their position, her footsteps silent on the forest floor. She crouched beside Liora, eyes fixed on the village. "The patrol patterns changed last week. They're more frequent now." Her words carried an edge of warning that made Liora's chest tighten.

The shadows lengthened across Arcadia's streets as the sun dipped lower. Liora watched a young girl mechanically hanging laundry, her movements jerky and unnatural. The sight stirred something deep within her - memories of her own village before Draven's attack, of laughter and life now silenced.

Rafe's hand brushed Liora's shoulder, gentle but firm. "We have an hour until dusk. Are you ready?" The question hung between them, heavy with unspoken concern. His touch anchored her, even as doubt threatened to pull her under.

A gust of wind carried the scent of woodsmoke from the village, along with fragments of conversation between the guards. Their casual discussion of dinner plans felt obscene against the backdrop of enslaved villagers. Liora's powers stirred in response to her rising anger, and she forced them back down.

Maya returned from her scouting position, her face tight with tension. "There's movement at the north gate. More soldiers arriving." She directed this information to Rafe, but her eyes flickered to Liora, measuring her reaction to this complication.

The news rippled through the group, shoulders tensing and hands moving to weapons. Derek muttered something under his breath, too low to hear but his meaning clear in the sharp glance he shot toward Liora. She pretended not to notice, focusing instead on controlling her breathing as Nero had taught her.

Rafe adjusted their plan, quick and decisive. "We'll split into three groups instead of two. Liora, you'll need to extend your cover further now." He spoke with confidence, but Liora caught the slight furrow in his brow. The change would strain her control, spreading her power thinner across more area.

Through the trees, Liora spotted one of Draven's lieutenants emerging from a building, his dark uniform adorned with silver symbols that seemed to absorb the fading light. The sight of those emblems sent a chill down her spine - she'd seen them in her nightmares, glowing with corrupt power.

The rebels began their final preparations, checking weapons and exchanging quiet words of encouragement. Liora closed her eyes,

reaching for that calm center Nero had helped her find during training. Her powers responded sluggishly, like thick honey refusing to
flow.

A bird's alarm call split the air, making everyone freeze. But it was
only a natural warning, not a signal from their lookouts. As the tension
eased, Liora caught Jayne watching her with an unreadable expression.
The spy's scrutiny reminded her that more than just the mission's
success rode on her control tonight - so did the rebels' fragile trust in
her abilities.

***

Shadows stretched like grasping fingers across the forest floor as Liora
crept forward with the rebels. The moon hung low and heavy, casting
just enough light to navigate by while staying hidden from Draven's
patrols. Her boots barely made a sound against the damp earth, yet
each step felt thunderous in her ears.

The weight of responsibility pressed down on her chest, making
it hard to breathe. This wasn't practice anymore—real lives hung in
the balance. Real consequences waited for any mistake. She caught
glimpses of the other rebels moving like ghosts through the trees, their
faces grim and focused.

Nero's words echoed in her mind: "Center yourself. Find your
purpose." But purpose felt elusive when doubt gnawed at her edges.
The sideways glances from the other rebels spoke volumes—they expected her to fail. Expected her to lose control just like she had during
training.

Her hands trembled as she pressed them against her sides, trying to
still the nervous energy coursing through her veins. The magic stirred

beneath her skin, responsive to her anxiety, threatening to spiral out of her grasp. Each breath came faster than the last.

The village's outline emerged through the trees—dark buildings hunched against the night sky like sleeping giants. Draven's flags hung limp in the still air, their presence a reminder of what they faced. What she had to overcome.

Ahead, a rebel shifted wrong, sending a cascade of pebbles down a small incline. The sound, though slight, made Liora's heart jump into her throat. She froze, certain they'd been discovered, certain she'd have to use her powers before she was ready.

The night remained quiet, but sweat beaded on her forehead. She could feel the others' tension, their readiness for action warring with the need for stealth. Their doubt in her abilities pressed against her like a physical weight.

A shadow detached itself from the darkness beside her—Rafe. His presence steadied her, even as his expression remained serious. He touched her shoulder briefly, a silent question in his eyes. Are you ready?

"Remember," he whispered, his voice barely a breath, "we're all counting on each other tonight. You've trained for this." The confidence in his tone helped ease the knot in her stomach, if only slightly.

He moved on to check the others, leaving Liora to wrestle with her fears. The magic pulsed beneath her skin, eager to be released. She clenched her fists, praying she could keep it contained until the right moment. Until she could prove herself worthy of their trust.

Liora's heart thundered against her ribs as Rafe's nod came. This was the moment—her chance to prove she belonged with the rebellion.

***

The guard's eyes glazed over as Liora focused her energy, channeling the dream magic just as Nero had taught her. The man swayed, caught in a waking dream that made the world tilt and blur around him. Relief flooded through her as he slumped against the wall, offering no resistance as two rebels dragged him into the shadows.

Rafe signaled from ahead, his fingers moving in the practiced patterns they'd rehearsed. Two guards at the storehouse. Heavy locks. Time running short. Liora crept forward, staying low beneath the windows where lamplight spilled onto the packed dirt.

Her magic stirred again as she reached for the guards' minds, but something felt different this time. The power surged stronger, feeding off her growing confidence. The guards' expressions went slack, their spears dipping as reality dissolved into dreams around them.

Sweat trickled down Liora's spine as she held the dream-state steady. The rebels moved like shadows, Rafe leading them past the entranced guards. Metal scraped against metal as they worked on the locks, each sound making her pulse jump.

The magic threatened to slip from her grasp, tugging at her control like a wild animal straining against a leash. She gritted her teeth, remembering Nero's lessons about purpose over power. These guards weren't her enemies—they were just men doing their jobs. She wouldn't let her power harm them.

Boxes and crates crashed together inside the storehouse as the rebels worked quickly to liberate Draven's supplies. Liora's concentration wavered with each sound, the guards' expressions twitching as reality threatened to break through the dreams she'd woven.

A shout from across the village square shattered the night's silence. Liora's heart stopped as she saw another patrol rounding the corner, their torches cutting through the darkness. Her hold on the nearby guards slipped, their eyes beginning to clear.

"Now!" Rafe's voice cut through her panic. The rebels burst from the storehouse, weapons drawn.

Liora's heart thundered against her ribs as the wave of dream energy rippled outward, precise and controlled for the first time since she'd discovered her powers. The soldiers stumbled, their eyes glazing over as the magic took hold, transforming the village square into a maze of shifting shadows in their minds.

Relief flooded through her as she watched the rebels press their advantage, moving swiftly past the disoriented guards. No one had been hurt by her magic this time - no allies caught in the crossfire, no unintended victims of her fear.

"Nice work, Liora! That's exactly what we needed!" Rafe's voice carried across the square, pride evident in his tone.

"I... I did it. I really did it!" The words escaped her in a breathless whisper, a smile tugging at her lips despite the chaos around them.

The success sang through her veins like liquid starlight, making her fingers tingle with newfound confidence. This was what Nero had tried to teach her - control born of purpose rather than fear, precision instead of raw power.

More soldiers rounded the corner, torchlight gleaming off their polished armor. Liora's magic responded instantly, no longer feeling like a wild beast straining against its chains but rather an extension of her will.

The world bent and wavered around the approaching guards, their steps faltering as dream-mist clouded their vision. One by one, they slumped against the walls or sank to their knees, lost in visions that kept them safely contained without causing harm.

Rafe flashed her a quick grin as he darted past, leading a group of rebels toward the storehouse. The operation was back on track, their objective within reach thanks to her controlled intervention.

Another patrol approached from the opposite direction, but this time Liora felt no panic, no crushing weight of doubt. Her power flowed smooth and steady, wrapping the new threats in dreams before they could raise the alarm.

The night air crackled with possibility as Liora maintained her focus, finally glimpsing the person she could become - not a danger to her allies, but a protector wielding her gift with precision and purpose.

A Dreamweaver.

***

The rebels moved like a well-oiled machine through Arcadia's square, their earlier doubts about Liora forgotten in the rush of success. She watched as they secured the perimeter, her magic still humming beneath her skin like a plucked bowstring.

Doors creaked open throughout the village, tentative faces peering out at the commotion. An elderly woman emerged first, her weathered features tight with suspicion until she recognized the rebellion's insignia on Rafe's coat. The woman's expression crumpled with relief, tears streaming down her cheeks as she stumbled forward.

More villagers followed, their movements cautious as newborn foals testing uncertain legs. They blinked in the torchlight, as if waking from a long, dark dream. Liora's chest tightened as she recognized the same haunted look she'd seen in Eldara's survivors.

A rebel she didn't know - a tall woman with close-cropped hair - clasped Liora's shoulder as she passed. "That was something else," she murmured, respect evident in her tone.

The praise felt foreign, like a coat that didn't quite fit. Liora managed a small nod, her attention caught by a group of children emerging from a nearby house. Their wide eyes darted between the fallen soldiers and the rebels, uncertain which side to fear.

Marcus approached, this one sporting a fresh cut above his eye. "Those guards won't remember a thing when they wake up," he said, gesturing to the sleeping soldiers. "Clean work." The words carried weight - an apology for his earlier skepticisms wrapped in professional admiration.

More villagers filled the square now, their voices a growing murmur of hope and disbelief. An old man gripped Liora's hand as he passed, his calloused fingers trembling. "Thank you," he whispered, voice rough with emotion. "We'd forgotten what it was like to dream our own dreams."

Rafe appeared at her side, his presence steady and warm. "The northern patrol will be making their rounds soon," he warned, but his proud smile took the edge off the words. "We should move quickly."

Two more rebels hurried past, each offering quick nods of acknowledgment to Liora. The gesture spoke volumes - she was no longer an outsider to be feared, but a comrade who'd proved her worth in battle. The realization settled like a warm stone in her chest.

Liora's fingers still tingled with residual magic as Nero approached through the crowd of freed villagers. His normally stoic features had softened, pride evident in the slight curve of his mouth. The weight of his approval settled over her like a warm blanket.

"You maintained control even when the second patrol appeared," he observed, his voice pitched low enough that only she could hear. "Your mother would have been proud of how you protected both sides - the rebels and the soldiers." The mention of her mother sent a familiar ache through Liora's chest.

"The true test of a Dreamweaver isn't in how much power they can unleash," he continued, gesturing to the sleeping guards who would wake with no memory of their defeat. "It's in knowing when to show restraint." His words echoed her earlier choices, when she'd chosen to incapacitate rather than harm.

A commotion near the village well drew their attention - more villagers emerging from hiding, their faces bearing the dazed expression of those newly awakened from a long nightmare. Nero's hand settled briefly on her shoulder, a gesture that carried the weight of years of tradition. "Come," he said, already turning toward the growing crowd. "There's more work to be done before dawn."

The square buzzed with controlled chaos as rebels and villagers worked together to gather supplies and treat minor injuries. But something tickled at the edges of Liora's awareness - a shadow of unease that didn't match the victory of the moment. She turned toward the village's eastern edge, where the pre-dawn sky had begun to lighten with unsettling speed.

***

The shadows shifted, and suddenly the air itself seemed to congeal with menace. These were no mere subdued guards. These were Draven's personal forces, like the ones that burned Eldara. They materialized from the darkness like nightmares made flesh, their weapons gleaming with unnatural light. Liora's stomach dropped - it was like they'd been lying in wait, letting the rebels taste victory before springing their trap.

But how did they know?

Steel clashed against steel as the square erupted into chaos. A rebel fell, clutching his throat. Blood sprayed across cobblestones. Another soldier crumpled under Marcus's blade. Nero was fighting as a dam holding back the soldiers from the villagers. The peaceful victory of moments ago shattered into screams and the metallic tang of violence.

"Liora!" Rafe's voice cut through the chaos. He parried a blow meant for his neck, spinning to face her. "Get these people out! Take the eastern path - we'll hold them here!" His eyes blazed with desperation as he turned back to the fight.

She grabbed the nearest villager - a young woman frozen in terror - and pulled her toward the eastern edge of the square. "This way!" Other villagers followed, stumbling in their haste. But each step away from the battle felt like a betrayal, every cry of pain from behind them a weight on her conscience.

A child's scream pierced the air. Liora whirled to see a small boy trip, his mother reaching for him as one of Draven's soldiers raised his blade. The distance was too great - no one would reach them in time.

Power surged through her veins, raw and electric. Nero's warnings echoed in her mind - control, restraint, purpose. But purpose stood right there in the square, about to die. Liora released her hold on the magic, letting it flood through her.

Her first strike cut through the air like lightning, dream-forged weapons slicing through the soldier threatening the child. The blade didn't draw blood - instead, it seemed to pass through armor and flesh alike, leaving the man collapsed in a heap, trapped in whatever nightmare Liora's power had conjured.

More weapons materialized around her - spears of pure dream energy, shields that rippled like water yet held firm against steel. Each manifestation felt more natural than the last, as if her body finally remembered a dance it had always known. The remaining soldiers turned toward her, recognizing the greater threat.

They never stood a chance. Liora moved through their ranks like a storm, each gesture unleashing another wave of dream weapons.

Some soldiers fell to phantom arrows, others crumpled beneath shields that crashed down like waves. Her power responded to every thought, every instinct, crafting exactly what she needed in each moment.

Marcus stared open-mouthed as three soldiers charging him simply collapsed, wrapped in tendrils of silvery energy. Rafe had lowered his sword entirely, watching with a mixture of awe and uncertainty as Liora systematically dismantled Draven's elite forces.

The square filled with the sound of falling bodies and clattering weapons. Not a single rebel had fallen since Liora's power had manifested. The soldiers who remained conscious began to retreat, scrambling over each other in their haste to escape the Dreamweaver's onslaught.

Dream-forged chains snaked out, wrapping around fleeing ankles and wrists. Liora couldn't let them report back - couldn't risk them leading more forces to the village. Each captured soldier slumped into unconsciousness as her power touched them, their minds overwhelmed by whatever visions her magic forced upon them.

The last soldier standing turned to run, only to find himself face-to-face with a wall of shifting, ethereal energy. He raised his hands in surrender, dropping his weapon. Liora felt no mercy - only cold certainty as another dream-blade manifested, sending him crumpling alongside his companions.

In the sudden silence, Liora's weapons began to fade, dissolving like mist in morning light. The square was littered with unconscious bodies, yet not a drop of blood had been spilled by her power. She stood in the center of it all, breathing hard, her hands still crackling with residual energy.

Her eyes found Nero at the edge of the square, and the sight of his expression made her stomach clench. He smiled, but it didn't reach his eyes. His fingers worried at the emblem on his coat - the mark of the Custodians she'd come to trust.

"Well done, Liora," he called out, his voice carrying across the square with practiced warmth. But beneath the praise, she caught an edge of tension, of careful restraint. Like a handler praising a dangerous animal that had performed its tricks well - while keeping one hand on the cage door. The realization settled cold and heavy in her gut: she hadn't just proved she could control her power. She'd proved how dangerous that power could be.

# The Power of Fear

T he forest path wound ahead through deepening shadows, but laughter and excited chatter brightened the air. Liora's feet ached from the march back to the road, yet her heart felt lighter than it had in weeks. Around her, rebels and newly-liberated villagers shared stories and hopes for the future, their voices carrying a note of triumph she'd never heard before.

A hand brushed her shoulder, and she turned to find Rafe falling into step beside her. His usual stern expression had softened into something warmer, pride radiating from his battle-worn features. "You were incredible back there," he said, voice low enough that only she could hear. "I've never seen anything like it."

Heat crept into her cheeks as she remembered the raw power that had flowed through her, how naturally it had responded to her will. "I just... knew what needed to be done. It felt different this time - like the magic was finally working with me instead of against me."

Rafe nodded, ducking under a low-hanging branch. "That's what real control looks like. Nero's been right about you all along - you just needed time to find your footing." His words carried the weight of genuine belief, washing away months of doubt and fear.

"We actually did it," Liora breathed, still hardly daring to believe it. "We freed them. And no one..." She trailed off, remembering the unconscious soldiers lying in the square, taken down without bloodshed.

"No one died by your hand," Rafe finished for her, understanding lighting his eyes. "That's what makes you different from Draven. You have all this power, but you choose how to use it. That's why the rebellion needs you - why I-" He caught himself, clearing his throat.

Behind them, one of the Arcadian children let out a peal of laughter as her father swung her onto his shoulders. The sound seemed to break some invisible tension, and Liora found herself smiling despite her exhaustion. "I couldn't have done it without everyone believing in me. Even when I didn't believe in myself."

The path curved around a massive oak, and Liora caught sight of Nero trailing at the back of the group. His shoulders were hunched, face drawn in that familiar expression of deep thought - but something felt off. Every time she glanced his way, his eyes darted elsewhere, as if avoiding her gaze.

"You're quiet," Rafe noted, studying her face.

"Just thinking." Liora kicked a stone from her path, watching it skitter into the underbrush. "Did you see Nero's face when I used that dream magic on the soldiers? He looked..." She struggled to find the right word.

A twig snapped beneath Rafe's boot as he considered her words. "Worried, maybe. But not about you - about what it means. Every time you grow stronger, it changes things. Makes people nervous." His hand brushed against hers, a fleeting touch of reassurance. "Doesn't mean you did anything wrong."

"I hope you're right." Liora stole another glance at Nero, but he had disappeared behind a cluster of villagers, leaving only questions in his wake.

The path ahead opened into a wider trail, and more rebels crowded around them, offering congratulations and friendly clasps on the shoulder. Each touch, each word of praise helped cement the reality of what she'd accomplished. For the first time since discovering her powers, Liora felt truly part of something larger than herself.

A scout appeared through the trees, signaling that it was time for them to take the villagers and a portion of the rebels back to Twilight Camp. Liora and Rafe stopped to watch them off, realizing that the real mission was about to begin.

As the group quickened their pace, eager for rest and celebration, Rafe caught Liora's eye one last time. "You've given them something they haven't had in a long time, Liora - real hope. Don't forget that."

Marcus walked up to Liora, his earlier skepticism replaced by an eager grin. "Hey, Dreamweaver! I owe you a drink. Least I can do after doubting you all this time."

The words had barely left his mouth when Rafe stepped between them, his shoulder creating a barrier that made Marcus take a half-step back. "She's already promised the first round to me," Rafe said, his voice carrying an edge that hadn't been there moments before. His hand found the small of Liora's back, the touch sending warmth spreading through her chest.

Heat crept up Liora's neck as she watched the two men size each other up. The possessive glint in Rafe's eye stirred something deep inside her, a flutter of excitement she hadn't expected. Marcus's gaze darted between them, understanding dawning on his features.

"Right, of course," Marcus said, backing away with his hands raised in mock surrender. "Another time then, maybe." He walked away to the fire Nero had started, leaving Liora acutely aware of Rafe's hand still resting against her back.

Rafe's fingers flexed slightly, drawing her closer as they walked. "Sorry if that was too forward," he murmured, but the slight smile playing at the corners of his mouth suggested he wasn't sorry at all. Liora found herself leaning into his touch, heart racing at this new tension between them. She did something unexpected to even herself.

She reached out to hold his hand.

Heat bloomed across Liora's palm as her fingers interlaced with Rafe's. The rough calluses from his sword work caught against her skin, sending tiny shivers up her arm. She kept her eyes forward, afraid that looking at him might break whatever spell had fallen over them in the gathering dusk.

The forest clearing stretched ahead, dappled with the last rays of sunlight filtering through the canopy. They would camp here tonight, and tomorrow they would begin the arduous journey over the Ashen Dunes. Beyond that, the Veilstone temple awaited her.

Power still hummed beneath her skin, a reminder of what she'd accomplished in Arcadia. But for the first time, it felt natural, like an extension of herself rather than something to fear. The magic moved with her heartbeat, steady and controlled, much like Rafe's presence beside her.

His thumb traced small circles on the back of her hand, each movement deliberate and gentle. It struck her how different this touch was from his usual intensity, how he could shift from fierce warrior to tender companion in the space of a breath. The contrast made her chest tighten with an emotion she wasn't ready to name.

Behind the growing fire, Jayne's disapproving stare cut through the twilight like a blade. Her arms crossed tightly over her chest, she watched their joined hands with narrowed eyes. The weight of that judgment should have bothered Liora, should have made her question this moment of vulnerability.

But the magic thrumming through her veins sang a different song. It whispered of possibility, of strength found in connection rather than isolation. Each pulse reminded her of how it had felt to finally trust herself, to let her power flow naturally instead of fighting against it.

Rafe's fingers tightened slightly around hers, as if sensing her thoughts. The gesture drew her attention back to him, to the way his shoulder brushed against hers with each step. His profile in the fading light looked softer somehow, the usual hard lines of determination gentled by something that might have been contentment.

Behind them, Derek broke into song – an old rebellion anthem about victory and hope. Nero was next, then other voices joined in, the melody weaving through the trees like wind through leaves. The timing felt right, as if the universe itself celebrated not just their success in battle, but this quiet moment of connection.

Liora's heart swelled with a joy so pure it almost hurt. This was what it felt like to belong, to find your place in the world and hold it close. The disapproval of others, the looming threat of Draven, even her own lingering doubts – none of it could touch this perfect slice of peace she'd carved out for herself.

***

The nightmare seized Liora before she fully surrendered to sleep. Colors twisted and bled together, reality bending until she found herself standing in a vast chamber bathed in otherworldly light.

The Eclipse of Dreams painted the world in shades of silver and shadow, its ethereal glow streaming through towering windows. At the chamber's center, Draven stood before the Ark of Dreams, his fingers hovering over its crystalline surface. The artifact pulsed with an inner light that seemed to reach out, tendrils of power wrapping around his outstretched hands.

Power radiated from the Ark in waves, each pulse distorting the air like heat rising from sun-baked stones. Draven's laughter echoed through the chamber as dream energy coursed through him, his form growing more imposing with each passing moment. The shadows at his feet writhed and stretched, taking on lives of their own.

Villagers from across Somnus appeared in the chamber, their eyes glazed and movements puppet-like. Liora recognized faces from Eldara among them - people she'd grown up with, had failed to protect. They moved in perfect unison, dreams and will bent to Draven's command through the Ark's amplified power.

The Eclipse's light caught the Ark's faceted surface, fracturing into a thousand points of radiance that pierced Liora's mind. Each beam carried fragments of dreams - hopes, fears, memories - torn from their owners and reshaped according to Draven's desires. The very fabric of reality seemed to crack and reform around him.

Bennet appeared among the controlled masses, his usually kind eyes now empty and cold. His gaze passed through Liora as if she were nothing more than another shadow, and something inside her chest shattered at the sight. The Ark's power had stripped away everything that made him who he was, leaving only an empty vessel for Draven's will.

Dream energy continued to build, the Eclipse amplifying the Ark's power beyond anything Liora had witnessed. The chamber's walls began to blur and shift, the boundary between physical world and dreamscape dissolving under the onslaught of raw power. Reality itself seemed to bow before Draven's corrupted authority.

Through the chaos, Draven's eyes found hers - dark pools of ambition and malice that threatened to drag her under. His smile widened as he raised the Ark higher, its light growing blinding. "This is what true power looks like," his voice resonated through her skull. "This is what you could never achieve with your weak attempts at control."

The dream energy surged again, and Liora felt her own powers responding, rising up within her like a tide she couldn't control. But instead of the usual chaos, she sensed something different - a deeper current of strength that seemed to whisper of balance and purpose. Even as Draven's display of power threatened to overwhelm her, this new awareness remained steady.

Draven's triumph turned to confusion as the Ark's light began to flicker, its power wavering for just a moment. In that instant of uncertainty, Liora glimpsed something in the artifact's depths.

The Veilstone materialized in Liora's hands, its surface cold against her skin. Unlike the Ark's corrupted light, the stone pulsed with a deeper radiance that seemed to reach inside her, drawing forth shadows she'd tried to bury.

Dark energy spiraled outward from the stone, wrapping around her arms like smoky tendrils. Each pulse brought forth another fear, another doubt, until they threatened to drown her. The weight of her failures - the mill's destruction, the chaos in Eldara, the rebels' mistrust - pressed down on her chest.

The chamber transformed around her, reality bending to reflect the darkness pouring from within. Where Draven had stood moments before, she now saw herself - a twisted version consumed by uncontrolled power. The other Liora's eyes blazed with raw energy as dream magic exploded outward in devastating waves.

Rafe appeared through the chaos, reaching for her with desperate eyes. The dark version of herself lashed out without hesitation, dream energy tearing through him like he was made of paper. His expression of betrayal burned itself into her mind as he crumbled to ash.

Gemini was next, her unwavering loyalty finally breaking as corrupted dream magic ripped away everything that made her who she was. The other Liora showed no remorse, no recognition of the friend who had stood by her through everything. Just cold purpose as she wielded power without restraint.

The rebels fell one by one, their bodies dissolving into shadow as her dark reflection carved through their ranks. Some tried to fight back, others begged for mercy, but none survived the onslaught. The chamber filled with screams that echoed endlessly in Liora's skull.

Nero appeared, his calm demeanor unchanged even as destruction rained down around him. "This is what happens when you let fear guide your power," he said, voice cutting through the chaos. The dark Liora hesitated for just a moment before unleashing a blast that erased him from existence.

Through the nightmare's chaos, Lyra Solari emerged like a beacon of silver light. Her presence cut through the dark energy swirling around Liora, creating a pocket of calm in the storm of corrupted dream magic. The other Liora snarled at the interruption, power crackling around her hands like lightning.

"The path you walk balances on a knife's edge," Lyra's voice resonated through the chamber, each word carrying the weight of ancient wisdom. "Your fear shapes the darkness, but it need not define you." The dark version of Liora launched a blast of raw energy at Lyra, but it passed through her form like smoke through sunlight.

The Veilstone pulsed in Liora's hands, its energy responding to Lyra's presence. Where before it had amplified her fears, now it seemed to resonate with something deeper - a chord of possibility that rang clear through the chaos. The other Liora faltered, her power wavering as the stone's light grew stronger.

"Power without purpose destroys everything it touches," Lyra continued, her form growing more substantial as she stepped between Liora and her dark reflection. "You've seen what becomes of those who let it rule them." Images of Draven flashed through the chamber, his corruption of the Ark of Dreams twisting into a mirror of Liora's own potential fall.

The dark Liora screamed in defiance, unleashing a wave of dream energy that threatened to tear reality apart. But Lyra remained unmoved, her calm presence anchoring Liora against the tide of her own fears. "Choose your path carefully, child," Lyra's words cut through the chaos. "For the power you fear can either break you or become the foundation of your strength."

As Lyra faded away, the Veilstone's pulse quickened in Liora's hands, matching her racing heart as she watched herself become everything she feared. The other Liora turned slowly, eyes meeting hers across the devastated chamber. A smile twisted her features as she raised her hands, dream energy gathering around her like a storm.

Power radiated from the stone, resonating with the darkness that had taken root in her chest. For a moment, Liora felt herself being pulled under, tempted to surrender to that raw strength. It would be so easy to let go, to stop fighting for control.

The dark version of herself stepped closer, hand extended in offering. "This is who we really are," she whispered, voice like broken glass. "Why keep denying it?" Dream energy crackled between them as the Veilstone pulsed once more, waiting for Liora's choice.

\*\*\*

The nightmare shattered as Liora bolted upright, sweat beading on her forehead despite the pre-dawn chill. Her hands trembled, still feeling the phantom weight of the Veilstone and its corrupting power. The dark version of herself lingered behind her eyes, a shadow that refused to fade.

"I would never," she whispered into the darkness, fingers clutching the rough blanket. The words felt hollow, unconvincing even to herself. But she wasn't Draven. She couldn't be. The Ark of Dreams might have twisted him into a tyrant, but she wouldn't let the Veilstone do the same to her.

A soft rustling beside her drew her attention as Gemini shifted in her sleep, brow furrowing as if sensing Liora's distress. The familiar sight of her friend's peaceful face helped ground her, pushing back against the lingering terror of watching her dark self destroy everything she loved.

Gemini's eyes fluttered open, immediately finding Liora's in the dim light. "Another nightmare?" she asked, voice thick with sleep but laden with concern. She pushed herself up, reaching out to squeeze Liora's trembling hand.

"What if they're right to fear me?" Liora's voice cracked. "What if I'm just lying to myself about being different from him?" The words tumbled out before she could stop them, giving voice to the doubt that she'd carried since that day in Eldara.

Gemini sat up fully, her eyes sharp despite the early hour. "You're not Draven," she said firmly. "He chose his path long ago. You're still choosing yours." Her quiet confidence wrapped around Liora like a warm blanket, pushing back against the cold fear in her chest.

"But the power..." Liora trailed off, remembering how easily her dark reflection had torn through everyone she cared about. "Sometimes it feels like it's waiting for me to slip, just once." The admission hung heavy in the darkness.

"Then don't face it alone," Gemini replied, her grip on Liora's hand tightening. "You have the rebellion. You have me." The simple truth in her words cut through some of the lingering darkness.

Liora squeezed back, drawing strength from her friend's unwavering support. But the restless energy from the nightmare still buzzed under her skin, making it impossible to consider more sleep. The dark version of herself waited behind her closed eyes, ready to remind her of everything she could become.

"I need some air," she murmured, already pulling away from Gemini's concerned gaze. The tent suddenly felt too small, too confined with the weight of her fears pressing in.

# The Hot Springs

Liora's bare feet ghosted across the damp earth, each step carrying her further from the suffocating confines of the tent. The camp lay silent around her, save for the occasional crackle of dying fires and the soft snores of exhausted rebels.

Steam rose from the hidden hot spring ahead, beckoning her with promises of warmth and solitude. Nero's earlier silence after the battle in Arcadia gnawed at her thoughts. He'd watched her wield her power with such intensity, then turned away without a word. His rejection stung worse than any reprimand could have.

The humid air clung to her skin as she approached the pool, remembering how Rafe had defended her abilities to the others. His faith in her felt both comforting and terrifying - what if she proved unworthy of that trust? The memory of his calloused hand closing over hers sent an unexpected warmth through her chest.

Moonlight filtered through the canopy, casting silver ripples across the spring's surface. Liora glanced over her shoulder, ensuring she was truly alone before reaching for the hem of her sleeping shirt. The cool night air raised goosebumps across her exposed skin as she shed her clothes.

The first touch of hot water against her toes drew a soft gasp. Liora eased herself deeper into the pool, letting the heat seep into her tired muscles. Steam curled around her like a lover's embrace, carrying away some of the tension that had knotted itself between her shoulders.

Submerging to her shoulders, Liora traced idle patterns in the water's surface. Why had Nero turned away? Was he disappointed in how she'd handled the soldiers, or afraid of what she might become? The questions circled like hungry wolves in her mind, offering no answers.

The spring's mineral-rich water softened the scrapes and bruises from their earlier fight. Liora's fingers found a particularly tender spot on her arm, remembering how Rafe had pulled her to safety when that last soldier had charged. His touch had lingered longer than necessary, sending her heart racing in a way that had nothing to do with battle.

A night bird called overhead, startling Liora from her thoughts. She sank deeper into the water, letting it lap at her chin. The heat worked its way into her bones, but did nothing to wash away the uncertainty that plagued her. Every victory seemed to bring new questions, new fears.

Water droplets glided down her neck as she tilted her head back, studying the stars through gaps in the leaves. The same stars had watched over her in Eldara, back when life had been simpler. Before she'd known what power truly meant, or how it could reshape everything she thought she knew about herself.

A soft splash from across the spring made Liora's heart stop. She whirled around, instinctively sinking deeper into the water.

"I didn't mean to startle you." Rafe's voice emerged from the shadows, low and husky. "I was here first, actually."

Heat flooded Liora's cheeks, and not from the spring's warmth. "I'm so sorry—I should go." She started to move toward the bank where her clothes lay.

"Stay." The word hung between them, gentle yet charged with something that made her pulse quicken. "There's plenty of room, and honestly, I could use the company."

Liora hesitated, then settled back into the water. The steam created a dreamlike barrier between them, obscuring details but highlighting the strong lines of his shoulders above the surface. "I thought everyone was asleep."

"Couldn't rest." Rafe moved closer, water rippling around him. "Keep seeing those soldiers, the way you handled them. It was..." His voice trailed off as their knees brushed beneath the surface.

The accidental touch sent electricity through Liora's body. She should move away, maintain some distance, but her muscles refused to cooperate. "It was what?" she whispered.

"Beautiful," he breathed, closing the remaining space between them. His chest pressed against her shoulder, solid and warm. Liora's fingers found their way to his skin, tracing the ridges of battle-hardened muscle.

Time seemed to stop as her hands explored on their own accord, mapping the terrain of scars and strength beneath her fingertips. Rafe's breath caught, a sound that sent shivers down her spine despite the heat.

Through the darkness and steam, Liora could barely make out his features, but she felt the intensity of his gaze. His hand found her waist beneath the water, and she bit back a moan at the contact. Everything else—her doubts, her fears, Nero's disappointment—faded away, leaving only the burning awareness of Rafe's touch and the dangerous possibility of what might happen next.

Liora's heart pounded in her ears as Rafe's lips brushed against hers. A rush of desire surged through her, and she leaned in, answering his kiss with equal fervor. Their lips moved in perfect sync, each touch igniting a flame that chased away the night's chill.

Rafe's hands roamed over her body, mapping the curves of her hips and waist. Liora's skin tingled everywhere he touched, sensations sparking along her nerves like tiny jolts of electricity. His body, hard and muscular, pressed against hers, the contrast sending a shiver down her spine.

She ran her hands up his chest, reveling in the feel of his skin beneath her palms. Scars crisscrossed his flesh, a testament to battles fought and won. Liora's breath hitched as her exploration ventured lower, her fingers tracing the contours of his abdomen.

Rafe's mouth moved to her neck, sending delicious shivers through her. His lips brushed along her sensitive skin, his breath warm against her damp flesh. Liora's head fell back, her fingers twisting in his damp hair as she surrendered to the sensations he invoked.

He murmured something unintelligible between kisses, his hands gentle yet insistent as they caressed her. Liora felt like she was drowning, but in the best possible way. Every rational thought fled as pleasure took over, leaving her acutely aware of Rafe and nothing else.

Their lips met again, tongues tangling in a dance that mirrored the one their bodies were performing beneath the water. Liora's heart raced as heat pooled low in her belly, a molten sensation that threatened to consume her.

Liora reached down, her fingers brushing against Rafe's arousal. She marveled at its solid presence, a force that demanded attention. With a gentle touch, she wrapped her fingers around him, exploring with a mixture of boldness and uncertainty.

The soft groan that escaped his lips at her touch sent a thrill through her. He captured her mouth with his, his kiss deep and hungry. Their tongues danced, echoing the rhythm of her hand as she stroked him slowly, tentatively.

Their bodies moved together in a silent symphony, each touch and kiss heightening the tension that arced between them. Liora felt her power stir at the edges of her consciousness, responding to the undercurrents of desire that surged within her.

Rafe's hands caressed her hips, then slid up her sides, leaving trails of fire in their wake. She felt his arousal press against her, his need as palpable as her own. Their kisses grew more fevered, each wanting to claim and be claimed.

With a soft moan, Liora shifted closer, wanting to feel every inch of him pressed against her. The spring's warm waters swirled around them, caressing their skin as their kisses deepened. She reveled in the sensations he inspired, wanting more of this—more of him.

She tilted her head back, exposing the fragile line of her throat. Liora arched into him, savoring the sensations he evoked with each touch. Her power whispered along her veins, a muted echo of the passion that raged between them.

Rafe's hands explored her curves, his touch both hungry and reverent. His lips brushed her earlobe, his breath warm against her skin as he whispered her name. It was a plea, a surrender, and a promise all at once.

Their bodies, slick with water and desire, moved together in perfect harmony. Liora's heart pounded in her chest, the cadence matching the thrumming of her magic beneath her skin. She felt powerful, alive, and utterly consumed by the moment.

Rafe's hand slipped between her thighs, eliciting a soft gasp. Liora arched against him, reveling in the exquisite torture of his touch. Her fingers tightened in his hair, guiding his mouth back to hers as their kisses grew more feverish.

The spring's water lapped at their bodies, forgotten in the heat of their passion. Liora's entire world narrowed to the feel of Rafe's skin against hers, the taste of his mouth, and the urgent need building within her. She wanted—no, needed—more.

Rafe's thumb brushed against her most sensitive spot, and Liora moaned, her hips instinctively moving against his hand. His fingers worked their magic, stoking the flames that threatened to consume her. She was close, so close, teetering on the edge of release.

But then reality intruded. Liora's eyes snapped open, and she stilled, suddenly aware of where they were. The spring, the rebels, the mission—all rushed back in a wave of mortification. She pulled away from Rafe, panting.

"What's wrong?" Concern filled his voice, his hands dropping away.

Liora wrapped her arms around herself, suddenly cold despite the spring's warmth. "I can't do this, Rafe. Not now." Her voice cracked on his name, betraying the storm of emotions raging beneath her calm exterior.

"Why not?" His eyes searched hers through the steam, filled with an intensity that made her heart stutter. "Because you're afraid?"

"Because I might be dead in days." The words tumbled out before she could stop them. "The Veilstone, Draven, this war—I can't promise anyone tomorrow. It's not fair to start something I can't finish."

Rafe moved closer, water rippling around his shoulders. "Life isn't about guarantees, Li. It's about moments like this—finding something worth fighting for, worth living for."

"The rebellion is counting on me." She backed away, feeling the rough stone of the spring's edge against her spine. "I can't let myself get distracted. I can't let my feelings compromise what needs to be done."

"What are we fighting for if not this?" His voice dropped lower, rough with emotion. "If not for the chance to love freely, to give ourselves to someone without fear?"

Liora's chest tightened at his words. The truth in them pierced her defenses, threatening to shatter the walls she'd built around her heart. "I don't know," she whispered, hating how vulnerable she sounded.

Water sloshed against the rocks as she pulled herself from the spring, not daring to look back at him. Her hands trembled as she grabbed her clothes, not bothering to dry off before pulling them on.

"Liora, wait." Rafe's plea followed her into the darkness, but she kept moving, her wet clothes clinging to her skin like the memories of his touch.

Her bare feet carried her swiftly through the undergrowth, leaving behind the warmth of the spring and the dangerous possibility of what might have been. But she couldn't outrun the echo of his words, or the growing certainty that maybe, just maybe, he was right.

***

Liora stumbled through the forest, her damp clothes clinging to her trembling form. Each step away from the spring felt like a betrayal—not just of Rafe, but of the part of herself that yearned for connection despite the looming shadow of war. The pre-dawn air bit at her wet skin, but she barely noticed, too consumed by the phantom sensation of Rafe's touch and the crushing weight of her responsibilities.

Golden tendrils of magic curled beneath her skin, responding to her turbulent emotions. The power felt different now, charged with an intimate energy she'd never experienced before. Liora clenched her fists, trying to steady the wild surge of her abilities. The last thing she needed was to lose control because of... whatever that had been with Rafe.

Through the tangle of tents and sleeping rebels, Nero's dwelling stood apart, a soft glow emanating from within. The flap hung slightly open, inviting yet somehow forbidding. No light burned within. Liora hesitated at the entrance, water dripping from her hair onto the frost-covered ground. What would her mentor think, seeing her like this? But the alternative—being alone with her thoughts and the lingering heat of Rafe's hands on her skin—seemed far worse.

"Master Thorne?" Her whisper cut through the silence, met only by the soft rustling of papers in the morning breeze. The tent's emptiness felt wrong, like walking into a temple after the priests had fled.

Something drew her forward - perhaps the lingering traces of her nightmare, or maybe the desperate need for answers that had driven her from her own bed. Her feet carried her inside before she could second-guess herself.

A book lay open on Nero's carefully made bed, its pages yellowed with age. The sight stopped her cold. This wasn't meant for her eyes. Yet she couldn't look away.

Ancient script crawled across the pages, interwoven with diagrams that seemed to pulse with their own inner light. One illustration in particular caught her eye - a figure holding what could only be the Veilstone, surrounded by swirling patterns that reminded her of her own dream magic.

Her fingers hovered over the page, trembling with the urge to touch. The air felt charged, as if the book itself held some fragment of power. This was wrong - she should leave, find Nero properly, ask her questions directly.

But the nightmare's shadow still loomed, and here, perhaps, lay answers. The figure in the illustration seemed to stare back at her, challenging her hesitation. Wasn't this what she needed? Understanding of what she truly was?

Soon others would wake, and this moment would pass. Whatever secrets the book held would remain hidden, unless she acted now.

The ink seemed to writhe beneath Liora's gaze as she traced the ancient words, her breath catching at each revelation. The prophecy unfolded like a flower made of shadows and light, each petal bearing whispers of possibility and doom.

Her fingers trembled over the weathered page where the Custodians had written of a final Dreamweaver - one whose power would tip the balance of Somnus itself. The words burned into her mind: "When darkness claims the dreaming throne, one shall rise from ashes of hope, bearing both salvation and destruction in their wake."

Sweat beaded on her forehead as she read further, recognizing herself in every carefully penned line. The prophecy spoke of a choice - the Veilstone's power channeled either to "shatter the chains of tyranny" or to "bind all dreams in eternal night."

The morning air grew thick and heavy around her as the full weight of the words settled into her bones. This wasn't just about fighting Draven anymore - it was about becoming him, or becoming something worse. The prophecy offered no certainty, no guarantee that her power would save rather than destroy.

Diagrams on the following pages showed the Veilstone's light fracturing in two directions - one path leading to broken chains and awakening, the other to shadows that devoured everything they touched.

Her own magic stirred restlessly beneath her skin as she studied them, as if responding to some ancient call.

"The bearer's heart shall guide the stone's light," she read aloud, her voice barely a whisper. "Through darkness or dawn, by fear or by love." Each word felt like a judgment, a reminder of how her own fears had already caused so much damage.

Time seemed to slow as she turned another page, revealing an illustration of a hooded figure consumed by the Veilstone's power. The figure's face was hidden, but something in its pose - something in the way shadow and light warred around it - made her stomach clench. It could have been Draven. It could have been her.

Behind her, footsteps crunched in the morning frost, growing closer to Nero's tent. Still, she couldn't tear her eyes from the prophecy's final lines: "When dreams and reality collide beneath the Eclipse, the choice must be made. All of Somnus hangs upon that single thread of fate."

Her hands shook as she touched the last illustration - a perfect rendering of the Veilstone suspended between light and shadow. It pulsed with an inner glow that seemed to reach out to her, calling to the magic that flowed through her veins. The same magic that had destroyed her village, that had nearly killed her friends.

The footsteps stopped just outside the tent. Liora's heart thundered in her chest as she stared at the prophecy's final words: "The power to save becomes the power to destroy, when fear eclipses love's pure light." The choice wasn't just about the Veilstone, she realized - it was about her own heart, and what truly drove her to fight.

Liora's fingers jerked away from the book as Nero's entered the tent. Her heart lodged in her throat, caught between guilt and defiance as she met his steady gaze.

"The springs can be quite alluring at dawn," Nero's voice carried a hint of amusement that made her cheeks burn. "Though I find most seek them for warmth rather than escape."

The knowing look in his eyes pierced through her defenses, seeing past her dripping hair and quaking shoulders to the turmoil beneath. Liora's magic stirred restlessly under her skin, responding to her shame and the lingering heat of Rafe's touch.

"I wasn't-" The lie died on her lips as Nero's gaze dropped to the prophecy laid bare before her. The ancient words seemed to pulse with renewed intensity, as if acknowledging their shared secret. Her fingers curled away from the weathered pages, but the damage was done.

A muscle twitched in Nero's jaw as he studied her, his expression shifting from mild amusement to something darker and more complex. "There are easier ways to dry off than reading forbidden texts." He moved further into the tent, letting the flap fall closed behind him with a soft whisper of canvas. "Though perhaps it's time we discussed what those pages contain."

"Is it true?" Liora's voice cracked. "Am I really meant to - to either save everyone or destroy them?" The words of the prophecy seemed to pulse on the page between them, each line a reminder of the impossible choice that lay ahead.

Nero settled onto his worn traveling chest, his shoulders bowing under an invisible burden. "Prophecies are like dreams, Liora. They show us possibilities, not certainties. The choice remains yours, always."

"But the Eclipse - it says when dreams and reality collide..." Her fingers traced the illustration of the Veilstone suspended between light and shadow. "What if I'm not strong enough? What if fear wins?"

A ghost of pain flickered across Nero's features. "Your mother faced similar doubts, similar fears. But she understood something crucial about power - it's not about being strong enough. It's about being true enough."

Liora's breath caught at the mention of her mother. "Was she - did she have to make a choice like this too?"

"When you were born, we - she realized what you were, what you could be. She chose to protect you, to hide you from those who would use your power for their own ends." Nero's voice softened. "The prophecy speaks of the Eclipse because that's when dream magic reaches its peak. When the boundaries between what is and what could be grow thin."

The morning light strengthened outside, casting long shadows through the tent's canvas. Liora stared at the prophecy's final warning about fear eclipsing love. "How do I know which choice is right? How do I keep from becoming what I'm fighting against?"

"That's what we're here to discover." Nero reached for the book, his fingers brushing the ancient pages with reverence. "But first, you need to understand that power - even the power to destroy - isn't inherently dark. It's the heart wielding it that matters. And your heart, Liora, is what Draven can never possess."

Liora's fingers curled into fists as Nero's words about her mother hung in the air between them. The weight of legacy, prophecy, and choice pressed down on her shoulders like physical chains.

"My mother died protecting me from this." Her voice came out rough, accusatory. "And now you're telling me it was all for nothing? That I have to face it anyway?"

Nero leaned forward, his eyes reflecting the growing dawn light. "She died protecting your chance to choose, Liora. There's a difference between destiny thrust upon you and destiny embraced."

"Choice?" The word tasted bitter on her tongue. "What choice is there when the prophecy says I'll either save everyone or destroy them?" Her gaze fell to the illustration of the hooded figure consumed by the Veilstone's power.

"I can barely control my power now," Liora whispered, staring at her trembling hands. "How am I supposed to handle the Veilstone during the Eclipse when everything will be amplified?" The memory of destruction in Eldara flashed through her mind - the mill collapsing, Bennet's broken body, the terror in villagers' eyes.

"Your mother knew the risks," Nero said, his voice gentler now. "But she also knew something Draven never will - that true power comes from love, not fear. She believed in you, Liora. In the strength of your heart."

The tent's air grew thick with unspoken grief and expectation. Liora's magic stirred beneath her skin, responding to her rising distress. Small objects around them began to tremble - papers rustling, cups rattling against each other.

"Stop." Nero's command cut through her spiral. "Breathe. Center yourself. This is exactly what we've been training for - control in the face of overwhelming emotion."

But the pressure kept building. The prophecy's words burned in her mind, mixing with images of her mother, of Draven, of everything she could become or destroy. Her magic pulsed stronger, making the tent's canvas walls shudder.

"I can't-" Liora choked out. "I can't be what everyone needs me to be. I can't bear this weight." The trembling around them intensified as her control slipped further.

The first rays of sunlight pierced through the tent's entrance just as Liora bolted, leaving Nero calling after her. She ran blindly, her magic trailing behind her like invisible smoke, while the prophecy's words echoed in her mind: "The choice must be made."

# Drowning in Prophecy

R afe's damp shirt clung uncomfortably to his skin as he paced
the perimeter of his tent, his heart still racing from the encounter at the hot spring. The memory of Liora's lips against his, the
way her body had pressed close, sent electricity coursing through his
veins.

He ran trembling fingers through his wet hair, trying to focus on
anything else - the mission, battle strategies, supply inventories. But
his mind kept drifting back to how the moonlight had painted silver
highlights across her shoulders, how her breath had hitched when he'd
pulled her closer.

Cursing under his breath, Rafe grabbed his sword belt and cinched
it tight, needing the familiar weight to ground him. The leather grip
felt cool against his palm as he drew the blade, examining the edge with
unfocused eyes. Even the routine of weapon maintenance couldn't
distract him from remembering how Liora's magic had sparked golden
between them, matching the heat building in his core.

His muscles coiled with restless energy as he moved through practice forms, steel whistling through the air. Each strike echoed the rhythm of his racing pulse, every thrust carrying the force of his frustrated desire. The physical exertion did nothing to cool the fire in his blood.

The tent canvas rustled in the night breeze, carrying hints of jasmine that reminded him of her hair. Rafe's grip tightened on the sword hilt until his knuckles whitened. He shouldn't be thinking about her like this - not with everything at stake, not with the danger they faced.

But the way she'd looked at him, vulnerable yet fierce, had stripped away his careful defenses. Her touch had awakened something primal in him, something that went beyond mere physical attraction. The need to protect her warred with his desire to know her completely.

Sweat beaded on his brow as he forced himself through another complex sequence of moves. The blade became an extension of his arm, cutting through memories of soft skin and searching hands. Yet each movement only served to remind him of how her body had moved against his in the water.

The sword clattered against the weapons rack as Rafe braced himself against the tent pole, his chest heaving. The physical exertion hadn't helped - if anything, it had intensified the ache of wanting her. His skin still tingled where Liora's fingers had traced.

Of course she'd pulled away. The weight of prophecy and power bore down on her shoulders like a physical burden. He'd seen it in her eyes at the hot spring - that flash of terror when her magic had sparked between them. The Veilstone's shadow loomed over everything, threatening to consume her just as Draven's power had corrupted him. Her fear made perfect sense.

The night air carried whispers of her name as Rafe sank onto his bedroll, head in his hands. His body burned with unfulfilled desire, every nerve ending alive with the memory of her pressed against him. But it wasn't just physical need that twisted his gut into knots. The way she challenged him, matched his stubborn pride with her own fierce determination, had carved a space in his heart that only she could fill.

Gods help him, he loved her. The realization hit like a sword thrust to the chest, leaving him breathless. He loved her strength and her vulnerability, her power and her fear. He loved how she fought to protect others even when it cost her everything. The depth of his feelings terrified him - he hadn't meant to fall, hadn't wanted to risk his heart again after losing so many.

Blood pounded in his ears as he reached for his water skin with shaking hands. The cool liquid did nothing to douse the fire in his veins. How could he protect her, support her through what was coming, when every fiber of his being yearned to pull her close and never let go? The tent walls seemed to close in around him as memories of her golden eyes and gentle touch threatened to overwhelm his carefully maintained control.

Rafe surged to his feet, his heart hammering against his ribs as he yanked the tent flap aside. The words burned in his throat, demanding release. He had to tell her, had to make her understand that whatever power coursed through her veins didn't matter - she mattered.

A blur of movement crashed into his chest, sending him stumbling back a step. Liora's wet hair plastered against his shirt as she collided with him, her skin still damp from the hot spring. Her breath came in ragged gasps, golden sparks crackling around her trembling fingers.

"Sorry, I wasn't - I'm fine," Liora stammered, trying to push past him. But Rafe caught the wild look in her eyes, the way her magic pulsed erratically around her like a wounded animal. Something was wrong. Very wrong.

His chest tightened as guilt crashed over him. Had he pushed too far at the spring? Made her feel trapped or pressured? "Liora, about what happened-" he started, reaching for her arm.

She jerked away from his touch, wrapping her arms around herself. "It's not - I can't -" Golden light flared between her fingers as she struggled to form words. That's when Rafe noticed the tear tracks on her cheeks weren't just from the spring water.

The protective instinct that had been simmering all night shifted into something sharper, more focused. This wasn't about their moment in the water - something else had shaken her to her core. "What happened?" he demanded, forcing his voice to stay steady despite the fear clawing at his gut.

Liora's eyes darted toward Nero's tent, and Rafe's hand instinctively moved to his sword hilt. "Did he-" The question died on his lips as another surge of magic rippled through the air around her, carrying whispers of ancient power and forgotten prophecies.

"The book," she choked out, her fingers curling into fists as she fought for control. "I saw - in the book - the last Dreamweaver." Golden light danced across her skin like lightning trapped beneath glass.

Rafe's heart clenched as understanding dawned. Of course Nero would have records of past attempts, warnings written in blood about the price of power. He'd seen how those kinds of revelations could break even the strongest spirit. "Whatever you saw," he said carefully, "whatever could happen - it doesn't have to be your story."

Her magic surged again, stronger this time, and Rafe caught her as her knees buckled. The confession he'd planned could wait. Right now, Liora needed his strength, not his heart's truth. He guided her further into his tent, away from prying eyes, as another wave of power crackled through the air around them.

Golden light pulsed around Liora's trembling form as Rafe guided her to sit on his bedroll. Her magic crackled against his skin, but he refused to let go. "What did you really see in that book?" The words came out rougher than intended, tight with concern.

"I saw what happens when - when the power takes over." Liora's fingers twisted in the fabric of her tunic. "I would want to protect everyone. But the power can corrupt. The people I love most..." Her voice cracked. "I can't bear the thought of hurting you like that. Any of you."

Rafe's chest tightened at the raw fear in her voice. He'd seen that same terror in soldiers' eyes before battle, that moment when doubt threatened to shatter their resolve. But this was different. This wasn't about facing an external enemy - this was Liora fighting herself. "Listen to me," he said, catching her chin with gentle fingers. "I've known people who want to hurt others. I've fought them, killed them. That's not who you are."

The golden light surrounding them flickered as their eyes met. Her magic hummed against his skin, warm and alive. "Your first instinct is always to protect," he continued, letting his hand drop to her shoulder. "Even when you lost control in Eldara, you were trying to save people. That matters, Liora. Intent matters."

Rafe's breath caught as Liora's magic pulsed against his palm, no longer chaotic but settling into a steady rhythm that matched her heartbeat. The golden light cast shadows across her face, highlighting the vulnerability in her eyes. His fingers tightened on her shoulder, anchoring her as another tremor ran through her body.

"When I first joined the rebellion," he said, his voice rough with memory, "I thought I had to carry every loss alone. Each failure, each death - I blamed myself." The confession scraped his throat raw. He hadn't meant to share this, but something in her broken expression demanded honesty. "It nearly destroyed me."

The magic surrounding them shifted, weaving between them like golden threads. Liora's shoulders relaxed slightly under his touch, her breath evening out. The terror in her eyes softened to something more manageable - not gone, but no longer threatening to consume her. Rafe fought the urge to pull her closer, to shield her from the weight of prophecy and power with his own body.

"You don't have to face this alone," he murmured, watching as her magic responded to his words, curling around them both like a protective cocoon. "Whatever comes, whatever choices you have to make - you have people who understand. Who'll stand with you." The unspoken 'I'll stand with you' hung in the air between them.

Her fingers unclenched from her tunic, one hand hesitantly reaching for his. As their skin connected, the golden light pulsed brighter, but it no longer felt dangerous. Instead, it wrapped around them with a warmth that spoke of trust and shared strength. Rafe's heart thundered against his ribs as Liora's magic settled into a steady glow, her fear giving way to something that looked almost like hope.

***

The walk back to her tent seemed to take forever, each step measured against Liora's racing thoughts. Rafe's hand rested at the small of her back, steadying her when occasional tremors of magic threatened her balance. The gesture felt protective rather than restraining, and she found herself leaning into his strength.

Flickering lamplight spilled from her tent, casting Gemini's shadow against the canvas as she paced inside. The moment they approached, she burst through the flap, worry etched across her features. Her eyes darted between Liora and Rafe, lingering on his hand at Liora's back.

"Where have you been?" Gemini's voice carried equal measures of relief and accusation.

Rafe's presence seemed to fill the small space outside the tent, his shoulders tensing at Gemini's tone. "She's safe now," he said, the words coming out more defensive than he perhaps intended. "That's what matters."

Liora felt Rafe's hand press slightly firmer against her back, as if preparing to defend her from Gemini's concern. The gesture, while touching, made her chest tighten - she couldn't bear the thought of them at odds over her.

Gemini's expression softened as she watched Liora lean unconsciously toward Rafe. Something shifted in her eyes, understanding replacing worry. Without warning, she stepped forward and wrapped her arms around both of them.

"Thank you," she whispered against Rafe's shoulder.

Rafe stood frozen for a moment, clearly caught off guard by Gemini's embrace. Then his free arm came up to return the hug, his other hand never leaving Liora's back. The tension drained from his shoulders as he accepted this unexpected peace offering.

"Take a moment to breathe," he said finally, stepping back. His eyes met Liora's, carrying a warmth that made her breath catch. "Both of you. We begin to cross the Ashen Dunes after breakfast."

As he disappeared into the darkness between the tents, Liora watched his retreating form until it blended with the shadows. Only then did she let Gemini guide her inside, where the world seemed a little brighter than before.

Liora's fingers traced invisible patterns on her blanket, avoiding Gemini's patient gaze. The morning light filtering through the tent canvas cast everything in muted gold, but it couldn't warm the chill that had settled in her bones since reading those words in Nero's tent.

"You're dancing around, Li," Gemini said, her voice gentle but insistent. She sat cross-legged on her own cot, hands folded in her lap with the stillness that made her such a gifted healer. "What happened with Rafe?"

Heat crept up Liora's neck as she picked at a loose thread on her blanket. "Nothing happened, exactly. We just..." The memory of Rafe's touch sent a shiver through her that had nothing to do with cold.

Gemini leaned forward, her eyes widening. "Li, your magic is practically sparking right now. Whatever happened between you two was definitely not 'nothing.'" A knowing smile played at the corners of her mouth.

"The hot springs," Liora blurted, then immediately buried her face in her hands. Golden light danced between her fingers as her magic responded to her embarrassment. "We were just talking, and then he was there, and..." She groaned, unable to continue.

"And?" Gemini prompted, but something in Liora's expression made her pause.

Liora seized the change of subject like a lifeline. "That's not why I'm upset. I went to Master Thorne's tent. There was this book..." Her voice trailed off as the weight of what she'd discovered there pressed down on her chest again. The spark of magic beneath her skin turned cold, and the playful atmosphere evaporated like morning mist.

The words of the prophecy echoed in Liora's mind, each syllable a weight pressing against her chest. "I found something," she whispered, her voice catching. "A prophecy about the last Dreamweaver - about me."

Gemini leaned forward, her dark eyes intent. "What kind of prophecy?" The question hung between them, heavy with implications.

"It said I could either save Somnus or destroy it completely." Liora's hands trembled as she spoke, and she clasped them together to still them. "The Veilstone... it's supposed to amplify my powers during the Eclipse. But if I can't control them..." She couldn't finish the thought.

Gemini crossed the space between their cots, settling beside Liora with the familiar warmth that had comforted her through countless storms in Eldara. "Whatever this prophecy says," she said, taking Liora's cold hands in her warm ones. "It doesn't define you."

"But what if it does?" Liora pulled away, standing to pace the small confines of their tent. "You've seen what happens when I lose control. If the Eclipse makes my powers stronger..." The tent's canvas walls seemed to pulse with her anxiety, dream magic responding to her distress.

"Everyone's counting on me to be this... savior." Liora stopped pacing, turning to face her friend. The morning light caught the tears threatening to spill from her eyes. "But what if I'm just the weapon Draven's been waiting for?"

Gemini stood, crossing to where Liora trembled. She took her friend's face between her hands, forcing Liora to meet her gaze. "Because I know you," she said firmly. "And the Liora I know would rather die than become what she fears."

The words struck something deep within Liora, releasing tears she hadn't realized she'd been holding back. They streamed down her cheeks, catching on Gemini's fingers as her friend held her face with unwavering certainty.

"Remember the flower crowns?" Gemini's voice carried the warmth of summer afternoons in Eldara. "How you'd spend hours weaving them for the children, making each one special?" Her thumbs brushed away Liora's tears. "That's who you are - someone who creates beauty, who protects innocence."

Liora's breath hitched as memories flooded back - the delight in children's eyes when she'd place delicate crowns on their heads, the way she'd carefully select each bloom to match their personalities. "But that was before-"

"Before nothing," Gemini cut her off, dropping her hands to grip Liora's shoulders. "Those hands that wove flowers still belong to you. The heart that wanted to make others smile hasn't changed. Your power doesn't define you - what you choose to do with it does."

The tent's canvas walls rippled with a gentle pulse of dream magic, but this time it felt different - less chaotic, more like the subtle rhythm of a heartbeat. Gemini smiled, recognizing the shift. "See? Even your magic knows who you truly are."

The tension melted from Liora's shoulders as Gemini's words sank in. Her magic settled into a gentle hum beneath her skin, no longer threatening to burst free. The familiar scent of herbs that always clung to Gemini's clothes brought back countless memories of comfort and healing, grounding her in the present moment.

Her fingers traced the rough canvas of her cot as she sank down onto it, the weight of prophecy and destiny feeling lighter than before. A smile tugged at her lips as she remembered how Rafe's touch had steadied her earlier, how his presence seemed to anchor her when everything else threatened to sweep her away.

Heat crept up her neck as she recalled the intensity in his eyes at the hot spring, the way his hand had felt against her skin. The magic within her stirred, responding to the memory with a warm glow that had nothing to do with fear or power. She caught herself touching her lips, remembering-

"Oh no you don't," Gemini interrupted her thoughts, a mischievous glint in her eye. "That dreamy look on your face has nothing to do with prophecies. What exactly happened with Rafe at those hot springs?"

Liora opened her mouth to respond, but the tent flap rustled with approaching footsteps, and Jayne's voice called out that breakfast was ready. The moment shattered like sunlight on water, leaving only the ghost of a smile on Liora's face as Gemini raised an eyebrow, clearly promising this conversation wasn't over.

# Ashen Dunes

Kael Varden traced the worn edges of his family crest pendant, its once-proud surface now dulled by years of broken promises and shattered loyalties. The candlelight in his quarters flickered across maps and battle plans scattered across his desk, casting dancing shadows that seemed to mock his indecision.

Draven's words echoed in his mind, a seductive whisper of power and certainty. The Emperor had seen right through him, recognized the ambition that burned beneath his carefully constructed facade of loyalty to the rebellion. How long had he been playing this role, pretending to believe in their naive dreams of freedom?

His fingers clenched around the pendant, its edges digging into his palm. The memory of his father's execution surfaced unbidden - another "loyal" general who had dared to question Draven's methods. Yet here he stood, contemplating the very alliance that had destroyed his family. The irony tasted bitter in his mouth.

The rebellion's idealistic notions of justice and equality had never truly resonated with him. They spoke of hope while cowering in forests, of freedom while binding themselves with rules and morality. Even now, they placed their faith in a girl who could barely control her own power, all because of some foolish prophecy.

Rising from his chair, Kael moved to the window, watching the rebels go about their evening routines. Their trust in him had been so easily won - a few strategic victories, some well-placed words of dedication to their cause. Fools, all of them, too blinded by hope to see the predator in their midst.

Kael paced the length of his quarters, the maps and battle plans blurring together as his mind wandered to Liora and her band of idealists. The girl's raw power was undeniable, but her weakness - her desperate need for control, for acceptance - would be her undoing. He'd seen it in her eyes during their conversations, that flicker of doubt that no amount of training could erase.

The Ashen Dunes would test them all. Kael had crossed that merciless expanse twice before, watched strong men crumble under the relentless sun and shifting sands. He knew what it had been before, and why it would never bear fruit again. Would Liora's untamed power protect them, or would it attract the very dangers they sought to avoid?

A cold smile tugged at his lips as he imagined their struggle. Rafe would lead them, of course, his unwavering faith in Liora blinding him to the futility of their mission. The rebels believed the Veilstone would give them the power to challenge Draven, but they didn't understand - couldn't understand - the true nature of power. It wasn't about artifacts or prophecies; it was about the will to use whatever means necessary to achieve one's goals.

The candle on his desk guttered, casting his shadow large against the tent wall. Kael's hand moved to the hidden pocket in his tunic, feeling the weight of the message he needed to send. The coordinates were already memorized, the timing calculated to perfection. Let them waste their strength crossing the Dunes - it would make the final betrayal all the sweeter.

Footsteps approached his quarters, and Kael quickly smoothed his features into the mask of concerned leadership he'd worn for so long. A young rebel entered with reports from the latest patrol, and Kael noted with satisfaction how the boy's eyes shone with admiration. Such blind trust would make his eventual betrayal all the sweeter.

The rebel left, and Kael returned to his maps, but his mind was already racing ahead, plotting the intricate dance of betrayal to come. His fingers brushed against the hilt of his sword - not the rebellion's standard-issue blade, but his old general's weapon, kept hidden all these years. Soon, very soon, it would taste blood again.

Kael's fingers trembled as he traced the worn edges of his family crest pendant one final time. The metal felt cold against his skin, a stark reminder of everything he was about to abandon. Years of shared battles, countless nights planning strategies around campfires, the genuine trust in Rafe's eyes when they'd last spoken - all of it would burn in the flames of his ambition.

The pendant's weight seemed to increase with each passing moment, as if the spirits of his ancestors were trying to pull him back from the precipice. His father had worn this same crest proudly, even as he faced Draven's executioner. What would he think of his son now, preparing to kneel before the very tyrant who had ordered his death?

A bitter laugh escaped Kael's throat as he placed the pendant on his desk. The irony wasn't lost on him - here he was, about to betray everything his father had died protecting. But his father's principles had earned him nothing but a shallow grave and a legacy of poverty for his family. Power, real power, required sacrifices.

The pendant caught the candlelight, throwing accusatory gleams across the room. Kael remembered the day his father had given it to him, speaking of honor and duty with such conviction. But what good had honor done for anyone? The honorable died while the pragmatic thrived. Draven had taught that lesson well.

Standing at his window, Kael watched the distant fires of the rebel camp flicker in the darkness. After the Eclipse, those same fires would paint the sky red for very different reasons. He picked up the pendant one last time, then deliberately placed it in his desk drawer. Some sacrifices were necessary for the power he craved, and sentiment had no place in the world he intended to build.

***

Rafe squinted against the harsh glare reflecting off the endless sea of sand before them. The Ashen Dunes stretched to the horizon like a golden ocean frozen in time, each ripple and wave carved by relentless winds. His grip tightened on his sword hilt, the familiar pressure offering little comfort against the alien landscape.

"The Dunes are alive," Nero's voice carried on the wind, drawing Rafe's attention. The old master's robes whipped around him, giving him an otherworldly appearance. "They shift and change with each passing hour, trying to lead travelers astray."

A chill ran down Rafe's spine despite the scorching heat as he watched Liora's face pale at Nero's words. Her golden energy flickered around her fingers - a tell he'd learned meant she was nervous. He fought the urge to move closer, to offer comfort. After their moment in the hot springs, everything felt different between them, charged with unspoken possibilities.

"The ancient texts speak of creatures that dwell beneath the sands," Nero continued, his eyes distant as if seeing beyond the physical realm. "They are drawn to dream energy, hunting those with power like moths to flame." His gaze settled meaningfully on Liora.

Maya cursed under her breath, while Derek shifted uneasily beside her. Rafe understood their fear - they'd all heard tales of entire caravans vanishing in the Dunes, leaving nothing but empty wagons half-buried in sand.

Marcus stepped forward, and jerked his head toward Liora. "Her powers will draw these creatures straight to us!"

"Her powers," Rafe cut in sharply, meeting Marcus's hostile glare, "might be the only thing that keeps us alive out there."

Jayne's cool voice broke through the standoff. "The Veilstone lies beyond the Dunes. We knew this wouldn't be easy." She pulled out a weathered map, the parchment crackling in the dry air. "Master Thorne, how long should we expect this crossing to take?"

Nero's expression grew grave as he traced their intended path across the map. "Three days, if the Dunes allow it." He paused, his next words carrying the weight of prophecy. "But time moves differently here, where dreams touch reality."

"How did it get like this?" Maya's voice cracked from the dry air. "The old stories talk about gardens and forests here."

Jayne's sharp laugh cut through the wind. "Draven happened." Her fingers tightened around the map until the parchment crinkled. "He turned this place into his personal graveyard when the southern provinces refused to bow."

Rafe's chest tightened at the mention of Draven's name. He'd seen firsthand what the tyrant did to those who defied him. But something in Nero's expression made the anger freeze in his veins. The old master's face had gone ashen, his eyes distant with a horror that made Rafe's skin crawl.

"Yes," Nero whispered, his voice barely carrying over the wind's moan. "But what happened here..." He shuddered, and Rafe noticed his hands trembling as he gripped his staff. "There are some crimes that leave scars on reality itself. The Dunes remember what Draven did - and they hunger for revenge."

Rafe caught the tremor in Liora's shoulders, her golden energy pulsing erratically around her fingers like a trapped bird seeking escape. Each of Nero's words about the Dunes seemed to strike her like physical blows. His feet shifted, instinct urging him to go to her, but Gemini was already there.

The healer's gentle hands found Liora's shoulders, and Rafe watched some of the tension ease from Liora's frame. A familiar twinge of - what, jealousy? - twisted in his gut at their easy intimacy. He pushed it aside, focusing instead on scanning the endless waves of sand for any sign of movement. The wind carried whispers that might have been voices, might have been threats.

Gemini's quiet murmur carried to him on the wind: "You're stronger than you know, Li." The nickname, spoken with such tenderness, made Rafe's chest ache. He remembered the feel of Liora's magic dancing across his skin at the hot springs, how right it had felt until she'd pulled away. Now wasn't the time for such thoughts, but they came unbidden anyway.

Rafe watched Nero trace their path across the map with a gnarled finger, his weathered hand casting spidery shadows across the parchment. The old master's voice carried an ancient weight as he spoke of the scattered settlements they'd encounter. Villages turned to graveyards, he called them - places where hope had withered under Draven's shadow.

"The people there..." Nero's voice cracked, and something in his eyes made Rafe's hand tighten on his sword hilt. "Those who survived Draven's wrath exist in a half-life, trapped between dreams and reality. We must pass through quickly, without engaging."

A muscle twitched in Jayne's jaw - so subtle Rafe might have missed it if he hadn't been watching her reaction. Her fingers traced the pommel of her dagger, a tell he'd learned meant she was fighting back memories. The fierce spy who never showed weakness suddenly looked haunted, and Rafe remembered rumors that she'd grown up in one of those border villages before Draven's purge.

"The children are the worst," Jayne whispered, her voice carrying an edge that cut deeper than any blade. "They play in the streets like nothing's wrong, but their eyes..." She stopped, swallowing hard. Rafe had never seen her this shaken, and it sent ice through his veins.

The wind picked up, carrying stinging sand that bit at exposed skin, but Rafe barely felt it. His attention fixed on the way Jayne's shoulders had drawn tight, how her knuckles whitened around the dagger hilt. There was history here - dark and personal - and he found himself wondering just how much of herself Jayne had buried in those dead villages along with her past.

"The temple lies across the Dunes," Nero explained, his voice carrying the weight of ancient knowledge. "But finding it..." He glanced at Liora, and Rafe noticed how she straightened under that penetrating gaze. "That task falls to you alone, child."

A muscle twitched in Rafe's jaw. He'd seen too many "simple" missions spiral into bloodbaths to trust anything that hinged on a single point of failure. But as he studied Liora's profile, the determined set of her shoulders despite the fear flickering in her eyes, something deeper than logic told him she could do this.

"The temple exists in both reality and dreams," Nero continued, his weathered hands sketching patterns in the air. "It will reveal itself only to one who carries the power of the Dreamweavers. Even then..." His voice dropped lower, forcing them to lean in. "It must choose to be found."

Marcus snorted, the sound sharp with derision. "So our entire mission depends on whether some ancient pile of stones decides to show itself?" His hand strayed to his weapon, a gesture Rafe didn't miss. "That's assuming we even survive crossing this wasteland."

Rafe's fingers itched to silence Marcus's doubts with steel, but Jayne's subtle head shake stayed his hand. She was right - they couldn't afford division now. Still, he shifted his position slightly, placing himself between Marcus and Liora. Just in case.

"The temple knows its own," Nero said, his calm voice cutting through the tension. "It was built by your fore bearers, Liora. Their power flows in your veins." The old master's eyes held something Rafe couldn't quite read - hope? Fear? "The question is: are you ready to embrace that legacy?"

Rafe held his breath, acutely aware of every eye fixed on Liora. He remembered her trembling hands at the hot springs, her whispered fears of becoming like Draven. But now, watching her golden energy dance around her fingers with growing confidence, he saw something else emerging - determination.

"I'm ready," Liora said, her voice steady despite the wind's attempt to tear the words away. The golden light surrounding her pulsed once, strong and sure, and Rafe felt an answering surge of pride in his chest. This was the woman he'd glimpsed in quieter moments - the one who could reshape the world if she believed in herself.

They moved as one toward the Dune's edge, where solid ground gave way to shifting sand. Rafe fell into step beside Liora, close enough to catch her if the treacherous ground betrayed her, but far enough to show his trust in her strength. Ahead, the endless waves of golden sand stretched toward a horizon that shimmered with heat and possibility. Behind them, the last traces of familiar territory disappeared into the wind-carved wasteland. There was no turning back now.

***

The sand whispered secrets in Liora's mind, each grain carrying promises of unlimited power. Her magic stirred beneath her skin, yearning to break free and dance with the swirling dunes that stretched endlessly before them. The golden light within her pulsed in rhythm with the desert's heartbeat, growing stronger with each step deeper into this broken place.

Sweat trickled down her back as she fought to maintain control. The desert's call grew more insistent, more seductive. Images flashed through her mind - herself standing atop the highest dune, arms raised as golden streams of dream energy reshaped reality itself. The vision felt so real, so attainable. Just one small surrender...

Her foot slipped on the shifting sand, and Liora stumbled. The momentary break in concentration sent her power surging, causing nearby dunes to ripple with reflected golden light. She clutched her chest, trying to cage the wild energy threatening to burst free.

"Something's wrong." Gemini's voice cut through the haze of whispered temptations. "Look at her hands - they're glowing. Master Thorne, we need to help her!"

The desert's song grew louder in Liora's ears, drowning out her friend's concerned words. Each breath drew in more of the ancient power that saturated this place. Her magic responded eagerly, pushing against her restraint like a living thing desperate to break free.

Through the golden haze clouding her vision, she glimpsed Nero's weathered face. His expression held neither surprise nor concern - only grim understanding. "This is her trial to face. The Ashen Dunes were left to test all who would wield great power. We cannot intervene."

The wind picked up, whipping sand against Liora's face as her power flared again. The dunes before her shifted, forming patterns that beckoned her forward, promising to show her secrets if she'd only release her careful control. Just for a moment...

"But she's suffering!" Gemini's protest barely registered through the desert's siren song. Liora's fingers sparked with golden light as another wave of power surged through her. The sand beneath her feet began to crystallize, transformed by the raw energy she could barely contain.

Nero's voice came as if from a great distance: "She must learn to resist the desert's temptations on her own. This is the price of wielding dream magic in this place. If she cannot wield it here, she will not be able to wield the Veilstone."

A particularly strong gust of wind sent more sand swirling around Liora, the grains now glowing with reflected power. Each one sang to her of destiny and greatness, of strength beyond imagining. Her magic swelled in response, and she could feel her control slipping further with each passing heartbeat.

The dunes stretched before her like an endless golden sea, and somewhere in their depths lay the Veilstone - calling to her, testing her, waiting to see if she was worthy. Liora gritted her teeth and forced another step forward, even as the desert's power threatened to overwhelm her entirely.

The desert's seductive whispers pulled at Liora's consciousness, urging her feet to wander from their chosen path. Golden tendrils of power beckoned from a distant dune, promising secrets and strength beyond measure. Her magic stirred in response, reaching toward that hypnotic call until a firm hand gripped her arm.

"Stay with us." Rafe's touch anchored her to reality, his calloused fingers warm against her skin. The desert's song faded slightly, allowing Liora to focus on his concerned face. Had she really started walking away from the group? The realization sent a chill down her spine despite the scorching heat.

"Look - ahead!" Marcus's voice cut through the wind. He stood atop a dune, pointing toward something in the distance. The rest of the group hurried to join him, Rafe keeping his steadying grip on Liora's arm as they climbed.

A cluster of buildings emerged from the heat-warped air, their walls bleached bone-white by endless sun. Liora's magic recoiled at the sight, sensing something wrong in the way the structures seemed to pulse with dark energy. The whispers in her mind turned to warnings, urging her to turn back.

"Dunrow." Jayne's voice cracked on the name, her face draining of color. She took an involuntary step backward, fingers clutching at the pendant around her neck. "We can't go there. We can't." The raw fear in her voice made Liora's power surge defensively, golden light sparking between her fingers as she stared at the cursed village that had stolen Jayne's childhood.

"We have no choice." Nero replied, a tone of understanding in his voice as he reached out to place a hand on Jayne's shoulder.

The empty streets of Dunrow stretched before them like an open wound. Liora's magic recoiled at the wrongness that permeated every shadow, every corner. Villagers shuffled past with vacant eyes, their movements mechanical and precise - puppets dancing to Draven's twisted dreams.

Her stomach churned as an elderly woman approached, face blank and movements jerky. Golden light sparked between Liora's fingers as her power responded to the corruption woven through the woman's dreams. The dark magic felt like oil against her skin, slick and suffocating.

A child stumbled past, eyes glazed and unseeing. The sight sent Liora's magic surging, golden energy crackling as she fought the urge to reach out and try to break whatever hold Draven had on these people. But fear held her back - fear of making things worse, of causing more harm than good.

Gemini moved forward with gentle determination, kneeling beside a trembling old man who had collapsed in the dusty street. Nero joined her, his weathered face grim as he examined the extent of Draven's corruption.

Liora stood rooted in place, her power thrashing beneath her skin like a caged animal. The weight of her failure pressed down on her chest. These people needed help - needed someone strong enough to break Draven's hold. Yet here she stood, paralyzed by doubt and fear.

The Veilstone's call echoed in her mind, a distant song of power and possibility. But how could she hope to master such power when she couldn't even help these villagers? Her magic flared in response to her turbulent emotions, causing nearby windows to rattle.

Yet as she watched another vacant-eyed villager shuffle past, something shifted inside her. Perhaps it wasn't her place to decide if she was worthy. The people of Dunrow needed someone to fight for them, whether that person felt ready or not.

"Master Thorne?" Her voice sounded stronger than she felt. "I need to speak with you." The words tumbled out before doubt could silence them. Nero looked up from where he knelt beside Gemini, his expression unreadable.

Golden energy crackled between her fingers as she waited for his response, her power responding to the corruption that saturated the very air around them. The wrongness of what Draven had done here demanded action, regardless of her fears.

Nero nodded and rose slowly, placing a reassuring hand on Gemini's shoulder before moving toward Liora. His eyes held understanding, as if he already knew the weight of the questions burning in her throat. Behind him, another villager shuffled past with that terrible vacant stare, reminding Liora why they couldn't afford to fail.

# Dunrow

Liora's magic recoiled as she followed Nero through the doorway of an abandoned shop. Dust coated every surface, and remnants of a life interrupted lay scattered across the floor - a child's toy, a half-finished letter, dishes left mid-meal. The dark energy of Draven's corruption pressed against her skin like oil, making her power spark defensively.

"I can't keep running from this." Her voice cracked as she turned to face Nero, golden light dancing between her trembling fingers. "Every time I close my eyes, I see their faces - the people I couldn't save in Eldara, and now these villagers. How many more will suffer while I hide from what I am?"

The weight of Nero's gaze settled on her as he considered her words. Through the grimy window behind him, she caught glimpses of more villagers shuffling past like puppets on invisible strings. Her power surged at the sight, no longer content to remain contained. "The Veilstone - I need to find it. Not because some prophecy says I should, but because these people need someone to fight for them."

Something shifted in Nero's expression - pride mixed with concern. "The path to the Veilstone isn't meant to be easy, Liora. It will test more than just your magic." His eyes took in the scene around them. "Are you prepared to face what lies within yourself?"

The question hung heavy in the stale air between them. Through the walls, Liora heard a child's broken laughter - hollow and wrong in a way that made her magic flare protectively. Her power responded to her resolve, golden light illuminating the dim room. "I'm done letting fear decide who I am. Show me what I need to know."

Nero's expression darkened. "The Veilstone isn't just a tool to be claimed, Liora. It's a mirror of the soul - it will amplify everything within you, including your fears. The prophecy states that the Veilstone will call to them when the time is right."

Liora's fingers tingled with suppressed energy. "How will I know? What am I supposed to look for?" The questions tumbled out, each one carrying the weight of her growing frustration.

"The signs will manifest through your dreams," Nero explained, his tone softening.

A memory flashed through Liora's mind - the strange, pulsing light she'd seen in the forest outside Eldara. Her heart raced as understanding dawned. "I've already seen something," she whispered, causing Nero to turn sharply toward her.

Nero's eyes narrowed. "Tell me everything," he commanded, his voice carrying an urgency she'd never heard before. "Every detail matters."

The tent's atmosphere grew heavy with tension as Liora began to describe her original vision. Each word seemed to draw them closer to a truth that had been waiting, hidden in plain sight all along.

The words caught in Liora's throat as Nero's face drained of color. He gripped the edge of a dusty table, knuckles white against the weathered wood. "The prophecy," he breathed, "it's further along than I realized."

Shadows danced across the walls as Nero paced, his usual composure cracking. "The vision you saw in Eldara wasn't just a dream or coincidence. The Veilstone was reaching out to you, calling to you." His voice dropped lower. "Your mother... she sealed away your powers to protect you from Draven. The stone broke through those barriers."

Liora's hands trembled as she pressed them flat against the table, steadying herself. "No more half-truths, Nero." The dream magic within her stirred, responding to her rising emotions. "Tell me everything. About my mother, about what really happened. I need to know, even if it breaks me."

Pain flickered across Nero's features as he leaned onto the table top. The weight of unspoken truths seemed to press down on his shoulders, aging him decades in moments. His fingers traced the Custodian's emblem on his coat - a nervous habit she'd noticed before.

"Your mother," he started, his voice rough with emotion, "was the most powerful Dreamweaver I'd ever known. She could shape dreams into reality with a mere thought." His eyes grew distant, lost in memories. "And that's exactly why Draven wanted her."

"I was there the night everything changed," he continued, each word seeming to cost him dearly. "I watched her face Draven, watched her choose to seal away your powers rather than let him corrupt them." A tear traced down his weathered cheek. "I failed her. Failed you both."

Liora's heart hammered against her ribs as pieces of her fractured past began sliding into place. Dream magic crackled in the air between them, making the building's walls ripple like water.

"Tell me how she died," Liora demanded, her voice barely above a whisper. The words hung in the air like smoke, waiting for the truth that would either break her or set her free. Nero's shoulders sagged as he lifted his gaze to meet hers, ready to unleash the burden he'd carried for so long.

∗∗∗

Gemini's hands trembled as she wrapped a bandage around the elderly man's burned arm, her healing magic flowing gentle and cool through her fingertips. The villager's vacant eyes stared past her, trapped in whatever nightmare Draven had woven into his mind. Movement caught her attention - Jayne's familiar silhouette drifting like a ghost through the doorway of a nearby house.

The wrongness of Jayne's movements sent a chill down Gemini's spine. The normally calculated spy moved as if pulled by invisible strings, her usual sharp awareness replaced by something distant and haunted. Gemini secured the bandage and whispered a soft promise to return to her patient.

Ash crunched beneath Gemini's boots as she followed Jayne into the dim interior of what had once been someone's home. Scorched walls told stories of violence, and the acrid smell of old smoke still clung to everything. Her throat tightened at the sight of a child's drawings scattered across the floor, their edges curled and blackened.

Jayne knelt in the center of the room, her shoulders curved inward as if bearing an impossible weight. In her hands, she cradled a stuffed rabbit, its once-white fur now gray with ash and age. A single tear carved a path through the dust on her cheek, falling to darken a spot on the toy's matted fur.

"Jayne?" Gemini kept her voice soft, gentle as when she spoke to wounded animals. "Are you alright?"

The spy's spine straightened with mechanical precision as she rose, her fingers still clutching the rabbit. Jayne's face transformed, emotions vanishing behind her usual mask of cool detachment. But Gemini caught the slight tremor in her hands, the way her throat worked to swallow back whatever memories this place had stirred.

Gemini stepped closer, each footfall stirring clouds of ash. The rabbit in Jayne's hands seemed to draw all light from the room, a gravity well of painful memories that threatened to pull them both under.

"I was seven when they came." Jayne's voice cracked, her usual calculated tone fracturing around the edges. "Right here, in this room. Mother had just finished braiding my hair." Her fingers traced the rabbit's torn ear, a gesture so childlike it made Gemini's heart ache.

The healer's instincts urged Gemini to reach out, to comfort, but something in Jayne's rigid posture warned against it. Instead, she settled against a scorched wall, letting the spy's words fill the heavy silence between them.

"Draven's soldiers didn't just kill everyone - they twisted them first." Jayne's knuckles whitened around the stuffed animal. "Made parents turn on children, friends against friends. The dreams they forced into people's minds..." She shuddered, and Gemini felt the echo of that horror in her own chest.

A bitter laugh escaped Jayne's throat. "This was Emma's." She held up the rabbit. "She lived next door. We used to pretend we were famous spies, hunting dragons in the village square." Her voice dropped to a whisper. "I watched her mother strangle her while screaming about monsters."

Gemini pressed her hand against her mouth, bile rising in her throat. The weight of Jayne's words seemed to press the air from her lungs, making it hard to breathe in the ash-filled room.

"Nero found me hiding in the cellar three days later." Jayne's eyes fixed on something distant, something only she could see. "I'd stuffed rags under the door to keep the smoke out. Kept so quiet, so still. Just like Emma and I practiced in our spy games."

The rabbit's head lolled as Jayne's hands began to shake. "Sometimes I wonder if I'm still in that cellar, if all of this - the rebellion, everything - is just another dream they put in my head." Her voice cracked again, a hairline fracture in her carefully maintained facade.

Gemini watched as Jayne's fingers worked through the matted fur, an unconscious gesture that seemed to anchor her to the present. The spy's next words came out barely above a whisper: "That's why I can't trust Liora's power. I've seen what dream magic can do. What it did here. What it made people do."

Gemini's heart constricted as she watched Jayne's fingers tremble against the rabbit's matted fur. The urge to reach out, to heal this wound that ran deeper than flesh and bone, pulled at her with an almost physical force.

Her feet carried her forward before conscious thought could intervene, ash swirling in her wake like disturbed ghosts. The distance between them felt vast, though it was only a few steps across the ruined room.

Jayne's shoulders tensed as Gemini drew near, but she didn't pull away. The spy's breath hitched, a tiny sound that seemed to echo in the dead air of the abandoned house. It reminded Gemini of injured birds, the way they went still when approached, torn between flight and surrender.

With infinite gentleness, Gemini placed her hand on Jayne's shoulder. The fabric beneath her fingers was cold, as if the chill of that long-ago cellar still clung to Jayne's skin. Through the contact, Gemini could feel the minute tremors running through the other woman's body.

"You survived," Gemini whispered, her voice barely disturbing the ash-laden air. She let her thumb trace small circles against Jayne's shoulder, the same soothing motion she used when treating shock victims. "You survived, and you're not alone anymore."

The stuffed rabbit slipped from Jayne's fingers, landing in the ash with a soft puff. Her hands hung empty at her sides, lost without the anchor of Emma's toy. Gemini's heart ached at the sight, at this glimpse of the seven-year-old girl still hiding in that cellar.

Without thinking, Gemini stepped closer, turning Jayne to face her. The spy's eyes were distant, haunted by ghosts that no amount of healing could banish. But Gemini had to try - it was written into her bones, this need to ease suffering wherever she found it.

She pulled Jayne into an embrace, feeling the other woman's body go rigid with surprise. For a moment, they stood frozen like that, Gemini's arms wrapped around Jayne's unyielding frame while ash continued to settle around them.

Then, like ice cracking in spring, something in Jayne began to give way. Her forehead dropped to Gemini's shoulder, and her hands came up to clutch at the back of Gemini's tunic. The tremors increased, and Gemini held on tighter, offering what shelter she could against the storm of memory.

Gemini felt every tremor that ran through Jayne's body, each one a testament to the pain this place held. The spy's fingers dug into her tunic, anchoring them both in the present while memories threatened to pull them under. Ash continued to settle around them like snow, coating their boots and turning the world gray.

A sound caught in Jayne's throat - not quite a sob, but something raw and wounded that made Gemini's heart clench. She ran her hand up and down Jayne's back, the same soothing motion she used with frightened children in her healing tent. The rigid tension in Jayne's spine began to ease, muscle by muscle, as if years of carefully maintained control were finally crumbling.

"I see them sometimes," Jayne whispered against Gemini's shoulder, her voice muffled. "In my dreams. Emma. Mother. Everyone." Her hands tightened in Gemini's tunic. "They ask why I lived when they didn't." The confession hung in the ash-filled air between them, heavy with guilt and grief. Gemini pulled back just enough to cup Jayne's face between her palms, forcing the spy to meet her eyes.

"You lived because you were meant to," Gemini said, her thumb brushing away a tear that had escaped down Jayne's cheek. "Because the world needs your strength, your courage." The words felt inadequate against the weight of such loss, but Gemini poured all her conviction into them. Jayne's eyes searched her face, looking for any sign of doubt or pity. Finding neither, something in her expression softened.

A shout from outside broke the moment - someone calling for the healer. But before Gemini could step away, Jayne caught her wrist. The spy's fingers were cool against her skin, her grip gentle but insistent. "Thank you," Jayne whispered, and in those two words Gemini heard everything that remained unsaid between them. She squeezed Jayne's hand once before turning toward the door, leaving the stuffed rabbit behind as a memorial to the ghosts of Dunrow.

***

Nero's fingers jerked with nervousness, his eyes refusing to meet Liora's. The light cast dancing shadows across his weathered face, deepening the lines of grief that seemed to appear whenever her mother came up.

"You don't understand what you're asking." His voice carried a weight that made Liora's chest tighten. "Some truths are better left-" He stopped as Liora's hand slammed against the wooden table.

"I understand perfectly." The words came out sharper than she intended, dream energy crackling in the air around her. "My entire life has been built on secrets. Every time I ask about her, someone changes the subject or tells me to wait." Her voice cracked. "I'm tired of waiting."

Nero's shoulders sagged, the light catching the glimmer of moisture in his eyes. "Your mother... she burned bright, just like you. The same fire, the same defiance." His fingers traced an invisible pattern on the table's surface. "She was the last trained in our ways, before Draven's purge began."

"Draven knew what she represented." Nero's voice hardened. "A threat to everything he'd built through fear and control. He sent his forces across Somnus, burning every village that might shelter her. Places like this one." His hand clenched into a fist. "I can still smell the smoke sometimes, hear the screams of those who refused to betray her."

Liora's vision blurred as phantom flames danced at the edges of her mind - memories not her own, yet somehow familiar. How many had died protecting the secret of her mother's existence? How many villages had burned because of the power that now coursed through her own veins?

"When you were born..." Nero's voice softened, thick with remembered pain. "She knew immediately what it meant. A daughter with the gift - it was everything Draven feared. Another Dreamweaver, one who might grow strong enough to challenge him."

The dream energy in the room pulsed with Liora's rising emotion, making the shadows leap and dance across the walls. Her mother had known, had carried that burden along with her infant daughter, understanding the danger that lurked in every shadow.

"She made me swear an oath." Nero's fingers brushed against an old scar on his palm. "Not just to protect you, but to give you something she never had - a choice." His eyes met Liora's, carrying decades of unspoken guilt. "She believed that power without purpose becomes a prison."

Liora's throat tightened as she pictured her mother, a woman she knew only through others' memories, planning her daughter's escape while Draven's forces closed in. The candlelight flickered, casting shadows that seemed to dance with her tumbling thoughts.

"Bennet wasn't chosen by chance." Nero's voice grew distant, lost in memory. "I searched every village in Somnus, looking for someone who could give you more than just safety - someone who could give you a home." The corner of his mouth lifted slightly. "He didn't hesitate, even when I warned him of the risks."

The image of Bennet's weathered face filled Liora's mind - his patient smile as he taught her to work the mill, his quiet strength when she woke screaming from nightmares she couldn't explain. He'd known all along what she might become, yet he'd never treated her as anything but his daughter.

"Eldara was as far from Draven's influence as I could get you." Nero's eyes looked through the window, as if remembering. "A simple village, where dream magic was nothing but bedtime stories. Where you could grow up free from the weight of your heritage."

The irony of it tasted bitter on Liora's tongue - how that very distance had left her feeling lost and alone when her powers first manifested, convinced she was some kind of monster. Yet that same isolation had protected her, kept her hidden until she was strong enough to face the truth.

Nero's voice cracked as he continued. "Your mother knew the price of power - how it can consume you if you're not ready for it." He closed his eyes, pain etching deeper lines in his face. "She wanted you to choose this path, not have it thrust upon you like she did."

A memory surfaced - Bennet teaching her to control the mill's mechanisms, his gentle reminder that power without precision was nothing but chaos. He'd been preparing her all along, in his own way, teaching her lessons that went far beyond grinding grain.

Liora's fingers curled around the edge of the table, steadying herself as the weight of her mother's sacrifice pressed down on her shoulders. The choice her mother had died to give her now lay before her, clear as the stars above Somnus.

"You still haven't told me how she died." Her voice trembled, but she forced herself to meet Nero's gaze.

Nero's shoulders hunched as if bearing an invisible weight. "The last time anyone saw your mother alive, she was walking this path, heading to confront Draven directly." The words seemed to age him, deepening the lines around his eyes. "She believed if she stopped running, he wouldn't seek you. And if she was powerful enough, she could end his tyranny before it spread further across Somnus."

Wind whistled through the tent's canvas. "Their powers clashed with such force that witnesses said the sky itself turned to fire." His voice dropped to barely above a whisper. "When it was over, your mother was gone. Draven remained emperor. And that region..." He gestured around them. "That became the Ashen Dunes."

Liora's knees buckled, and she gripped the table's edge to steady herself. The Ashen Dunes were not just calling to her because of her power. They called to her because that vast wasteland of shifting sands and bitter winds - was her mother's tomb. Her power, combined with Draven's, had scarred the very earth itself.

Liora's mind reeled with images of her mother facing Draven alone, wielding the same dangerous power that now coursed through her veins. How many had died that day? How many villages had been reduced to ash in their final confrontation?

"Many died for her," Nero's eyes softened as he gazed into the dancing flame. "Your mother had that effect on people - everyone who met Lyra fell in love with her spirit, her determination to protect others."

The name struck Liora like lightning. Her breath caught in her throat as pieces clicked into place. "Lyra? Lyra Solari?" The words tumbled out before she could stop them.

Nero's head snapped up, his expression shifting from nostalgic remembrance to sharp focus. "How do you know that name?" His voice carried an edge of urgency she'd never heard before.

"She's been..." Liora's fingers twisted in her lap as she struggled to explain. "She appears in my dreams. Guiding me, teaching me about my powers." The candlelight flickered across Nero's face as his complexion grew pale.

His hands trembled as he gripped the edge of the table, knuckles turning white. "Lyra Solari," he whispered, voice thick with emotion, "was your mother." Tears gathered in the corners of his eyes, threatening to spill over.

Liora's world tilted on its axis. The ethereal woman from her dreams - the one who spoke with such gentle wisdom and understanding - was her mother? The room seemed to spin as memories of those dream encounters took on new meaning.

Nero's voice cracked as he continued. "She always said the dreamscape transcended death itself." He pressed a hand to his mouth, struggling to maintain composure. "But to think she found a way to reach you..."

Liora's knees gave out, and she sank onto a nearby crate. The dream energy that had been crackling around her moments ago settled into a gentle hum, matching the rhythm of her thundering heart. Her mother. All this time, the woman in her dreams had been her mother. The guidance, the gentle encouragement, the way she seemed to understand Liora's struggles with her power - it all made sense now.

"Why didn't you tell me sooner?" The words caught in her throat as she looked up at Nero. His face was a mask of regret and something deeper - fear. Not of her, but for her. The same fear she'd seen in her mother's - in Lyra's - eyes during their dream encounters.

The door creaked open, spilling harsh sunlight into the dim room. Rafe's silhouette filled the doorway, his hand resting on the hilt of his sword. His eyes darted between Liora and Nero, reading the tension in the air. "Everything alright?" The question hung heavy in the silence.

Nero straightened, composing himself with visible effort. His eyes met Liora's, carrying the weight of unspoken truths and promises yet to be revealed. "We should make a decision," Rafe continued, shifting his weight. "Camp here for the night or push on through the dunes?"

"We move on." Nero's voice carried a finality that brooked no argument. His gaze flickered to where Jayne stood in the shadows beyond Rafe. "We've asked enough of this place." The words seemed to carry a double meaning, and Liora noticed Jayne's slight nod of acknowledgment.

# Lonely Desolation

The sand shifted beneath Rafe's boots as they left the cursed village of Dunrow behind, its haunted streets fading into the haze of the desert. His hand rested on his sword hilt, muscles tense despite the lack of immediate threat. Years of combat had taught him that safety was often an illusion, especially in these wastes.

Derek and Maya's faces flashed through his mind - their determined expressions as he'd given the order to stay behind. Had he made the right call? The two were among his most capable fighters, veterans who'd survived countless battles against Draven's forces. But someone needed to secure their retreat path, and they were the best choice for that task. Still, their absence left the group more vulnerable.

The wind howled across the dunes, carrying stinging particles that bit at any exposed skin. Rafe pulled his scarf tighter around his face, watching Liora's figure ahead of him. Her golden magic flickered around her like a shield, keeping the worst of the sand at bay. If they failed to reach the Veilstone, if Draven's forces overwhelmed them,

Derek and Maya would be the only chance for any survivors to escape. The thought sat heavy in his gut.

A distant screech echoed across the wasteland - one of the desert's many horrors making itself known. Rafe's grip tightened on his sword as he scanned the horizon. The sound reminded him of the last time he'd split his forces. That decision had cost lives, good people lost because he hadn't been there to protect them. The memories of their faces still haunted his dreams.

Movement caught his eye - just Nero adjusting his pack, but it made Rafe's heart race all the same. Every shadow, every sound could mean death in the Ashen Dunes. He'd fought too many battles, lost too many friends to take any threat lightly. What if Derek and Maya encountered Draven's forces back in Dunrow? What if leaving them behind had just sentenced them to death? The questions gnawed at him like desert scavengers picking clean a corpse.

Ahead of him, Liora's shoulders hunched against an invisible weight. Her steps dragged in the sand, lacking their usual grace. The revelation about her mother had clearly shaken her more than she let on. His chest tightened with the urge to comfort her, but he kept his distance. Sometimes space was the kindest gift you could give.

"The Ember Ruins lie east," Nero announced, his voice carrying over the whisper of wind through the dunes. "What remains there is the last bit of civilization, if you can call it that, before desolation greets us." The old master's cryptic words did nothing to ease the tension that radiated from their group.

Jayne practically vibrated with nervous energy, her usual measured pace replaced by quick, urgent steps that carried her far ahead of the group. But what caught Rafe's attention more was how Gemini kept pace with her, their shoulders occasionally brushing. Something had shifted between them in Dunrow's broken streets.

The wind picked up, carrying stinging grains of sand that forced them to pull their scarves tighter. Through the billowing fabric, Rafe watched Gemini's hand brush against Jayne's arm - a gesture so subtle he might have missed it if he hadn't been looking. Jayne's rigid posture softened just slightly at the touch.

"You're going to strain something if you keep frowning like that," Marcus said, falling into step beside him. The younger man's attempt at levity felt forced, but Rafe appreciated it nonetheless.

Rafe adjusted his pack, buying time to organize his thoughts. "We need to be ready for whatever is waiting in those ruins. Draven's forces won't be far behind." The words tasted like sand in his mouth, dry and bitter.

"Already ahead of you," Marcus pulled a crude map from his vest. "I've been marking possible defensive positions since we left camp. The ruins might offer better cover than these open dunes." His finger traced a path across the weathered parchment.

The discussion of tactics should have focused Rafe's mind, but his attention kept drifting to Liora. She walked alone now, her golden magic occasionally flickering around her fingers like nervous lightning. Each flash made his heart clench with worry.

"Listen," Rafe cut off Marcus's strategic planning mid-sentence, "get the others ready for a rest stop ahead. That ridge should provide some shelter from the wind." He didn't wait for a response, already moving to close the distance between himself and Liora. Some things were more important than planning the next move.

Rafe's boots crunched through the sand as he drew alongside Liora, matching her pace. The wind whipped at their clothes, and he fought the urge to shield her from it. Her magic still sparked around her fingers, dancing like trapped fireflies seeking escape.

"That looked like a heavy conversation back there," he kept his voice casual, though his heart hammered against his ribs. The space between them felt charged with unspoken words, crackling like the magic that surrounded her.

Shadows played across her face as she turned to him, and his chest tightened at the strain he saw there. But she smoothed her features quickly, pulling on a mask of composure that didn't quite reach her eyes. The gesture reminded him of soldiers before battle, armoring themselves against fear.

"I'm fine," Liora's voice carried the same forced steadiness as her expression. Her fingers curled into fists, extinguishing the dancing lights. "Just processing what needs to be done." The words fell between them like stones dropping into still water.

Sand stung Rafe's face as another gust tore across the dunes. He wanted to reach for her, to break through that careful facade. Instead, he watched her withdraw further behind her walls, each second widening the gulf between them.

"Whatever Nero told you," he started, then hesitated as her shoulders stiffened. "You don't have to carry it alone." The words felt inadequate against the weight he could see pressing down on her.

Liora's steps never faltered, but something in her posture shifted, becoming more rigid. "I'm just preparing myself," she said, each word measured and distant. "For what I have to do." The finality in her tone cut deeper than any blade.

The rejection stung more than he wanted to admit. Rafe had faced down armies without flinching, but this quiet dismissal left him feeling oddly vulnerable. His jaw clenched against words that wanted to spill out – pleas, demands, confessions.

"Right then," he managed, forcing his voice to remain neutral. "I'll leave you to your preparation." Each syllable tasted like ash in his mouth. He'd learned long ago when to retreat from a losing battle.

As he fell back, letting the space between them grow, Rafe caught a flicker of something in her expression – regret maybe, or pain. But before he could be sure, she'd turned away, leaving him with nothing but questions and the endless whisper of sand against sand.

***

Rafe pressed his back against the weathered stone ridge, grateful for even this brief respite from the relentless sand. His parched throat burned as he took careful sips from his waterskin, rationing each precious drop while watching Gemini pull medical supplies from her pack.

"No camp setup," he called out, his voice rougher than intended. "Just water and a quick breather." The look Gemini shot him spoke volumes about her concern for their exhausted group, but she nodded, tucking the supplies away.

Marcus paced the perimeter, one hand never far from his sword hilt. "Two hours till sunset," he reported, squinting at the sun's position through the hazy air. "If we push hard, we might make the ruins before dark." The unspoken alternative hung heavy between them - being caught in open dunes after nightfall was a death sentence.

Rafe's muscles protested as he pushed off from the ridge, scanning their surroundings with practiced vigilance. The eclipse loomed over them like a shadow, just over a day away. Time slipped through their fingers like the endless grains of sand surrounding them.

His gaze drifted to Liora, who stood apart from the group, her back straight despite the exhaustion he knew she must feel. The distance she'd placed between them ached like an old wound, but he forced his attention back to their immediate concerns.

"Five minutes," he announced, catching Marcus's eye. "Then we move." The younger man nodded, already gathering the others. Rafe had chosen him as second for moments like these - when orders needed to be carried out without question.

The wind changed direction, carrying with it a scent that made Rafe's hand tighten on his sword hilt. Something acrid and wrong rode the air currents, reminding him of battlefields he'd rather forget. The Ember Ruins were close, their ancient magic seeping into the very atmosphere.

Rafe watched Liora's silhouette against the darkening sky, her shoulders taut with an invisible burden. The urge to go to her clawed at his chest, but he forced himself to turn back to Nero and Marcus as they hunched over a crude map sketched in the sand.

"The ruins stretch for miles underground," Nero traced a path with his finger. "Most entrances have collapsed, but there's one here-" he tapped a spot, "that should still be accessible."

A few paces away, Jayne sat cross-legged beside Gemini, both women silent as they shared a meager portion of dried meat. The healer's usual warmth seemed dimmed, and Rafe noticed how she kept glancing at Liora's back with poorly concealed hurt.

"We'll need to move fast," Rafe dragged his attention back to the strategy session. "The eclipse is tomorrow night, and the General will be attacking Somnara, a suicide mission if we don't succeed in ours."

Rafe studied the group's fragmented dynamic - Liora isolated by choice, Gemini rejected by her closest friend, clustering in uncertain alliances. If they couldn't pull together, they surely wouldn't succeed.

Jayne broke the tense silence. "We should have encountered resistance by now." Her voice carried across their makeshift rest stop, drawing everyone's attention. "Draven's elite guard these dunes like hawks, yet we haven't seen a single patrol."

The observation made Rafe's stomach knot. He'd been trying to ignore that same nagging concern since they'd entered the Ashen Dunes, hoping the others wouldn't notice. But of course Jayne would pick up on it.

Marcus shifted his weight, sand crunching beneath his boots. "She's right. Even accounting for the eclipse preparations, there should be scouts at minimum." His fingers drummed against his weapon, a nervous tell Rafe had noticed during their years fighting together.

"Perhaps," Nero interjected, his weathered face grave, "the Emperor is allowing us passage." The words hung in the air like poison, and Rafe felt the hair on the back of his neck rise. The old master's implications were clear - they were being led into a trap.

Rafe's gaze darted to Liora, still standing apart from them. Her silence spoke volumes, shoulders rigid as she stared out across the endless dunes. He wanted to go to her, to share his growing unease, but the wall she'd built between them seemed insurmountable.

"Think about it," Gemini added, moving to stand beside Jayne. "When have Draven's forces ever shown restraint?" The healer's usual gentle tone carried an edge of steel, and Rafe noticed how Liora's hands clenched at her friend's words.

The wind picked up, carrying stinging sand that masked the group's expressions. But Rafe saw how Jayne and Gemini exchanged knowing looks, their temporary alliance born of shared suspicion. It was unlike Gemini to side against Liora, and the shift in dynamics set his teeth on edge.

A memory surfaced - the last time he'd seen Draven's forces pull back, it had been to draw rebels into an ambush that still haunted his dreams. The parallel was too strong to ignore, but they had no choice but to press forward. The Veilstone waited, and without it, they had no hope of stopping Draven during the eclipse.

"We keep moving," Rafe announced, cutting through the growing tension. "But in tighter formation. No one strays." He met each person's eyes in turn, lingering on Liora's back, willing her to turn around. She didn't.

The group gathered their supplies in silence, the unspoken fear of what awaited them in the ruins weighing heavily on their shoulders. As they prepared to move out, Rafe couldn't shake the feeling that they were being watched - not by scouts or soldiers, but by something far more dangerous. Something that was counting on their desperate push forward.

Rafe pulled Nero aside as the others gathered their gear, keeping his voice low to avoid drawing attention. "The ruins are our best option, but..." He gestured toward the darkening horizon where ancient stone structures pierced the sky like broken teeth. "What aren't you telling us?"

The old master's eyes crinkled at the corners, but not with his usual warmth. "We'll shelter there tonight. The walls still hold power - enough to shield us until dawn." His gaze drifted to the endless expanse of dunes beyond. "Then we enter the desolation."

Sand whispered against stone as the wind picked up, and Rafe fought the urge to check on Liora again. Instead, he watched Nero's weathered face, noting how the man's expression grew more grave with each passing moment.

"Tonight is crucial," Nero continued, his voice barely audible above the wind. "Liora must forge a connection with the Veilstone. It's the only way to divine its location before the eclipse." The words carried the weight of prophecy, making Rafe's skin prickle with unease.

Nero turned toward Liora, who stood at the edge of their group, her hair whipping in the strengthening gusts. "Tonight," he called out to her, "you must open yourself to the stone's power. Everything depends on it."

Liora's only response was a slight nod, her face turned away from them both. The gesture twisted something in Rafe's chest, reminding him of how she'd withdrawn since their moment at the hot spring. The memory of her pulling away from him still burned.

He watched her shoulders tense as Nero approached her, speaking words too quiet for him to hear. Whatever bond they'd formed in those precious moments by the water seemed to have evaporated like morning dew in the desert heat.

The others began moving toward the ruins, Marcus taking point while Jayne covered their rear. Rafe remained rooted in place, caught between his duty to lead and his desire to bridge the growing chasm between himself and Liora.

A particularly violent gust of wind sent sand stinging against his face, forcing him to shield his eyes. When he lowered his hand, Liora had already started walking, her steps purposeful as she followed Nero toward the looming ruins. She didn't look back.

Rafe's fingers brushed the hilt of his sword, finding comfort in its familiar grip as he fell into step behind the group. The rejection sat heavy in his gut, but he pushed it aside. They had a mission to complete, and his personal feelings couldn't matter - not with the fate of Somnus hanging in the balance.

***

The sand shifted beneath Liora's feet as she walked ahead of the group, each step carrying the weight of Nero's revelations. Her mother's face flickered through her mind—not the hazy memory she'd carried for years, but the ethereal presence from her dreams. Lyra Solari. The Dream Warden. The truth burned in her chest like swallowed fire.

Golden wisps of power curled around her fingers, responding to the storm of emotions she fought to contain. The magic felt different now, knowing it was her mother's legacy. Knowing that Nero had kept this from her, had watched her struggle and doubt herself while holding these secrets close.

The wind picked up, whipping sand against her face, but Liora welcomed the sting. It gave her something tangible to focus on, something other than the hollow ache where her anger sat. The ruins loomed ahead, their broken spires reaching toward the darkening sky like accusing fingers.

Footsteps crunched behind her—lighter than Rafe's, more deliberate than Gemini's. Nero. Her jaw tightened as he drew alongside her, his presence carrying the weight of unspoken words.

"The Veilstone must be located tonight," Nero said, his voice low enough that the others wouldn't hear. "And retrieved tomorrow. Before the Eclipse. Your mother—"

"Don't." The word came out sharp enough to cut. "You don't get to use her name now."

Nero's breath caught, the smallest tell of impact. "Liora, I understand your anger. But the Veilstone—"

"I know what needs to be done." Her power flared, golden light dancing across the sand before she reined it back. "I'll find it. I'll do what's necessary."

The sand whipped harder around them as Nero stepped closer, his weathered face creased with concern. "Pushing away those who care for you isn't the path to victory, Liora. Gemini, Rafe—they give you strength, not weakness."

Heat rose in her chest, the magic responding to her spike of anger. How dare he speak of strength when he'd hidden so much? When he'd watched her fumble in the dark while holding all the answers? "Strength?" The word tasted bitter on her tongue. "What good is strength to someone being sent to die?"

Nero's shoulders stiffened, and something flickered across his face—pain, perhaps, or remembrance. "Your mother had loved ones too," he said softly, then turned and walked away, leaving her alone with the howling wind.

The sand settled in his wake, golden grains catching the last rays of sunlight. They reminded her of her magic, of the power that hummed beneath her skin—her mother's power. Her mother's sacrifice.

Understanding crashed through her like a wave breaking against stone. This wasn't about Nero's secrets or her own fears. It wasn't even about the prophecy that hung over her like a sword.

The magic stirred within her, no longer chaotic but purposeful. She thought of Gemini's unwavering faith, of Rafe's protective presence, of all the people who believed in her even when she couldn't believe in herself.

Her mother had faced this same choice—had chosen to fight knowing she might not return, because some things were worth dying for. Some people were worth protecting, no matter the cost.

The wind died down, as if responding to her clarity of purpose. Ahead, the ruins stood stark against the darkening sky.

She flexed her fingers, watching golden light dance between them. The power felt different now—not a burden to be feared, but a tool to be wielded. A legacy to be honored.

# The Ember Ruins

G emini's boots crunched over scattered debris as they entered the Ember Ruins, her fingers instinctively tightening around her satchel. Ancient stone pillars rose like sentinels against the darkening sky, their surfaces etched with symbols that seemed to pulse with a faint, ethereal glow. The air felt thick with untold stories, pressing against her skin like a tangible force.

Power thrummed through the ruins, older, wilder - a symphony of forgotten magic that made her breath catch in her throat. Her gaze traced the intricate patterns carved into fallen columns, wondering if they held secrets that had been lost to time.

Memories of her father's teachings surfaced as she studied a partially crumbled wall. He'd spoken of places like this, where the earliest healers had learned to channel energy from the earth itself. What wisdom had been shared in these halls? What discoveries had been made beneath these weathered arches? The questions echoed in her mind, unanswered.

Ahead, Liora walked beside Nero, her shoulders tense and her steps measured. Gemini's heart ached at the distance that had grown between them since leaving Dunrow. Where once they'd shared everything, now walls of silence stretched between them, built from secrets and uncertainties. She longed to reach out, to offer comfort as she always had, but something held her back.

The sound of boots scuffing stone drew her attention to Jayne, who walked slightly apart from the group. Since their moment in the burned house, something had shifted between them - a crack in Jayne's carefully maintained armor. Gemini caught her eye, and Jayne's usual guarded expression softened for just a moment before she looked away.

Marcus cursed as he stumbled over a fallen stone, the sound echoing off the ancient walls. Rafe shot him a warning glance, his hand tightening on his sword hilt. The ruins seemed to absorb their presence, wrapping them in shadows that grew deeper with each step.

Wind whistled through broken windows, carrying the scent of age and decay. Gemini's fingers brushed against a wall, and she jerked back at the spark of energy that passed between stone and skin.

Liora paused ahead, her hand raised as golden light flickered around her fingers. The sight made Gemini's chest tighten with worry. She'd seen how each use of power seemed to drain something from her friend, leaving behind shadows in eyes that used to shine with joy.

Jayne moved closer to Gemini as they passed through a partially collapsed doorway, their shoulders nearly touching. Neither spoke, but Gemini felt the weight of unspoken words between them - of shared pain and understanding that had bloomed in Dunrow's ashes.

The corridor opened into a vast chamber, and Gemini's breath caught at the sight of massive columns stretching toward a ceiling lost in darkness. Nero raised his torch, illuminating fragments of what might have once been magnificent murals.

Gemini watched Rafe's torch cast dancing shadows across the weathered walls as he gestured down a long hallway. "These rooms should be safe enough for the night. I'll take first watch." His voice echoed off ancient stone, making the ruins feel even more vast and empty.

Something in Liora's stance made Gemini's chest tighten as her friend practically fled into the nearest chamber, closing herself off yet again. The familiar urge to follow, to comfort, to heal rose up - but this time, Gemini squared her shoulders and strode past Liora's door.

"I'll take this one," she announced, perhaps more forcefully than necessary. The words tasted strange on her tongue - how many nights had she and Liora shared space, sharing whispered conversations until sleep claimed them? But things were different now.

Marcus and Jayne exchanged glances at her tone, but Gemini ignored them as she pushed open the heavy stone door. The room beyond was surprisingly intact, with delicate carvings still visible on the walls despite centuries of dust.

Her pack hit the floor with a dull thud that seemed to reverberate through the entire chamber. The bed - if it could be called that - was little more than a stone platform with ancient cushions that had long since rotted away.

Gemini's fingers traced one of the wall carvings as she crossed to sit on the edge of the platform. The stone was cool beneath her, but she could feel traces of old magic humming through it, like the whispered echoes of long-forgotten songs.

Her mother's pendant felt heavy against her chest as she leaned back against the wall. How many times had she watched her mother disappear into the night, only to return days later with new scars and darker shadows in her eyes? Was this what it felt like, to choose solitude over comfort?

The sounds of the others settling into their rooms filtered through the thick walls - Jayne's quiet footsteps, Marcus's muffled curse as he presumably stubbed his toe, Nero's soft murmuring that might have been a prayer. But from Liora's room, only silence.

Gemini's heart skipped as the door creaked open, revealing Liora's silhouette against the dim light of the corridor. Her friend's shoulders were hunched, fingers twisting together in that familiar nervous gesture that hadn't changed since they were children.

"I'm sorry," Liora whispered, her voice cracking. "I've been awful, pushing everyone away." She crossed the room slowly, as if afraid Gemini might send her back out into the darkness.

Gemini patted the stone platform beside her, relief flooding through her as Liora settled next to her. Their shoulders brushed, and Gemini felt some of the tension ease from her friend's frame. The silence stretched between them, comfortable this time, like the quiet moments they used to share in the garden back home.

"Nero told me about my mother," Liora finally said, her words barely audible above the whisper of wind through ancient stone. "About how she wielded dream magic, how she..." Her voice caught. "How she died fighting Draven."

The pieces clicked into place in Gemini's mind - Liora's withdrawal, the haunted look in her eyes since Dunrow. Her hand found Liora's, squeezing gently. "Is that why you've been pulling away? To protect us?"

Liora nodded, tears catching the faint light as they slid down her cheeks. "I couldn't bear the thought of you or Rafe feeling what her loved ones must have felt when she..." She trailed off, unable to finish.

A smile tugged at Gemini's lips despite the gravity of the moment. "Oh? Rafe specifically, is it?" She bumped her shoulder against Liora's playfully. "I've seen the way you two look at each other when you think no one's watching."

Color flooded Liora's cheeks as she sputtered, "That's not - I didn't mean -" She broke off with a watery laugh, some of the darkness lifting from her expression. "You're impossible."

"Someone has to be," Gemini replied softly, her heart lightening at the sound of her friend's laughter. "We're stronger together, Li. Whatever comes next, whatever we face - you don't have to carry it alone."

Gemini reached for Liora's trembling hands, wrapping them in her own steady grip. The familiar calluses and scars beneath her fingers brought back memories of countless nights spent healing scrapes and bruises, sharing secrets in whispered conversations. "If you need to walk this path alone, I understand. But know this - I'll be here, waiting, whenever you need me."

Tears welled in Liora's eyes, reflecting the faint magical glow that seemed to pulse through the ruins' ancient walls. Gemini's throat tightened at the sight of such raw vulnerability on her friend's face. How long had Liora been carrying this weight alone?

The stone beneath them hummed with old magic as Liora launched herself forward, wrapping her arms around Gemini in a fierce embrace. Gemini held her friend close, feeling Liora's tears dampen her shoulder as years of held-back emotion finally broke free.

Something shifted in the air between them - a tension Gemini hadn't even realized was there until it dissolved. This was the Liora she remembered, the one who'd crawl through her window late at night after nightmares, seeking comfort in shared silence.

Liora pulled back, wiping her eyes with the heel of her hand. The determination in her expression reminded Gemini of the day they'd first met, when a young Liora had stubbornly insisted on helping tend to an injured bird despite her fear of failure.

"I'm tired," Liora whispered, her voice gaining strength with each word, "of holding everything back. Of being afraid to feel, to want, to..." She trailed off, color rising in her cheeks.

A smile tugged at Gemini's lips as she watched her friend struggle with words that had clearly been building for some time. The same look had been mirrored in Rafe's eyes whenever he thought no one was watching him watch Liora.

"You know," Gemini said, keeping her voice carefully casual as she traced a pattern in the dust coating the stone platform, "Rafe will be patrolling the halls after dark. All those shadows to check, corridors to secure..."

Liora's breath caught, and Gemini bit back a laugh at how predictable her friend could be. The golden sparks that sometimes accompanied Liora's stronger emotions flickered briefly around her fingers.

"I should probably get some rest," Gemini said, stretching with exaggerated weariness. She gave Liora a gentle push toward the door, pretending not to notice how her friend's hands shook slightly as she smoothed her tunic.

***

Rafe's footsteps echoed through the ancient corridors of the Ember Ruins, his shadow dancing against weathered stone walls in the flickering torchlight. The musty air pressed against his skin like a damp shroud, carrying whispers of long-forgotten secrets that made his neck prickle with unease.

Each passageway looked identical to the last, forcing him to mark his path with small chalk crosses. The ruins reminded him of the abandoned villages after Draven's attacks - hollow shells stripped of life and warmth. His hand tightened around the hilt of his sword, finding comfort in its familiar weight.

The distant sound of settling stone made him freeze, muscles tensing as he listened. Nothing followed except the soft whisper of wind through cracks in the walls. These ruins felt wrong, as if they were watching him with ancient, hungry eyes. He'd rather face a hundred of Draven's soldiers than spend another night in this cursed place.

His thoughts drifted to Liora, as they always did during these lonely watches. The way she'd withdrawn from him cut deeper than any blade. Rafe understood loss - gods, did he understand - but watching her suffer alone twisted something inside his chest.

Moonlight filtered through a crumbling section of ceiling, casting silver patterns across the floor. Rafe traced them with his boot, remembering how Liora's magic had danced with similar ethereal beauty during her training sessions. Back then, she'd still looked at him with trust, before the weight of prophecy and legacy had built walls between them.

A cool breeze carried the scent of sand and sage, reminding him of their moment at the hot spring. The memory of her closeness, followed by her retreat, still burned. Rafe pressed his palm against the cold stone wall, letting its chill ground him in the present. He couldn't afford such distractions, not here, not now.

The sound of shifting sand drew his attention to a partially collapsed corridor. Rafe approached cautiously, torch extended. Only darkness greeted him, but something about the shadows felt wrong. These ruins held too many secrets, and he couldn't shake the feeling that they were about to discover something they shouldn't.

Rafe's boots scuffed against ancient stone as exhaustion pulled at his limbs. The night watch stretched endlessly, each hour marked only by the gradual dimming of his torch. He pictured Liora cross-legged on the floor of her chamber, lost in meditation as she searched for traces of the Veilstone's power.

His fingers traced another chalk mark at an intersection, the simple act requiring more focus than it should. Sleep beckoned like a siren's call, but the ruins held too many dangers to let his guard down. The memory of Nero's warnings about creatures drawn to dream magic kept his sword hand ready.

The torch's flame guttered in a sudden draft, and Rafe cursed under his breath. These ruins played tricks on the senses - every shadow seemed to move, every whisper of wind carried phantom voices. He'd rather face an honest fight than this constant state of tension.

When he rounded the corner back to their sleeping quarters, the sight of Liora standing in the hallway stopped him cold. The moon-light streaming through a crack in the ceiling caught in her hair, cre-ating a silver halo that made his chest tighten. She wasn't supposed to be awake - wasn't supposed to be here.

Their eyes met across the darkness, and the weight of unspoken words pressed against his lungs. Liora's face held a look he'd never seen from her before - fear, perhaps, or determination. Hunger. The last time they'd stood this close, at the hot spring, she'd run from him. The memory still stung, but he forced it down, focusing on the present danger.

The shadows seemed to deepen around them as they stood in weighted silence. Rafe searched for words that wouldn't push her fur-ther away, but exhaustion made his thoughts sluggish. Every instinct screamed to close the distance between them, to offer the comfort she so clearly needed.

Rafe's heart hammered against his ribs as he studied Liora's face in the moonlight. Something wild and desperate lurked behind her eyes, setting off warning bells in his mind. "Li, are you alright?" His voice came out rougher than intended. "Should I get Nero-"

Her finger pressed against his lips, the touch sending electricity down his spine. The torch trembled in his grip as her other hand found his chest, right above his thundering heart. Every survival instinct screamed at him to step back, to maintain the careful distance they'd built, but his boots felt rooted to the ancient stone.

The air between them crackled with tension, thick enough to cut. Rafe caught the scent of wildflowers and magic that always clung to her skin, making his head spin. The walls he'd carefully constructed since the hot spring crumbled like sand in a storm.

His free hand moved of its own accord, fingers brushing her cheek. Her skin burned fever-hot against his calloused palm. The moonlight caught in her eyes, turning them to liquid silver, and Rafe forgot how to breathe.

The torch clattered to the floor as Liora surged forward, her lips crashing into his. Fire exploded through his veins, consuming every thought except the feel of her pressed against him. His hands tangled in her hair as he backed her against the wall, lost in the taste of her mouth.

She made a small sound in the back of her throat that nearly undid him. The kiss deepened, desperate and hungry, as if they could devour each other's fears and doubts. Golden light flickered beneath her skin, her magic responding to the intensity between them.

Rafe's sword belt caught on her tunic as she pulled him closer. The rational part of his mind tried to surface, to remind him of all the reasons this was dangerous. But then her teeth grazed his bottom lip, and coherent thought scattered like autumn leaves.

The ruins seemed to pulse around them, shadows dancing in time with Liora's glowing magic. Rafe could feel her power humming against his skin, wild and intoxicating. Part of him wondered if this was another trick of the ancient place, some dream or illusion meant to break him.

Her fingers dug into his shoulders as if she could anchor herself against a storm. The kiss turned almost violent, edged with the desperation they both carried. All the unspoken words between them poured out in touches and tastes instead.

The fallen torch sputtered, casting their shadows huge against the walls. Somewhere in the darkness, stone shifted and settled, but Rafe couldn't bring himself to care. The world had narrowed to this moment, to the feel of Liora in his arms and the taste of magic on his tongue.

# Rafe and Liora

Liora pressed forward, her heart thundering against her ribs as she guided Rafe through the doorway. The stone walls of his quarters swallowed the dim torchlight, casting dancing shadows across his hesitant features. Her fingers trembled against his chest, feeling the rapid beat of his heart matching her own.

His breath caught as she traced her fingertips along his jaw. "Li," he whispered, the word carrying a weight of uncertainty. But when she lifted onto her toes, brushing her lips against his, that uncertainty crumbled.

The golden threads of her magic hummed beneath her skin, sparking like starlight where they touched. Rafe's initial restraint melted as he pulled her closer, one hand tangling in her hair while the other traced patterns at the small of her back.

Time seemed to fracture and spin as their kiss deepened. Liora poured every unspoken word, every moment of longing into the press of her lips against his. Her magic responded to her racing emotions, filling the air with shimmering motes of light that danced around them like fireflies.

Rafe broke away, his breathing ragged. "We shouldn't—" But Liora silenced his protest with another kiss, softer this time, letting her actions speak the words her throat couldn't form. His resistance wavered, then shattered completely.

Their next kiss ignited like wildfire, fierce and consuming. Rafe's fingers tightened in her hair as he backed her against the cool stone wall. The contrast between the cold stone and his warmth sent shivers racing down her spine.

Every brush of his lips against hers felt like coming home and stepping off a cliff all at once. Liora's magic surged and swirled, responding to the storm of emotions crashing through her. Golden light wrapped around them both, creating a cocoon of warmth and possibility.

His hands framed her face with a gentleness that made her heart ache. When he pulled back to study her features, his dark eyes reflected the shimmer of her magic. "You're incredible," he breathed, thumb brushing across her lower lip.

Liora leaned into his touch, letting herself forget about prophecies and responsibilities for just this moment. Here, with Rafe's heartbeat thundering against her palms, she wasn't the last Dreamweaver or a weapon against Draven. She was simply herself.

Her fingers traced the line of his jaw, down the strong column of his neck, lingering at the hollow of his throat. The faint pulse fluttering beneath her touch sent a thrill through her. Unlike their encounter at the hot springs, shrouded in darkness and uncertainty, now she could see him, every detail illuminated by the soft glow of her magic. The sculpted planes of his chest, the gentle curve of his biceps, the way the firelight danced across his skin—it was a feast for her senses.

With a newfound boldness, Liora reached for the ties of his tunic, her breath catching as she fumbled with the knots. His hands, calloused and warm, settled on her waist, sending shivers down her spine. A gasp escaped her lips as his fingers brushed against the exposed skin above her nightdress. His touch, a spark of electricity that set her nerves alight.

He leaned in, his lips brushing against her ear, sending a wave of goosebumps rippling across her skin. His whisper, warm against her ear, sent a thrill through her. "Li," he murmured, the sound a caress against her senses.

Her hands, now steadied by his presence, worked at the fastenings of his tunic. The fabric parted, revealing the smooth expanse of his chest. Her gaze lingered, tracing the contours of his muscles, the play of light and shadow across his skin. Each touch, each stolen glance, stoked the flames of desire within her.

His hands wandered lower, settling on the curve of her hips. A gasp escaped her lips, not from surprise, but from the sheer pleasure of his touch. His fingers slipped beneath the hem of her nightdress, sending a wave of heat through her core. The world narrowed down to the sensation of his hands on her skin, a symphony of touch and desire.

The fabric of her nightdress bunched around his and her hands as together, they pulled the straps off each shoulder, allowing the straps to fall. Her breath hitched as she waited for him to look up and see her. His gaze lingered as she bared all to him under the soft glow.

"More beautiful than I could have ever imagined," he whispered, his eyes tracing the curve of her, from the swell of her breasts to the dip of her collarbone. He leaned back, pulling her down with him into the mattress that was his bed.

His lips found hers again, the sweet taste returning once-more. Rafe's fingers brushed against the sensitive skin of her, eliciting a tremble of anticipation. She arched into his touch, feeling her body come alive under his gaze, a pleasure she'd never known she craved. This time was far different from the hot springs, there was no fear, only want, longing, and pure electric need.

His lips moved to her neck, trailing a path of fire down to the hollow between her breasts. She moaned softly, her fingers tangling in his hair, pulling him closer. Every touch, every kiss, sent tremors of pleasure through her. Liora was drowning in his, and she wanted to ensure that he'd drown deeper.

He lifted his head, his eyes dark with desire, and met her gaze. "You're sure?" he asked, his voice husky with emotion, and Liora knew, with a certainty that resonated deep within her soul, that this was where she wanted to be, in his arms, surrendering to the moment.

His question hung in the air, a silent plea for reassurance. Liora didn't answer, her actions speaking louder than any words. With a boldness she hadn't known she possessed, she reached for the ties of his pants, her fingers fumbling with the knots. His breath hitched as her hands brushed against his skin, the warmth radiating from him a tangible force.

Liora tugged at the strings, her touch sending a shiver through his body. Rafe leaned back against the bed, his eyes never leaving hers. The firelight danced across his features, illuminating the desire burning in his dark eyes. With a final tug, the fabric parted, revealing the lean strength of his legs.

Liora's gaze lingered, her heart pounding against her ribs. This was new territory, a vulnerability she hadn't anticipated. Yet, there was no fear, only a growing sense of anticipation. Her fingers traced the line of Rafe's hip, down his thigh, each touch sending a ripple of awareness through both their bodies.

She reached for him, her hand cupping him gently. Her touch was hesitant at first, exploring the unfamiliar contours of his body. Rafe's breath grew shallow, his muscles tensing beneath her fingertips. A low moan escaped his lips, the sound a mixture of pleasure and surprise.

Liora marveled at the feel of Rafe's thickness in her hand, the smooth skin, the heat radiating from him. Her touch grew bolder, her fingers stroking him with a newfound confidence. Her magic sparked and swirled, responding to the intimacy of the moment. Golden light filled the room, casting dancing shadows across their intertwined bodies.

She lowered her head, her lips brushing against his skin. A sharp intake of breath echoed in the stillness of the room. The taste of him, salt and musk, filled her senses. She moved her mouth, her tongue tracing the contours of his body.

Rafe's hands found purchase in her hair, his fingers tightening as she continued her exploration. A low growl rumbled in his chest, the sound vibrating against her lips. Liora's magic surged, responding to his growing arousal. The air crackled with energy, the world narrowing down to the two of them.

Each movement of her mouth, each flick of her tongue, elicited a groan from deep within him. Liora lost herself in the sensations, the taste, the texture, the sheer power she held in her hands. This was a dance of intimacy, a language spoken without words.

Rafe's body trembled beneath her touch, his breathing ragged and uneven. Liora felt a thrill course through her, a sense of control mingled with a burning desire. His pleasure was hers, and she reveled in the power she held over him.

The power that coursed between them was overwhelming, and Liora found herself relishing the way it surged through her veins. But just as she was about to take him into her mouth again, Rafe stopped her. "Wait," he gasped, his voice hoarse with desire. "If you keep doing that, I won't last."

A flush crept up Liora's cheeks at his words, but she didn't pull away. Instead, she ran her fingers teasingly along his length, relishing the way he squirmed beneath her touch. "I could always make you come again," she said, her voice a soft purr.

Rafe growled, his eyes dark with hunger. With a swift motion, he lifted her up and deposited her onto the bed. His hands moved to the ties of her nightdress, quickly undoing them and pushing the fabric aside. Liora shivered as the cool air kissed her skin, sending goosebumps racing across her exposed flesh.

Their gazes locked, a silent communication passing between them. In that moment, Liora saw the desire burning in Rafe's eyes, but also something more—a depth of emotion that went beyond physical attraction. It was as if he was seeing into her soul, and she, his.

Without breaking eye contact, Rafe lowered his head, pressing a kiss to the hollow of her throat. His lips trailed downward, leaving a trail of fire across her collarbones and down to the swell of her breasts. Liora arched her back, her body pleading for more even as her mind spun with uncertainty. She had never wanted anyone like this before, with such a fierce intensity that it bordered on desperation.

Rafe's hands settled on her hips, his thumbs stroking the sensitive skin of her inner thighs. "You're so beautiful," he murmured against her skin, his breath ghosting across her sensitive peaks. "I want to worship every inch of you."

Liora whimpered at his words, her body aching for him. She wanted to feel him everywhere, to erase the distance between them until they were consumed by the flames of their passion. "Please," she begged, her voice hoarse with need. "I need you."

Rafe chuckled, the sound vibrating against her sensitive skin. "Impatient, aren't you?" He nuzzled her neck, his breath teasing the sensitive spot below her ear. "But I aim to please."

His lips continued their path downward, planting soft kisses along her abdomen and dipping into her navel. Liora squirmed beneath him, her fingers tightening in his hair. She wanted him to hurry, even as she reveled in the torture of anticipation.

With agonizing slowness, Rafe kissed the tops of her thighs, his breath ghosting across the dampness between her legs. Liora whimpered, her hips bucking slightly as her body begged for release. "Rafe," she pleaded, her voice a mere breath.

Finally, he granted her unspoken request. His tongue traced slow, deliberate patterns along her folds, teasing her with gentle flicks and languid strokes. Liora moaned, her head falling back as pleasure rocked through her. His mouth was pure magic, igniting every nerve ending, causing her to burn with an intense, desperate hunger.

"More," she gasped, her fingers tightening in his hair. "Please, I need more."

Rafe chuckled, the vibrations sending shivers of pleasure through her. "As you wish." He obliged, his tongue delving deeper, his lips sucking and tasting her most intimate core.

Liora's back arched off the bed as wave after wave of pleasure rolled through her. Rafe's tongue flicked and teased, stoking the flames of her desire until she was sure she would burn up from the inside out. Her hands gripped his shoulders, her nails digging into his skin as she struggled to maintain her tenuous hold on reality.

"Rafe," she breathed, her voice a mere whisper. It was as if she were floating outside her body, every sensation heightened and amplified. She was keenly aware of the contrast between the cool air on her skin and the hot brand of Rafe's mouth against her core.

His fingers dug into her hips, holding her in place as he continued his relentless assault. Liora squirmed, her body arching and twisting as she sought release. Her magic crackled and snapped around them, filling the room with a wild energy that mirrored the chaos within her.

"Please," she begged, not even sure what she was asking for. More? Less? She didn't know, she just knew she was teetering on the edge of something monumental, and she wanted—no, needed—to take the leap.

Rafe sensed her impending climax, his mouth working her with an intensity that mirrored the storm raging within her. Liora's breath hitched as pleasure coiled tighter and tighter, building like a wave about to crash. The world narrowed to the feel of his tongue against her sensitive flesh, the warmth of his breath, the sound of his soft groans.

And then, suddenly, she was falling. Pleasure washed over her in relentless waves, crashing against her with an intensity that left her breathless. Liora cried out, her body trembling as the climax ripped through her.

Rafe gentled his touch as she came down, his tongue lapping softly at her sensitive flesh. Liora lay against the bed, her skin tingling with the aftershocks of her release. She felt boneless, and at the same time, as if she were floating, suspended in a sea of pleasure.

Gradually, her breathing slowed, and her heart stopped pounding quite so hard. She became aware of the dampness between her legs, the slickness of Rafe's skin where he had joined her on the bed. A hint of self-consciousness crept in, but it was quickly chased away by the heat in Rafe's eyes as he hovered over her.

"That was—" She struggled to find the words to describe the intensity of what she had just experienced. "Incredible," she finished, her voice a mere breath.

Rafe chuckled, his eyes sparkling with mischief. "I aim to please." He leaned down, brushing a soft kiss against her lips. "But I'm not done yet."

Liora felt a thrill course through her at his words. She wanted more, craved it with an intensity that surprised her. Her body, which should have been sated, was already coiling tight once more, ready for another round.

"Rafe," she murmured, her fingers tangling in his hair as she pulled him closer. "I need you." It was a plea, a demand, and an admission of her own desires all rolled into one.

"I know," he whispered, his eyes searching hers.

Their lips met in a hungry kiss, mouths moving in desperate unison. Liora could taste herself on his lips, a heady reminder of the pleasure he had just given her. Liora's gaze drank in the sight of Rafe's body, the lean strength of him, the dusting of dark hair that trailed down his chest and below.

She reached for him, her hand wrapping around his thickness. Rafe groaned, his head falling back as he gave himself over to her touch. Liora explored him with bold strokes, relishing the way he squirmed and moaned beneath her fingers.

But soon, even that wasn't enough. She wanted to feel him inside her, stretching her, filling her. With trembling hands, she guided him to her entrance, feeling a thrill at the anticipation gleaming in his eyes. "Please," she breathed, her voice husky with need.

Rafe didn't need any further encouragement. He thrust into her with one smooth motion, burying himself deep. Liora gasped, her back arching off the bed as she felt him stretch and fill her. It was intense, overwhelming, and utterly perfect.

He stilled, waiting for her to adjust to his size. Liora's body pulsed around him, a tight heat that seemed to pull him in deeper. She lifted her hips, eager for more. "Yes," she whispered, her fingers tightening in his hair. "Oh gods yes."

Rafe obeyed, withdrawing slowly before thrusting back in. Liora moaned, her head falling back as pleasure washed over her. Rafe's movements were slow and deliberate, each stroke driving her deeper into the mattress.

She met his thrusts with abandon, her hips lifting to meet each one. The bed creaked beneath them, the only sound in the room aside from their ragged breathing and soft moans. Liora's fingers dug into Rafe's shoulders, her nails leaving crescents in his skin.

"Harder," she begged, her voice hoarse with need. "Please, Rafe."

Rafe growled, his eyes darkening with desire. He grabbed her hips, lifting her slightly as he plunged into her. Liora cried out, her body trembling on the edge of another climax. The heat between them was scorching, burning away any hesitation or uncertainty. Their rhythm was fierce and frenzied, a desperate race toward release.

"Rafe, I—" Liora's words were cut off as her orgasm crashed over her, even more powerful than the first. She clenched around him, her body riding the wave of pleasure as it swept her away.

Rafe groaned, his own release coming fast on the heels of hers. "Li," he gasped, his voice a strangled mix of pleasure and desperation. His body stiffened as he thrust into her one last time, burying himself as deep as he could go.

Liora felt him pulsing inside her, his warmth spreading through her. She tightened her legs around his hips, wanting to keep him as close as possible. Their breathing slowed, the only sound in the room the gentle thump of their heartbeats.

The warmth of Rafe's skin against hers anchored Liora to this moment, his steady heartbeat a rhythm that matched the pulse of her magic. Her fingers traced the scars on his chest, each one a story of battles fought and survived. The golden threads of her power danced between them, responding to the contentment that filled her chest.

This feeling - this connection - defined her more than any prophecy or destiny ever could. Her magic had always frightened her, made her feel isolated and different. But here, wrapped in Rafe's arms, she understood that her power came from these moments of pure emotion, of trust and vulnerability. The realization settled into her bones like a truth she'd always known but forgotten.

A shiver ran through her as Rafe's fingers traced lazy patterns along her spine. Her magic responded, sending sparks of golden light dancing across their skin. No more running from what she felt, from who she was. The strength of her emotions, the depth of her connections - these weren't weaknesses to be feared but foundations to build upon.

The ancient timepiece on the wall chimed softly, pulling Liora from her reverie. The sound reminded her of what awaited - she must find the Veilstone's hidden location. Her muscles tensed slightly, aware that this peaceful moment would soon end.

The shadows in the corner of the room seemed to deepen, and her magic stirred restlessly beneath her skin. Something waited, something that would test everything she'd just discovered about herself. Liora pressed closer to Rafe, memorizing the feel of his arms around her, gathering strength for what was to come.

# Wraiths of the Ruins

R afe traced lazy circles on Liora's bare shoulder, watching the faint golden shimmer of her magic dance beneath her skin like starlight. Her breath came in soft, even pulls against his chest, her dark hair spilling across his arm in silken waves. The memory of her touch still burned against his skin, electric and fierce.

In sleep, the worry lines that usually creased her forehead had smoothed away. Her full lips, still slightly swollen from his kisses, curved into a gentle smile. The sheet had slipped down to her waist, revealing the elegant arch of her spine and the scattered beauty marks that mapped constellations across her back.

Heat bloomed in his chest as he recalled how she'd moved against him, all grace and raw power. Her magic had sparked between them, intensifying every caress until he'd lost himself completely in her storm. Even now, hours later, aftershocks of that energy pulsed through his veins.

The candlelight caught the curve of her hip, painting her skin in amber and gold. She was art brought to life - strong yet soft, powerful yet vulnerable. His fingertips ghosted over a small scar near her ribs, wondering at its story, at all the pieces of her he had yet to discover.

Her hair smelled of lavender and something uniquely her - like summer rain and lightning. Rafe buried his face in those dark strands, breathing her in. The way she'd whispered his name, voice breaking with need, would echo in his dreams for years to come.

He'd been with others before, but nothing compared to this, of trust freely given and passion unleashed. The memory of her eyes, dark with desire, fluttering closed as pleasure overtook her, sent another wave of heat through his core.

A soft murmur escaped her lips as she shifted closer, seeking his warmth even in sleep. Her leg tangled with his, skin like silk against the rough scars that marked his thigh. The contrast of her softness against his battle-hardened body struck him as perfectly right.

Her hand rested over his heart, as if even unconscious she needed to feel its steady rhythm. The simple intimacy of that gesture squeezed something in his chest. She'd chosen to share not just her body but her vulnerability, her fears, her magic - everything that made her uniquely Liora.

Dawn's first light began creeping through the high windows, painting her skin in rose gold. Soon they would need to face whatever challenges awaited, but for now, Rafe allowed himself to simply exist in this moment, memorizing every detail of her peaceful expression.

His fingers found the pulse point at her throat, steady and strong like the woman herself. Whatever came next, whatever battles they faced, this night had changed everything. Rafe pressed a gentle kiss to her temple, silently vowing to protect not just her life, but this newfound peace she'd found in his arms.

Rafe's heart thundered against his ribs as the words "I love you" caught in his throat. He shifted to wake Liora, to finally confess what he'd held back, when a metallic screech echoed through the ancient halls.

The sound jolted him upright, years of combat training taking over. He snatched his sword from beside the bed and pulled on his breeches, careful not to disturb Liora's peaceful sleep. The cold stone floor bit at his bare feet as he crept toward the door.

Ethereal blue light seeped under the doorframe like ghostly fingers reaching for him. Rafe's grip tightened on his sword hilt, the leather wrapping creaking under his white-knuckled grasp. Another crash rang out, followed by Marcus's muffled curse.

The corridor stretched before him like a throat to hell. Wraiths peeled themselves from the walls, their translucent forms crackling with corrupted dream energy. Their hollow eyes fixed on Marcus, who stood with his back against a pillar, sword raised in trembling hands.

"Marcus, don't move," Rafe hissed through clenched teeth, inching forward. The nearest wraith turned its eyeless face toward him, jaw unhinging to reveal an endless void. The temperature plummeted, frost crystallizing along Rafe's bare chest.

Three more wraiths emerged, their armor crafted from nightmares and shadow. They moved like smoke on water, weapons materializing from the corrupted dream energy that formed their essence. Marcus's blade passed harmlessly through one's chest.

"Get back to Liora!" Marcus shouted, parrying a spectral blade that left frost crackling along his sword edge. "We need her magic!" Blood trickled down his arm where a wraith's touch had frozen his skin.

The wraiths pressed closer, their hollow voices whispering promises of eternal sleep. Rafe retreated step by step, keeping himself between the creatures and Liora's door. His breath came in visible puffs as the temperature continued to drop.

Rafe's heart slammed against his ribs as another wraith materialized between him and Liora. The creature's hollow eyes fixed on him, promising an eternity of frozen nightmares. His muscles screamed to move, to fight, to protect her - but the crushing cold of the wraith's presence held him in place.

Silver light exploded through the corridor as Nero emerged from the shadows, his hands wreathed in ancient magic. The wraiths recoiled, their ethereal forms wavering like smoke in a storm. "These are no ordinary spirits," Nero's voice cut through the supernatural silence. "The ruins remember more than we knew - every death, every horror Draven inflicted here."

The silver energy pulsed outward in waves, pushing the wraiths back step by agonizing step. But still they blocked Rafe's path to Liora, their weapons raised in silent challenge. Blood froze in the cuts across his chest where their blades had found purchase. Was she safe? Had they reached her already? The questions burned through his mind like acid.

"Focus, Delacroix!" Nero commanded, his magic flaring brighter as he engaged three wraiths at once. "She can handle herself - we need to contain these memories before they spread! And wake the others!" The words did nothing to ease the knot in Rafe's gut. He'd sworn to protect her, and now these nightmare creatures stood between them.

A wraith's blade whistled past Rafe's ear, leaving frost crystals in his hair. He ducked and rolled, trying to circle around toward Liora's door, but two more spectral forms rose from the floor to block his path. Their armor, crafted from corrupted dreams, gleamed with an inner light that spoke of ancient pain and endless suffering. Rafe raised his useless sword, muscles coiled to spring - but where could he strike against creatures made of memory and shadow?

***

Gemini jolted awake as her door exploded inward, wood splinters flying across the stone chamber. Marcus's silhouette filled the doorway,
his sword already drawn and gleaming in the dim light.

"Wraiths! We need to move now!" His voice cracked with urgency
as metallic screeches echoed through the ancient corridors.

Her instincts kicked in as she grabbed her satchel, fingers finding
the familiar pouches of herbs and bandages. The sounds of combat
grew louder - the clash of steel, shouts of warning, and that bone-chill-
ing screech that made her skin crawl.

"Where's Liora?" Gemini's heart raced as she thought of her friend.

Marcus grabbed her arm, pulling her toward the door. "Rafe's with
her. We need to get to the main chamber before they cut us off." His
grip was too tight, betraying his fear of the creatures he claimed to
distrust more than Liora's magic.

The corridor outside stretched into darkness, broken only by sput-
tering torchlight that cast writhing shadows on the ancient walls.
Gemini's bare feet found the cold stone as she ran, following Marcus's
lead while her mind raced through preparation for the injuries she
knew would come.

Another screech, closer now, sent vibrations through the stone
beneath her feet. Marcus cursed, shoving her behind him as a dark
shape emerged from an intersecting passage. The wraith's form seemed
to absorb the torchlight, its metallic limbs moving with unnatural
grace.

Gemini's fingers found the small vial of blessed water in her satchel
- a gift from an old priestess who'd warned her of dark days ahead. She
uncorked it with trembling hands as Marcus engaged the creature, his
blade singing through the air.

The wraith's claws scraped against Marcus's sword with a sound
that set Gemini's teeth on edge. She waited for her opening, remembering lessons about timing and trust. When Marcus forced the
creature back, Gemini threw the vial, watching it shatter against the
wraith's core.

Holy water hissed and steamed where it struck the darkness, and
the wraith's screech turned to a wail of agony. Marcus didn't waste the
opportunity, his blade finding the gap in its defense. As the creature
collapsed into shadows, Gemini was already running again, prayers for
her friends' safety mixing with the sound of her racing heart.

Gemini's feet carried her through the twisting corridors, each turn
revealing new horrors. The wraiths' ethereal forms caught the torchlight, their movements jerky and wrong as they pressed forward.
Ahead, Rafe and Nero stood back-to-back, Nero's magic finding purchase against the creatures' shadowy forms.

Her heart lurched at the sight of the shirtless Rafe's blood-streaked
arm. Even as she assessed his injury from afar, her healer's instincts
cataloging the severity, her thoughts raced to Liora. Where was she?

The corridor leading to Liora's chamber was barren. Instead, it
Rafe's door blocked by three wraiths, their claws leaving deep gouges
in the ancient stone as they advanced. Rafe's desperate attempts to
break through their line spoke volumes - Liora was trapped behind
that door.

Nero's voice cut through the chaos, ancient words of power that
made Gemini's skin prickle. Silver light erupted from his staff, forcing
one of the wraiths back, but two more emerged from the shadows to
take its place. This wasn't a random attack - they were targeting Liora
specifically.

"Gemini, stay back!" Rafe's warning came too late as a wraith noticed her presence, its head snapping toward her with that horrible

mechanical precision. She fumbled for another vial of blessed water, her last one, as the creature stalked forward.

The sound of splintering wood drew everyone's attention. Rafe's door shuddered in its frame as something struck it from within. Gemini recognized the golden glow seeping through the cracks - Liora's magic was building.

Rafe must have sensed it too. He redoubled his efforts as he pressed forward with renewed desperation. "Liora!" His voice carried equal measures of warning and fear. They all knew what could happen if her power exploded unchecked in these ancient halls.

Gemini's fingers closed around the vial just as the wraith lunged. She ducked under its first swipe, feeling the rush of air as those deadly claws passed inches from her face. The creature's momentum carried it past her, giving her the opening she needed.

The blessed water struck true, eating through the wraith's shadowy form like acid through cloth. Its screech of pain was cut short as Marcus's blade separated its head from its shoulders, the darkness dissipating into nothing.

Gemini's feet refused to move as she watched golden light pulse beneath Rafe's door. Her heart screamed to run toward Liora, to help her friend contain the magic threatening to burst free. But before she could take a step, Jayne's calloused fingers wrapped around her wrist.

"We have to go." Jayne's voice carried the weight of experience, of having seen too many friends fall to hesitation. Her grip tightened as another wraith emerged from the shadows at the far end of the corridor.

Marcus shouldered his way past them, his blade already singing through the air. "Get her out of here. I'll help Rafe get Liora." The determination in his voice left no room for argument, even as doubt gnawed at Gemini's resolve.

Jayne pulled harder, forcing Gemini to stumble backward. The wraith's screech echoed off the ancient stones as Marcus engaged it, buying them precious seconds. Gemini's healer's instincts warred with the reality of their situation - she couldn't help anyone if she died here.

Her feet finally remembered how to run as Jayne led her down a side passage. The sounds of combat grew fainter, replaced by their ragged breathing and pounding footsteps. But the golden light from Liora's magic seemed to follow them, seeping through cracks in the stone walls like a reminder of what - and who - they were leaving behind.

***

Rafe's heart hammered as he watched Gemini and Jayne disappear around the corner. The ethereal forms of wraiths blocked his path back to Liora's chamber, their spectral weapons gleaming with an otherworldly light. His fingers tightened around the hilt of his sword, knowing it would do little good against these incorporeal nightmares.

Golden light seeped beneath Liora's door, pulsing like a frightened heartbeat. The magic called to something deep within him, an echo of their shared intimacy just hours before. He needed to reach her, to protect her, but the wraiths stood between them like a wall of shifting shadows and malevolent intent.

Marcus appeared at his side, breath ragged and sword drawn. "We need to get through," Marcus growled, his usual skepticism about Liora's powers absent in the face of immediate danger. The wraiths shifted, their forms rippling like smoke in a breeze, but their weapons remained deadly solid.

Rafe cursed under his breath, missing Gemini's blessed water that could make these creatures vulnerable to steel. The corridor felt impossibly long, stretched by the presence of these ancient guardians. More golden light spilled from beneath Liora's door, and with it came a wave of power that made his skin prickle.

"There!" Marcus pointed to a gap in the wraiths' formation, but as they moved toward it, the spirits closed ranks. Their hollow eyes fixed on Rafe with ancient malice, as if they recognized something in him that deserved their wrath. The air grew colder, heavy with the weight of centuries of trapped nightmares.

A scream echoed from Liora's chamber, and Rafe's blood turned to ice. He launched himself forward, blade sweeping through the nearest wraith. The spirit dissipated like mist only to reform, its ghostly sword slashing toward his exposed side. Marcus barely deflected the blow with his own blade, the clash of steel on spectral energy sending sparks flying.

"We need another way!" Marcus shouted, backing away from a second wraith's attack. But Rafe couldn't tear his eyes from Liora's door, where the golden light had taken on a darker hue. The magic felt wrong, twisted somehow, and fear clawed at his throat.

The wraiths pressed forward, forcing them back step by step. Each swing of their weapons came closer to finding flesh, and Rafe could feel the cold burn of their presence seeping into his bones. He remembered Nero's warnings about the ruins, about the corrupted magic that lingered here, and wondered if they'd walked straight into a trap.

Another cry from Liora's room, this one filled with power rather than fear, made the very stones beneath their feet tremble. The wraiths paused, their forms wavering as if caught in a strong wind. Rafe seized the moment, charging forward again, Marcus right behind him. But the spirits recovered too quickly, their ranks closing once more.

Sweat trickled down Rafe's back as he parried another ethereal blade. Without Gemini's holy water, they were fighting shadows, and each moment they delayed was another moment Liora faced whatever horror had invaded her chamber alone. He met Marcus's gaze, saw his own desperation reflected there, and knew they needed a new strategy - fast.

Rafe caught a flash of movement down the corridor - Nero's dark robes billowing as he charged toward them. The old master's face was set in grim determination, his hands already weaving patterns of protective magic in the air.

Marcus didn't wait for orders. He hurled himself at the wraiths, creating an opening. A spectral blade caught him in the shoulder, and his cry of pain echoed off the ancient stones. Blood darkened his shirt as he stumbled back, but he'd made enough space for Nero to reach them.

"Get out of here, Rafe!" Nero commanded, his voice carrying the weight of years of authority. "I'll get Liora and Marcus to safety." His magic flared, pushing back the nearest wraiths with surprising force.

The order struck something primal in Rafe's chest, a rebellion against leaving Liora behind. "I'm not leaving her!" His sword swept through another wraith, useless but defiant. The golden light under her door had grown darker, more unstable.

A crash echoed from the temple entrance, followed by the unmistakable sound of armored boots on stone. Rafe's blood ran cold as he recognized the precise, disciplined footfalls of Draven's elite guard. They'd been followed, tracked through the desert like prey.

Marcus clutched his wounded shoulder, face pale but determined. "They're coming up the east corridor," he gritted out. "We're about to be surrounded." The wraiths pressed closer, their hollow eyes reflecting the corrupted golden light seeping from Liora's room.

Nero's magic pulsed again, stronger this time, creating a barrier between them and the approaching soldiers. "They're here for her," he said, his voice tight with strain. "We can't let them reach her while she's vulnerable to the ruins' power."

Rafe's mind raced through options, each worse than the last. They were trapped between wraiths and Draven's finest killers, with Liora caught in some magical nightmare behind that glowing door.

Another wave of dark energy pulsed from Liora's room, making the wraiths shudder and twist. Their forms began to change, becoming more solid, more real. Rafe remembered Nero's warnings about corrupted dream magic and felt fear claw at his throat. This was wrong. All of it was wrong.

Through the chaos, Rafe caught movement at the far end of the corridor - the gleam of polished black armor and the blood-red capes of Draven's personal guard. Their measured advance spoke of absolute confidence, of hunters who knew their prey was cornered. Rafe raised his sword, knowing it wasn't nearly enough, but unwilling to give up while Liora still needed him.

# Unexpected Help

The stale air of the catacombs pressed against Gemini's skin as she followed Jayne's hurried footsteps through the darkness. Her fingers trembled against the rough stone walls, using them as guides while distant screams and metallic clashes echoed from above. The sounds reminded her of that terrible night in Eldara, when everything had changed.

Jayne's hand squeezed her wrist, pulling her to a stop. In the dim light filtering through ancient grates, Gemini caught the tension in Jayne's jaw, the way her eyes darted between shadows like a cornered animal. Something about this place seemed to unnerve the usually stoic rebel far more than the battle raging above.

"Listen," Jayne whispered, her voice barely a breath. Gemini strained her ears, catching the rhythmic thud of boots against stone. The pattern stirred something in Jayne's expression - recognition, then fear. "Elite guard. I'd know that march anywhere."

Gemini's heart hammered against her ribs as Jayne pressed them both into an alcove, the cold stone biting through her thin sleeping clothes. The thundering steps grew closer, accompanied by the distinctive rattle of armor that had haunted Eldara's streets. Her healer's instincts screamed at the memory of treating victims who'd survived encounters with those guards.

A sob caught in Gemini's throat as shadows danced across the wall ahead - too many shadows. Jayne's fingers dug into her arm, grounding her in the present moment. The touch reminded her of how she'd steadied Liora through countless fears, and now she needed that same strength.

"We need to move," Jayne breathed against her ear, the words barely audible over Gemini's pounding heart. "There's something worse than ghosts down here." The tremor in Jayne's voice sent ice through Gemini's veins - she'd never heard fear from the hardened rebel before.

They crept forward, each step measured against the echoing battles above. Gemini's bare feet found every sharp stone, but she bit back her whimpers. The darkness felt alive, watching, waiting. Her fingers brushed something soft and powdery - she jerked back, refusing to think about what centuries of death had left behind in these passages.

A crash from above showered them with dust and debris. Gemini stifled a cough, tasting ash and decay on her tongue. Jayne's grip tightened as voices carried down the corridor - voices speaking in the clipped, formal tones of the Imperial court. The elite guard weren't just passing through; they were searching.

"This way," Jayne mouthed, tugging Gemini toward a narrow passage she hadn't noticed before. The walls pressed in closer, forcing them to turn sideways to squeeze through. Gemini's chest constricted with each step, her breaths coming in shallow gasps as the space grew tighter.

The passage opened suddenly into a chamber, moonlight spilling through a partially collapsed ceiling. But before Gemini could draw a full breath, Jayne's hand clamped over her mouth. There, illuminated by the silver light, stood three figures in polished black armor, their backs turned but their presence promising death if they turned around.

Gemini's throat closed as one of the elite guards shifted, moonlight glinting off his sword. Her mother's face flashed through her memory - the cold efficiency in those eyes whenever she'd prepared for a mission. Gemini had sworn never to become that, never to hold a weapon meant for ending life rather than preserving it.

Jayne pressed something cold and metallic into her palm - a dagger - but Gemini shook her head violently, pushing it back. Even now, with death mere steps away, she couldn't betray her healer's oath. The disappointment in Jayne's eyes stung, but not as much as becoming what she feared most.

The guards spoke in low tones, their words lost in the chamber's hollow acoustics. Gemini focused on controlling her breathing, the way she'd taught countless patients during difficult procedures. In, hold, out. Each breath threatened to give away their position, but panic would kill them faster than any blade.

Dust tickled her nose as more debris rained down from above. The urge to sneeze built with agonizing slowness. Gemini pressed her face into her sleeve, tears streaming down her cheeks as she fought against her body's natural response. Jayne's hand found hers in the darkness, squeezing gently - understanding without words.

One of the guards moved toward their hiding spot, armor creaking with each step. Gemini's heart seemed to stop altogether as his shadow fell across their alcove. She could smell the oil used to maintain his armor, hear the leather of his gloves flex as he gripped his weapon.

A crash echoed from somewhere above, followed by shouts and the distinctive crackle of magic. The guard's head snapped up, attention

him, more wraiths emerged, their corrupted magic pulsing through the ancient stones. His back hit the wall - nowhere left to retreat.

The elite guard's eyes gleamed with triumph through his helmet's visor. Rafe's sword arm trembled, muscles screaming from deflecting the relentless assault. Another of Liora's cries echoed through the ruins, and his heart clenched. He'd failed her.

A shadow dropped from above - Maya, moving like liquid darkness. Her daggers found gaps in the guard's armor with deadly precision. The man's triumphant look turned to shock as blood spurted from his throat.

"Move!" Maya grabbed Rafe's collar, yanking him aside as a wraith's spectral blade passed through the space where his head had been. The ghost-steel would have done worse than draw blood. They stumbled together down a side passage, the wraiths' haunting wails following.

Rafe's chest heaved as they ran. "Liora - I have to get to her." He tried to turn back, but Maya's grip was iron on his arm. More soldiers' shouts echoed from the direction they'd fled, along with the distinctive sound of Nero's magic clashing with something dark and ancient.

"You'll be no good to her dead," Maya hissed, pulling him around another corner. Her eyes darted to the shadows, tracking threats. "We need to regroup. This was a trap."

The ruins groaned around them, as if the very stones felt the corruption of the wraiths seeping in. Rafe's jaw clenched as he heard more fighting in the distance. Every instinct screamed at him to go back, to fight through to Liora, but Maya was right. He'd be cut down before he made it ten steps.

Another wraith phased through the wall ahead of them. Maya shoved Rafe down a different corridor, her daggers already in motion. "Run! I'll hold it off!" He hesitated for a heartbeat, then turned and sprinted into the darkness, Liora's name a prayer on his lips. He'd find another way to her. He had to.

Rafe's boots skidded on the ancient stones as Maya pulled him around another corner. His heart hammered against his ribs, each beat screaming at him to turn back. The wraith's otherworldly shriek echoed through the passage behind them, raising the hair on his neck.

"Derek and I found another way in when we followed them from Dunrow," Maya whispered, her grip still iron-tight on his arm. "We can circle around, come at them from behind." The certainty in her voice didn't match the tremor in her hand.

Blood from his wound trickled down his sleeve, each drop marking their path like breadcrumbs. Rafe clenched his jaw against the pain, forcing himself to think past the fog of exhaustion and worry. "How long have you been tracking them?" His voice came out rougher than intended.

Maya pressed them both flat against a wall as heavy footsteps thundered past an intersecting corridor. "Since they left the village. Derek spotted their scout first - they weren't as subtle as they thought." Her eyes met his in the dim light, hard with determination. "We called the General to help. You can still help her, Rafe, but not if you get yourself killed trying to break through their line."

The stones beneath Rafe's palm vibrated with the distant clash of magic - Nero's silverlight against something darker, more corrupt. He closed his eyes for a moment, remembering how Liora had felt in his arms just hours ago. Safe. Whole. Now she faced Draven's elite guard without him.

"Marcus is with her," Maya said, reading his expression. "And Nero's no slouch in a fight. We have to trust them." She tugged him forward again as another wraith's wail pierced the darkness behind them.

Rafe's sword felt heavier with each step away from Liora. The blood loss wasn't helping, making his head swim. But Maya's logic cut through his desperate need to charge back in - a suicide run wouldn't save anyone. "Tell me about this other entrance."

They descended a narrow staircase, the air growing thick with dust and decay. Maya moved with practiced silence, her daggers ready. "There's an old temple entrance, half-buried in sand. The troops didn't spot it - too focused on following your trail." A hint of pride crept into her voice.

A distant explosion shook loose debris from the ceiling. Rafe's heart lurched - was that Liora's magic? Or something worse? Maya's grip tightened on his arm, sensing his impulse to turn back. "Five more minutes," she promised. "Then we'll hit them from behind while they're focused on the main corridor."

The passage ahead split into three branches. Maya didn't hesitate, pulling him toward the rightmost path. Rafe forced his feet to follow, each step away from Liora feeling like a betrayal. But Maya's plan was their best chance - maybe their only chance - to turn this ambush around. He just prayed they wouldn't be too late.

If only something didn't nag at him in the back of his mind.

***

Golden light pulsed beneath Liora's skin as her eyes snapped open, heart hammering against her ribs. The space beside her held only cold emptiness where Rafe's warmth should have been. Metal scraped against stone outside - screams and clash of steel piercing the darkness.

Ethereal shapes oozed from the ancient walls, their translucent forms twisting into mockeries of warriors. Liora's magic flared instinctively, creating a barrier of shimmering gold between her and the wraiths. Her bare skin prickled with goosebumps as she scrambled for her clothes, never taking her eyes off the approaching spirits.

A familiar voice cried out in pain beyond the door - Marcus. Liora's magic surged stronger, responding to her fear for him. Another wraith lunged, passing through her shield like smoke before her power pushed it back, its hollow screech echoing off the stone walls.

"Hold them back!" Nero's command cut through the chaos, followed by Marcus's grunt of effort. Were they fighting more wraiths out there? Or something worse? Liora yanked her tunic over her head, hands trembling as she fought to focus her power.

The spirits pressed closer, their empty eyes fixed on her with haunting intensity. Her mother's energy coursed through her veins, instinct taking over as she wove dreams into weapons. Golden threads lashed out, dispersing two wraiths into wisps of shadow.

Heavy boots thundered down the corridor - too many sets to be friends. Elite guards. Draven's men. How had they found them? Liora's breath caught in her throat as she remembered Gemini and Jayne. Please let them be safe, she silently begged as she pulled on her boots.

Another wraith dove for her throat. Liora's magic exploded outward, shredding the spirit into nothing. But more emerged from the walls, an endless tide of nightmare fuel. Her power wouldn't last forever against this many.

The door handle rattled. Voices barked orders on the other side - Imperial voices. Liora gathered her magic close, ready to fight her way out if needed. She wouldn't let them take her, wouldn't let them use her power the way they'd tried to use her mother's.

A scream of pure agony ripped through the air - Marcus? Or Rafe? Liora's heart clenched as her magic responded, golden light blazing brighter. She had to get out there, had to help them. But the wraiths blocked her path to the door, their ghostly forms pressing closer despite her barrier.

Liora's magic thrummed beneath her skin, begging for release as she fought to contain it within the ancient walls of the Ember Ruins. The wraiths pressed closer, their hollow faces twisted in eternal agony. She couldn't risk unleashing her full power here - not when the ruins themselves seemed to pulse with volatile energy that could amplify her magic beyond control.

Golden threads of dream energy wove through her fingers as she carefully picked off the nearest spirits, trying to clear a path to the door. The haze of ghostly forms swirled thicker with each dispersed wraith, making it harder to see through the supernatural fog. Her power burned in her chest, demanding to be unleashed, but Liora gritted her teeth and held it back.

The door exploded inward in a shower of splinters. Liora's magic gathered instinctively before she recognized Nero's commanding presence. Behind him, Marcus stumbled, clutching his bloodied shoulder as he gasped for breath. Their faces were tight with urgency that made her stomach clench.

"Move!" Nero grabbed her arm, his grip steel as he pulled her toward the door. Chaos erupted around them as they emerged into the hall. Imperial guards in gleaming armor clashed with more wraiths, their weapons passing harmlessly through the spirits while ghostly blades left very real wounds. Blood already stained the ancient stones beneath their feet.

Marcus grunted in pain as he deflected a guard's sword with his good arm. His shoulder wound leaked fresh crimson down his chest. Liora's magic surged protectively, but she forced it back, knowing one wrong move could bring the unstable ruins down around them.

"This way!" Nero pulled them left, away from the thickest fighting. A wraith materialized through the wall beside them, its hollow screech piercing Liora's ears. She sent a careful tendril of power to push it back, just enough to clear their path without risking the ruins' reaction.

More guards rounded the corner ahead, their armor reflecting the ethereal glow of the wraiths. Liora's heart hammered against her ribs as she recognized the elite insignia on their breastplates. These were Draven's personal soldiers.

Marcus stumbled, his face pale from blood loss. Liora caught his uninjured arm, helping support his weight as they changed direction. The guard's shouts echoed behind them, mixed with the otherworldly wails of the wraiths.

Dream energy crackled along Liora's skin as another spirit lunged for them. She deflected it with the smallest push of power she dared use, feeling the ruins' energy pulse ominously in response. They had to get out of here before her magic triggered something worse than wraiths. But where were Rafe and the others? The thought of him facing these horrors alone made her power spike dangerously close to breaking free.

Liora's magic surged through her veins as another wraith emerged from the crumbling walls. The spirit's hollow eyes fixed on her with an unsettling familiarity that made her skin crawl. Behind her, Marcus's labored breathing reminded her of their desperate situation.

"Through here." Nero's voice carried a strange mix of reverence and urgency as he guided them down a narrow corridor. Ancient carvings lined the walls, their intricate patterns seeming to pulse with each flash of her power. "The altar chamber lies ahead - I spent years studying the Custodians' teachings within its walls."

The corridor opened into a circular room dominated by a weathered stone altar. Ghostly light filtered through cracks in the ceiling, casting eerie shadows that danced across the floor. Liora's magic responded to something ancient here, humming beneath her skin like a forgotten melody.

Three more wraiths materialized around them, their translucent forms twisting into battle stances. But as Liora reached out with her power, she sensed something different in these spirits - not just hatred and pain, but fragments of who they'd been before Draven's corruption. Her heart ached at the realization.

Golden threads of dream energy wove between her fingers as she focused on the nearest wraith. Instead of attacking, she gentle reached for the spark of humanity still trapped within its twisted form. The spirit's hollow eyes widened as her power touched it, its form shimmering with newfound awareness.

"That's it," Nero murmured, his own magic providing a steady anchor as she worked. "Free them from his control. Show them the way back to themselves." The wraith's form began to glow, its agonized expression softening as her power unraveled Draven's corruption.

Marcus positioned himself near the entrance, sword ready despite his injury. "More guards coming," he warned, voice tight with pain. "Whatever you're doing, do it fast." Blood still seeped from his shoulder, but his grip on his weapon remained steady.

Liora's power flowed stronger as she turned to the second wraith, finding the process easier now that she understood what she was looking for. This spirit had been a woman once - she could sense fragments of memories, of love and loss and sacrifice. The wraith's form blazed with golden light as she severed Draven's hold.

The third spirit fought against her magic, its form rippling with darkness that made her stomach churn. Sweat beaded on her forehead as she pushed harder, trying to reach past the corruption to the person

trapped within. Her power strained against Draven's influence, neither willing to yield.

Boots thundered in the corridor outside as Liora poured more
energy into freeing the spirit. The wraith's form flickered between
darkness and light, its screech of agony echoing off the ancient stones.
Marcus raised his sword as shadows appeared in the doorway, but
Liora couldn't spare attention for the approaching guards - not when
she was so close to breaking Draven's hold over another lost soul.

Golden light blazed through Liora's fingers as the third wraith finally yielded, its form dissolving into peaceful mist. But before relief
could settle, darkness gathered at the altar, coalescing into a towering
figure that made her magic recoil. The wraith knight's armor gleamed
with corrupted dream energy, its hollow eyes fixed on Nero with terrible recognition.

Her mentor's face drained of color as he stepped forward. "My
darkness," he whispered, voice heavy with ancient guilt. "My shame
given form. I feared this might happen." The wraith knight drew a
spectral blade that pulsed with the same corrupted power that had
nearly consumed Liora's own magic.

"Get her out of here," Nero commanded Marcus without taking
his eyes off the approaching knight. "This is my battle - the price of
my cowardice when I abandoned my post as Custodian." His hands
glowed with pale silver light as he raised them in a defensive stance.

Liora's protest died in her throat as armored figures burst through
the doorway. "Target acquired!" one shouted, his elite guard insignia
catching the ghostly light. "Secure the Dreamweaver!" Steel rasped
against leather as blades cleared sheaths.

Her magic surged instinctively, but Nero's sharp command cut
through her panic. "No! Your power could bring the ruins down on us

all." He deflected the wraith knight's first strike with a barrier of light. "Go! I'll hold them here."

Marcus grabbed her arm with his good hand, pulling her toward a half-hidden passage behind the altar. Guilt and fear warred in her chest as she glimpsed Nero standing alone against his past. The wraith knight's blade crashed against his defenses, dark energy spiderwebbing through the protective light.

"Stop them!" An elite guard's order sent his men charging forward, as the wraith knight pressed its advantage, its corrupted blade leaving trails of darkness in the air as it sought to break through Nero's weakening barrier. Liora had to help him.

Somehow, she had to.

# Nero's Regret

R afe stumbled through the crumbling passageway, his shoulder
scraping against rough stone as he followed Maya's flickering
torch. Blood trickled down his arm from where the elite guard's blade
had caught him, each step sending fresh waves of pain through his
body.

Maya moved like a shadow, her footsteps nearly silent despite their
hurried pace. The ruins groaned around them, ancient stones shifting
in ways that made Rafe's combat-honed instincts scream warnings.
Something felt wrong - more than just the obvious disaster unfolding
behind them.

"Wait," he gasped, pressing his palm against the wall to steady
himself. The stone felt warm beneath his touch, thrumming with an
energy that shouldn't have been there. His heart pounded against his
ribs as realization struck - Liora.

Maya turned back, her face half-hidden in shadow. "We don't have
time to rest, Delacroix. Those wraiths will be on us in minutes." Her

voice carried an edge he hadn't heard before, something that made the hair on the back of his neck rise.

The ground shuddered beneath their feet, sending cascades of dust raining from the ceiling. Rafe's fingers tightened around his sword hilt as golden light flared somewhere deep within the ruins, casting their shadows in multiple directions at once. Liora's magic - but twisted somehow, warped into something that felt fundamentally wrong.

"That's not possible," Maya muttered, her eyes widening as she stared back the way they'd come. "The General said she wouldn't be able to access that kind of power yet." The words slipped out before she could catch them, and Rafe saw her jaw clench in sudden tension.

Ice formed in Rafe's gut as pieces clicked into place - Maya's convenient arrival, her insistence on this particular escape route, the way she'd positioned herself between him and any path that might lead back to Liora. "The General," he repeated, his voice dropping to a dangerous whisper. "What exactly did the General order?"

Maya's hand dropped to her weapon, but Rafe was already moving. His blade cleared its sheath as he lunged forward, ignoring the protest of his wounded shoulder. Maya barely managed to deflect his strike, her eyes now holding a calculating coldness that confirmed his worst fears.

Another tremor rocked the passage, stronger this time. Stones began to fall around them as the very foundations of the ruins seemed to shake apart. Through it all, Rafe could feel Liora's power building to impossible levels, and with it came a soul-deep certainty that he'd made a terrible mistake in leaving her behind.

A chunk of ceiling crashed down between them, and Maya seized her chance. Her boot connected with Rafe's injured shoulder, sending white-hot agony lancing through his body. His sword clattered against stone as his grip failed.

Armored hands seized Rafe's arms before he could recover, yanking them behind his back with brutal efficiency. The elite guards' armor seemed to absorb the golden light still pulsing through the ruins, making them look like moving shadows.

Maya's torch illuminated her satisfied smirk as she retrieved his fallen blade. "You really should have just kept running, Delacroix." She tested the weapon's weight in her hand before sliding it into her own belt.

The guards dragged Rafe backward through the corridor, his boots scraping against debris. He struggled against their grip until one of them drove a gauntleted fist into his wounded shoulder, leaving him gasping and seeing stars.

Harsh sunlight assaulted his eyes as they emerged from the ruins. Through watering vision, Rafe made out masses of Imperial troops - far more than should have been possible given their remote location. Standards bearing Draven's crest fluttered in the hot desert wind.

Something wasn't right. The soldiers moved with practiced precision, but none made any aggressive moves toward him or the ruins. They simply held their positions, as if waiting for something. Or someone.

The realization hit Rafe like a physical blow. These weren't reinforcements arriving to attack - they were an escort, already in position. Which meant this entire assault had been coordinated long before they'd entered the ruins.

"Where's the General?" Maya called out to a nearby officer. Rafe's blood ran cold as pieces of the puzzle slotted into place.

The guards forced Rafe to his knees in the sand, but he barely noticed the pain. His eyes remained fixed on the crumbling ruins as golden light continued to pulse from within, each flash feeling like a knife in his chest. He'd failed her. Again.

The officer shifted his weight as he finally addressed Maya. "The General went down personally to retrieve the girl. Said something about her being too valuable to trust to anyone else."

Rafe's heart hammered against his ribs. Nero and Marcus were still down there - they'd protect Liora, help her escape. They had to. Nero's wisdom and Marcus's strength could give her the chance she needed to break free of whatever trap Varden had laid.

Golden light pulsed from the ruins again, stronger this time, and Rafe felt the desert itself seem to tremble. Something was wrong with that light - it carried an edge of darkness he'd never felt in Liora's magic before.

The sound of boots crunching on sand drew Rafe's attention. His stomach dropped as he saw Derek emerging from another entrance, leading a column of Imperial guards. Between them stumbled Jayne and Gemini, their hands bound behind their backs.

Gemini's eyes met his, wide with fear and confusion. A bruise was already darkening along her jaw, and Rafe's fingers curled into fists at his sides. Derek's betrayal shouldn't have surprised him - there had been too many coincidences, too many convenient moments of Imperial intervention.

The ruins shuddered again, and this time Rafe could hear screaming beneath the rumble of shifting stone. The sound carried notes of both rage and anguish that made his blood run cold. What were they doing to her down there?

Maya barked an order, and the guards yanked Rafe to his feet. His wounded shoulder screamed in protest, but he barely noticed the pain. All he could focus on was the way the golden light was starting to take on a sickly tinge around the edges.

"Cover him," Maya commanded, her voice tight with urgency. "The General doesn't want him seeing what comes next."

Rough hands forced a black cloth over Rafe's head, plunging him into darkness. The fabric was thick enough to block out even the intense flashes still emanating from the ruins, but it couldn't muffle the sounds.

Through the cloth, Rafe heard another scream - this one filled with such profound grief that it felt like a physical blow to his chest. Then the world seemed to explode with power, and everything went silent.

***

The wraith knight's blade crashed against Nero's barrier again, sending dark energy crackling across the chamber's ceiling. Liora's chest tightened as her own magic surged in response, threatening to break free. The underground chamber felt too small, too confining for the power building beneath her skin.

Marcus shoved her behind a fallen pillar as elite guards poured through the doorway. The passage that had promised escape now lay blocked, forcing them to watch as Nero faced down his past made manifest. Blood dripped from Marcus's injured shoulder onto the ancient stones, but his grip on her arm remained firm, anchoring her when every instinct screamed to help her mentor.

Silver light flared as Nero deflected another strike, but Liora saw the tremor in his hands, the way his barrier flickered with each impact. The wraith knight's corrupted blade left trails of darkness in its wake, each slash eating away at Nero's defenses like acid through cloth. Her magic pushed against her control, resonating with the darkness that filled the chamber.

"We have to help him," Liora whispered, golden energy dancing between her fingers. But Marcus's grip tightened, his eyes fixed on the hairline cracks spreading across the chamber's ceiling with each clash of power. One wrong move, one burst of uncontrolled magic, and tons of ancient stone would bury them all. The elite guards seemed to realize this too, hanging back as the two powerful beings dueled.

The wraith knight's blade found a gap in Nero's defense, drawing a line of blood across his arm. Her mentor stumbled, his barrier flickering dangerously thin. Dark energy pulsed from the spirit's armor, and Liora felt an answering surge in her own power. The walls seemed to press closer, the air growing thick with conflicting magics. They needed to act soon - but one wrong move would bring the ruins down around them.

Liora watched in horror as Nero stumbled back, blood dripping from his arm. The wraith knight's corrupted blade hummed with dark energy that made her skin crawl. Her magic surged against her control, wanting to help, to protect, but Marcus's iron grip kept her behind the fallen pillar.

"You couldn't save her," the wraith's hollow voice echoed through the chamber, its words cutting deeper than any blade. "You failed her, just as you'll fail this one." The spirit's armor shifted, revealing glimpses of a familiar face - Liora's mother.

Nero's barrier flickered, his shoulders sagging under the weight of old guilt. But then something changed in his stance. His spine straightened, and the tremor in his hands stilled. "No," he said, voice steady despite the blood staining his sleeve. "Lyra made her choice. She knew what had to be done."

The wraith knight charged, its blade a blur of corrupted energy. Nero met the attack with renewed purpose, his silver magic blazing bright enough to cast stark shadows across the ancient walls. Their powers clashed in a display that made Liora's teeth ache, the very air seeming to vibrate with competing energies.

Stone cracked overhead as Nero drove the wraith back, each blast of power more controlled, more focused than before. "I couldn't save her," he acknowledged, deflecting another strike. "But that was never my role to play. She chose her path, and I choose mine."

Golden light erupted from Nero's hands, wrapping around the wraith like chains of pure energy. The spirit struggled, its armor creaking as Nero's power sought the corrupted core of its being. "I honor her choice," Nero declared, "by protecting what she died to save."

The chamber filled with blinding light as Nero poured everything he had into one final surge of power. Liora felt the moment the corruption broke, felt the rush of relief as another lost soul found peace. The wraith knight's armor collapsed with a thunderous crash, empty now of the spirit that had powered it.

Nero swayed on his feet, drained but standing tall. The elite guards tensed, weapons raised, but uncertainty showed in their stance.

"Master Thorne!" Liora called out as Nero's knees buckled. She broke free from Marcus's grip, magic ready to defend her mentor. But Nero waved her back, his eyes fixed on the unstable ceiling above them.

Liora's heart hammered against her ribs as Draven's elite guard fanned out around them, their black armor gleaming in the flickering light of her magic, a half-dozen crossbows now trained on their small group.

The ruins groaned overhead, a constant reminder of their precarious position. Her power thrummed beneath her skin, begging for release, but she couldn't risk it. Not here. Not with tons of ancient stone ready to collapse at the slightest provocation.

Blood dripped from Nero's arm, each drop echoing in the tense silence. He stood between her and the guards, shoulders squared despite his exhaustion. Marcus pressed against her back, his breathing ragged from his own wound, but his presence steadied her racing thoughts.

They were trapped, cornered like animals, and her magic could do nothing but watch.

A slow clap echoed through the chamber, making Liora's skin crawl. General Varden emerged from the shadows, his polished boots clicking against ancient stone as he approached.

"No," she muttered, shocked to her core. Her heart thundered against her ribs as disbelief coursed through her veins.

"I must admit, Master Thorne, that was quite the display of power." Varden's smile didn't reach his eyes as he circled their group. "Though I expected nothing less from someone who failed to protect Lyra Solari." His gaze shifted to Liora, cold and calculating. "Like mentor, like student, I suppose."

Marcus spat blood at Varden's feet. "Traitor!" The words drew a flash of rage across Varden's features before his mask of control slipped back into place.

"Traitor?" Varden's laugh held no warmth. "I chose the winning side, Marcus. While you rebels chase fairy tales and prophecies, Draven offers real power." He turned to Liora, his voice dropping to a dangerous whisper. "Power you could have shared, if you weren't so afraid of your own potential."

Nero stepped forward despite his wounds, silver magic crackling around his hands. "The only thing Draven offers is corruption and death." Blood dripped from his sleeve as he positioned himself between Liora and Varden. "But then again, you always did prefer the easy path to power, didn't you, Kael?"

Liora's magic coiled inside her like a trapped storm as Varden stepped closer, his boots echoing against ancient stone. The torchlight caught the insignia on his chest - the same one she'd trusted, the same one that had promised safety for her people. Her power pulsed in response to his proximity, and she fought to keep it contained as debris crumbled from the ceiling.

"You've shown such promise, Liora." Varden's voice carried the same hollow warmth she remembered from Twilight. "The Emperor sees it too. Lead us to the Veilstone, take your rightful place in his court, and your friends will be spared." He gestured to where Nero stood bleeding, to Marcus's labored breathing behind her. "You could have everything - safety, security, the chance to truly master your powers without fear."

The offer slithered through her mind like poison. Images flashed before her - Eldara in flames, villagers screaming as darkness consumed them, her own magic spiraling out of control. Would serving Draven really keep everyone safe? Her power flickered between her fingers as she glanced at Nero, saw the faith in his eyes despite his wounds. The faith she'd earned.

"And if I refuse?" The words tasted like ash in her mouth. Golden light danced across her skin, responding to the anger building in her chest. How dare he stand there, offering false mercy after his betrayal?

Varden's smile turned cruel as he drew his sword. "Then you'll watch them die, one by one, knowing their blood stains your hands. And in the end, you'll lead us to the Veilstone anyway." The blade gleamed in the torchlight as he pressed it against Nero's throat. "The choice is yours, Liora. But choose quickly - I'm not known for my patience."

Golden light exploded from Liora's hands as fury and betrayal crystallized into raw power. "I choose them," she snarled, her magic surging outward in a wave that knocked Varden away from Nero. The ceiling groaned above them, ancient stone shifting ominously, but she couldn't stop now. Not with everything at stake.

The chamber erupted into chaos. Crossbow bolts whistled through the air as elite guards opened fire. Liora's barrier flickered into existence just in time, the golden shield absorbing the deadly projectiles. But the effort drained her, each impact sending tremors through her arms. Nero's silver magic joined hers, strengthening the barrier even as blood continued to drip from his wound.

Marcus lunged forward, his blade finding gaps in the guards' armor with deadly precision. Pride and fear warred in Liora's chest as she watched him fight - pride at his skill, fear for his safety. She reached for her power again, ready to help, when Varden's voice cut through the chaos. "Take them down!"

The warning cry died in her throat. Time seemed to slow as Varden's blade sliced through the air. Marcus turned too late, his eyes widening in shock as the sword plunged into his chest. The sickening sound of steel meeting flesh echoed off the ancient walls.

"No!" Liora's scream tore through the chamber as Marcus crumpled to the ground, blood pooling beneath him.

Power surged through her veins, raw and uncontrolled. Golden light pulsed from her skin as Marcus's blood stained the stones. The ceiling cracked above them, chunks of rock raining down as her magic responded to her grief. Varden's satisfied smirk burned into her memory as he pulled his blade free. Marcus's eyes found hers, filled with pain and something else - trust, even now. His lips moved, forming words she couldn't hear over the roar of her power, before his head fell back against the blood-stained floor.

The world exploded in golden light as Liora's magic erupted, raw power tearing through her veins like liquid fire. She felt Marcus's blood stain her hands as if she had killed him herself, his final expression of trust burning behind her eyes. The chamber shuddered as her power lashed out, sending elite guards flying into ancient walls with sickening crunches.

"Liora, stop!" Nero's voice barely penetrated the roaring in her ears. Her mentor's silver magic tried to contain her fury, but she shrugged it off like paper in a storm. Nothing mattered except making Varden pay. The traitor's smug expression had vanished, replaced by the first flickers of fear as her power wrapped around him in writhing tendrils of gold.

Her consciousness slammed into Varden's mind with the force of a battering ram. His mental defenses crumbled beneath her assault as she pushed deeper, past the surface thoughts of terror and into the dark corners where his true self lurked. Images flashed through her awareness - his childhood fears, his desperate grab for power, his betrayal of everything he'd once held dear.

Blood trickled from Varden's nose as he struggled against her invasion. This went beyond anything she'd been taught, beyond even what Draven did to his puppets. She didn't want to control Varden - she wanted to unmake him, to tear apart the very essence of who he was until nothing remained but empty flesh.

The chamber's foundations groaned as her power continued to build. Somewhere distant, she heard Nero shouting her name, felt Marcus's cooling blood beneath her feet. But all she could focus on was the feeling of Varden's mind splintering beneath her assault, his memories fracturing like glass under her relentless pressure.

Varden's screams echoed off the ancient walls as she pushed deeper, golden light pouring from his eyes and mouth. His betrayal had cost Marcus his life - her friend, who had believed in her despite his fears. She would ensure nothing remained of the man who had destroyed that trust.

Her magic surged through Varden's consciousness, seeking out every trace of who he had been. Childhood memories dissolved like smoke.

"Liora, this isn't you!" Nero's voice cracked with desperation. "Don't let vengeance corrupt what your mother died to protect!" The words barely registered through her fury, but something in them tugged at her conscience. Would her mother have wanted this? To see her daughter become something worse than what she'd fought against?

Varden's body convulsed as his mind continued to fragment. His eyes rolled back, showing only gold where pupils should be. She could feel him trying to scream, but his voice had long since given out. Soon there would be nothing left - no memories, no personality, no soul. Just an empty shell where General Kael Varden had once existed.

Golden light pulsed through Liora's veins as she held Varden's mind in her grasp. His consciousness splintered beneath her power, memories dissolving like dawn's mist. The ruins trembled around them, but she couldn't stop - not after what he'd done to Marcus. Her friend's blood still stained the ancient stones, his final expression of trust burned into her memory.

Through the haze of her fury, she heard Nero calling her name. His silver magic wrapped around her like a protective embrace, trying to pull her back from the edge. The pressure of his power against hers felt like a lifeline in a storm, reminding her of who she was meant to be. Her grip on Varden's mind wavered as Nero's words penetrated her rage.

The moment's hesitation cost everything. Varden's body jerked, his eyes clearing just enough to show a flash of triumph. Before Liora could react, he twisted away from her magical grip, silver blade glinting in the golden light. Time seemed to slow as she watched the steel arc through the air, finding its mark in Nero's unprotected back.

"I should have done this years ago," Varden snarled, driving the blade deeper. Blood bloomed across Nero's chest like a crimson flower as her mentor's silver magic flickered and died. His eyes met hers, filled with pain and something else - not disappointment, but faith. Even now, he believed in her.

Power erupted from Liora's core as Nero collapsed, her scream of rage drowning out Varden's cruel laughter. Golden light exploded outward in a wave of pure energy, slamming into walls already weakened by their battle. The ceiling groaned overhead as ancient stone shifted, but she didn't care anymore. Let it all come crashing down.

Golden energy tore through Liora's veins like molten fire as her magic exploded outward, shattering ancient columns and sending Varden's troops scrambling for cover. The ruins trembled around her, dust and debris raining down as her power lashed out in waves of raw grief. Her consciousness stretched beyond its limits, seeking Varden's mind again, but he had already retreated beyond her reach.

Through tear-blurred vision, she watched the traitor and his men disappear into the shadows of a crumbling passage. Her legs gave out beneath her as the last of her strength drained away, leaving her collapsed beside Nero's body. Blood soaked into her clothes - she couldn't tell anymore if it was his or Marcus's or her own. The metallic scent filled her nose, mixing with the dust that choked the air.

The ceiling groaned overhead, ancient stone shifting as her magic continued to pulse weakly through the chamber. Nero's unseeing eyes stared past her, that final look of faith frozen on his face. She reached for him with trembling fingers, desperate to find some spark of life, but his skin felt cold beneath her touch. The silver magic that had always surrounded him like an aura had vanished completely.

Marcus lay crumpled nearby, his blood painting elaborate patterns across the stone floor. He looked smaller somehow, younger, the fierce warrior replaced by something fragile and broken. Her fault. They had died protecting her, believing in her, and she had failed them both. The weight of that knowledge pressed against her chest until she could barely breathe.

Stone crashed down around her as the ruins began to collapse in earnest. Liora curled around Nero's body, her magic flickering weakly as she tried to shield them from the falling debris. But she had nothing left to give. Darkness crept at the edges of her vision as exhaustion dragged at her limbs. The last thing she saw before consciousness fled was a shaft of golden light breaking through the dusty air, illuminating the faces of those she had failed to save.

# The Whispering Woods

G olden light pulsed beneath Liora's skin as grief tore through her chest. The weight of Nero's cooling body pressed against her legs, grounding her in a reality she no longer wanted to face. Power surged through her veins, different from before - not the violent explosion of rage, but something deeper. Ancient. Her consciousness stretched beyond the physical world as she surrendered to the crushing despair.

The ruins dissolved around her, stone walls melting into swirling mists of silver and gold. The metallic scent of blood faded, replaced by the sharp tang of ozone and starlight. Her body felt lighter, almost translucent, as if she existed between heartbeats. Was this death? The thought brought no fear, only a hollow acceptance.

But the darkness didn't claim her. Instead, reality shifted and re-formed like clay beneath a sculptor's hands. The air hummed with possibility, thick with untapped potential. Through tear-blurred vision, Liora watched as golden threads of energy wove themselves into familiar shapes - the mill in Eldara, Bennet's smile, her mother's garden. Not memories, but something more tangible. More real.

The Dreamscape. She had crossed into it without sleeping, without the usual barriers between worlds. Power thrummed through her core, different from anything Nero had taught her. This wasn't about controlling dreams or bending them to her will. This was about becoming the bridge between worlds, letting reality reshape itself through her grief. Golden light spilled from her fingertips, painting new constellations across the ethereal sky.

The golden threads of the Dreamscape dissolved like morning mist, leaving Liora standing in a vast chamber that stretched beyond sight. Ancient stone pillars rose into darkness, their surfaces etched with flowing script that pulsed with a familiar energy. Her footsteps echoed across worn flagstones as she moved deeper into the temple's heart, each step carrying the weight of prophecy.

Pain lanced through her chest with every breath, memories of Nero's final moments threatening to overwhelm her. But something pulled her forward - a resonance that sang through her bones and made her power flutter beneath her skin. The temple felt alive, watching her progress with the weight of centuries. Was this what her mother had seen, in those final days before facing Draven?

A massive doorway loomed ahead, its surface carved with intricate patterns that seemed to shift and flow like water. The air grew thick with power, pressing against her skin like storm-heavy clouds. Her heart thundered in her chest as she recognized the symbols - the same ones that had marked the stone in Eldara's forest, the ones that had first awakened her power. They pulled at something deep within her core, demanding recognition.

Lyra Solari stood before her, silver hair floating in an unfelt breeze, her presence both comforting and overwhelming. The woman's eyes held wisdom, and something else - a profound sadness that made Liora's heart ache. Her mother had given everything to be here.

"You've finally allowed yourself to see," Lyra's voice resonated through the chamber, each word carrying layers of meaning that settled into Liora's consciousness like falling snow. "The path has always been here, waiting."

Questions tumbled through Liora's mind, fighting for precedence. About her mother, about the Veilstone, about her own destiny. But what emerged was simpler, more fundamental: "Why me?"

Lyra's smile held both warmth and sorrow. "The gift chooses its bearer, dear one. Your fear wasn't weakness - it was wisdom. You saw through Kael Varden, but you did not allow yourself to accept it. But now you understand that power without purpose is like a storm without direction."

The runes on the nearest pillar flared brighter, casting Lyra's face in sharp relief. Liora saw then how much they resembled each other - the same determined set of the jaw, the same questioning look in their eyes.

The symbols on the temple walls pulsed brighter as Lyra glided forward, her ethereal form casting no shadow despite the otherworldly light. Liora followed, her footsteps echoing against the ancient stone while her mother's made no sound at all.

A massive archway loomed ahead, its surface carved with intricate patterns that seemed to shift and dance whenever Liora tried to focus on them. The air grew thicker here, heavy with the weight of centuries of dreams.

"I don't know where to find the Veilstone, even though it keeps calling to me," Liora's voice wavered slightly. "You found it, didn't you?"

"The Whispering Woods have opened to you, child," Lyra's voice took on an urgent edge. "There, you will find a hidden entrance to a place forgotten by all but the oldest dreams. The Veilstone awaits you."

A distant rumble shook the temple foundations, sending cascades of glittering dust raining down around them. The dreamscape was becoming unstable, their time growing short.

Lyra reached out, her hand passing through Liora's cheek in a gesture that felt like a cool breeze. "Be careful, my daughter. The path to the Veilstone is treacherous - not just because of what lies ahead, but because of what lies within."

The rumbling intensified, and the temple walls began to blur at the edges. Liora could feel the dream starting to fade, reality tugging at her consciousness like an insistent tide.

Through the growing haze, she caught one last glimpse of her mother's face - proud, worried, and filled with a love that transcended even death. The runes flashed once more, searing their ancient wisdom into Liora's mind before the dreamscape dissolved completely around her.

Liora's eyes snapped open, dust and debris raining down as consciousness slammed back into her. Golden light still pulsed beneath her skin, a protective dome shimmering around her and the bodies of her fallen friends. The magic that had exploded outward had somehow curved back to shield them, preserving what remained of Nero and Marcus in death's terrible stillness.

Her legs trembled as she pushed herself up, tears cutting clean tracks through the grime on her face. Nero's peaceful expression twisted something deep in her chest - he looked as if he were merely sleeping, though the blood staining his robes told a different story. Marcus lay nearby, his young face forever frozen in determination, the wound from Varden's blade stark against his chest.

Rubble stretched in every direction, the ancient ruins reduced to little more than scattered stone and memories. Her power had torn through the temple like a golden storm, leaving nothing but destruction in its wake. The thought of Varden made bile rise in her throat - had he escaped? Or was his body buried somewhere beneath the chaos she'd unleashed?

"Gemini?" Her voice cracked as she called out, the name echoing off broken pillars. "Rafe?" Nothing but silence answered, broken only by the settling of displaced stones. Fear clawed at her throat - had they made it out? Or had her magic...? No. She couldn't let herself think about that possibility.

Liora stumbled forward, picking her way through the devastation. Her boots crunched over shattered tile and splintered wood, each step carrying her further from the friends she couldn't save. Guilt pressed against her ribs like a physical weight, but she forced herself to keep moving. She had to find the others.

The pre-dawn air hit her face as she emerged from what remained of the temple entrance, and Liora froze. Where there should have been endless dunes of the Ashen Desert stretching toward the horizon, an impossible sight greeted her instead.

Trees. Hundreds of them, their ancient trunks wider than houses, stretched upward until their branches disappeared into mist. Leaves in impossible shades of silver and gold rustled in a wind she couldn't feel. The Whispering Woods - they shouldn't be here, couldn't be here. Yet somehow they had manifested, as if called forth by her power or her mother's guidance.

The forest seemed to breathe, an ancient presence that pressed against her consciousness. Whispers drifted between the trees, too faint to make out but carrying an undercurrent of urgent purpose. This was where her mother had led her - the path to the Veilstone lay somewhere in those mysterious depths.

Her feet carried her forward before conscious thought could intervene, drawn by both hope and destiny. The first step past the tree line sent a shiver of power through her body, and the whispers grew louder. Whatever waited in these woods - friends or foes, answers or more questions - Liora knew with bone-deep certainty that this was where she needed to be.

***

The temple emerged from the mist like a ghost, its weathered stone columns rising through tangles of ancient vines. Liora's breath caught in her throat as moonlight filtered through the canopy, casting strange patterns across worn carvings that spiraled up the temple's face. Her power hummed beneath her skin, responding to the sacred energy that saturated every stone.

Crumbling steps led to a massive doorway, its arch decorated with symbols that seemed to shift and dance in her peripheral vision. When she tried to focus on them directly, they settled into familiar patterns - the same ancient language she'd seen in her dreams, telling stories of Dreamweavers long past.

Twin statues flanked the entrance, their features worn smooth by centuries of wind and rain. Yet their eyes remained sharp, seeming to track her movements as she approached. One held an orb that pulsed with a faint, golden light; the other clutched a blade wreathed in shadow. Choice and consequence, power and protection - the duality of dream magic carved in stone.

The temple's walls stretched upward, disappearing into the darkness above. Impossibly tall windows punctuated the stone, their colored glass long since shattered. What remained cast prismatic shadows across the ground, like tears frozen in time. The air grew thicker as Liora moved closer, heavy with the weight of forgotten memories and ancient power.

Recognition struck her like lightning. This was the temple from the dreamscape - every detail exactly as she'd seen it with Lyra. The pillars wrapped in starlight, the runes that seemed to breathe with their own life, even the way shadows pooled in the corners like liquid darkness. Her mother had been showing her the way all along, leading her to this moment.

Moss-covered tiles formed intricate patterns across the floor, spiraling toward a central altar that stood bathed in moonlight streaming through a hole in the domed ceiling. Unlike the rest of the temple, the altar looked untouched by time - its polished surface gleaming as if it had been tended only yesterday.

The walls held massive murals, their colors still vibrant despite their age. They depicted the history of the Dreamweavers - their rise, their fall, and the prophecy that spoke of one who would either save or doom them all. Liora's hand trembled as she traced the image of a solitary figure holding what could only be the Veilstone, wondering if she was looking at her own fate.

A soft breeze whispered through the temple, carrying the scent of old magic and something else - something familiar. It reminded her of summer flowers and gentle hands braiding her hair, of comfort and safety and home. Her mother's presence lingered here, as if some part of Lyra had been waiting for her daughter to find this place.

Energy thrummed through the stone beneath her feet, responding to her presence. The temple itself seemed to wake, stirring from
centuries of slumber. Runes began to glow along the walls, their light
spreading like veins of gold through ancient rock. This place knew her,
recognized her bloodline, her purpose.

Liora's footsteps echoed through the vast chamber, each sound
rippling back to her like waves in a still pond. The temple's air hung
thick with ancient magic, making her skin tingle as she traced the path
she'd walked so many times in her dreams.

Worn stone columns stretched into darkness above, their surfaces
etched with spiraling patterns that seemed to move in the corner of
her vision. When she turned to look directly at them, they stilled, as if
playing some ancient game of statues with her presence.

Her heart thundered against her ribs as she followed the pull of
power deeper into the temple's depths. The familiar path from her
dreams took on new weight in reality, each step carrying her closer to
what she'd seen so many times with Lyra's guidance.

A soft glow beckoned from an archway ahead, drawing her forward
like a moth to flame. The shadowed chamber beyond felt both foreign
and achingly familiar, as if she'd walked this path in another life.

The Veilstone hovered above its pedestal in the chamber's heart,
bathing the room in ethereal light that pulsed like a sleeping heartbeat.
Its surface rippled with colors she had no names for, each wave sending
whispers of power through her bones.

This moment felt too simple, too clean. After everything - the
prophecies, the warnings, the trials - here sat the Veilstone, unguarded
and waiting. Her mother's voice echoed in her memory, warning of
deceptions hidden in plain sight.

The chamber's shadows seemed to deepen, pulling away from the Veilstone's light as if retreating from its power. Or perhaps gathering, preparing for something she couldn't yet see.

Sweat beaded on her forehead despite the chamber's chill. Everything she'd learned from Nero screamed that power never came without price, that easy paths often led to the hardest falls.

The stone steps felt worn beneath Liora's feet as she crossed the threshold into the inner chamber, centuries of footfalls having smoothed deep grooves into the ancient rock. Ancient magic thrummed through the air, making her skin prickle with awareness, raising goosebumps along her arms. The Veilstone's light painted shifting patterns across weathered walls, its glow intensifying as she drew closer, casting her shadow in multiple directions at once.

Her heart thundered against her ribs as memories of Nero's warnings echoed in her mind, each beat seeming to match the pulse of light before her. Power always demanded sacrifice. The question was whether she could bear its cost, whether she was truly ready for what claiming the Veilstone would mean. The stone pulsed in response to her presence, its ethereal light dancing like captured starfire, beckoning her forward with promises of strength beyond measure.

Shadows retreated from her path as she approached the hovering stone, yet something about their movement felt deliberate, almost watchful. They seemed to gather in the corners, coalescing into deeper patches of darkness that defied the stone's radiance. The chamber itself seemed to hold its breath, waiting to see what choice she would make, the very air growing thick with anticipation.

Each step brought fresh waves of energy washing over her skin, like walking through invisible curtains of power. The Veilstone's energy called to something deep within her, resonating with her own abilities in a way that felt both familiar and foreign, sending whispers of power through her bones. Like recognizing a face in a dream, only to find it changed upon waking, the stone's magic sang to her blood while simultaneously setting her teeth on edge with its otherworldly nature.

The prophecy's words whispered through her thoughts: liberation or tyranny, salvation or destruction. All hanging on the intent in her heart when she claimed this power. The weight of that choice pressed down on her shoulders like a physical thing.

Sweat beaded on her forehead despite the chamber's chill. The Veilstone's light seemed to pulse in time with her heartbeat now, as if already forging a connection. Yet there was resistance too, a sense of being measured, judged.

Her hands trembled as she raised them toward the stone. This was what she'd fought for, what Nero had died protecting. The key to either mastering her powers or being consumed by them. There would be no turning back from this moment.

The air grew thick with potential, making each breath feel like drawing in liquid light. Static electricity danced across her skin as the chamber's atmosphere became almost syrupy with magical energy. The Veilstone's power reached out to her in gossamer threads, tentative tendrils of ancient magic testing her resolve, her worthiness to wield what it offered, probing for any weakness in her determination.

"This is it," she whispered to the watching darkness, her fingers trembling in the ethereal glow. "The key to control... or the path to ruin. I have to choose." Her voice sounded strange in the chamber's heavy silence, as if the very air absorbed her words, turning them into echoes of possibility that rippled through the space between worlds.

Time seemed to slow as she stretched out her hand that final distance, each heartbeat lasting an eternity. The Veilstone's surface rippled like disturbed water at her touch, its crystalline structure seeming to melt and reform beneath her fingertips. Its light flared brilliant white, casting stark shadows that danced across the chamber walls. Power surged through the connection, raw and ancient and overwhelming in its intensity, flooding every nerve with the accumulated magic of centuries. Then everything changed.

# The Veilstone

The Veilstone's brilliance faded to absolute darkness, leaving Liora suspended in a void where even her own body seemed to vanish. Her mother's voice echoed through the emptiness, carrying the weight of prophecy and promise.

"Look beyond the veil, to what is beneath." Lyra's words rippled through the darkness like stones dropped in still water. The void shifted, revealing glimpses of memory - or perhaps possibility - that flickered past too quickly to grasp.

Power thrummed through Liora's awareness, raw and ancient. It felt different from her previous encounters with dream magic, more primal somehow. This wasn't just about wielding power - it was about understanding its source, its true nature beneath the surface.

The darkness pressed against her consciousness, testing her resolve. Was this what her mother had faced in her final moments? Had she too stood at this precipice between mastery and madness, trying to pierce the veil between what was and what could be?

The darkness rippled and took form, solidifying into a scene that made Liora's heart stutter. She stood atop Draven's tower in Somnara, but not as herself - as a witness to what could be.

The Eclipse of Dreams hung above, casting its ethereal glow across the city. Dream energy pulsed through the air like a living thing, responding to the celestial alignment that would amplify its power beyond measure.

Draven stood at the tower's edge, his dark robes billowing in the wind as he held the Ark of Dreams aloft. Its crystalline surface caught the Eclipse's light, fracturing it into thousands of shadow-tinged rays that rained down upon the city below.

But what made Liora's blood run cold wasn't Draven - it was the figure standing beside him. Another version of herself, but twisted, corrupted by power and ambition. This dark reflection wore an expression of cold satisfaction as she wielded the Veilstone with casual brutality.

Below them, the citizens of Somnara writhed as dream magic wrapped around them like chains. The other Liora raised her hand, and the Veilstone pulsed in response, amplifying Draven's control over the population.

"Beautiful, isn't it?" the dark Liora purred, her voice carrying an edge that made the real Liora's skin crawl. "All that fear of power, when we should have embraced it from the start."

Draven turned to his protégé with approval in his eyes. "You've learned well," he said. "Together, we'll reshape Somnus into what it should have been - a realm where dreams serve order, not chaos."

The citizens below began to still, their movements becoming mechanical and uniform as their wills were stripped away. The other Liora watched with satisfaction, as if their suffering was nothing more than a necessary step toward some greater purpose.

Through it all, Liora felt the weight of choice pressing down on her. This wasn't just a vision - it was a warning, a glimpse of what she could become if she let fear drive her toward control rather than protection.

The dark reflection's eyes glittered with an unnatural light as she stepped closer, the Veilstone pulsing in rhythm with her movements. Her voice carried the seductive promise of absolute power, wrapping around Liora like silk-covered steel.

"Look at them," Dark Liora whispered, gesturing to the citizens below. "No more chaos. No more pain. One command, and all their suffering ends." The words slithered through Liora's mind, carrying echoes of every doubt she'd ever harbored.

The Veilstone in Dark Liora's hands flared brighter, its faceted surface reflecting possibilities - a unified Somnus, a world without rebellion or resistance, peace enforced through absolute control. The vision was terrifyingly beautiful in its simplicity.

Draven stood at the tower's edge, a dark sentinel watching the exchange with calculating eyes. His presence served as a stark reminder of where this path led, of power corrupted by the very fear it sought to control.

"Think of Eldara," Dark Liora continued, her voice softening with false sympathy. "If you'd had this power then, you could have protected everyone. No more hiding, no more running." The words struck deep, touching the wound that still ached in Liora's heart.

The Eclipse's light seemed to dim as Dark Liora extended her hand, offering the Veilstone. Its surface rippled with dream energy, promising answers to every question that had haunted Liora since her powers first manifested.

"One choice," Dark Liora purred. "That's all it takes. Take the power. Use it. Show them all that you're not weak - that you can bring the peace they never could." The air grew thick with possibility, with the weight of destiny hanging in balance.

The vision pulled at Liora's core, whispering promises of certainty and control. Her dark reflection's words resonated with a truth she'd tried to deny - how often had she wished for the power to protect those she loved, no matter the cost?

The Veilstone pulsed in Dark Liora's outstretched hand, its faceted surface reflecting fragments of possibility. A world without fear, without doubt, where her powers served a clear purpose. The promise felt intoxicating, like sweet poison sliding through her veins.

Memories of Eldara's destruction flickered through her mind, tinged with the bitter taste of helplessness. If she'd had this kind of power then, could she have saved them all? The thought wrapped around her heart like thorned vines, squeezing until she could barely breathe.

Dark Liora's smile widened, reading the conflict in her expression. "You feel it, don't you?" she purred. "The rightness of it. The clarity." The words echoed with seductive certainty, each syllable striking a chord of longing in Liora's chest.

The vision shifted, and suddenly Rafe materialized beside Dark Liora. His eyes held that same intensity Liora remembered from their night together in the ruins, but something was wrong. The fire in them seemed hollow, manufactured, like a perfect reflection without depth.

Dark Liora's fingers trailed down Rafe's chest, and his body responded with mechanical precision. "Remember how he made you feel?" she whispered, her voice dripping with dark promise. The air grew thick with dream energy as memories of passion flooded through Liora - the heat of Rafe's skin, the pressure of his lips, the way he'd felt inside her.

The Veilstone pulsed, and suddenly Liora felt everything - every touch, every kiss, every moment of ecstasy amplified a thousandfold. Dark Liora's power wrapped around her like a lover's embrace, showing her how easy it would be to have this forever. To never lose him, to keep him bound to her through dreams and desire until the end of time.

The Eclipse's light seemed to bend around them, creating a cocoon of shadow and possibility. Liora took a step forward, drawn by an inexorable pull. The air between her and her dark reflection shimmered with potential, with the promise of unity and purpose.

The Veilstone's energy reached out to her, familiar yet foreign, like looking into a mirror and seeing a stranger's eyes staring back. Dark Liora's form began to blur at the edges, as if ready to merge with her, to make them whole.

Power thrummed through the air, making Liora's skin tingle with anticipation. One step closer, and she could end the struggle. No more doubt, no more fear of losing control. Just pure, focused purpose.

The citizens below continued their mechanical movements, a living testament to the peace that absolute control could bring. Their vacant expressions should have horrified her, but in that moment, they seemed almost peaceful - free from the burden of choice.

Liora reached out, her fingers inches from the Veilstone's surface. Dark Liora's smile turned triumphant as their reflections began to blur together, the line between what she was and what she could become growing thinner with each heartbeat.

Rafe moved toward her, and Liora suddenly saw the truth beneath the perfect surface. His movements were too smooth, too practiced - a puppet dancing on dream-forged strings. The passion in his eyes was an illusion, carefully crafted to match her deepest desires. This wasn't love - it was imprisonment dressed up in beautiful lies.

The real Rafe would never submit so completely, would never let his fire be tamed into such careful obedience. He was wild and fierce and free, and the thought of breaking that spirit, of turning him into this hollow reflection of himself, made bile rise in Liora's throat. The Veilstone's promise turned to ash in her mouth as she watched Dark Liora puppet him through another perfect, soulless kiss.

The Veilstone's surface rippled like dark water, and suddenly Liora's hand froze mid-reach. A different kind of warmth bloomed in her chest - the memory of Gemini's laughter during their shared meals in Eldara, of quiet evenings spent weaving flower crowns while trading stories of their dreams.

Rafe's face flashed through her mind, not with the calculated approval her dark reflection offered, but with genuine trust and affection. The way he'd looked at her before, believing not in her power, but in her heart.

The memories came faster now, a cascade of moments that defined her. Bennet teaching her to grind grain at the mill, his patience never wavering even when her frustration sparked uncontrolled bursts of power. The village children who once brought her wildflowers, unafraid despite knowing she was different.

The Dreamweavers hadn't been tyrants or saviors - they had been guardians, understanding that true power lay in the choice to serve rather than rule.

Nero's voice cut through the seductive whispers of her dark reflection: "You're more than a weapon, Liora. Remember that." His voice carried the weight of wisdom bought with sacrifice, of faith paid for in blood.

The vision of enslaved citizens below shifted, and Liora saw them as they truly were - not peaceful, but hollow. Empty vessels stripped of the very dreams that made them human. This wasn't protection; it was extinction of the spirit.

Dark Liora's smile faltered as the Veilstone's light began to change, responding to the shift in Liora's heart. "They'll destroy themselves without guidance," she hissed, desperation creeping into her voice. "Without control, there is only chaos."

But Liora saw through the lie now. Chaos wasn't the enemy - fear was. Fear of loss, fear of pain, fear of the very power meant to protect. The same fear that had driven Draven to become what he fought against.

The Eclipse's light seemed to brighten, cutting through the shadows of doubt. Liora stepped back from her reflection, understanding blooming like dawn after a long night. Power wasn't meant to eliminate choice - it was meant to protect it.

Her dark reflection's form began to fragment, the seductive promises of control dissolving like mist in morning light. The Veilstone pulsed once more, but this time its energy felt different - not a weapon to be wielded, but a gift to be shared.

"I won't be a weapon. I'm not here to conquer, but to free." The words rang through the chamber with quiet certainty, each syllable striking against her dark reflection like hammer blows on heated steel.

Dark Liora's face contorted, the mask of seductive confidence cracking to reveal the fear beneath. The Veilstone in her hands pulsed erratically, its light dimming as Liora's conviction grew stronger. The promise of absolute control that had seemed so alluring moments ago now felt hollow, like a beautiful fruit rotting from within.

Around them, the vision of enslaved citizens began to blur and fade. The tower's imposing walls became transparent, Draven's approving smile dissolving into nothingness. Each element of the dark future unraveled like poorly woven cloth, leaving only the pure, unwavering light of the Eclipse above.

The chamber air crackled with residual energy as Dark Liora's form finally shattered, scattering like dust in a sudden breeze. But the Veil-stone remained, its faceted surface now glowing with a warm, steady light that spoke not of dominion, but of protection.

The Veilstone retreated from her sight as the darkness once again swallowed Liora whole, pressing against her skin like cold silk. Her heart still thundered from rejecting her darker self, the echo of her own corrupted voice lingering in her mind like a fading nightmare.

Lyra's presence filled the void, bringing with it the scent of night-flowers and the warmth of a mother's embrace. "You have conquered your doubt, but that is not all that haunts you." The words resonated through Liora's bones, stirring memories she'd tried to bury.

*** 

The next vision shimmered into focus, transforming the darkness into the familiar warmth of Twilight camp. Lanterns swayed gently in the evening breeze, casting dancing shadows across the weathered tents and worn paths that had become home.

Nero emerged from between two tents, his stride purposeful yet gentle as always. His presence brought a fresh wave of grief to Liora's chest, the memory of his sacrifice still raw and bleeding in her heart.

Liora rushed forward, arms outstretched toward her mentor. The familiar scent of sage and old books enveloped her as she embraced him, tears of joy springing to her eyes. But something felt wrong. Wet warmth seeped through her tunic where their bodies met.

She stumbled backward, her hands coming away sticky and crimson. The wound in Nero's chest gaped like a hungry mouth, dark blood flowing freely down his robes. His kind eyes hardened as he stared at her, accusation replacing the warmth she remembered. Heat rippled through the air around him, distorting his form like a mirage. Flames licked up his legs, consuming his robes. The fire cast his face in harsh shadows, transforming his features into something grotesque and unfamiliar.

"You killed me, Liora." His voice crackled like burning wood. "Your lack of control, your weakness - they brought this end." The flames climbed higher, blackening his skin, but his eyes remained fixed on her, boring into her soul.

Her throat closed as guilt crashed over her. "No," she whispered, but the word felt hollow. She had failed to protect him. Failed to control her powers when it mattered most.

The fire spread across his shoulders, turning his silver hair to ash. "I died because you weren't strong enough. Because you couldn't master what was given to you." Each word struck like a physical blow, forcing her back another step.

Smoke curled from his mouth as he spoke again, his voice roughening. "How many more will die for your weakness? How many others will burn while you struggle with powers you don't deserve?"

The flames consumed him completely now, his form a pillar of fire that reached toward the ceiling. Yet his eyes still blazed through the inferno, pinning her in place with their merciless judgment.

Heat scorched her face as she raised her arms against the blaze. This wasn't real. This wasn't her mentor - the man who had believed in her, taught her, sacrificed himself to protect her. This was her guilt given form, her fears made manifest.

Marcus materialized from the smoke, his scarred face twisted with hatred. Blood trickled from his chest - the same wound that had killed him. His accusatory glare joined Nero's, doubling the weight of guilt pressing down on Liora's chest.

"Look what you brought to us," Marcus spat. "We took you in, trusted you, and this is how you repay us? With destruction?" The heat from the fire made his scars appear to writhe across his skin like living things.

The world tilted and spun around Liora as Twilight crumbled. Each falling beam, each burning tent represented another failure, another life she'd put at risk. The smoke burned her lungs, but she couldn't look away from the devastation her powers had caused. Her legs trembled as waves of shame and regret threatened to overwhelm her.

"Your power is poison," Marcus growled, advancing through the flames. "Everything you touch turns to ash. Everyone who believes in you ends up dead." Behind him, more figures emerged from the smoke - villagers from Eldara, fallen rebels, their wounds stark and accusatory in the firelight.

The ground beneath her feet began to crack and splinter. Twilight wasn't just burning - it was being consumed, devoured by the same destructive force that lived within her.

Through the inferno, a familiar silhouette emerged. Bennet's weathered face appeared, etched with disappointment that cut deeper than any blade. His miller's clothes were singed, and his eyes held none of the warmth she remembered from their days at the mill.

The flames parted around him as he stepped forward, his presence commanding even in this nightmare realm. "I raised you better than this, Liora." His voice carried the weight of every lesson unlearned, every warning unheeded. "Look what your recklessness has brought to our home."

The burning camp of Twilight shifted and warped, transforming into the familiar streets of Eldara. The flames consumed the thatched roofs of her childhood, turning the peaceful village into a mirror of her darkest fears. The mill wheel creaked one final time before collapsing into a shower of burning splinters.

"You thought you could control it?" Bennet's words dripped with bitter disappointment. "The Veilstone will only amplify what's already there - chaos, destruction, death. Everything you touch turns to ash, just like our mill, just like our home."

Around them, villagers fled from their burning homes, their screams mixing with the roar of the flames. Each face was familiar - the baker who'd given her warm bread on cold mornings, the weaver who'd taught her to mend her clothes, the children she'd played with in happier days.

Bennet gestured at the devastation, his hand trembling with barely contained anger. "This is your legacy, Liora. Not protection, not salvation - just ruins and regret. The Veilstone doesn't belong in the hands of someone who can't even protect her own village."

The heat pressed in from all sides as Eldara crumbled around them. The apothecary's shop collapsed, releasing clouds of burning herbs that filled the air with acrid smoke. The marketplace, where she'd spent countless mornings helping Bennet sell their flour, disappeared beneath a wave of flames.

Liora watched helplessly as her childhood home was consumed, each burning building a testament to her failures. The weight of Bennet's accusations pressed down on her chest, making it hard to breathe through the smoke-filled air.

"The Veilstone requires wisdom," Bennet continued, his voice cutting through the chaos. "It demands control, purpose, understanding. You possess none of these. You'll destroy everything, just as you're destroying Eldara now."

The flames rose higher, forming a wall of fire that separated Liora from her surrogate father. Through the blaze, she could see his face hardening into a mask of judgment, his final condemnation hanging in the air between them as Eldara continued to burn.

Heat pressed in from all sides as the three apparitions circled Liora, their forms wavering like mirages in the desert. Nero's blood-soaked robes left crimson footprints in his wake. Marcus's wounds gaped fresh and angry in the flickering light. Bennet's disappointed gaze cut deeper than any blade.

"Look at what you've done." Nero's voice crackled like burning wood, each word stabbing into her heart. The scent of his funeral pyre filled her lungs again, choking her with memories of failure.

"Every step, you leave destruction." Marcus's scarred face twisted as he gestured at the phantom ruins of Twilight surrounding them. Blood dripped from his chest wound, each drop echoing against the stone floor like an accusation.

"Do you really believe you're any different from Draven?" Bennet's words carried the weight of every shattered dream, every broken promise. The phantom flames of Eldara reflected in his eyes, turning their familiar warmth to burning judgment.

Memories assaulted her from all sides - the collapsed mill wheel, the chaos at Twilight, Nero's final sacrifice. Each failure, each moment of lost control played out in the air around her like a twisted performance. The apparitions' accusations tangled together, their voices rising to a crescendo that threatened to drown her in a sea of guilt and regret.

The stone floor bit into Liora's knees as she collapsed, her legs no longer able to hold her against the weight of accusation and memory. Through the inferno of guilt, Rafe's form shimmered into view. His gentle smile cut through the haze of smoke and regret like a blade of sunlight.

"I forgive you," he whispered, reaching toward her with an outstretched hand. The gesture, so familiar and warm, made her chest ache. His fingers glowed with the same golden light she'd seen that first night in Eldara, when he'd defended her against Draven's forces.

Tears burned hot trails down her cheeks as she shook her head. The words of forgiveness felt wrong, undeserved. How could he forgive what she'd done? The destruction she'd brought to everyone who dared to care about her?

The scene warped and shifted, the burning ruins of Twilight dissolving into the peaceful afternoon light of Eldara's past. Young Liora sat on the mill's steps, her small hands covered in flour and tears streaming down her face. She'd ruined an entire batch of grain, letting it spoil because she'd forgotten to check the moisture levels.

Bennet knelt before her younger self, his weathered face creased with understanding rather than anger. "The hardest person to forgive is yourself, little one," he said, his voice carrying the same warmth it always had when sharing wisdom. "But without that forgiveness, we can never grow beyond our mistakes."

The memory crystallized around her with painful clarity - the scent of fresh-cut wheat on the breeze, the distant sound of the mill wheel creaking, the rough wood of the steps beneath her small hands. She remembered how his words had soothed her child's heart, making the weight of failure lighter.

Present-day Liora watched the scene unfold, feeling the truth of Bennet's words echo across the years. The apparitions of Nero, Marcus, and Bennet still circled her, but their accusations seemed to fade against the simple wisdom of that long-ago afternoon.

Her younger self looked up at Bennet with trust shining in her eyes, accepting his gentle lesson about forgiveness. The sight stirred something deep within Liora's chest - a reminder of who she had been before fear had twisted her relationship with her power.

The peaceful memory began to fade, reality bleeding back in around the edges. The stone chamber's cool air replaced the warm afternoon breeze, and the Veilstone's steady glow cut through the phantoms of flame and smoke.

Liora drew in a shaking breath, feeling the weight of both past and present pressing against her heart. Forgiveness, she realized, wasn't about deserving - it was about choosing to move forward, about allowing growth to emerge from the ashes of failure.

Liora pushed herself to her feet, legs trembling but stance firm as she faced the apparitions that circled her like smoke. The phantom flames cast dancing shadows across the chamber walls, but their heat no longer scorched her skin. Her failures hung in the air between them - visible, acknowledged, but no longer crushing.

"I've failed," she said, her voice growing stronger with each word. "But I've learned, too. My mistakes don't define me—they guide me. I choose to protect, even if I stumble." The words tasted like truth on her tongue, washing away the bitter ash of guilt.

The apparitions flickered like dying candles, their accusing faces melting into wisps of shadow. Liora's chest expanded as the crushing weight of guilt lifted, allowing her to breathe freely for the first time since Nero's death.

Around her, the forms of Nero, Marcus, and Bennet dissolved into mist. Their final expressions shifted from judgment to something softer - perhaps pride, or acceptance. The image of young Liora on the mill steps lingered longest, a reminder of innocence not lost but transformed through experience and growth.

Darkness swept through the chamber like a tide, extinguishing the last traces of the apparitions. The cool stone beneath Liora's feet vanished, leaving her suspended in the void once more. Yet this darkness held no terror - it embraced her like an old friend, cradling her in its depths.

Silver light bloomed in the distance, coalescing into Lyra Solari's ethereal form. Her hair floated as if underwater, threads of starlight weaving through the strands. A smile graced her lips as she regarded Liora with eyes that held a mother's love.

"Your guilt bound you to the past. It is no more." Lyra's voice resonated through the void, each word rippling like waves on a midnight lake. "Now you must face the final trial."

# A Mother's Love

The impact drove the air from Liora's lungs as she crashed onto the scorching sand. Grit filled her mouth, tasting of ash and copper. Her vision swam, the world tilting sideways before settling into a nightmare landscape of scattered bodies stretched across the dunes.

Blood stained the sand in dark patches, seeping outward like spilled ink. The metallic scent mixed with smoke, creating a suffocating fog that burned her throat. These weren't illusions or phantoms - the corpses were real, their vacant eyes staring accusingly at the sky.

Wind whipped across the dunes, carrying the acrid stench of death and scorched earth. The temple entrance should have been visible from here, but only endless waves of sand stretched toward the horizon. Movement caught her eye - a figure standing motionless among the carnage, their form blurred by the heat rising from the sand. Liora's breath caught in her throat. The silhouette seemed familiar, yet wrong somehow, like a reflection in troubled water.

She took a hesitant step forward, sand shifting treacherously beneath her feet. The figure remained still, facing away from her, their clothes rippling in the hot wind. Something about their stance sent warning signals racing through her mind, but she couldn't look away.

Another step brought the person's features into sharper focus. Dark hair whipped around their shoulders, and their posture held a regal bearing that seemed out of place in this wasteland. Recognition dawned slowly, like ice spreading through Liora's veins.

The figure began to turn, movement fluid and deliberate. Liora's muscles tensed, ready to run or fight, though her feet remained rooted to the spot. The world seemed to hold its breath, waiting for the revelation she somehow knew would shatter her.

Liora's heart stuttered in her chest as she stared at the figure before her. The ethereal glow that had surrounded Lyra Solari in the dreamscape was gone, replaced by something raw and human. Her mother's shoulders slumped beneath the weight of unseen burdens, her eyes fixed on the carnage stretching across the dunes.

Sand crunched beneath Liora's feet as she took another step forward. The bodies seemed to multiply with each passing moment, their empty faces turned skyward in silent accusation. Some wore rebel colors, others the dark uniforms of Draven's forces. Some wore no colors at all. Innocents caught in the carnage. Death had made them equals.

Tears carved clean tracks down Lyra's ash-stained cheeks. Her hands trembled at her sides, and for the first time, Liora saw her not as a infallible being, but as a woman who had fought and lost and carried those scars within her.

The wind caught Lyra's hair, whipping it around her face like dark wings. She made no move to brush it away, standing as still as the corpses surrounding them. Her presence felt solid, real in a way it never had during their dream encounters.

Liora's throat tightened as she navigated between the fallen. Each step required careful placement, a macabre dance to avoid disturbing the dead. The closer she got, the more details emerged - a wedding ring glinting on a lifeless hand, a letter peeking from a bloody pocket, small tokens of lives cut short.

Another step brought her within arm's reach of her mother. Lyra's shoulders tensed, but she didn't turn. Her gaze remained fixed on the horizon where heat waves distorted the boundary between earth and sky. The silence stretched between them, filled with unspoken words and shared grief.

A sob caught in Liora's throat as she reached out, her fingers trembling inches from Lyra's shoulder. Would her hand pass through, proving this another cruel illusion? Or would she finally feel the warmth of her mother's embrace after all these years of absence?

The bodies seemed to watch their reunion, their blank eyes reflecting the merciless sun. Some wore expressions of surprise, others of terror - final moments frozen in death. They formed a grotesque audience to this meeting of mother and daughter.

Before Liora's fingers could make contact, Lyra spoke. Her voice carried none of the otherworldly resonance it had held in dreams. Instead, it cracked with very human pain as she whispered, "I'm so sorry, my dear. I never wanted you to see this."

The words hit Liora like physical blows, each syllable driving the air from her lungs.

"The plan was doomed to fail from the beginning." Lyra's voice cracked, her gaze still fixed on the horizon where heat waves distorted reality. "All of this - the ruins, the bodies, the darkness consuming Somnus - it's the price of that failure. Draven won long before today."

Sand shifted beneath Liora's feet as she stumbled back, her mother's words carving holes in her chest where hope had lived moments before. If she had already failed, if everything was already lost, what was the point of continuing?

"When?" Liora's voice emerged as a whisper, barely audible above the moaning wind. "How did I fail? Tell me so I can fix it, please." The desperation in her tone surprised her, raw and bleeding like an open wound.

Lyra's head snapped toward her, eyes widening as if truly seeing Liora for the first time. Something shifted in her expression - recognition, confusion, then a flash of something Liora couldn't name. The ethereal distance that had marked their previous encounters vanished, replaced by an intensity that made Liora take another step back.

"Liora?" Her mother's voice held a note of wonder now, mixed with disbelief. "My child, how are you-" She reached out, fingers trembling, then pulled back as if burned. "No, this isn't possible. You shouldn't be here."

The bodies surrounding them seemed to press closer, their presence suffocating. Liora fought the urge to run, to escape this nightmare version of her mother and the crushing weight of failure. But her feet remained rooted to the spot, sand slowly burying her boots.

"I don't understand." Liora forced the words past the lump in her throat. "You said the plan failed - that I failed. That Draven won." Each word felt like glass in her mouth, cutting deeper with every syllable.

Lyra's laugh held no humor, only a bitter edge that seemed to slice through the air between them. "Oh, my dear." She shook her head, dark hair whipping around her face. "I wasn't speaking of you. I was speaking of myself."

Understanding crashed over Liora like a wave of icy water. The bodies stretching across the dunes weren't from her future - they were echoes of the past. Her mother's past. The day Lyra Solari had fallen trying to stop Draven. Each corpse represented a friend, an ally who had fought beside her mother in that final, devastating battle.

The wind picked up, carrying stinging particles of sand that mixed with the tears on Liora's cheeks. Her mother's form seemed to flicker before her, like a candle flame caught in the breeze, yet the pain etched across Lyra's face remained sharp and real. This wasn't the serene guide from her dreams - this was a warrior at the moment of her deepest despair.

"In the end, why did I try?" Lyra's voice cracked, her hands clenching into fists at her sides. "Everything I've done will mean nothing. Somnus is doomed. Why struggle against what you cannot change?" The words fell like stones into the silence between them, heavy with the weight of shattered hope.

Sand swirled around their feet as Liora stepped forward, reaching out to bridge the gap between them. The heat from the now Ashen Dunes rose in shimmering waves, distorting the air and making Lyra's form waver like a mirage. But Liora could still see the tears tracking down her mother's face, could feel the crushing weight of failure pressing down on both their shoulders.

Her mother's words echoed in her mind, each syllable carving deeper wounds than any blade. The crushing weight of despair in Lyra's voice felt familiar - how many times had Liora herself questioned whether fighting was worth the cost?

But beneath the pain, something else stirred in Liora's chest. She thought of Rafe's unwavering faith, of Gemini's steadfast friendship, of all the small acts of defiance that kept hope alive in Somnus. Each one was a tiny flame pushing back against the darkness. Her mother had chosen to fight alone, but Liora wasn't alone anymore.

"You didn't fail." Liora's voice grew stronger with each word, cutting through the moaning wind. "You protected me. You gave me the chance to grow up, to find my own strength." She took another step forward, sand shifting beneath her feet. "Even if Draven killed you, he couldn't destroy everything you fought for. I'm still here. The rebellion is still fighting. Hope still exists because of what you did."

Lyra's head snapped up, her eyes widening as they met Liora's steady gaze. The wind whipped her dark hair around her face, but couldn't hide the flicker of something - recognition, pride, or perhaps hope - that crossed her features. The air between them seemed to crackle with unspoken emotions, with all the years of absence and longing that separated mother and daughter.

The laugh that burst from Lyra's throat held no warmth, slicing through the air like shattered glass. Her head turned with an unnatural fluidity, dark hair writhing like serpents in the hot wind. The motion transformed her features, twisting her mother's familiar face into something darker, more sinister.

"How successful has my plan been, really?" Lyra's words dripped with mockery. "Look at yourself - a child playing at being a Dreamweaver, stumbling through powers you can barely control." Her lips curved into a cruel smile that made Liora's stomach clench.

The bodies surrounding them seemed to shift closer, their blank eyes reflecting accusation. Sand whirled around Liora's feet as she took an involuntary step backward, her mother's words cutting deeper than any blade.

"You think you can control the Veilstone?" Lyra's voice rose above the moaning wind. "You can't even control your own magic without hurting those around you. How many more must die before you accept the truth?"

Memories flashed through Liora's mind - the destruction at Eldara, the chaos during training, Nero's sacrifice. Each one struck like a physical blow, making her shoulders curl inward under their weight.

"Why play into Draven's game?" Lyra advanced, her movements predatory. "He orchestrated this entire moment - drawing you here, letting you believe you could succeed where I failed." The air around her rippled with dark energy that felt wrong, tainted.

The wind picked up, stinging Liora's eyes with sand and ash. Her mother's form seemed to grow larger, more menacing, casting a shadow that stretched impossibly long across the dunes.

"He wants you here," Lyra hissed, her voice distorting. "Wants you to feel the same despair that broke me. And look how well it's working." Her laugh echoed across the wasteland, hollow and cruel.

Heat shimpered between them as Lyra's words found their mark. Doubt crept through Liora's veins like poison, each heartbeat spreading it further. Had she walked willingly into Draven's trap, leading her friends to their deaths?

The corpses pressed closer, their presence suffocating as Lyra towered over her daughter. "Your weakness is your despair," she sneered, reaching out with fingers that seemed too long, too sharp. "And you've let it consume you completely."

The vision slammed into Liora with the force of a tidal wave. Her mother's despair flowed through her veins, bitter and sharp as broken glass. The sand beneath her feet transformed, becoming the battlefield of years past where Lyra had made her final stand against Draven.

Ghostly figures materialized around them - rebels and soldiers locked in desperate combat. At the center stood Lyra Solari, her power radiating in waves of pure light as she faced down Draven. The Emperor held the Ark of Dreams aloft, its crystalline surface pulsing with an otherworldly glow that seemed to drink in the very air around it. The artifact's power felt wrong, corrupted by Draven's twisted ambitions.

The scene played out like a nightmare in slow motion. Draven's laughter echoed across the dunes as he channeled the Ark's power- er, turning dreams into weapons. Rebels fell screaming as their own nightmares materialized, tearing them apart from within. Lyra fought desperately, her magic a brilliant shield against the darkness, but for every soldier she saved, two more fell to Draven's corrupted dream magic.

Through her mother's eyes, Liora felt the crushing weight of each death, each failure to protect those who had trusted her. The Ark's power grew stronger with every fallen rebel, feeding on their terror and despair. Draven wielded it like a conductor leading a symphony of horror, his control absolute as he shaped reality itself to his will.

Blood stained the sand crimson as Lyra made her final charge, gath- ering every last spark of power she possessed. But the Ark's corruption was too deep, too complete. As Lyra's magic clashed with its taint- ed energy, the resulting explosion transformed the dunes into glass, shattering both the land and her mother's hope in a single devastating moment. The echo of that despair threatened to pull Liora under, to drown her in the same darkness that had claimed her mother.

The vision shifted, fracturing like broken glass before reforming into a new scene. Through the haze of memory, Liora watched as her mother - younger, less haunted - cradled a blanket-wrapped bundle. Tears streaked down Lyra's face as she extended the precious cargo toward a younger Nero Thorne, whose expression held a gravity Liora had never seen before.

"Promise me, Nero." Lyra's voice cracked, her fingers lingering on the blanket's edge. "Promise me you'll keep her safe until she's ready."

The baby - Liora herself - stirred in the bundle, one tiny hand reaching up to grasp at empty air.

The scene dissolved, reforming in the familiar shadows of the Whispering Woods. Lyra moved with purpose through the ancient trees, her steps sure despite the darkness pressing in around her. The same temple entrance Liora had discovered hours ago loomed before her mother, its stone archway seeming to pulse with an inner light.

Inside, Lyra faced her first trial - a mirror of herself wielding corrupted dream magic, tempting her with promises of unlimited power. Her mother's rejection was immediate and absolute, her voice ringing with conviction as she denounced the false path.

The second trial manifested as a swarm of shadow creatures, each bearing the face of someone Lyra had failed to protect. She stood firm, acknowledging her guilt while refusing to let it consume her. Her magic blazed bright, dispelling the apparitions with unwavering resolve.

As Lyra approached the third trial chamber, understanding struck Liora like lightning. The timeline collapsed, past and present merging into a single moment. This wasn't just a vision of the past - this had been her mother's third trial.

Liora staggered back as understanding crashed over her. The ghostly figures surrounding them weren't just memories - they were echoes of her mother's failure, trapped in an endless loop of despair. Lyra hadn't fallen to Draven's power or even his corruption. She had fallen to her own broken heart.

The wind howled through the chamber, carrying whispers of the past. Through the maelstrom of memories, Liora watched her mother face this same trial, saw her crumble under the weight of having to choose between her daughter and her duty. The Veilstone had rejected Lyra not because she lacked power or courage, but because she couldn't reconcile sacrificing her child for the greater good.

Sand swirled around them as the apparition of Lyra twisted, its form flickering between mother and monster. "You see now?" it hissed, voice distorting. "I chose you over Somnus, and that choice doomed everything. My love became my weakness." The words cut deeper than any blade, carrying the bitter truth of years of regret.

Heat shimmered between them as the full impact of her mother's sacrifice took hold. Lyra had hidden her away, choosing to face Draven alone rather than risk her daughter's life. But that same protective instinct had shattered her resolve when she needed it most, leaving her vulnerable to the very despair that now threatened to consume Liora.

The chamber seemed to pulse with dark energy as her mother's form loomed closer, radiating waves of hopelessness and guilt. "You'll fail just as I did," the apparition whispered, its features melting into something darker, more sinister. "Love will be your undoing, just as it was mine." But even as the words sliced through her defenses, Liora felt something else stirring in her chest - not despair, but a fierce determination.

"I don't know the future," Liora's voice cut through the moaning wind, steady and clear. "But I'm taking this Veilstone. I'm going to fight Draven." Her feet shifted in the sand, planting themselves more firmly as she lifted her chin. "What happens after that, happens. I won't give in to despair, no matter how dark it gets."

The apparition shuddered, its dark edges dissolving like smoke in sunlight. The cruel twist of its features softened, melting away to reveal the serene presence Liora had known in her dreams. Lyra Solari stood before her daughter, radiant and whole, her ethereal form glowing with an inner light that pushed back the shadows.

The darkness began to recede, revealing that Liora never left the chamber she began in. The chamber itself seemed to exhale, ancient stones groaning as the oppressive darkness lifted. Behind Lyra, the Veilstone blazed to life, its crystalline surface pulsing with pure, untainted power. The artifact's light painted the walls in shifting patterns, as if celebrating Liora's triumph over despair.

Tears streaked down Lyra's face, but her smile held nothing but pride and love. She stepped forward, her movements fluid and graceful, no longer bound by the weight of guilt and regret. The air around her shimmered with dream magic in its purest form, untouched by corruption or fear.

"My brave, beautiful daughter," Lyra whispered, reaching out to cup Liora's face with hands that felt like morning sunlight. "You've done what I never could. You faced your despair and chose hope instead of surrender." Her touch was gentle, carrying echoes of all the embraces they'd never shared.

The Veilstone's glow intensified, casting mother and daughter in a soft, golden light. Lyra pulled Liora into an embrace that felt like coming home, like finding a piece of herself she hadn't known was missing. Dream magic swirled around them, responding to their shared connection.

"I let my fear of losing you become stronger than my faith in the future," Lyra murmured against Liora's hair. "But you - you've learned to draw strength from love instead of letting it become your weakness." Her form flickered slightly, like a candle flame caught in a gentle breeze.

Sand whispered across the chamber floor as Lyra pulled back, her eyes shining with unshed tears and fierce determination. "The path ahead won't be easy," she said, her voice carrying the weight of prophecy. "But you won't walk it alone. I'll always be with you, in every dream, every moment you need guidance."

The air grew thick with emotion as Lyra's form began to fade, becoming translucent around the edges. Her smile never wavered as she stepped back, her figure starting to dissolve into motes of light that danced like stars in the chamber's air. "It's time for you to forge your own destiny, my daughter. Make it one worthy of the hope you carry."

Dream magic surged through the chamber as Lyra's presence dimmed, her final words echoing with power and promise. "I love you, Liora. Never forget that love is your strength, not your weakness." Her form shimmered one last time before dissolving completely, leaving behind only the lingering warmth of her embrace.

The chamber fell silent save for the steady pulse of the Veilstone, waiting on its ancient pedestal. Liora stood alone now, tears drying on her cheeks as she faced the artifact that had drawn her to this moment.

# Liora's Choice

The Veilstone pulsed beneath Liora's fingertips, its crystalline surface warm and alive. Her heart thundered in her chest as she wrapped her fingers around it, feeling the ancient power respond to her touch.

Energy surged through her veins like liquid starlight, filling every corner of her being. The chamber's shadows retreated as the Veilstone's glow intensified, casting everything in a brilliant golden radiance that seemed to emanate from within her as much as from the stone itself.

Dream magic coursed through her body, no longer the wild, untamed force she'd struggled to control. The Veilstone acted as an anchor, a focusing lens through which her power flowed with newfound precision. Each breath brought deeper understanding of the connection between her will and the magic that had always lived inside her.

The stone's surface shifted beneath her grip, its facets realigning themselves as if recognizing its new wielder. Memories that weren't her own flickered through her mind - ancient Dreamweavers who had held this power before her, each leaving their mark on the artifact's legacy.

Clarity washed over her like a cool spring rain, sweeping away the last traces of doubt and fear. She understood now why the Veilstone had called to her, why it had waited all this time. It wasn't just a tool or a weapon - it was a bridge between what she was and what she could become.

The chamber's ancient walls seemed to hum in response to the union of Dreamweaver and Veilstone. Patterns of light danced across the stone surfaces, telling stories of past and future in a language Liora somehow understood without words. Every shadow held meaning, every glimmer of light spoke of possibility.

Power thrummed through her arms, but it didn't overwhelm her as she'd feared. Instead, it settled into her bones like it had always belonged there, waiting to be awakened. The Veilstone's energy merged with her own, amplifying her strength while tempering it with wisdom accumulated over centuries.

She lifted the stone higher, watching as threads of golden light wove themselves around her fingers. Each strand responded to her thoughts, bending and flowing with a grace she'd never managed before. Control came as naturally as breathing now, guided by the Veilstone's ancient knowledge.

The chamber's air grew thick with dream magic, but Liora didn't feel the usual strain of maintaining such power. The Veilstone balanced the flow of energy, allowing her to direct it with nothing more than focused intent. Shadows and light danced at her command, no longer fighting against her will.

Dream energy pulsed outward in controlled waves, touching the chamber's furthest corners without causing harm. Liora felt tears sliding down her cheeks - not from fear or exhaustion, but from the pure joy of finally understanding what she was truly capable of. The Veilstone had shown her the way, and there would be no turning back.

The Veilstone's energy coursed through Liora's veins, but beneath its golden radiance, shadows stirred. Her demons hadn't vanished - they'd merely retreated, waiting in the corners of her mind where doubt still lingered.

Each pulse of power from the stone brought whispers of temptation, echoes of the trials she'd faced. The tyrant's voice still promised absolute control. The guilt still wrapped cold fingers around her heart. The despair still threatened to drown her hope in darkness.

She lowered the Veilstone, studying its shifting surface. The artifact responded to her touch, but she sensed it would amplify whatever lived within her - both light and shadow. Her fears hadn't disappeared; they'd become part of the power she now wielded.

The chamber's air grew heavy with possibility as Liora tested the connection. Dream magic flowed through her with new precision, but maintaining control required constant vigilance. One slip of concentration, one moment of weakness, and those inner demons could surge forth through the very power meant to contain them.

Liora's hands trembled as understanding settled over her. The trials hadn't been about defeating her demons, but about accepting their existence. The Veilstone wasn't a cure for her struggles - it was a tool that would make them more acute, more demanding of her attention.

Dream energy pulsed outward, touching the chamber walls. Where before such display might have spiraled into chaos, now the power bent to her will - but she felt the cost. Each use of the stone would require her to face those inner battles anew, to choose her path again and again.

The stone's warmth pulsed against her palm like a second heartbeat, reminding her that this was just the beginning. The real test wouldn't be in claiming the Veilstone, but in wielding it.

***

Kael paced before the row of bound prisoners, his boots crunching against sand and broken stone. The desert wind howled through the ruins, whipping his cloak around him as he studied Rafe's defiant glare. Blood still trickled from the gash above the rebel's eye where Maya had struck him. Behind Rafe, Gemini and Jayne knelt in silence, their hands bound tight enough to leave marks.

The weight of his family's pendant pressed against his chest beneath his armor. He'd worn it through every battle, every victory, but now it felt like a mockery of everything he'd thrown away. Nero's final words echoed in his mind - not anger or hatred, but disappointment. The old master had seen through him long before anyone else.

The pendant grew heavier with each passing moment. His father would have been ashamed to see what remained of their noble house - a turncoat who'd abandoned not one cause, but two. First Draven's empire, then the rebellion that had taken him in. The irony wasn't lost on him.

Derek shifted nervously beside him, hand tight on his sword hilt. "General, what if she doesn't come?" The young man's voice wavered. Kael shot him a sharp look that made him flinch. Of course Liora would come - her weakness had always been her attachments to these people.

Kael stared at the ethereal treeline that had materialized where only sand existed hours ago. The Whispering Woods shouldn't be here.

Yet there they stood, their branches swaying with an otherworldly grace that made his skin crawl. Only the Veilstone's power could have drawn them here, which meant Liora had entered there. His plan was working perfectly.

Maya approached, her boots scuffing against the broken stone. "The perimeter is secured, General. No sign of movement from the woods." The words carried an edge of fear that Kael understood all too well. Even Draven's elite soldiers gave the Whispering Woods a wide berth, their ancient magic too unpredictable to risk. But they had their orders - no one entered, no one left without his knowledge.

Maya's knife pressed against Rafe's throat, drawing a thin line of blood when he tried to speak. "Quiet," she hissed. But Kael saw the truth in Rafe's eyes - not fear, but pity. As if he understood the hollowness eating away at Kael's core, the price of power paid in betrayal and blood.

The pendant burned like ice against his skin. His mother's final words rang in his ears: "Stay true to yourself, my son." But which self? The loyal general? The dedicated rebel? The ambitious traitor? Perhaps they were all masks, and underneath lay nothing but hunger for control.

Kael's breath caught as golden light exploded from the depths of the Whispering Woods, so bright he had to shield his eyes. The radiance pulsed with ancient power, sending tremors through the ground beneath his feet. Even Maya stepped back, her knife wavering at Rafe's throat.

The light began to coalesce, drawing inward like liquid gold being poured into a mold. Kael's skin prickled with electricity as the air itself seemed to bend and twist around the ethereal display. This was old magic - deeper and more primal than anything he'd witnessed in Draven's court.

Something was emerging from the woods. No, someone. Kael's hand instinctively went to his sword hilt as a figure took shape within the golden nimbus. The stories of Lyra Solari's attempts to claim the Veilstone flashed through his mind - how its power had rejected her, driven her mad with visions of failure.

But this was different. Where Lyra had fought against the Veilstone's will, this power sang in harmony with its wielder. Kael watched in disbelief as Liora stepped from the treeline, golden energy swirling around her like a living cloak. Her eyes blazed with inner light, and the very air seemed to resonate with her presence.

Kael watched as Liora advanced, her power rippling through the air like heat waves off desert sand. The display stirred something deep within him - not fear, but hunger. This was the raw potential he'd sensed in her from the beginning, finally unleashed. His fingers tightened around his sword hilt, though he knew steel would be useless against such magic.

"She did it!" Gemini's voice rang out, breaking the tense silence. "She mastered the Veil-" The rest of her words cut off as Derek pressed his blade against her throat. A thin line of blood appeared where the edge bit into her skin. Kael fought the urge to tell Derek to ease up - showing mercy now would only undermine his authority.

The golden light surrounding Liora pulsed brighter at the threat to her friend. Kael felt the surge of protective energy roll across the ruins like a wave, making his teeth ache. He'd seen that same fierce devotion in Lyra's eyes years ago, right before she'd torn through Draven's forces to protect her people. Like mother, like daughter.

Maya shifted closer to Rafe, her knife steady against his throat. Smart girl - she understood that Liora's attachments were both her greatest strength and her fatal weakness. One wrong move, one burst of uncontrolled power, and her friends would pay the price. Kael allowed himself a small smile. Everything was proceeding exactly as planned.

The pendant grew colder against his chest as Liora's gaze locked onto his. There was something new in those glowing eyes - not just power, but understanding. She saw through him now, past the masks of loyalty and duty to the hollow core beneath. His smile faltered. The pendant at his chest grew ice-cold. This wasn't supposed to happen. Draven had assured him the Veilstone would overwhelm her, break her will as it had broken her mother's. Yet there she stood, radiating more raw power than Kael had ever sensed from even the emperor.

Derek made a strangled sound beside him, taking an involuntary step backward. Kael couldn't blame him - every instinct screamed to retreat from this display of barely contained energy. But pride and ambition kept his feet planted firmly in place. He hadn't come this far to show weakness now.

"Impossible," Maya whispered, her usual confidence cracking. The knife at Rafe's throat trembled slightly. Even the elite guards shifted uneasily, their training warring with primal fear. Kael forced his breathing to remain steady, though his heart hammered against his ribs.

The golden light pulsed in time with Liora's steps as she approached, each footfall leaving briefly glowing impressions in the sand. Kael searched her face for signs of the struggle he'd expected - the strain of containing the Veilstone's power. Instead, he found only serene determination that sent a chill down his spine.

Rafe's quiet laughter cut through the tension. "You didn't expect this, did you, Kael?" Blood still trickled from his wound, but his eyes shone with fierce pride as he watched Liora advance. Kael fought the urge to strike him silent, knowing it would only prove the rebel's point.

Kael forced a calm smile as Liora approached, though every nerve in his body screamed at the raw power emanating from her. "Well done. I knew you had the strength to claim it." The words tasted like ash in his mouth. This wasn't how it was supposed to go - she should have been broken, desperate, not radiating controlled power that made his skin crawl.

Golden tendrils of energy drifted from Liora toward her bound friends. Kael watched as their faces relaxed slightly, some of the pain and fear easing from their expressions. Even now, she thought of others first - a weakness he could exploit. Derek's hand tightened on his weapon while Maya shifted her stance, ready to strike. But Liora made no aggressive moves, simply standing there with that unnervingly serene expression.

The pendant at his chest grew colder with each passing moment. Kael squared his shoulders, pushing aside the gnawing doubt that threatened to undermine his resolve. "I'm offering you the same choice as before," he said, keeping his voice steady despite the electricity crackling in the air. "Surrender the Veilstone to Emperor Draven, and your friends walk free."

"Don't you dare!" Rafe's voice rang out, raw with desperation. Maya's blade pressed deeper against his throat, but he didn't flinch. "He's lying, Liora! Don't trust him!"

Gemini's voice joined the chorus of protest. "We're not worth the price, Li! You know what Draven will do with that power!" Blood trickled down her neck where Derek's blade bit into her skin, but her eyes blazed with fierce determination.

"Better dead than slaves to his nightmares!" Jayne spat the words with such venom that the guard holding her took a step back.

The golden light surrounding Liora pulsed brighter with each cry from her friends. Kael's hand instinctively went to his sword hilt as the power rolled over him in waves. The very air seemed to vibrate with potential energy, making it hard to draw a full breath.

Derek's nervous energy was becoming problematic. Kael could see the young man's sword hand trembling as he pressed the blade against Gemini's throat. One wrong move, one flinch, and blood would flow - destroying any chance of negotiation. But Kael couldn't show weakness by calling him off.

Maya, at least, maintained her professional composure. Her knife remained steady at Rafe's throat despite the crackling energy filling the air. Her eyes never left Liora's face, watching for any sign of aggressive movement. Kael appreciated her discipline, even as he wondered if steel would have any effect against such power. He forced his voice to remain steady as he added, "Choose quickly. My soldiers' patience isn't endless." But even as he spoke the words, he wondered who truly held the power in this confrontation.

Kael's skin crawled as Liora's gaze drifted over him, through him, as if he were made of smoke. The golden light surrounding her pulsed with each heartbeat, but she made no move to attack. No attempt to defend her friends. She simply stood there, studying him with those unnervingly bright eyes.

His hand tightened on his sword hilt until his knuckles went white. This wasn't how it was supposed to go. Where was the fear, the desperation he'd counted on? The pendant at his chest grew colder with each passing moment of her scrutiny.

Memories of the Ember Ruins flickered through his mind - fragments of gold light and searing pain as she'd torn through his thoughts. The violation of it still made his stomach churn. Yet this felt different. Then, she'd been raw power and rage. Now she radiated a calm that set his teeth on edge.

Derek shifted nervously beside him, the blade at Gemini's throat wavering. Kael wanted to snap at him to stay still, but he couldn't tear his gaze away from Liora's face. From those eyes that seemed to see straight through every mask he'd ever worn.

The wind picked up, whipping sand around them, but the golden light surrounding Liora remained undisturbed. Perfect. Controlled. Nothing like the chaos he'd witnessed in the ruins. Nothing like what Draven had promised would happen when she claimed the Veilstone.

Maya's voice cut through his thoughts, tight with tension. "General?" The question hung in the air between them. What were his orders if negotiation failed? What orders could possibly matter against power like this? The pendant grew heavier with each passing moment of indecision.

The golden light pulsed again, stronger this time, and Kael had to fight the urge to step back. Pride kept his feet planted firmly in the sand, even as every instinct screamed at him to retreat. To run from that penetrating gaze that stripped away every lie he'd ever told himself.

"Well?" he demanded, hating how his voice cracked on the word. But Liora didn't respond, didn't even seem to register his question. She simply continued to look through him, into him, with those blazing eyes that promised judgment without mercy. The pendant burned like ice against his skin.

Kael's grip tightened on his sword hilt as Liora's voice cut through the howling wind. The sound carried an otherworldly resonance that made his teeth ache.

"You offer my friends' freedom in exchange for the Veilstone." Golden light pulsed with each word, casting strange shadows across the ruins. Her calm acceptance sent a chill down his spine. This wasn't the desperate negotiation he'd expected. The pendant grew colder against his chest.

Protests erupted from the prisoners. Rafe struggled against Maya's blade, fresh blood trickling down his neck. Gemini's eyes filled with tears as she shook her head. Even Jayne, who'd always been the most pragmatic, spat curses at him. But Liora's serene expression never wavered as she continued, "Very well."

The words hung in the air like smoke, making his skin crawl. Where was the anger, the pleading he'd counted on? Derek shifted uneasily beside him, the young man's sword trembling against Gemini's throat. Maya's professional mask cracked slightly as uncertainty crept into her eyes. None of this followed Draven's predictions.

Power radiated from Liora in waves, each pulse stronger than the last. Kael fought to maintain his commanding stance even as dread pooled in his stomach. The pendant felt like a block of ice now, a constant reminder of every betrayal that had led to this moment. He'd expected to face a broken girl desperate to save her friends. Instead, he found himself staring into eyes that held both infinite power and terrible understanding.

Kael watched in disbelief as Liora stepped forward, the Veilstone's golden light dimming with each movement. His heart thundered against his ribs as Maya gestured for the guards to bring forth the containment box. This surrender felt wrong - too easy, too clean. The pendant at his chest grew colder with each step Liora took toward them.

The ornate box's runes flickered to life as the elite guard approached, their faces masks of professional detachment despite the crackling energy in the air. Kael's fingers tightened around his sword hilt as Liora reached out, golden tendrils of power still dancing around her hands. One wrong move, one burst of defiance, and blood would stain the sand. But she simply placed the Veilstone into the waiting container with deliberate care.

A sharp click echoed across the ruins as the box sealed shut, cutting off the golden radiance. Kael released a breath he hadn't realized he'd been holding. The weight of the moment pressed down on him like a physical thing - victory achieved without the expected battle, without the resistance Draven had warned him to expect. Something about it made his skin crawl.

Maya's blade wavered slightly at Rafe's throat as she glanced toward Kael, awaiting orders. Derek's grip on Gemini had grown white-knuckled, the young man's uncertainty plain on his face. Even Jayne's defiant glare held a hint of confusion now. Kael forced his voice to remain steady as he commanded, "Release them." The words tasted like ash in his mouth.

Kael watched his elite guard retreat through the ruins with practiced efficiency, the containment box secure in their grasp. The Veilstone's capture had gone smoother than expected - almost too smooth. Yet victory thrummed through his veins as he imagined presenting the artifact to Draven. With its power, the Eclipse would reshape Somnus itself.

Sand whipped around him as he walked away, the pendant cold against his chest despite the desert heat. His soldiers moved with mechanical precision, their training evident in every motion. Soon they would reach the Imperial roads, where speed would matter more than stealth. The thought of Draven's approval quickened his pulse. The Eclipse was hours away, and together, they would harness powers beyond imagination.

The word "together" snagged in his mind like a splinter. Kael's fingers tightened on his sword hilt as doubt crept in unbidden. When had he started thinking of Draven's victory as his own? The emperor had promised him power, position, recognition - but promises were as shifting as the desert sands beneath his feet.

Memory flashed of Liora's penetrating gaze, seeing through every mask he'd constructed. Her surrender had been too easy, too controlled. Nothing like the desperate struggle Draven had predicted. The pendant grew colder still as uncertainty gnawed at him. Was he truly securing his own future, or merely exchanging one master for another?

Kael pushed the thoughts aside as he marched forward. Doubt was a luxury he couldn't afford, not when victory lay within grasp. Yet even as he led his forces toward Somnara, the question lingered like poison in his veins: in Draven's new world, would there truly be room for anyone else's ambitions but his own?

# Open Minds

The sand shifted beneath Liora's feet as she sprinted across the clearing, her heart thundering against her ribs. Power still hummed through her veins from the Veilstone, but nothing mattered except reaching her friends.

Gemini's arms wrapped around her first, fierce and desperate. The healer's shoulders shook with silent sobs, and Liora buried her face in her friend's hair, breathing in the familiar scent of herbs and healing balms. "I thought—" Gemini's voice cracked. "When they took us, I feared—"

"I'm here," Liora whispered, her own tears falling freely now. The weight of everything—the Veilstone's trials, losing Nero, the fear of losing everyone else—crashed over her like a wave. She clung tighter to Gemini, anchoring herself in her friend's solid presence.

A warm hand settled on her shoulder, and she looked up to find Rafe hovering close, his dark eyes scanning the perimeter even as he kept contact with her. His jaw was clenched tight, a muscle twitching beneath the skin. When his gaze finally met hers, the intensity there stole her breath.

"We need to move," he murmured, though his hand didn't leave her shoulder. "Varden's forces may have withdrawn, but we're still exposed here." His fingers tightened briefly, as if reassuring himself she was real.

Jayne appeared at Gemini's side, her usual sharp edges softened by concern as she touched the healer's arm. "He's right. You're exhausted, Gem." The nickname slipped out naturally, and Liora noticed how Gemini leaned slightly toward Jayne's touch.

"I'm fine," Gemini protested, though she still hadn't fully released Liora. Her fingers clutched the fabric of Liora's tunic, trembling slightly. "We need to tend to your wounds first."

Jayne's expression darkened at the mention of injuries, and she shifted closer to Gemini, almost protective. "The cuts aren't deep. They can wait." Her eyes met Liora's briefly, a silent message passing between them about keeping Gemini safe.

"Why?" Jayne's voice cut through the air, sharp as a blade. "After everything we went through, why give it to him?" Her eyes narrowed, searching Liora's face for answers.

Heat rose in Liora's chest, not from anger but from something deeper—certainty. The power hummed through her, a symphony of light and shadow that connected her to every dream within reach. Even now, she could sense the Veilstone's presence growing distant, but its energy remained woven through her being like golden threads in a tapestry.

"I don't need to hold it," Liora explained, watching understanding dawn in Gemini's eyes. "The Veilstone isn't just a tool or a weapon—it's a conduit. And now, so am I." She lifted her palm, letting dream energy dance across her fingers like starlight.

Jayne's breath caught as the golden light reflected in her eyes. "You're saying you can still use its power? Even with Varden taking it to Draven?"

A smile tugged at Liora's lips as she remembered her mother's words in the temple. The Veilstone had never been about possession—it was about connection. "The power was never in the stone itself," she said softly. "It was always about understanding how to channel it."

"But how can we possibly stop Draven now?" Rafe's hand reached for his sword hilt, recoiling upon realizing he had no weapon. "The Eclipse is hours away, and thanks to Varden, the rebllion is no more. We have no army." His eyes flickered to where Varden's forces had disappeared into the darkness. "And now our one weapon is in the hands of our enemy."

A smile tugged at Liora's lips as awareness flowed through her veins like liquid gold. The Veilstone's gift had opened her senses far beyond what she'd imagined possible. Even now, she could feel the pulse of dreams across the desert—hundreds of minds linked by hope and determination.

"When Varden left to come after us," she began, her voice steady with newfound certainty, "he didn't just abandon his post. He revealed his true colors to everyone at Twilight." The golden energy danced between her fingers as she spoke, casting warm light across their faces.

Rafe's brow furrowed as he processed her words. Behind him, Jayne's eyes widened with realization, and she gripped Gemini's hand tighter.

"The rebel forces aren't scattered or broken," Liora continued, feeling the truth of it resonating through her connection to the dreamscape. "They're gathering. I can sense them—their dreams, their determination." She closed her eyes briefly, letting the sensation wash over her. "The ranks are thin, yes. They're tired. Under-fed and under-armed. But ready."

The energy pulsed stronger as she opened her eyes, meeting Rafe's gaze. His expression shifted from doubt to something fiercer—hope kindling like a flame in darkness.

"Though," Liora added, a hint of steel entering her voice as she glanced in the direction Varden had fled, "it seems they might need a new general." Her eyes locked with Rafe's, seeing the same fire there that burned in her chest.

Gemini stepped forward, her healer's hands steady despite her exhaustion. "You're saying the rebellion isn't lost? That we still have a chance?"

The smile came naturally to Liora's lips as she met Gemini's worried gaze. Her friend's anxiety rippled through the dreamscape like waves on a pond, but beneath it lay an unshakeable core of determination. The same strength that had kept Gemini healing others even when exhausted still burned bright.

Golden threads of dream energy wove through the air around them, invisible to the others but blazing in Liora's heightened awareness. Each person's thoughts and emotions painted distinct patterns—Gemini's steady warmth, Jayne's sharp-edged protectiveness, Rafe's burning intensity. The connections flowed between them like rivers of light, impossible to ignore.

Unlike the violent invasion of Kael's mind, this felt as natural as breathing. The Veilstone's power had transformed her consciousness, expanding it until she could read the surface of their thoughts as easily as seeing their faces. Rafe's concern for her safety colored his thoughts deep crimson, while Jayne's strategic mind calculated escape routes in cool blues and grays.

The constant input threatened to overwhelm her. Liora tried to push it away, to close whatever mental door had opened, but the awareness remained. Every fleeting worry, every spark of hope, every unspoken fear—all of it poured into her mind in an endless stream. She gritted her teeth, forcing herself to focus on the physical world around them.

The power thrumming through Liora's veins wavered as Jayne stepped forward, her boots kicking up small clouds of sand. "If they're ready, we need to be too." Her eyes darted toward the horizon where the dunes stretched endlessly. "We've got a long walk ahead of us if we want to reach them before the Eclipse."

The golden threads of dream energy pulsed with each step as they made their way across the shifting sands. Liora's newfound awareness picked up every flutter of exhaustion, every spike of determination from her companions. Rafe led their small group, his shoulders tense as he scanned for threats, while Jayne brought up the rear with the same sharp-eyed vigilance that had kept them alive in the ruins.

A gentle touch on Liora's arm pulled her attention away from the kaleidoscope of others' emotions. Gemini's familiar presence felt like a cool stream in her mind, soothing the chaos of her expanded senses. "Li?" Her friend's voice carried the same gentle concern that had comforted her after countless nightmares in Eldara. "Are you okay?"

The question hit harder than Liora expected, breaking through the strange detachment that had settled over her since claiming the Veilstone's power. Was she okay? The energy coursing through her felt both foreign and achingly familiar, like remembering a song heard in childhood. Her mother's voice echoed in her memory, speaking of choices and consequences. "I'm not sure," she admitted, watching golden sparks dance between her fingers. "But I know what I have to do now."

Gemini's hand squeezed her arm, and Liora felt her friend's worry mix with fierce pride through their connection. The healer didn't press further, seeming to understand that some transformations required space to settle. They walked on in silence, their footprints disappearing behind them as the ever-shifting dunes reclaimed the sand.

***

The sun beat mercilessly against Liora's back as she trudged through the shifting sands of the Ashen Dunes. Each step sank deeper than the last, the terrain fighting against their progress. Ahead, Rafe's broad shoulders cut a path through the wind-whipped granules, while Gemini and Jayne flanked their small group, all of them pushing forward despite the exhaustion evident in their movements.

The twin moons hung low on the horizon, their alignment growing closer with each passing minute. Liora's chest tightened at the sight. The Eclipse of Dreams loomed before them, its power building like a storm about to break. They had precious little time to reach Draven's stronghold before the celestial event reached its peak.

Memories of her trial in the temple flickered through her mind - the dark version of herself, drunk on power and control, ruling alongside Draven. The vision had shown her how easily she could slip into tyranny, how seductive the path of dominance could be. But it had also revealed something else: the strength that came from choosing protection over power.

A whisper brushed against her consciousness, and Liora stumbled, catching herself before she fell. The thought wasn't her own - it belonged to Gemini, a worried litany about having no supplies. The realization struck Liora like lightning: the Veilstone hadn't just amplified her power, it was expanding it, allowing her to catch glimpses of her companions' thoughts.

Liora pulled back from Gemini's thoughts, but another consciousness brushed against hers - Jayne's sharp, analytical mind cutting through the desert haze. The spy's thoughts were a complex tangle of mission parameters and contingency plans, but underneath lay something softer, warmer, centered around the healer walking beside her.

Heat crept up Liora's neck that had nothing to do with the desert sun. The tenderness in Jayne's typically guarded thoughts when they landed on Gemini felt intimate, private - stolen moments of longing wrapped in layers of duty and restraint. She shouldn't be witnessing this, shouldn't be privy to the way Jayne's heart quickened whenever Gemini stumbled in the sand, how her hand twitched with the desire to reach out and steady her.

Liora tried to shut out the impressions flooding her mind. But Gemini's thoughts drifted through again, tinged with concern - not for their mission or dwindling supplies, but for Jayne's rigid posture and the dark circles under her eyes. The healer's desire to soothe, to comfort, to understand the layers beneath Jayne's carefully maintained facade resonated through the connection.

A particularly strong gust of wind sent sand stinging against their faces. Liora felt Jayne and Gemini's simultaneous impulse to shield each other, followed by their mutual restraint. The push and pull between them vibrated like a plucked string, neither willing to act on what hummed beneath the surface.

Rafe glanced back, his brow furrowing at whatever he saw in her expression. Liora forced her features into something she hoped looked less intrusive, less knowing. The last thing their group needed was this delicate dynamic disturbed by her newfound ability to peer behind carefully constructed walls.

Gemini's thoughts shifted again, remembering the gentle way Jayne had spoken to her in Dunrow, how their relationship had shifted to something almost tender. The memory carried an undercurrent of warmth that made Liora's cheeks flush darker. She shouldn't be here, shouldn't be witness to these private moments.

Through Jayne's eyes, Liora caught the way sunlight caught in Gemini's hair, how it transformed ordinary brown into threads of copper and gold. The observation came with a swift surge of self-re-crimination - Jayne berating herself for such indulgent thoughts when they should be focused on surviving the desert, on reaching Draven's stronghold before the Eclipse.

With effort, Liora wrenched her awareness back to herself, to the physical sensation of wind and sand against her skin, though she could still feel the echo of that delicate tension, that careful dance between duty and desire. She had to master this new aspect of her power, had to learn to control it before she invaded any more private moments.

As much as she wanted to, Liora couldn't stop herself from brushing against Rafe's consciousness. His thoughts washed over her like a wave - determination tinged with barely contained anticipation. Through his eyes, she saw herself as he saw her: powerful, purposeful, transformed by her trials in ways that both thrilled and terrified him.

But there was something else. Liora saw her own image reflected in Rafe's mind, transformed by his desire into someone bold and confident. In his eyes, she stood taller, her body not a collection of emotional scars but a landscape of strength and resilience. She saw herself as he did, her curves emphasized by the dust that coated her, the wind playing with loose strands of her hair.

Images flashed through his mind, a tangle of memories and impulses. Rafe remembered the way she'd looked at him in the hot spring, the raw desire in her eyes, and how it had driven him to claim her lips, to explore her body with a desperation that surprised them both. The memory came with an edge of frustration too - how he'd wanted to confess his love, to tell her everything that was in his heart, but had been interrupted.

But it was more than just memory. As Rafe looked at her now, Liora felt the throb of his barely restrained arousal, the swift rush of his pulse, and the warmth coiling low in his stomach. She recognized his physical reaction because it echoed her own, a yearning that had simmered steadily since being back in his presence.

The connection between them thrummed with unspoken desires, with images of tangled limbs and whispered confessions. Liora's breath caught as she felt Rafe's desperation for the chance to be alone with her, to explore the depths of their connection without the weight of the world on their shoulders.

She knew, without a doubt, that he saw her as beautiful, desirable, and worthy of being loved and cherished. The thought sent a jolt of warmth through her, something that started in her chest and spread outward, a tingling sensation that left her skin sensitized. It was like standing too close to a fire, except this heat didn't burn. It illuminated, giving her courage and strength.

And for the first time since gaining this new depth of perception, Liora let herself sink into the sensation, into the warmth of another person's want. She held that knowledge close like a secret treasure, letting it anchor her even as the desert wind whipped around them, carrying the promise of the Eclipse and the fight to come.

His other memories flickered through her mind - the girl she'd been in Eldara, scared of her own shadow, contrasted sharply with who she'd become. Pride and fear tangled together in his thoughts, pride in her growth warring with fear of losing her to the very power that made her extraordinary. The emotion behind it staggered her, raw and unfiltered without his usual careful restraint.

Through his eyes, she watched herself walking through the desert, the Veilstone's golden light threading through her hair like a crown. His breath caught at the sight, and Liora felt his struggle to remain focused on their mission when all he wanted was to protect her from what lay ahead. The force of his concern wrapped around her like a physical embrace.

Memories of her mother surfaced unbidden - stories of Lyra's final battle with Draven, how she'd fought to protect Somnus until her last breath. The weight of that legacy pressed down on Liora's shoulders, heavier than the desert heat. Would she prove stronger than her mother had been? Or would she fail as Lyra had, leaving others to carry on the fight?

Her mother had been powerful too, had fought with everything she had, and still Draven had prevailed. The thought of leaving Rafe - leaving any of them - to face Draven alone filled her with a dread that threatened to overwhelm her.

The wind picked up, driving sand against their faces, and Liora felt Rafe's instant impulse to shield her from it. His protective instinct ran soul-deep, woven into every thought and action. Yet he held himself back, respecting her strength even as it pained him to watch her face these challenges alone.

Through their connection, she caught the edge of a memory - Rafe standing over his father's grave, swearing vengeance against Draven. The parallel to her own loss struck her hard. They were both fighting to honor fallen parents, both carrying the weight of impossible promises. But where her mother had fought alone, Liora had something Lyra didn't allow herself: a team willing to stand beside her, to share her burden.

Sand crunched under her boots as Liora forced herself to pull back from Rafe's thoughts. The intimacy of the connection left her breathless, but she couldn't afford to lose herself in it. She had to focus on what lay ahead, had to find a way to succeed where her mother had failed. The twin moons crept closer to alignment overhead, and time was running out.

# War Approaches

The rebel army's banners snapped in the wind, a sea of defiance spread across the plains before Somnara's walls. Rafe's heart lifted at the sight. Liora had sensed their gathering through the Veil-stone's power, but seeing the army with his own eyes kindled fresh hope within him. These weren't just soldiers - they were farmers, merchants, and craftsmen who'd lost everything to Draven's tyranny.

Commander Vale's weathered figure cut through the crowd, his presence drawing respectful nods from the gathered rebels. The man carried himself with quiet dignity, so different from Varden's pompous strutting. Vale had always put his men first, even when it meant standing up to the General's more ruthless commands.

A memory flashed through Rafe's mind - Vale stopping Varden from executing a young scout who'd failed his mission. The Commander had argued that fear bred mistakes, while trust inspired loyalty. That moment had revealed the stark difference between the two men's leadership.

The setting sun cast long shadows across Vale's face as he approached their small group. His eyes lingered on Liora for a moment, widening slightly at the golden energy that seemed to shimmer around her. But unlike others who'd seen her power, there was no fear in his gaze - only a soldier's measured assessment.

Blood stained Vale's armor, and fresh scars marked his exposed skin. Whatever battles they'd fought to reach this point had clearly taken their toll. Yet the Commander's spine remained straight, his jaw set with determination. Here was a man who understood the weight of command but refused to let it break him. Rafe felt the tension in his shoulders ease - with Vale leading them, they stood a real chance against Draven's forces.

Rafe stepped forward to greet Vale, muscles aching from days of hard travel. The older man's lined face cracked into a rare smile as he clasped Rafe's forearm.

"It's about damn time," Vale growled, though warmth colored his gruff tone. His grip tightened for a moment before releasing, and Rafe fought back a wince as the pressure aggravated his wounds.

"What happened with Varden?" The question had burned in Rafe's mind since their escape. Had the General's betrayal torn the rebellion apart, or united them against a common enemy?

Vale's expression darkened. "When he left Twilight without warning, everyone put two and two together. Instead of falling apart like he probably hoped, we decided to mass anyway. Turns out his treachery did us a favor - showed us who our real allies are."

"You all look like you've been dragged through hell," Vale said, eyes tracking over their battered group. He gestured to a cluster of healers' tents behind him. "We've got skilled medics who can-" but Liora cut him off, her voice carrying an edge of urgency that made Rafe's spine straighten. "There's no time. The Eclipse approaches, and Draven won't wait."

"The Eclipse festival has begun," Jayne reported, her voice carrying across the gathered rebels. "It means the streets are packed with civilians. I guess Draven's using them as shields." The spy's calculating gaze met Rafe's, sharing an unspoken concern about what that might mean for their assault.

"We'll need to split our forces," Vale continued, spreading a crude map across a flat rock. "Hit multiple gates, draw out the guards-" He stopped mid-sentence as Liora approached.

"Your men will die needlessly," she stated, her voice carrying an otherworldly certainty that made Rafe's skin crawl. "I can sense Draven's thoughts. He expects this."

Rafe caught glimpses of the old Liora beneath the power - a flicker of uncertainty, a moment of compassion. But then her eyes would meet his, and he'd see galaxies of raw energy swirling in their depths. The woman he'd grown to love was wielding forces that could reshape reality itself.

"Then what do you suggest?" Vale challenged, though Rafe noticed how the commander's hand trembled slightly.

Thunder rolled overhead, and Liora turned toward Somnara's gates. "I suggest," she said, power rippling through her words, "that you let me show Draven what the Veilstone is truly capable of." Around them, the very air seemed to hold its breath, waiting for the chaos about to unfold.

Rafe watched Jayne step forward, her usual calculated demeanor replaced by raw determination.

"We didn't come this far to watch you martyr yourself," Jayne declared, earning murmurs of agreement from rebels that had gathered around. The words struck a chord in Rafe's chest. He'd seen too many good people sacrifice themselves in this war, starting with his own family in that burning village years ago.

"You misunderstand," Liora said, her voice carrying that unsettling echo that made Rafe's spine tingle. "I'm not sacrificing myself. I'm ensuring Draven can't use you against me." Rafe felt her power brush against his mind - gentle with him, unlike the brutal force she'd used on Draven's guards. But what truly chilled him was the smile playing at her lips, reminding him too much of Varden before his betrayal.

The scout's boots kicked up dust as she skidded to a halt before Rafe, her chest heaving. "The astronomers say less than an hour until the Eclipse begins," she gasped, pointing to where the twin moons had begun their celestial dance. Rafe's gut twisted as he watched their slow convergence, knowing what it meant for them all.

***

The rebel leaders huddled around a makeshift table, their faces illuminated by flickering torchlight. Liora traced her fingers along the table's edge as Rafe outlined their assault plan on Somnara. Through the enhancement of her abilities, the fears and doubts of those around her pressed against her consciousness like a physical weight.

The new lieutenant, a scarred woman named Serra, radiated skepticism that felt like needles against Liora's skin. The woman's thoughts leaked through - memories of other failed assaults, of comrades falling to Draven's forces. Liora caught fragments of Serra picturing her own death, imagining her body decorating Somnara's walls as a warning to others.

"We hit the Market District hard and fast," Rafe said, his calloused finger drawing a line across the crude map. "Varden knows our usual patterns, so we change them. No formations, no standard tactics. Pure chaos."

The strategy stirred memories of Eldara's festival, of chaos erupting into destruction. Liora pushed the thoughts away, focusing instead on the steady confidence radiating from Rafe. His faith in her felt like a warm ember against the cold press of responsibility.

"Once we draw their forces," Rafe continued, "Liora makes her move through the tunnels beneath the Fortress of Woe." His gaze met hers, carrying an unspoken weight. "Everything we do, every life risked, is to get you to Draven."

The pressure constricted her chest, but Liora refused to let it show. She sensed the mix of fear and hope surrounding her. These people, who once shunned her uncontrolled power, now staked everything on that same force.

Serra's voice cut through the murmurs. "And if she fails?" The question hung sharp as a blade, but Liora felt the genuine concern beneath the woman's harsh tone.

"Then we all fail," Rafe answered before Liora could speak.

Jayne unrolled a detailed sketch of the tunnel system, her fingers tracing the path they'd take. "These passages haven't been used since the Mason Rebellion. They'll be watching the obvious routes, expecting us to come straight through the gates."

The reality of what awaited settled over Liora like a shroud. Hundreds would fight and die as a distraction, their only purpose to clear her path to Draven.

"Gather your weapons, say your goodbyes. We move on Somnara now," Rafe declared, his hand briefly touching Liora's shoulder. Through that contact, she felt his fear - not of failure, but of losing her. She met his gaze, silently promising to return, even as her mind whispered of futures where such promises shattered like glass.

***

Liora watched the rebels disperse into the shadows, their armor gleaming dully in the fading light. Each farewell felt like another weight added to her shoulders, knowing their lives hung on her success. She caught fragments of their thoughts - prayers to forgotten gods, memories of loved ones, flashes of homes they might never see again. She willed her mind to withdraw, shielding herself from their intimate reflections.

"You're doing that thing again," Gemini said softly beside her, reaching out to touch Liora's arm. "Where you try to carry everyone's burden at once."

Liora turned to her friend, struck by how the approaching twilight softened Gemini's features, making her look more like the girl from their shared childhood in Eldara. Before powers and prophecies had complicated everything. "I can feel what they're all thinking, Gem. Their faith in me, their fear..."

"And what am I thinking?" Gemini's gentle smile carried echoes of countless quiet moments they'd shared, of herb gardens and flower crowns and whispered secrets.

Liora deliberately didn't reach for the Veilstone's power. "You're thinking I'm being too hard on myself. Again."

"I'm thinking how proud I am of you," Gemini corrected, pulling Liora into a fierce embrace. "That scared girl who once hid from her own power? She's grown into someone amazing."

The words caught in Liora's throat as Gemini's pride and love washed over her, more powerful than any magical insight the Veilstone could provide. She clutched her friend tighter, remembering all the times Gemini had believed in her when she couldn't believe in herself.

A horn sounded in the distance, signaling the first wave of rebels moving into position. Liora reluctantly pulled back from Gemini's embrace, seeing her own mix of fear and determination mirrored in her friend's eyes.

"You've never once looked at me with fear," Liora managed, her voice thick with emotion. "Even when I destroyed half the mill, even when my powers were completely out of control - you just saw me. Just Li."

"Because that's who you are," Gemini squeezed her hands, her touch grounding and real amid the swirling tension of pre-battle preparations. "All this talk of prophecies and destinies - they don't change the girl who used to weave flower crowns with me by the river. The one who nursed that injured fox kit back to health. The one who always, always tries to protect others, powers or no powers."

"Promise me something, Li. When you face him - when you're holding all that power in your hands - remember that girl. Remember that your strength comes from your heart, not just your magic."

The warmth of Gemini's embrace couldn't chase away the chill that had settled in Liora's bones.

"That girl you remember," Liora pulled back, her voice catching. "The one who made flower crowns and healed injured animals - I'm not sure she can survive what's coming." The words tasted like ash in her mouth, but the truth of them echoed in her heart. Already she felt changed by the Veilstone's power, by the weight of so many lives depending on her.

Gemini's face crumpled, a flash of pain crossing her features before she masked it. The expression cut deeper than any of Draven's attacks could have. Liora caught a stray thought - Gemini's desperate fear that she was losing her friend to something darker than death. The insight made Liora step back, creating distance between them.

"Li, please-" Gemini reached for her, but Liora turned away, unable to bear the pain in her friend's eyes. The space between them felt like a chasm now, wider than any physical distance.

***

Kael shifted uneasily atop the palace ramparts as crimson banners snapped in the wind. Below, the festival crowds filled Somnara's streets with their mindless revelry, their movements as mechanical as puppets dancing to Draven's strings. The sight churned his stomach.

The Ark of Dreams pulsed with an otherworldly glow before Draven, its crystalline surface reflecting the gathering darkness of the approaching Eclipse. Less than an hour, now. Kael's fingers twitched near his sword hilt as he watched his Emperor reach towards the box beside it.

Kael's jaw clenched as he watched the Veilstone pulse with an ethereal light, its crystalline facets casting haunting shadows across Draven's features.

The Emperor's fingers hovered inches from the Veilstone's surface, trembling with barely contained desire. Kael recognized that look - he'd worn it himself in those quiet moments alone with the stone during their journey to Somnara. The raw power it promised, the whispered temptations of absolute control. But where Kael had wrestled with his conscience, Draven showed no such internal struggle.

A guard shifted positions nearby, and Kael's hand instinctively moved to his sword hilt. The movement drew Draven's attention, those cold eyes fixing on him with predatory intensity. "Does something trouble you, General?" The words dripped with subtle venom, and Kael forced his fingers to relax.

"Beautiful, isn't it?" Draven's voice carried a hint of madness. "Soon, their dreams will fuel our ascension." His eyes gleamed with an intensity that reminded Kael of his father's final moments - that same desperate hunger for power that had led to his destruction.

The crowd's vacant cheering echoed off the palace walls as performers danced through the streets. Kael recognized faces he'd known since childhood, now twisted into grotesque masks of forced joy. Was this truly the protection he'd convinced himself he was fighting for?

A guard captain approached with news of the rebellion and Liora's advance. Kael's heart hammered against his ribs as Draven's lips curved into a predatory smile.

"Your loyalty has served us well, General Varden." Draven's words slithered down Kael's spine. "When the Eclipse reaches its peak, you'll have your reward." The promise rang hollow, like all the others that had led him down this path.

Shadows lengthened across the palace roof as the twin moons began their fatal dance. Kael watched a group of children below, their movements jerky and unnatural as they scattered flower petals. He'd told himself this was necessary, that order required sacrifice. Now, the cost seemed impossibly high.

The Veilstone's pulse quickened, matching the rhythm of Kael's growing dread. Each beat sent ripples through the air, distorting the reality around them like heat waves rising from sun-baked stones. He could feel its power reaching for him, promising everything he'd ever wanted.

Draven's consciousness slammed abruptly into Kael's thoughts, ripping open the scars Liora had left behind. The invasion forced him to his knees, and the festival crowds below blurred into a nauseating swirl of color and sound.

"Yes," Draven hissed, forcing Kael to relive every excruciating moment of Liora's assault. "Show me again how she broke you, my faithful general. Show me how she laid bare every fear, every weakness, every betrayal. How she ripped your memories from you."

Through the haze of remembered pain, Kael watched his own hands trembling against the stone floor. The shame of that defeat burned hotter than Draven's mental probe, reminding him of how far he'd fallen from the proud warrior he'd once been.

This time, the Ark's pulse quickened, matching the rapid beating of Kael's heart as Draven released his hold. Above them, the twin moons crept closer to alignment, their approaching convergence promising power beyond measure - or destruction beyond imagining.

"She was supposed to be desperate, broken," Draven snarled, pacing like a caged beast. "Your betrayal should have shattered her resolve, not strengthened it." Each word carried an accusation that pierced deeper than any blade.

Kael pushed himself back to his feet, legs unsteady as phantom echoes of Liora's power rippled through his mind. The festival continued its eerie performance below, but all he could hear was the approaching storm of a girl who'd learned to turn her pain into purpose - and the growing certainty that he'd chosen the wrong side in this war.

"Prepare my guard, General Varden." Draven's fingers traced patterns across the Ark's surface, leaving trails of ghostly light in their wake. "These rebels think themselves clever, they will attack when the Eclipse begins. Crush them. Make an example that all of Somnus will remember."

The order twisted in Kael's gut like a rusted blade. He'd led countless public executions before, but now the thought of more blood
spilled across Somnara's cobblestones made bile rise in his throat.

"And what of the girl?" The question slipped out before he could
stop it, his voice rougher than intended.

"I'll show her exactly how I broke her mother." Draven's smile
stretched wide, revealing too many teeth. "Again and again, until she
begs for death." The Emperor's eyes gleamed with a madness that
made Kael's skin crawl.

Draven paused, the Ark's pulse quickening beneath his palm. "Actually, before you marshal the guard..." His voice dropped to a silken
whisper that promised violence. "Bring me the miller from the Fortress
of Woe."

Ice spread through Kael's veins. He'd interrogated Bennet himself,
had seen the old man's unwavering loyalty to Liora. Now that loyalty
would become another weapon in Draven's arsenal.

The twin moons crept closer to alignment overhead as Kael bowed
stiffly, each movement sending fresh waves of pain through his skull.
"As you command, Emperor." The words tasted like ash on his tongue.

Festival dancers twirled below, their movements growing more
frenzied as the Eclipse approached. Their vacant eyes and fixed smiles
reminded Kael of corpses he'd seen on battlefields - bodies arranged in
grotesque poses by cruel hands.

He turned toward the palace stairs, his shadow stretching long and
dark across the stones. Behind him, Draven's laughter mingled with
the Ark's otherworldly hum, a discordant symphony that promised
only horror in the hours to come.

# For Somnus

G emini's tears blurred the flickering torchlight as she slumped against a weathered oak, her heart aching from Liora's parting words. The girl she'd grown up with, shared secrets and flower crowns with, seemed to be slipping away like water through cupped hands. Her fingers traced the familiar pattern of her healer's satchel, seeking comfort in its worn leather.

A shadow fell across her boots, and Jayne's distinctive footsteps crunched in the gravel. The spy's usual sharp edges seemed softer in the dying light. "May I join you?" Jayne's voice carried none of its usual steel.

"She's changing." Gemini's words caught in her throat. "The V eilstone... it's like watching someone drown, but they think they're learning to breathe underwater." Her hands trembled as she wiped away fresh tears.

Jayne settled beside her, their shoulders nearly touching. "You see it too, then." It wasn't a question.

"I've known her since we were children." Gemini pulled her knees to her chest. "She used to weave daisy chains and leave them on sick people's doorsteps, too shy to give them in person. That girl would never..." She trailed off, unable to voice her fears.

"Power changes people," Jayne murmured, but then added, "Though sometimes it just reveals who they truly are." Her hand found Gemini's shoulder, squeezing gently. "Your friendship grounds her. I've seen it."

Gemini turned to study Jayne's face, surprised by the warmth there. "You're not as cold as you pretend to be, are you?" The words slipped out before she could stop them.

A ghost of a smile touched Jayne's lips. "Perhaps not." She pulled something from her pocket - a small, wrapped bundle. "Here. Chamomile tea. For later, when this is over. We all need something to hold onto."

The simple gesture broke something in Gemini's chest. Fresh tears spilled as she accepted the tea, but these felt different - cleansing rather than desperate. "Thank you," she whispered, clutching the bundle like a lifeline.

Shouts erupted from the rebel camp - orders being given, weapons being distributed. The moment shattered like glass. Jayne stood, offering her hand to Gemini.

Gemini stared at Jayne's outstretched hand, her heart still raw from their conversation about Liora. The spy's usual stern expression had softened into something more vulnerable, more human. Taking the offered hand, Gemini pulled herself up from the ground, brushing dirt from her robes.

"I owe you both an apology," Jayne said, her voice barely above a whisper. "When we first met, I saw Liora as a weapon and you as..." She paused, shame coloring her features. "As someone who would hold her back. I was wrong."

Heat crept up Gemini's neck. Part of her wanted to agree, to let Jayne feel the full weight of her earlier coldness. But she thought of the tea bundle in her pocket, this unexpected gesture of kindness. "Fear makes us all do things we regret. The rebellion taught me that much."

Jayne reached beneath her cloak and withdrew a slender dagger in an ornate sheath. The metalwork caught the torchlight, dancing like captured stars. "This was my sister's," she said, holding it out. "Before Draven's forces..." Her voice cracked. "You're one of us now, Gemini. You should be able to protect yourself."

Gemini stared at the dagger, its metalwork catching the torchlight like trapped fireflies. Her stomach churned at the thought of wielding a weapon. "I'm a healer, Jayne. I took an oath to preserve life, not take it."

The spy's eyes hardened, though not unkindly. "And how many lives will be lost if you're cut down before you can reach them?" Jayne pressed the sheathed blade into Gemini's trembling hands. "Draven's forces won't spare you for your noble intentions."

"Better to die with a sword in your hand than in your back." Jayne's voice carried the weight of personal experience. "I've seen too many healers cut down while tending the wounded. Their deaths helped no one." The spy's hand covered Gemini's, adjusting her grip on the weapon. "Sometimes protecting life means being ready to fight for it."

Heat crept up her neck as Jayne's hand remained over hers, adjusting her grip on the ornate hilt. The spy's touch was gentler than expected, belying her usual sharp edges. Through their connected hands, Gemini sensed a tremor in Jayne's usually steady demeanor - was she remembering her sister?

Jayne's hand tightened over hers, steadying her grip on the dagger. "Remember," Jayne said, "your healing saves lives. This-" she tapped the blade's pommel "-ensures you live long enough to do it." Their eyes met, and Gemini saw something raw and vulnerable in Jayne's gaze.

The moment stretched between them like spun glass, fragile and precious. Jayne's hand slipped away, leaving Gemini's skin tingling where they'd touched. But before the spy could step back, Gemini caught her wrist. "Thank you," she whispered, meaning more than just the dagger. "For seeing me."

***

Gemini's pained eyes were burned into her mind as Liora watched the first forces marching off. Behind her, Rafe's footsteps crunched through the sand, hesitant yet determined. She didn't need to turn around to know the worry etched across his face.

"I should be protecting you," Rafe's voice cracked slightly. "Getting you as far from here as possible, not watching you walk into his trap." His hand reached for her shoulder but stopped short, trembling in the space between them.

Liora turned to face him. Shadows danced across his features, highlighting the fresh scars from their journey across the dunes. She saw the man who'd defended her in Eldara, who'd believed in her when she couldn't believe in herself. But now his strength seemed fragile, like autumn leaves clinging to their branches before the first frost.

"For once," Liora stepped closer, letting her power wrap around them both like a shield, "I'll be the one keeping you safe." The certainty in her voice surprised her. The girl who'd hidden from her powers in the mill seemed like a stranger now. She reached up, her fingers brushing his cheek, feeling the roughness of his stubble. "Trust me to be strong enough for both of us."

Words formed on his lips but died unspoken as horns blared from Somnara's walls, announcing the start of the Eclipse in mere minutes.

Liora's fingers lingered against Rafe's cheek. Her pulse thundered as the weight of unsaid words pressed against her throat.

"Rafe, I-" The confession caught, tangled with fear and hope and the crushing awareness that these moments might be their last. She forced herself to meet his gaze, finding the same mix of terror and tenderness mirrored there. "Whatever happens up there, I need you to know that I've fallen in love with you."

His sharp intake of breath cut through the distant sounds of the gathering army. Rafe's hand tightened around hers, still pressed against his face, and she felt him trembling.

"Liora," her name fell from his lips like a prayer, "I've loved you since that night in Eldara, when you chose to stay and fight rather than run." He pulled her closer, his free hand tangling in her hair. "I think I'll love you until the day I die, whether that's today or fifty years from now."

The pressure of his lips against hers sent sparks across Liora's senses, and for a moment, everything else faded into the background. The whispers of the Veilstone fell silent, and even the distant preparations for war melted away. There was only Rafe and the taste of his mouth, the feel of his calloused hands against her skin.

When they finally pulled apart, breathless, Liora's cheeks were flushed, and her heart raced. She pressed a hand to her chest, feeling like the emotions bubbling under her skin might overflow. If she could have bottled this feeling and kept it forever, she would have. It was dangerous, to be sure, but it was also freeing. In that moment, she wasn't the last of the Dreamweavers, burdened with prophecy and feared by her own people. She was just a girl, kissing the boy she loved.

A breeze stirred, carrying the sweet scent of desert flowers, and she shivered slightly, goose bumps rising on her arms. Rafe noticed and pulled her closer, his fingers tangling with hers. She stepped into the circle of his arms, and her heart stuttered as she remembered the feel of his body against hers.

The night before, Liora had explored his muscles with her hands, tasted the salt of his skin with her tongue. She had discovered a multitude of sensations and experiences, and yet here he was, offering more. She closed the distance between them, her lips finding his again as she leaned into him. His mouth opened under hers, a silent invitation, and she accepted, stepping forward to press their bodies together. Their kiss deepened, becoming more urgent, more needy. She felt his desire like a physical touch, and her skin flushed with heat.

Liora pulled away, breathless. She felt raw and exposed, but somehow that only made her want more. This was what it meant to be alive, to feel everything so deeply. She didn't know how long they stood there, clutching each other in the fading twilight, but when they finally separated, the world felt different. She was different.

The warmth of Rafe's kiss lingered on Liora's lips as she watched him disappear into the gathering shadows. Her fingers traced where his touch had been moments before, the ghost of their connection still humming through her veins.

Above, the twin moons crept closer to their fateful alignment with the sun. The air itself seemed to hold its breath, charged with an electric tension that made her skin prickle. Through the Veilstone's enhanced awareness, she felt the dream magic saturating the atmosphere growing stronger with each passing second. It called to her like a siren's song, promising power beyond measure.

Memories of her mother's sacrifice flickered through her mind - not the twisted visions Draven had planted, but the true ones she'd uncovered in the temple. The same choice lay before her now: to wield this power for protection or dominion. The fear she'd carried since discovering her powers in Eldara fell away. She was ready. With the Veilstone's power thrumming through her veins and love burning in her heart, she turned toward the city and took her first step toward destiny.

***

Rafe's boots crunched against the gravel path, each step carrying him further from Liora and closer to the inevitable battle ahead. His chest ached with a peculiar mix of elation and dread. Her whispered confession of love still echoed in his ears, a bittersweet melody that threatened to unravel his composure.

Commander Vale's silhouette materialized through the pre-dawn mist, his battle-worn armor reflecting the dim torchlight. The commander's presence anchored Rafe back to reality, reminding him of the weight of their mission. Hundreds of rebels waited in formation behind Vale, their nervous energy palpable in the darkness.

Those three words from Liora had changed everything and nothing at once. Rafe had always known, somewhere deep in his soul, that his heart belonged to her. But hearing her say it aloud made the impending assault on Somnara's gates feel different – more desperate, more vital.

His hand brushed against the hilt of his sword, feeling the familiar worn leather grip. The weapon had been his constant companion through countless battles, but none as crucial as this. The fate of Somnus hung in the balance, and with it, his future with Liora.

Vale's grim expression spoke volumes as Rafe approached. "The eastern group is prepared?" the commander asked, his voice barely above a whisper. Rafe nodded, pushing thoughts of Liora to the back of his mind. There would be time for love after they'd won – if they won.

The first hints of the Eclipse painted the sky in unsettling hues, casting strange shadows across the assembled forces. Rafe couldn't help but glance back toward where he'd left Liora, though she was now hidden from view.

"Your men are ready?" Vale's question cut through Rafe's thoughts. He turned back to face his commander, noting the lines of worry etched deeper than usual around the older man's eyes. They both knew the cost of failure.

Memories of their last intimate moment threatened to overwhelm him – the warmth of her touch, the tremor in her voice as she confessed her feelings. Rafe clenched his jaw, forcing himself to focus on the mission. Love was a luxury they couldn't afford, not until Draven was defeated.

A scout materialized from the shadows, breathing heavily. "Imperial guards are changing shifts," he reported. "We have our window." Vale's hand tightened on his sword hilt, and Rafe felt his pulse quicken in response.

Rafe caught Vale's piercing gaze through the gloom, the commander's weathered face betraying a hint of concern. "You understand we're walking straight into Draven's trap?" Vale's question hung in the air between them, heavy with implications.

A familiar rush of anticipation coursed through Rafe's veins, and he couldn't suppress the grim smile that tugged at his lips. "Whatever trap he's laid, I know you'll lead us through it."

Vale's calloused hand gripped Rafe's shoulder, the pressure firm and grounding. "No, Delacroix. You're closer to this than any of us." The commander's voice carried an unexpected weight. "You know Liora's capabilities, her strengths. You understand what's at stake."

The reality of Vale's words struck Rafe like a physical blow. Every moment with Liora – training sessions, shared dangers, intimate confessions – had prepared him for this. He knew her power, her determination, and most importantly, her heart.

Memories of their last embrace threatened to distract him, but Rafe forced them aside. The scout shifted nervously nearby, awaiting orders, while the assembled rebels maintained their tense formation behind them.

"The eastern approach will be heavily guarded," Rafe found himself saying, his tactical mind taking over. "But if Liora's vision is correct, the sewers beneath the market district will be lightly defended." The words flowed naturally now, pieces falling into place.

Vale nodded slowly, a glimmer of approval in his eyes. "Your command, then. What are your orders?" The question carried both trust and challenge, and Rafe felt the weight of responsibility settle onto his shoulders.

The first rays of the Eclipse painted the sky in ethereal colors, casting strange shadows across the gathered forces. Rafe's hand tightened on his sword hilt as he surveyed the men and women who would follow him into battle.

Time seemed to slow as Rafe absorbed the magnitude of the moment. These weren't just soldiers anymore – they were his to lead, to protect, to guide through whatever hell Draven had prepared for them.

Rafe's sword sang as he drew it from its scabbard, the familiar weight settling into his palm like an old friend. The assembled rebels stood before him, their faces a mix of determination and fear in the strange light of the approaching Eclipse. His heart thundered against his ribs as he stepped forward to address them.

"Look around you," he called out, his voice carrying across the gathered forces. "Each of you stands here because you've lost something to Draven's tyranny. Your homes, your families, your freedom." The words poured from somewhere deep within, fueled by years of pain and purpose. "Today, we take it all back."

Murmurs of agreement rippled through the crowd as Rafe continued, his grip tightening on his sword. "We are not just rebels anymore. We are the dawn that breaks through Draven's endless night. We are the hope that survives in the darkest corners of Somnus." The troops straightened, shoulders squaring as his words ignited their resolve.

"When they tell stories of this day," Rafe's voice grew stronger, "they won't speak of how many we were, or what weapons we carried. They'll tell of how we stood together, how we fought for something greater than ourselves." The Eclipse cast strange shadows across the assembled faces, but their eyes burned bright with determination.

His gaze found Liora among the crowd, her golden energy shimming around her like a halo in the ethereal light. Their eyes locked across the distance, and in that moment, everything else fell away. "Ready?" he mouthed, his heart clenching at the sight of her.

She gave a single, firm nod, her chin lifting with quiet determination. Rafe felt a surge of pride mixed with fear. This was what they'd trained for, what they'd sacrificed everything to achieve.

Turning back to face Somnara's imposing gates, Rafe raised his sword high. The metal caught the Eclipse's light, throwing scattered reflections across the assembled rebels. The moment stretched thin as a bowstring, pregnant with possibility and danger.

"For Somnus!" The battle cry tore from his throat, raw and powerful. A hundred voices took up the call, the sound swelling into a deafening roar that shook the very ground beneath their feet.

Rafe's boots pounded against the earth as he charged forward, leading the assault on the gates. Behind him, the rebel army surged like a tide, their combined footfalls creating a thunder that rivaled the storm in his heart.

The distance to the gates vanished with each stride, and Rafe could see the Imperial guards scrambling to respond. His world narrowed to the space between one heartbeat and the next, between one breath and another. As arrows began to rain down from the battlements, Rafe's voice joined the continuing battle cry, and the rebellion crashed against Somnara's defenses like a wave breaking against stone.

# The Eclipse of Dreams

The market square erupted into chaos as Rafe's forces charged through the festival crowds. Liora's heart hammered as she ran behind him, her magic already weaving protective barriers around their band of rebels. The screams of civilians pierced the air as they scattered, leaving abandoned stalls and trampled decorations in their wake.

Dream-twisted arrows rained down from the palace walls, their corrupted magic seeking to entangle the rebels in nightmares. Liora reached out with her enhanced powers, catching the arrows in a web of golden light before they could touch her companions. The strain of maintaining the shield while running made her muscles burn, but she refused to let it drop.

She sensed Gemini and Jayne moving through the sewers below, their presence like flickering candles in her mind. The fear radiating from Gemini felt like ice in her veins, but her friend's determination burned even brighter. Jayne's cold focus provided an anchor for them both as they led their force toward the palace foundations.

A squad of Draven's elite guard emerged from an alley, their armor gleaming with corrupt sigils. Liora's magic surged instinctively as one charged at Rafe, throwing the soldier backward into his companions. The power felt different now - controlled, precise, an extension of her will rather than a wild force to be feared.

Blood splashed across cobblestones as rebels and guards clashed in the narrow streets. Liora caught glimpses of familiar faces twisted in combat, but she couldn't stop to help them all. The palace loomed closer, Draven's presence at its peak a dark stain against her magical awareness. Each step toward it made her heart pulse faster.

Another wave of guards poured from the surrounding buildings, threatening to cut off their advance. Liora reached deeper into her power, drawing out threads of golden energy that wrapped around the soldiers' minds. Their eyes glazed over as she forced them into peaceful dreams, their weapons clattering to the ground as they slumped unconscious.

The effort left her gasping, but Rafe's hand on her arm steadied her. Through their connection, she felt Gemini's group encountering resistance below, the clash of steel echoing through the tunnels. The urge to help her friend tore at her, but she knew her path led upward, toward the growing shadow of Draven's power.

A massive explosion rocked the square as rebel forces breached another section of the city. The distraction they'd planned was working - Draven's forces were being drawn away from the palace, spread thin across multiple fronts. But the cost was written in the bodies already littering the streets, rebels and citizens alike caught in the crossfire.

The palace gates stood before them now, their ancient metal writhing with corrupt dream magic. Liora's power clashed against Draven's defenses, golden light meeting twisted shadows in a spectacular display.

The palace gates loomed ahead, surrounded by Draven's most elite guards. Liora sensed the twisted threads of Draven's control woven through their minds. Their thoughts felt wrong - muffled and distorted like voices underwater.

Golden light flowed from her hands as she reached for the nearest guard's consciousness. The man's eyes widened in terror as her power brushed against Draven's hold, but she pressed deeper, untangling the dark magic strand by strand. His face transformed as awareness returned, horror dawning as he realized what had been done to him.

Each mind she touched revealed new horrors - memories of being forced to hurt loved ones, to betray their own people. These weren't just soldiers, they were victims. As she freed them, their rage at Draven's violation fueled their decision to join the rebel assault, turning their weapons against their former master.

A young woman in officer's armor stumbled forward as Liora broke Draven's hold over her. Tears streamed down her face as she remembered ordering her own brother's execution. Her anguish hit Liora like a physical blow, but the officer's next words came out steady: "The throne room. I'll show you the fastest way." More freed guards rallied behind her, their combined knowledge of the palace layout becoming a crucial advantage.

Blood and sweat stung Liora's eyes as she worked her way through the ranks of controlled soldiers. Each liberation drained more of her strength, but left more allies in their wake. She felt Draven's fury building above them as his forces turned against him. His presence pressed down like a storm cloud, growing darker with each mind she stole from his grasp. But the growing army of freed soldiers at her back gave her the strength to continue pushing forward, up toward the final confrontation that awaited.

Liora's heart stopped as Bennet's presence flickered on the edges of her consciousness. He radiated fear and pain from the palace's highest tower, where Draven's dark power coiled around him like a serpent. The bond between them, forged through years at the mill, stretched taut with his suffering.

Liora's magic flared as another guard collapsed before her, their mind freed from Draven's control. Through the chaos of battle, her eyes found Rafe's across the blood-stained marble floor. His sword flashed as he parried a strike, but his gaze locked with hers for a heartbeat. In that moment, she poured all her unspoken feelings into a single look - love, fear, determination.

The pull of Bennet's presence tugged at her consciousness like a hook in her chest. His pain radiated through their connection, each wave making her stomach clench. Rafe would understand why she had to leave, why she couldn't stay to help him fight. The memory of Bennet's gentle guidance at the mill, his unwavering faith in her even when she doubted herself, drove her forward.

Guards tried to block her path as she sprinted toward the grand staircase, but her magic lashed out instinctively. Golden light wrapped around their minds, sending them slumping to the floor in peaceful dreams. Each use of power drained her further, but she couldn't stop - not with Bennet's agony pulsing through her awareness like a beacon.

Draven's power now felt like a physical force that made the air thick and hard to breathe. But Liora pushed through it, drawing on everything she'd learned since that first night in Eldara when her power awakened. This time, she would not let fear hold her back.

***

Blood sprayed across Rafe's face as his blade found another of Draven's soldiers. Through the chaos of battle, his heart seized - Liora had entered the palace. Alone. The crowd of fighting bodies surged around him, but that golden shimmer that marked her presence had vanished completely.

"Damn it, Li," he muttered, parrying a wild swing from another guard. Her choice to face Draven alone shouldn't have surprised him. The kiss they'd shared still burned on his lips, and now he understood it had been a goodbye.

A rebel cry pierced the air as more of their forces poured into the market square. Rafe's blade sang as he cut through the press of bodies, his muscles burning with each strike. He couldn't follow her - his place was here, leading the assault that would give her the chance she needed.

The metallic tang of blood filled his nostrils as he pressed forward, watching their rebels clash with Draven's forces. Each soldier they faced seemed to wake from a dream-induced haze as Liora's influence spread through the city. Some turned on their former comrades, while others fled in confusion.

"For Somnus!" Rafe's voice carried over the din of battle. His men responded, surging ahead with renewed vigor. Above them, the twin moons crept closer together, the Eclipse's approach marking their dwindling time.

The weight of the Veilstone's power still lingered in his mind - he'd felt it when Liora had looked into his thoughts. That kind of power could corrupt, could destroy. But he'd seen the strength in her eyes, the determination to remain herself despite it all.

Another guard fell to his blade as memories of Twilight Camp flashed through his mind. He'd watched her nearly break under the weight of her power then. Now she faced an even greater challenge, alone on that palace roof with Draven and his Ark of Dreams.

"Commander!" His second called out. "The eastern quarter is secured!" Rafe nodded, dispatching another soldier with a quick thrust. Their plan was working - the rebellion's attack drew Draven's forces away from the palace, spreading them thin across the city.

A fresh wave of guards poured from a side street, their eyes glazed with Draven's control. Rafe raised his blade, roaring a challenge that his rebels echoed. He couldn't protect Liora now, but he could ensure she had the time she needed. The thought steeled his resolve as he charged forward, blade flashing in the eclipse-darkened sky.

A flash of movement caught Rafe's attention - Kael Varden's distinctive armor gleaming at the head of a column of elite guards. The sight of his former mentor sent rage coursing through Rafe's veins. Every death, every betrayal could be traced back to that man's treachery. The guard beside Rafe crumpled under an elite's blade, but Rafe barely registered the loss, his focus locked on Varden's approaching figure.

"Form up!" Rafe's command cut through the chaos as elite guards crashed into their lines. These weren't the mindless puppets they'd faced before - these were Draven's finest, their movements precise and lethal. Three rebels fell in the first clash, their screams lost in the din of steel on steel. Rafe parried a thrust meant for his heart, his counter-strike hampered by exhaustion that made his sword feel like lead.

Kael's voice carried over the fighting, ordering his men to encircle the rebel force. The bastard's tactical brilliance hadn't diminished with his betrayal. Rafe caught glimpses of him through the press of bodies - always just out of reach, directing his troops with the same cold efficiency that had once earned Rafe's admiration. Now that calculating nature served Draven, turning this street into a killing ground for rebels who'd once called him commander.

A rebel archer fell beside Rafe, an elite guard's sword buried in his chest. The man's eyes locked with Rafe's as life fled them, adding another weight to the burden of command. They were being cut to pieces, yet retreat would doom Liora's mission. Rafe roared a challenge at Kael, but his voice was swallowed by the clash of steel and screams of the dying. Above them, the Eclipse crept closer, casting an other-worldly pall over the bloodshed below.

Blood trickled down Rafe's blade as he cut through the last guard between him and Kael. His former mentor stood with that same cal-culating posture he'd used during training sessions, sword held in a deceptively casual guard. The sight made Rafe's stomach turn.

Rafe spat blood onto the cobblestones, his sword tracking Kael's every movement. The man who'd once taught him everything about warfare now stood as his enemy, that familiar half-smile twisting into something cruel.

"You taught us to fight for what's right," Rafe kept his blade angled, watching for the telltale shift in Kael's stance that always preceded his attacks. "Was that just another lie? Like everything else?"

Kael's sword gleamed in the eclipse light. "Right? Wrong? Those are luxuries for people who've never had to make real choices." His blade whipped out, testing Rafe's guard. "You're still so naive, thinking the world divides neatly into good and evil."

"This isn't about philosophy." Rafe circled left, feeling the ache of old wounds Kael had helped him earn. "You betrayed us. Led Draven's forces straight to the ruins. Marcus, Nero - their blood is on your hands."

A flash of something - regret maybe - crossed Kael's features before vanishing behind that mask of indifference. "And what of the blood on yours? How many have died following your orders today?" His sword rose to point at Rafe's heart. "At least I chose power over pretty ideals. What's your excuse for leading these fools to slaughter?"

Kael's lip curled. "I taught you to recognize weakness, to exploit it. The rebellion is weak - clinging to outdated ideals of freedom while Draven shapes a new future." His voice carried that same instructional tone he'd used in countless practice sessions. "You could still join us. The girl's power will break her, just as it broke her mother."

The mention of Liora sent fresh rage coursing through Rafe's veins. His grip tightened on his sword until his knuckles went white. "You don't get to speak her name. Not after what you did." The faces of the dead flashed through his mind - Marcus, Nero, countless others who'd trusted Kael. "She's stronger than you'll ever understand."

Their blades met with a resounding clash that seemed to shake the very air. Kael's technique was flawless as ever, each movement flowing into the next with practiced precision. But Rafe saw something new in his former mentor's eyes - a shadow of doubt, a flicker of fear that hadn't been there before. The sight fueled Rafe's attacks as their deadly dance began in earnest.

***

The marble halls of Draven's palace echoed with Liora's footsteps despite her attempts at stealth. No guards blocked her path - not even a servant scurried through the corridors. The emptiness felt deliberate, mocking.

Light from the Eclipse filtered through stained glass windows, casting fractured shadows across the floor. Liora's powers stretched out, testing the air, seeking the telltale signs of Draven's magic. Nothing. The absence of resistance only confirmed what she already knew - he waited above, believing he'd lured her into his trap. A ghost of a smile played across her lips as she climbed another sweeping staircase.

The Veilstone's energy surged stronger with each step toward the palace roof. Its power called to something deep within her, something that had always been there but only now fully awakened. Draven thought he understood her power, thought he could break her like he broke her mother. But he hadn't seen what the stone had shown her in those ancient ruins - hadn't witnessed her embrace both light and shadow within herself.

Whispers of memory - Bennet's voice, his pain - pulled at her consciousness from somewhere above. The bait in Draven's trap. Her heart clenched, but she forced herself to maintain focus. Every corridor she passed through remained suspiciously clear, leading her exactly where Draven wanted. Let him think he was in control. Let him believe she was rushing blindly to save her mentor.

The final door to the roof lay ahead, sunlight bleeding through its edges. Liora paused, feeling the Veilstone's power coiling inside her like a spring waiting to be released. Draven expected her to burst through, emotional and unprepared. Instead, she closed her eyes, reaching out with her mind.

Liora pushed through the heavy door, and the full force of the Eclipse's golden light washed over her. Her eyes found Bennet first - slumped forward on his knees, trembling as dark tendrils of Draven's corrupted dream magic wrapped around his mind.

The Ark's corrupted magic made her skin crawl, its crystal surface casting sickly patterns in the Eclipse's light. Beside it, the Veilstone pulsed golden, calling to her power. She felt Bennet's fractured thoughts through his nightmare but stayed focused, remembering the Veilstone's revelations. Draven understood only corruption and control, never creation or protection.

The Eclipse's light grew, making the Veilstone pulse with energy. Its power resonated in her blood, echoing her mother's legacy and all prior Dreamweavers. Though Draven controlled the Ark of Dreams, he couldn't grasp true dream magic's potential when wielded by one who accepted its duality.

"Let him go." The words left her mouth before she could stop them. Draven's lips curved into a cruel smile as he tightened his grip on the Ark, causing Bennet to cry out. The sound pierced through her, and the Veilstone flared in response to her surge of anger. Its warmth spread up her arm, whispering of power, of vengeance.

Dark magic crackled between them as Draven took a step forward. "Your mother made similar demands." His voice carried across the roof, smooth as silk and sharp as steel. "Before I showed her the true cost of defiance." Another twist of power wracked Bennet's body. Through their connected minds, Liora felt an echo of his agony, felt him trying to tell her to run.

The Veilstone's energy coiled tighter within her, ready to strike. But Nero's teachings echoed in her memory - power without purpose was just destruction waiting to happen. She forced herself to breathe, to think past the rage building in her chest. Draven wanted her to attack blindly, to lose control. No. She wouldn't give him what he wanted. She wouldn't become what he expected.

The Veilstone's warmth pulsed against Liora's mind as Draven circled closer, his shadow stretching across the sun-bleached stones. Her powers sensed the dark tendrils of his magic wrapping around the rooftop like hungry serpents, waiting to strike.

"Did you think finding the Veilstone was your own choice?" Draven's lips curled into a knowing smile. "Every step of your journey - the attack on Eldara, your training with that fool Nero, even your touching romance with the rebel captain - all orchestrated to shape you into the weapon I required." The Ark of Dreams gleamed in his grip, its corrupted surface reflecting the Eclipse's golden light.

Through their connected minds, Liora felt Bennet trying to warn her, but Draven's magic crushed his thoughts into whispers. Her heart thundered as understanding crashed over her. The convenient timing of Rafe's arrival in Eldara, Kael's careful manipulation of the rebel council, the suspiciously clear path to the Veilstone - she'd walked right into his web, exactly as he'd planned.

"Your mother believed she could resist too." Draven's voice softened with false sympathy as he gestured to the Ark. "But in the end, she understood her place. As will you, Liora Solari."

The name struck Liora like a physical blow. Solari. Her mother's name, her true inheritance. Not the broken pieces Draven had tried to forge into a weapon, but something deeper, more profound. The Veilstone hummed against her skin, its power resonating with the truth in her blood.

Memories flooded through her - her mother's face, backlit by golden dream magic as she wove protective barriers around their home. The way Lyra's hands had moved, creating not destruction but shelter, sanctuary. The Veilstone's energy shifted, no longer a coiled spring waiting to strike, but a flowing river of possibility.

Draven's smug expression faltered as Liora straightened, power radiating from her in waves that matched the Eclipse's pulsing light. She felt Bennet's pride cutting through his pain, felt the strength of his belief in her. The name Solari echoed in her mind, carrying with it generations of Dreamweavers who had understood that true power lay not in domination, but in protection.

Golden light erupted from the Veilstone as it tore free from its place beside Draven, shooting across the space between them like a falling star. The stone slammed into Liora's palm with enough force to make her stumble, but its warmth spread up her arm like coming home. Power surged through her veins, familiar yet different from before - no longer fighting to break free, but flowing in harmony with her intentions.

Draven's face contorted, the composed mask cracking to reveal the rage beneath. His fingers tightened around the Ark of Dreams until his knuckles turned white. "Insolent child." Dark energy crackled around him, making the air taste like metal and ash. "You think having the stone makes you its master?"

Dark magic crackled between them as he raised his hand, and Liora felt invisible bonds tightening around her limbs. The Veilstone's power strained against his control, but his grip on the Ark gave him the advantage. "Kneel before your Emperor, little Dreamweaver. Accept your destiny as my instrument."

Pain lanced through Liora's body as Draven's power pressed down, forcing her to one knee. The Veilstone's energy flickered wildly, responding to her distress. She glimpsed Bennet's anguished expression through her tears, saw the triumph blazing in Draven's eyes as he towered over her. But beneath the agony, beneath the crushing weight of his control, something else stirred - a deeper power that the Veilstone had awakened, one that Draven couldn't possibly understand.

She felt Bennet's pain through their mental link, drawing strength from memories of peaceful mornings and his steady guidance. The Veilstone's power flowed through her in waves that matched those memories.

Golden light threaded between her fingers as she worked beneath Draven's magic, finding the paths he'd corrupted. The Veilstone guided her to restore rather than destroy, unlocking what he'd forced closed. She dissolved the dark tendrils from Bennet's mind one by one with her light.

Draven clutched the Ark harder, pouring more power into his control. But Liora had found her opening, and the Veilstone's energy swept through like cleansing rain. She felt Bennet's mind reaching back, helping break the final bonds.

The final tendril snapped with a crack that echoed across the rooftop. Bennet slumped forward, gasping as his thoughts became his own again. Through their connected minds, Liora felt his relief, his gratitude - and his warning.

Liora's triumph evaporated as Draven's hand shot out, hurling Bennet across the rooftop like a discarded toy. Her mentor's body crumpled against the far wall, and their mental connection snapped with a pain that made her teeth clench. The Veilstone pulsed against her palm, responding to her spike of fear.

"Impressive." Draven's voice carried no trace of anger at her success. If anything, he sounded pleased. "You've learned to untangle my work without destroying the mind beneath." The Ark of Dreams gleamed in his hands, its crystalline surface drinking in the Eclipse's light. "Your mother never managed that level of... finesse."

The casual mention of her mother sent a fresh wave of rage through her body. The Veilstone's energy surged in response, but Liora forced it back, remembering Nero's warnings about letting emotion drive her power. "You have no idea what I'm capable of." Her voice remained steady despite the thunder of her heart.

Draven's smile widened, revealing teeth that seemed too sharp in the golden light. "Oh, but I do." He raised the Ark, and its surface began to ripple like disturbed water. "I've been waiting for someone worthy of witnessing the Ark's true potential."

The world shifted between one breath and the next. The Eclipse's light vanished as if someone had drawn a curtain across the sun. Darkness crashed over her in a wave, and the Veilstone's warmth became her only anchor as reality dissolved around her. Through their brief connection, she heard Bennet's desperate warning fade into nothing.

# Liora's True Potential

G emini's boots splashed through filthy water as she followed
Jayne's lead through the winding sewers. The dagger at her hip
felt foreign, wrong - a healer carrying a weapon seemed like a cruel
joke. But Jayne's words echoed in her mind: better to die fighting than
helpless.

The stench made her eyes water, but she pressed on, watching
Jayne's graceful movements ahead. Their small force moved with
practiced stealth, though Gemini felt clumsy in comparison. Her
thoughts drifted to Liora, praying her friend's strength would hold
against whatever awaited above.

A shaft of light pierced the darkness ahead - their exit point. Gemini's heart thundered against her ribs as they approached. Something
felt wrong. The air carried an electric tension that made her skin
prickle with warning.

Jayne raised her fist, signaling them to halt. The spy's body language
screamed danger, but before she could voice her concern, chaos erupt-

ed. Elite guards poured from hidden alcoves, their armor gleaming in the dim light.

"It's a trap!" Jayne's voice cut through the sudden clash of steel. She spun, blade flashing, taking down two guards in rapid succession. Gemini pressed herself against the slimy wall, terror freezing her in place as rebels fell around her.

Derek and Maya stood among the elite guards, their rebel uniforms a mockery of loyalty. Of course they'd known about the sewers. Her stomach twisted with betrayal.

Blood and sewage mingled at her feet as watched Derek cut down a rebel he'd once shared a bed with. His movements carried no hesitation, just brutal efficiency. This was his true nature, revealed at last. Maya's twin daggers found their mark with deadly precision, picking off rebels who'd trusted her with their lives days ago.

"Healer Estelle," Derek's voice carried a mocking edge as he approached through the chaos. "Lord Draven sends his regards." His sword dripped red, and his eyes held none of the warmth she'd once mistaken for friendship. Gemini's grip tightened on her dagger as she searched desperately for Jayne in the melee. They needed a miracle, and fast.

Gemini's fingers trembled against the dagger's hilt, unable to draw the weapon as Derek advanced. Around her, the sewer tunnel had transformed into a killing ground, the splash of boots in putrid water now mixed with screams and the ring of steel.

The tunnel walls pressed in around her, the stench of death and sewage making her head spin. Her instincts screamed to help the fallen rebels, but survival locked her muscles in place. Derek's boots splashed through the filthy water, deliberate steps bringing death closer with each moment.

Sweat trickled down her spine as she pressed harder against the slimy wall. Her mind raced through everything Jayne had taught her about self-defense, but terror scattered the lessons like leaves in a storm. The dagger might as well have been a child's toy for all the good it would do her now.

Derek's lips curved into a cruel smile as he raised his sword. "Nothing personal, Healer." The blade whistled through the air, and Gemini squeezed her eyes shut, waiting for the bite of steel.

Instead, a wet gurgle filled her ears. Her eyes flew open to see Derek's face twisted in shock, the tip of a blade protruding from his chest. Blood bubbled from his lips as he dropped his weapon, the clang echoing off the tunnel walls.

Jayne's voice cut through the chaos as she yanked her sword free. "That was for Marcus." Derek's body crumpled into the filthy water, his betrayal repaid in full measure. The spy's normally composed features held a fierce satisfaction as she kicked his corpse aside.

Blood spattered Jayne's face and clothes, but her movements remained fluid and deadly as she dispatched another elite guard who charged their position. The precision of her strikes spoke of years of training, so different from Gemini's fumbling attempts with the dagger.

Gemini's legs threatened to give out as the reality of her near-death experience hit her. The tunnel spun slightly, the metallic scent of blood mixing with the sewage to create a nauseating cocktail. Her fingers finally released their death grip on the unused dagger.

Jayne's blood-streaked face softened with concern as she turned back to Gemini. "Are you hurt?" Her eyes scanned for injuries with the intensity of a hawk, while her sword remained ready for any new threats. The sounds of fighting continued further down the tunnel, but their immediate area had cleared.

The question seemed to come from very far away as Gemini stared at Derek's body floating face-down in the murky water. She'd treated his wounds, shared her food with him, trusted him. Her stomach lurched as she realized how close she'd come to joining him in death. "I..." The words stuck in her throat as shock set in, the tunnel walls wavering around her.

Her eyes darted between shadowy figures, trying to distinguish friend from foe in the chaos. Years of training as a healer had taught her where to strike to save a life - now those same lessons whispered darker knowledge of where to strike to end one. The thought made bile rise in her throat.

A rebel fell nearby, clutching a crimson-stained side. Instinct drove Gemini to step forward, but she caught herself. In this madness, stopping to heal would only create two corpses instead of one. The guilt of inaction burned in her chest like acid.

The tunnel echoed with Jayne's controlled voice, directing their remaining forces. Even in crisis, the spy moved like a deadly dancer, her blade finding gaps in armor with practiced precision. Gemini found herself mesmerized by the lethal grace, her heart stuttering for reasons beyond fear.

Gemini's heart slammed against her ribs as Maya launched herself at Jayne with a feral snarl. The betrayer's daggers flashed in the dim light, forcing Jayne to leap backward or be gutted. Water splashed around their feet, turning pink with blood from earlier kills.

Maya fought like a woman possessed, her strikes coming faster and more vicious with each passing moment. "He was worth ten of you!" Her voice cracked with rage as she pressed her attack, forcing Jayne closer to the tunnel wall. The confined space left little room for fancy footwork.

The metallic ring of steel on steel echoed off the slimy walls as Jayne parried another flurry of strikes. Her usual grace seemed hampered by fatigue from the earlier fighting, her movements a fraction slower than normal. A dagger slipped past her guard, drawing a thin line of red across her bicep.

Gemini's fingers clenched uselessly around her own dagger, her body refusing to move. She'd seen Jayne train countless times, but this was different. Maya fought with the desperate fury of someone with nothing left to lose, and it showed in every savage thrust and slash.

Blood dripped steadily from Jayne's arm, her breaths coming in controlled but heavy bursts. She'd always made fighting look like a dance, but now each movement carried the weight of exhaustion. Maya's twin daggers kept finding gaps in her defense, adding small cuts that would soon add up.

The betrayer's blade whistled past Jayne's throat, missing by a hair's breadth. Gemini's breath caught in her throat - one slip, one moment of hesitation, and it would be over. Her medical knowledge painted vivid pictures of exactly how quickly someone could bleed out from a throat wound.

Maya pressed her advantage, backing Jayne into a corner where the tunnel curved. "I'll send you to join him," she spat, her features twisted with grief and hatred. Her next strike drew blood from Jayne's shoulder, deeper than the previous cuts.

Tears blurred Gemini's vision as she watched Jayne stumble slightly on the uneven floor. Her healer's instincts screamed to help, but her legs remained frozen in place. She'd seen death before, but never like this - never so personal, never so brutal.

The spy's back hit the wall, and Maya's lips curved in triumph as she raised both daggers for a killing blow. Time seemed to slow as Gemini

saw death reaching for Jayne with steel fingers. Her heart threatened
to burst from her chest.

Gemini's hand found the dagger's hilt without conscious thought.
Her feet carried her forward through the filthy water, every lesson
about preserving life screaming in protest. But watching Jayne struggle
awakened something primal, something that burned hotter than fear.

Maya never saw her coming. Gemini guided the blade between her
ribs with surgical precision, her free hand steadying Maya's body to
muffle the sound of her fall. The action felt simultaneously foreign
and familiar, like a nightmare version of her usual work.

Jayne's eyes widened in recognition as her foe crumpled. For a
heartbeat, their gazes locked across the dying guard's body - recognition, gratitude, and something deeper passing between them. The
moment shattered as more shouts echoed from further down the
tunnel. Gemini stared at her bloodied hands, her mind struggling to
reconcile the healer she'd been with what she'd just done. The dagger's
weight felt different now - no longer foreign, but transformed into
something more complex.

Blood dripped from Gemini's trembling fingers, each crimson drop
disappearing into the filthy water at her feet. Her stomach heaved as
the reality of what she'd done crashed over her - she'd taken a life.
Everything she believed in, everything she'd trained for, shattered in
that single moment of violence.

Maya's last breath played on repeat in her mind, a wet, surprised
gasp that would haunt her forever. Her knees buckled, sending her
splashing down into the putrid water. The dagger slipped from her
nerveless fingers, the clatter lost in the ongoing sounds of battle echoing through the tunnel.

Jayne's strong hands gripped her shoulders, pulling her up with
surprising gentleness. "Look at me, not her." The spy's voice cut

through Gemini's spiral of horror. "You saved my life. Now save your-self." The words were harsh but the touch lingering on her shoulder spoke of understanding.

The tunnel spun as Gemini fought to steady herself, her healer's oath warring with the primal need to survive. More shouts echoed from behind them, growing closer. Her fingers found the dagger again, the metal warm and slick with evidence of her transformation.

"Mourn later," Jayne commanded, already moving forward through the tunnel. "Survive now." The words struck something deep in Gemini's chest, a truth she couldn't deny. She forced her legs to move, following Jayne's lead while her soul ached with the weight of what she'd become. The sounds of pursuit grew louder, driving them deeper into the darkness of Somnara's underbelly.

***

The darkness pressed against Liora's skin like thick oil, coating her senses until even breathing felt like drowning. This wasn't just any darkness - it was the dreamscape, twisted and corrupted by Draven's influence through the Ark of Dreams. The Veilstone pulsed against her chest, its warmth the only anchor in this void.

"Look around you, child." Draven's voice echoed from everywhere and nowhere. "This is what true power feels like. The ability to shape reality itself." The darkness shifted, forming shapes of her past - the mill in Eldara, the rebel camp, faces of those she'd lost.

Liora's fingers tightened around the Veilstone, drawing on its strength to push back against Draven's influence. Golden light sparked from her hands, cutting through the oppressive dark. But each tendril of light seemed to feed the shadows, making them grow darker, more substantial.

"You feel it, don't you?" Draven materialized before her, his form flickering between solid and shadow. "That rush when you bend reality to your will. The thrill of holding lives in your grasp." His smile twisted, cruel and knowing. "Just like you did with Kael Varden in the Ember Ruins."

The memory of that power surge hit Liora like a physical blow. She had enjoyed it - the complete control, the way his mind crumbled before her. Shame burned in her throat, but she forced it down. "I'm nothing like you."

Draven circled her, his laughter echoing through the void. "No? We both know what it's like to be feared. To be treated as something other than human." His words slithered into her mind, finding purchase in her deepest insecurities. "The only difference is that I embraced it."

"You'll become what I am, whether you want to or not. The power you hold... it's meant to rule." Draven's form solidified, the Ark of Dreams glowing with an unholy light in his hands. "Fighting it only prolongs the inevitable."

Liora felt the Veilstone's power surge through her veins, raw and tempting. For a moment, she saw the path Draven described - a future where her power knew no bounds, where none would dare question her. Where she'd never feel weak or afraid again.

But then she remembered Gemini's words: she was still human, Veilstone or not. She thought of Rafe's unwavering faith, of Nero's sacrifice, of all those fighting below who believed in her not because of her power, but despite it.

"No, I won't. This ends now." Golden light erupted from her hands, pushing back the darkness inch by inch. The dreamscape trembled around them as two opposing forces of will clashed, neither willing to yield.

The darkness rippled around Liora as she channeled another burst of golden energy through the Veilstone. Her power collided with Draven's shadowy tendrils, sending shock waves through the twisted dreamscape. The void pulsed with each impact, reality bending and warping at the edges of her vision.

Draven's laughter echoed as he wielded the Ark of Dreams, sending a torrent of corrupted memories washing over her. Liora saw herself at the mill again, the day it collapsed, but this time the destruction spread further, consuming all of Eldara. She gritted her teeth, recognizing the manipulation. The Veilstone grew warm against her chest as she pushed back, turning his illusions to mist.

A wave of raw power slammed into her defenses, nearly driving her to her knees. Draven's presence pressed against her mind, trying to break through her mental barriers. But Nero's training held firm - she visualized her thoughts as a flowing river, letting Draven's attacks wash past without finding purchase.

"Your mother tried to resist too," Draven taunted, his form shifting like smoke. "She believed power should serve rather than rule." He hurled another assault of dark energy that Liora barely deflected. "Look where that got her."

Rage flared in Liora's chest, and the Veilstone responded, its light intensifying until it nearly blinded her. She channeled that fury into a focused beam of golden energy that cut through Draven's defenses, making him stagger back. For a moment, she glimpsed fear in his eyes.

The dreamscape trembled as their powers clashed again, reality fraying at the edges. Liora felt the temptation to fully unleash the Veilstone's power, to let it consume both her and Draven. The raw energy sang in her blood, begging to be released.

Instead, she remembered Gemini's words about remaining human. She pulled back, focusing her power inward rather than out. Golden light spiraled around her in intricate patterns as she began creating dreams rather than destroying them. Draven's next attack splashed harmlessly against her defenses.

"What are you doing?" Draven snarled, unleashing another barrage of corrupted memories. But this time, Liora caught them, transforming his darkness into light. Each nightmare he threw at her became a beacon of hope.

The Ark of Dreams pulsed with angry red light as Draven poured more power into his attacks. The void around them started to crack, reality bleeding through the fissures. Liora felt the strain of maintaining her defenses, sweat beading on her forehead as she continued weaving dreams to counter his assault.

The darkness rippled with visions of chaos below, and Liora's heart clenched as she watched her friends fighting for their lives. Draven's cruel laughter echoed through the dreamscape as he forced her to witness their struggles. The Veilstone burned against her chest, its power begging to be unleashed.

"You could save them all with a thought," Draven's voice slithered through her mind. "Just let go. Embrace what you truly are." His words struck too close to the fear she'd carried since that day in Eldara - the fear of losing control, of becoming the monster everyone thought she was.

Through the swirling void, she saw Rafe stumbling backward, blood streaming from a gash above his eye as Varden pressed his advantage. The general's blade flashed in the eclipse-light, each strike driving Rafe closer to the edge of a market stall. The Veilstone pulsed harder, and Liora felt its power surge through her veins.

Another vision materialized - Gemini crouched behind a fallen pillar, clutching her bloody dagger with shaking hands as elite guards closed in. Jayne stood before her, sword moving in deadly arcs, but even her skill couldn't hold back the overwhelming numbers forever. One guard's blade slipped past her defense, drawing a line of red across her arm.

The power built inside Liora like a storm, and she could feel how easy it would be to reach out, to crush their enemies with a single thought. The temptation was almost overwhelming. She could end this all now, save everyone she loved. But Nero's words echoed in her memory: "Power without purpose is just another form of destruction."

Draven's presence pressed closer, his darkness seeping into the edges of her mind. "You see? This is the cost of your restraint. Their blood will be on your hands." The Ark of Dreams pulsed with malevolent energy, forcing more visions into her mind - rebels falling to elite guards, the streets running red with sacrifice.

Liora's hands trembled as she watched Varden's blade slice through Rafe's defenses, drawing another line of blood. The Veilstone's energy surged again, and for a moment, her vision tinged with gold. It would be so easy to reach out, to tear Varden's mind apart like she'd nearly done before. The power was there, waiting.

Below, Gemini finally broke from her hiding place, trying to reach a fallen rebel who lay bleeding nearby. An elite guard turned, his sword rising. Jayne shouted a warning, but she was too far away, locked in combat with two other guards. The Veilstone's power screamed through Liora's blood.

"Choose, girl," Draven's voice cut through her thoughts. "Choose between your principles and their lives." His darkness pressed harder, showing her more visions of death and defeat. Each one struck like a physical blow, feeding the desperate need to act, to unleash everything she had.

Golden light poured from Liora's skin as she collapsed to her knees, the Veilstone's power surging through her veins like molten metal. Each heartbeat sent fresh waves of raw energy cascading through her body, begging to be unleashed. Draven's darkness pressed closer, his presence an oily whisper in her mind.

"Yes," he breathed, his voice resonating with dark triumph. "Feel it consuming you. This is what you were meant to be." The Ark of Dreams pulsed in sync with the Veilstone, their energies intertwining in the corrupted dreamscape. Through the void, she could still see flashes of the battle below - Rafe bleeding, Gemini in danger, her people dying.

The power built inside her chest until breathing became almost impossible. It would be so easy to let go, to allow that golden fury to explode outward and reshape reality itself. She could save them all, protect everyone she loved. Destroy Draven and all her enemies. The Veilstone's energy sang through her blood, promising everything she'd ever wanted - strength, control, the ability to ensure no one she loved would ever suffer again.

Draven's darkness coiled around her like a serpent, encouraging, tempting. The golden light intensified until it filled her vision, burning away everything else. Liora felt herself slipping, the barriers between her consciousness and the raw power of the Veilstone beginning to crack. Part of her wanted to fight it, to remember Gemini's words about staying human. But a larger part yearned to embrace this transformation, to become something greater than human. The power pulsed again, stronger than ever, and she began to let it in.

Golden light blazed through Liora's veins as the Veilstone's power threatened to tear her apart. Through the dreamscape's shadows, she watched helplessly as Rafe stumbled, blood streaming from a gash in his side. Varden pressed forward, his blade seeking the killing blow. The power surged again, begging to be unleashed.

A scream pierced the darkness - Gemini's voice. Liora's heart clenched as she saw her friend backing away from approaching guards, the bloody dagger trembling in her inexperienced hands. Jayne fought desperately to reach her, but there were too many enemies between them. The Eclipse cast everything in an otherworldly glow, making the blood on the cobblestones gleam like black mercury.

The Veilstone pulsed harder, its energy intertwining with the Ark of Dreams' corrupted power. Draven's presence pressed against her mind, showing her more visions of death and defeat. Each one struck like a physical blow, feeding the desperate need to act. To save them all, she'd have to give in. Let the power consume her. Become something else entirely.

"Your mother was weak," Draven's voice slithered through her thoughts. "She chose death over embracing her true potential." The words found purchase in Liora's deepest fears - that she too would fail, would watch everyone she loved die because she was afraid to become what the power wanted her to be. The golden light burned brighter, threatening to blind her.

Another cry rang out - this time from one of the rebel leaders as they fell to an elite guard's blade. The sound snapped something inside Liora, and she felt the last threads of her control beginning to fray. The Veilstone's power sang through her, promising salvation through transformation. As darkness pressed in from all sides, she began to let the barriers between herself and that raw power crumble. Maybe Draven was right. Maybe this was what she was meant to become.

A familiar presence brushed against her consciousness - warm, gentle, like sunlight breaking through storm clouds. Lyra Solari materialized before her, her form translucent yet steady amidst the chaos. The sight of her mother made Liora's heart clench with a mixture of longing and fear.

"Liora, remember who you are," Lyra's voice carried the weight of failure. "The Veilstone is not only strength but a mirror of your heart. To wield it, you must embrace the purity of your purpose."

"But... what if I lose myself?" Liora's voice cracked as tears burned behind her eyes. "What if I become just like him?" The question that had haunted her since discovering her powers finally escaped her lips, raw and desperate.

Lyra stepped forward, her ethereal form radiating a calm that cut through the surrounding darkness.

"We all carry shadows, Liora," Lyra's words settled into her soul like autumn leaves on still water, "but it is how we use our light that defines us. Recognize your doubts, but do not let them bind you. You are the last Dreamweaver. Be a Dreamweaver."

Memories flooded in - sharing tea with Gemini on quiet mornings, Rafe's steady hand holding hers, even Jayne's reluctant smile when Liora had first controlled her magic. The Veilstone's wild energy began to calm, its golden light shifting from a desperate blaze to a steady glow that matched her heartbeat.

The vision of a peaceful Somnus shimmered before Liora - children playing in sun-dappled streets, dream magic used to heal rather than harm, the twin moons casting their gentle light over a land free from fear. The Veilstone's energy shifted within her, no longer a desperate inferno but a steady flame that matched the rhythm of her heart.

Lyra's presence began to fade like morning mist, but her warmth remained, settling into Liora's bones like a forgotten lullaby finally remembered. The love in her mother's eyes spoke of sacrifice, of choices made not from fear but from an unshakeable belief in something greater than power.

"I believe in you, Liora. Trust your heart, and it will guide you." The words echoed through her soul as Lyra's form dissolved completely, leaving behind a certainty that filled the spaces where doubt had lived.

Opening her eyes, Liora found her fear had transformed into an iron resolve. The Veilstone pulsed in perfect harmony with her heartbeat as she gathered her power - not to destroy, but to protect. With a single thought, she shattered Draven's dreamscape like glass, golden light piercing through the artificial darkness.

Draven's roar of rage shook the very foundations of the palace as he unleashed a torrent of corrupted dream energy. The Ark of Dreams blazed with sickly purple light in his hands, but Liora stood her ground. This time, she knew exactly who she was and what she fought for.

# Emperor Draven

S teel clashed against steel as Rafe drove Kael back up the palace steps. Blood trickled down his arm where Kael's blade had found purchase, but the pain only fueled his rage. Each strike carried the weight of betrayal, each parry reminded him of the faces of those who'd died trusting this man.

Kael's boots scraped against the marble as he retreated, his usual calculated demeanor cracking under Rafe's relentless assault. The traitor's sword work remained precise, but Rafe saw the fear bleeding through his mask of confidence. Good. Let him feel what their fallen companions felt in their final moments.

"You destroyed everything we built—your friends, your allies! Tell me, was it worth it?" Rafe's blade whistled past Kael's ear, taking a few strands of hair with it. The sounds of battle echoed from the streets below, a cacophony of death that Kael had orchestrated.

"I did what I had to, Delacroix. Survival isn't about loyalty." Kael's counter-strike nearly caught Rafe's shoulder, but years of fighting alongside the man had taught Rafe his patterns. He twisted away, letting momentum carry him into a savage backhand strike.

The blow connected with Kael's jaw, sending him staggering. Blood sprayed across the pristine steps as Kael spat out a tooth. Rafe pressed forward, his sword becoming an extension of his fury. Marcus's face flashed in his mind, Nero Thorne as well.

The traitor's casual dismissal of their fallen comrades twisted like a knife in his gut. His blade moved faster, each strike carrying the weight of a dozen memories—shared meals, battle plans, victories celebrated together. All of it poisoned by Kael's betrayal.

The palace steps grew slick with their mingled blood, forcing Rafe to adjust his footing. Each clash of steel sent vibrations up his arm, but he welcomed the pain. It kept him focused, kept him from losing himself completely to the rage that threatened to consume him. Above, golden light pulsed against the darkening sky—Liora fighting her own battle with Draven. The thought of her steadied his hand.

"They trusted you," Rafe spat, deflecting a thrust aimed at his ribs. "Nero, Marcus, every rebel who followed you—they believed in you." His counter-strike nearly took Kael's ear. The general's usually perfect form was deteriorating, exhaustion and perhaps guilt finally showing through his mask of indifference.

Kael attempted to create distance, but Rafe stayed on him, refusing to let him recover. Each step brought them closer to the palace's grand entrance, where ornate columns cast deep shadows in the Eclipse's strange light. Part of him wanted to end this quickly, to rush to Liora's aid. But the faces of the dead demanded justice, and Rafe's blade sang with their memory as he pressed his attack.

***

The wave of dark energy rushed toward Liora like a tide of nightmares, threatening to drown her in its depths. She raised the Veilstone, its light pulsing in harmony with her heartbeat as she crafted a shield of pure dream essence. The collision sent ripples through the air, causing the very fabric of reality to shudder.

"You don't own me, Draven. I choose my path." Liora's voice carried across the space between them, steady despite the strain of holding back his assault.

Draven's laugh echoed with hollow malice. "And you have chosen death." His power surged again, darker and more intense, pressing against her defenses like a thousand razor-sharp claws.

The Veilstone hummed against her palm, offering more power - so much more than she was using. Liora felt it calling to her, promising swift victory if she'd only unleash its full potential. But her mother's words echoed in her mind, reminding her that true strength lay in restraint.

Dark tendrils of Draven's magic snaked around her shield, probing for weaknesses. Each one that touched her defense withered away, turned to golden dust by the Veilstone's pure light. Draven's frustration manifested as storm clouds of corrupted dreams swirling above them.

Sweat beaded on Liora's forehead as she maintained her defensive stance. The Veilstone's energy flowed through her like a river, controlled but powerful. She could feel Draven's confusion at her refusal to match his aggression, his certainty wavering for the first time.

Another assault crashed against her shield, this one filled with visions of her friends falling in battle. Liora recognized the manipulation and pushed back, not with force but with clarity, dispersing the false images like morning mist before the sun.

The air crackled with competing energies - Draven's corruption versus Liora's steadfast light. Each clash sent sparks of dream essence scattering across the rooftop, some manifesting as brief, beautiful visions before dissolving away.

Draven's attacks grew more frenzied, less controlled. His power lashed out wildly, no longer focused solely on breaking through but on causing as much destruction as possible. Debris from the palace roof began to crack and float upward, caught in the maelstrom of his rage.

The Veilstone pulsed once more, its light steady and true in Liora's grasp. She felt its approval of her restraint, even as Draven gathered himself for another devastating attack. This time, his power coalesced into a spear of pure darkness, aimed straight at her heart.

The dark spear of energy dissipated as Draven spun away, the Ark of Dreams glowing with malevolent purpose in his hands. The Ark of Dreams pulsed with an otherworldly glow in Draven's hands, its crystalline surface reflecting twisted versions of reality. Liora's stomach dropped as she realized he had not yet played his last trick - this battle had merely been a distraction.

"Did you think I needed you?" Draven's lips curled into a cruel smile. "The Ark will give me Somnus. After I'm done, your precious Veilstone will spread my rule past to this whole forsaken world." His words dripped with contempt as he raised the artifact higher, its light casting grotesque shadows across his features.

"Watch as I remake this world." Draven's voice boomed across the rooftop, amplified by the Ark's power. His laughter echoed across the rooftop as he raised it skyward, unleashing waves of corrupted dream magic that spread like a plague across Somnara.

Screams erupted from the streets below as citizens collapsed, their minds trapped in Draven's manufactured nightmares. Liora felt each connection snap into place through the Veilstone's resonance - thousands of souls being twisted and bound to his will.

A mother clutched her child before both crumpled to the ground. Market vendors dropped their wares, eyes glazing over as Draven's influence took hold. Even the fighting rebels succumbed, their weapons clattering against cobblestones as darkness claimed their minds.

Draven's power continued to spread beyond Somnara's walls, reaching toward distant villages and settlements. Each new victim added to his strength, their trapped consciousness feeding the Ark's terrible purpose. His face twisted with maniacal glee as he felt his influence growing.

The Veilstone's light pulsed faster, more urgently. Liora knew what it was telling her - only by fully opening herself to its power could she hope to save everyone. But doing so might burn away everything she was, leaving nothing but a hollow vessel of pure energy.

***

Kael's blade clashed against Rafe's with brutal force, sending shockwaves through his already aching arms. The rebel fought differently now, his earlier rage replaced by something far more dangerous - purpose. Each strike carried deliberate weight, each movement calculated to drive Kael back up the palace steps.

Sweat trickled down Kael's neck as he parried another precise thrust. The battle below raged on, but up here, isolated on these ancient stairs, only the ring of steel and their labored breathing filled the air. He recognized the shift in Rafe's technique - the same focused determination he'd once admired in the younger warrior during their shared days in the rebellion.

"Getting tired, General?" Rafe's voice carried no mockery, only cold certainty. The words stung more than any blade could. Kael retreated another step, his boots scraping against worn stone. Above them, dream energy crackled across the sky as Liora and Draven's battle raged, but Kael couldn't spare a glance upward.

His counter-attack faltered as memories of his betrayal flashed through his mind - the faces of those who'd trusted him, who'd believed in his dedication to their cause. Rafe seized the opening, his blade singing past Kael's guard and drawing a line of fire across his ribs. The pain brought clarity, but not the kind Kael wanted.

The palace entrance loomed behind him now, its shadows promising false sanctuary. Kael's breath came in ragged gasps as he deflected another series of strikes. Blood seeped through Kael's shirt where Rafe's blade had found him, each movement pulling at the wound. Pride warred with practicality as he considered his options. He could feel his strength ebbing, matched against Rafe's seemingly inexhaustible resolve. The younger man's eyes held no hatred now, only the cold promise of justice.

Another step back, and Kael's heel caught on the top stair. He stumbled, barely bringing his sword up in time to prevent Rafe's blade from finding his throat. The clash of steel echoed off the palace walls, a sound that seemed to mock his faltering defense. Here, at the very doors of power he'd sacrificed everything to grasp, his betrayal was catching up to him.

Rafe pressed forward, his attacks flowing with increasing confidence. Each strike forced Kael to give ground, his practiced formations crumbling under the assault. The irony wasn't lost on him - his own teachings being used to dismantle his defense, piece by piece. His arms trembled with exhaustion, every parry coming slower than the last.

The weight of his choices pressed down on Kael as heavily as Rafe's relentless assault. He saw now the path that had led him here - each compromise, each betrayal, each step away from honor - all leading to this moment of reckoning. His blade felt heavier with each passing second, while Rafe seemed to grow stronger, more assured.

With another strike, his sword clattered down the palace steps, each metallic bounce echoing Kael's hammering heart. Cold steel pressed against his throat, right above his family crest - the weight of generations bearing down on that single point of contact. The pendant felt heavier than ever, its metal burning against his skin with the shame of his choices.

"You don't deserve to wear this." Rafe's words cut deeper than any blade could. The truth in them stripped away Kael's last defenses, leaving him naked before the weight of his betrayals. He'd dishonored everything the crest represented - loyalty, duty, sacrifice.

His knees struck the stone steps without conscious thought, the impact jarring through his exhausted body. The point of Rafe's sword never wavered from his throat, steady as the younger man's conviction. Kael closed his eyes, waiting for the final stroke that would end his legacy of failure.

Memories flashed behind his closed lids - his father's proud smile when he'd first earned his commission, the weight of responsibility when he'd received his general's stars, the moment he'd chosen to betray it all. Each memory carried the bitter taste of opportunities squandered, honor abandoned.

The pendant shifted against his chest as he swallowed, its familiar weight now an anchor of guilt. Above them, dream energy crackled across the darkening sky, but Kael barely registered it. His world had narrowed to the cold bite of steel against his throat and the crushing weight of his shame.

A strange sensation rippled through the air, like reality itself holding its breath. The hairs on the back of Kael's neck stood up as an unnatural silence descended, drowning out even the sounds of battle below. Something fundamental was changing in the world around them.

Reality buckled under the weight of whatever power had been unleashed. The palace steps seemed to ripple like water, solid stone becoming fluid beneath them. Kael's stomach lurched as gravity itself seemed to hesitate, uncertain which way was down.

The family crest grew ice-cold against his skin as darkness descended, bringing with it a bone-deep certainty that everything was about to change. In that moment, facing what felt like the end of the world, Kael Varden realized execution might be the least of his concerns.

*** 

The blade trembled in Gemini's hand as she plunged it into another soldier's side. His eyes widened, mouth forming a silent 'oh' before he crumpled at her feet. Her stomach lurched, but she forced herself to keep moving through the chaos of battle, Jayne's words echoing in her mind: survive now, mourn later.

Blood stained her robes - both from those she'd tried to save and those she'd been forced to kill. The dagger Jayne had given her felt foreign in her grip, so different from the herbs and bandages she usually wielded. A scream tore through the air, and Gemini spun to find an elite guard bearing down on a fallen rebel. Without thinking, she threw herself forward, blade finding the weak spot in his armor just as Jayne had shown her.

Tears blurred her vision as she fought alongside the rebels, each death by her hand adding another crack to her heart. But when she glimpsed Jayne fighting three guards at once, something fierce and protective rose within her. She wouldn't let anyone else she cared about die today. The dagger moved with newfound purpose as she rushed to aid her friend.

Through the haze of battle, Gemini caught sight of golden light erupting from the palace roof - Liora's power clashing with Draven's darkness. Her best friend was fighting alone up there, while down here Gemini struggled with taking lives to save others. Another guard charged, and this time when Gemini's blade found its mark, her tears were not just for the life she took, but for the innocence she was losing with each strike.

The world suddenly shifted, reality bending as power washed over the city. Was it Liora or Draven? Gemini staggered, catching herself against a wall as she watched horror spread across the faces of those around her. Even as darkness crept at the edges of her vision, she gripped her bloodied dagger tighter. Her hands might never be clean again, but at least they would be stained protecting those she loved.

Gemini's world exploded in agony as a deafening roar shattered the sky above. Her dagger clattered to the blood-stained cobblestones as she clutched her head, feeling as if invisible hands were trying to tear her skull apart. The sensation of another presence - cold, dark, and violating - slithered through her mind like poisoned honey.

Draven's invasion felt like thousands of needles piercing her thoughts, each one carrying memories of death and darkness. The healing prayers her father had taught her crumbled to ash in her mind, replaced by visions of violence that threatened to overwhelm her gentle nature. She tried to hold onto images of Liora's smile, of peaceful days in her garden, but they slipped away like water through trembling fingers.

Through tear-blurred vision, she saw Jayne collapse nearby, the fierce spy's face contorted in the same excruciating pain. The woman who had taught her to fight, to survive, now looked as vulnerable as a wounded bird. Without thinking, Gemini crawled toward her, each movement sending fresh waves of agony through her splintering consciousness.

Their hands found each other in the chaos, fingers intertwining with desperate strength. Gemini pulled Jayne close, pressing their foreheads together as they both shook with the force of Draven's mental assault. The touch anchored her, gave her something real to hold onto as her mind threatened to shatter completely.

"Stay with me," Gemini whispered, though she wasn't sure if she spoke the words aloud or only thought them. Jayne's grip tightened in response as darkness crept across Gemini's vision. Together they huddled on the bloody ground, two hearts beating in terrified unison as Draven's power threatened to consume them both. In what felt like their final moments, Gemini found a strange comfort in not facing the end alone.

# The Last Dreamweaver

T he screams of thousands tore through Liora's mind as Draven's power reached across all of Somnus. Below, Gemini collapsed into Jayne's arms. Rafe staggered back from Kael, his sword dropping from trembling fingers. Their agony ripped into her heart, each cry a knife twisting deeper.

Draven's laughter cut through the chaos. "Watch them break, little one. Feel their minds shatter as they realize who truly rules them." His power, dark and oppressive, pushed against her defenses, trying to crush the light she emanated.

The Veilstone's energy coursed through her veins, no longer fighting her control but beckoning her to embrace it fully. Her mother's words whispered at the edges of her mind, about choice and purpose, but they grew fainter with each passing heartbeat. Below, thousands of minds bent under Draven's will, their thoughts turning dark and hollow.

Golden light spilled from between her fingers as she gripped the stone tighter. If she gave herself to its power completely, would there be anything left of her? The question burned in her chest as she watched Rafe collapse to his knees, fighting against Draven's invasion of his mind. She couldn't lose him - couldn't lose any of them.

The power built within her, a tide rising to drown everything she was. But as she stared at Draven's triumphant smile, she knew there was no other choice. Better to sacrifice herself than watch everyone she loved become puppets in his twisted game. The Veilstone's light grew brighter, responding to her acceptance.

Tears rolled down her cheeks as she opened herself fully to the stone's power. "I'm sorry," she whispered, though no one could hear her over the cacophony of suffering. The crystal's energy surged through her, threatening to burn away everything that made her human. But she held onto one thought as the power consumed her: she chose this, not for dominance, but for love.

Liora stretched out with her consciousness, touching the minds of those suffering below. She felt Rafe's determination even as he fought against Draven's invasion, saw Gemini's tears as she clung to Jayne. Their pain became her anchor, their resistance her strength.

The Veilstone's power surged through her veins like liquid sunlight. This time, she didn't fight it. Instead, she became it, letting the ancient magic of the Dreamweavers fill every fiber of her being. Her feet lifted from the palace roof as the golden light intensified.

Draven's attack faltered. His grip on the Ark of Dreams tightened as he witnessed her transformation. "Impossible," he snarled, pouring more power into his assault. The dark energy crackled between them like lightning in a storm.

Liora reached out to the minds of Somnara's people, not to control but to protect. Her consciousness touched each one, a gentle barrier against Draven's invasion. She felt their relief as her light pushed back his darkness, their gratitude as she eased their pain.

The battle for Somnus's collective consciousness raged like a tempest. Where Draven sought to dominate, Liora defended. Where he tried to break, she mended. Their powers clashed in the sky above Somnara, golden light against writhing shadows.

Through the Veilstone, Liora sensed the truth of Draven's power - built on fear, sustained by control. But her power came from something else entirely. Love for her friends, hope for Somnus's future, the desire to protect rather than rule. It flowed through her, pure and unstoppable.

Sweat beaded on Draven's forehead as he poured more power into the Ark. "You cannot resist forever," he growled, but uncertainty crept into his voice. The darkness around him flickered as Liora's light grew stronger, pushing back against his assault with the combined will of thousands who chose freedom over fear.

The battle for control tore through the minds of Somnus like a storm, and Liora felt each surge of power ripple through the thousands caught between her and Draven. Golden light pulsed from the Veilstone, meeting the dark energy of the Ark in violent crashes that shook the palace towers. Each collision sent shockwaves of agony through the people below.

Through her expanded consciousness, she felt Rafe stumbling on the palace steps, his mind a fortress under siege. His thoughts reached for her through the chaos - memories of quiet moments shared, of trust built in darkness, of love discovered in war. But even his iron will began to crack under the pressure of their clashing powers. Blood trickled from his nose as he fought to maintain control of his own mind.

Jayne and Gemini's linked consciousness burned like a beacon in the square below. They clung to each other, their joined hands white-knuckled as they endured wave after wave of psychic assault.

Gemini's heart tried to absorb the pain of others even as her own mind threatened to splinter. Jayne's carefully constructed walls of suspicion and distance crumbled, leaving her raw and vulnerable, her only anchor Gemini's unwavering presence.

Even Kael Varden, who had chosen Draven's path of power, writhed in torment. His betrayal had not earned him immunity from this battle. His thoughts were a maze of regret and justification, pride and shame tangling together as the two forces fought for dominion over his consciousness. Through their connection, Liora felt the weight of his choices crushing him, felt the moment his carefully maintained facade began to crack.

The Veilstone grew hotter in Liora's grasp as she witnessed their suffering. Each mind that fractured under the strain sent spikes of pain through her expanded awareness. She could feel them all - friends, enemies, innocents - their agony becoming her own as the battle for Somnus's soul raged on. The power building within her threatened to consume everything, but she couldn't stop. Not while they still needed her protection.

Through the chaos of battling minds, Liora felt a new disturbance rippling through her expanded consciousness. The dreamscape itself began to tear, reality fraying at the edges where Draven's power pressed too hard against the fabric of dreams. Golden threads that had always connected the sleeping and waking worlds started to snap, each break sending shockwaves of distortion through her awareness.

Her mother's presence, which had been a constant whisper since claiming the Veilstone, suddenly cried out in pain. Lyra's spirit form flickered like a candle in a storm as Draven's assault battered against the very foundations of the dream realm she protected. Through their connection, Liora felt her mother's essence beginning to fragment, threatening to scatter into the void between worlds.

The Veilstone pulsed harder in Liora's grip, its heat now almost un-
bearable. Cracks appeared in the air around them, showing glimpses of
nightmares seeping through - twisted versions of reality where darkness held permanent sway. A child's scream echoed from one such rift,
and Liora felt her heart constrict at the sound.

"You see?" Draven's voice carried a note of madness now. "The
dreamscape bends to my will!" His laughter echoed across multiple
planes of existence as another section of the dreamscape shattered
beneath his onslaught.

Nero's last lessons surfaced in Liora's mind, cutting through her
panic with crystal clarity. "Power isn't about force," he had told her,
his eyes gentle but urgent. "It's about balance. The dreamscape exists
between reality and imagination, between light and shadow. Tip too
far in either direction, and everything collapses."

The Veilstone's energy surged through her veins as understanding crystallized in her mind. Two worlds, with a veil between - the
dreamscape and reality. Draven sought to dominate both, using one
to control the other. The Custodians had created the Veilstone as
a shield, a barrier between realms. But they had missed something
fundamental.

Golden light pulsed from her hands as the truth settled into her
bones. She wasn't meant to be a wall between worlds or a weapon
to control them. The power flowing through her spoke of something
else entirely - of bridges rather than barriers, of harmony rather than
dominion.

Draven's dark energy pressed against her defenses, making the air
crackle with conflicting magics. "Your end has come," he snarled,
his voice echoing across multiple planes of existence. "The last
Dreamweaver will fall."

A smile touched Liora's lips as the Veilstone's warmth spread through her chest. "That's where you're wrong, Draven," she called out, her voice steady despite the strain. "Where you've been wrong this entire time."

The palace roof trembled beneath them as she gathered her power, no longer fighting against its nature but embracing it fully. "Lyra Solari was the last Dreamweaver," Liora declared, golden light streaming from her eyes. "I am the first of something new."

Reality rippled around them as her power built, the very air seeming to hold its breath. Below, she felt thousands of minds turn toward her, drawn by the shift in energy. Even Draven hesitated, his grip on the Ark faltering for just a moment.

The Veilstone's light grew brighter, responding to her acceptance of this new truth. She was neither guardian nor conqueror - she was a bridge, born to unite rather than divide.

Golden light pulsed from Liora's hands as the Veilstone's power surged through her veins. The ancient magic no longer fought her control - instead, it sang in harmony with her newfound purpose. Through her expanded consciousness, she felt the threads connecting all of Somnus: dreams and reality, light and shadow, past and future.

Through the Veilstone's expanding awareness, Liora felt the boundaries of Somnus dissolving. The magic stretched beyond their realm, touching other realms, other people held back by the veil. The connections blazed like golden threads in her mind, each one leading to another story, another struggle between light and shadow.

A young man stood at the edge of a cliff, his clothes tattered and windswept. Above him, a city floated among the clouds, its crystalline towers catching the light like scattered diamonds. His longing pierced through Liora's consciousness - the desperate need to reach something that seemed forever out of grasp. His dreams resonated with her own memories of staring up at Draven's palace, feeling small and powerless.

Near a molten lake of fire, a girl perched on black volcanic rock. Ash drifted around her like snow, settling in her dark hair. Despite the heat emanating from the crater below, loneliness radiated from her in waves that Liora felt across the worlds. The girl's isolation echoed through the Veilstone, reminding Liora of countless nights spent hiding from her own power, believing she was the only one of her kind.

In a temple that seemed built from pure light, a priestess knelt before an altar. Her white robes pooled around her like liquid moonlight, but beneath her serene exterior, Liora sensed conflict. The woman's prayers were tinged with doubt, her faith wrestling with duty. The struggle touched something deep in Liora's heart - the weight of expectations, the fear of failing those who believed in you.

These glimpses of other worlds rippled through Liora's consciousness as the Veilstone's power continued to build. Each connection strengthened her resolve, showing her that the battle between light and shadow, between control and freedom, stretched far beyond Somnus. The magic hummed through her veins as she turned her attention back to Draven, knowing that what happened here would echo across all these connected realms.

"The veil must fall." The words left her lips with absolute certainty. The Veilstone's glow intensified, responding to her declaration as if it had waited centuries for this moment.

"No!" Draven's face contorted with rage and fear. "You'll destroy everything!" His grip on the Ark tightened as dark energy crackled around him, but his power felt hollow now, built on control rather than understanding.

Liora stretched out with her consciousness, letting the Veilstone's energy flow through her and into the fabric of reality itself. The barrier between worlds - not just dreams and waking, but all the realms that magic touched - had grown too rigid, too controlled. She felt the truth of it in her bones: magic wasn't meant to be contained or controlled, but to flow freely between all worlds.

Draven's shock rippled through their connected minds as she touched the Ark of Dreams, its dark energy initially recoiling from her light before yielding to her touch. His grip on the artifact tightened, but he couldn't prevent the connection that formed between the two relics. Power flowed between them like water finding its level, neither light nor dark but something entirely new.

"Magic is for all," Liora breathed, her voice carrying across multiple planes of existence. The words felt right in her mouth, an echo of something older than memory. Through her expanded awareness, she felt her mother's approval like sunshine breaking through storm clouds.

Reality shimmered around her as she gathered the frayed edges of both worlds in her mind. The dreamscape pulsed with familiar warmth, while the physical realm hummed with solid certainty. Where they touched, sparks of possibility danced in the air. Instead of forcing them apart or trying to dominate one with the other, she began to weave them together like the childhood quilt that still lay on her bed in Eldara.

Golden threads of dream-stuff twisted through the warp and weft of reality, creating patterns that spoke of both worlds without belonging fully to either. Each pass of her power mended another tear in the fabric of existence, sealing the rifts that Draven's assault had created. Through their connection, she felt his growing panic as he realized what she was doing.

The Ark of Dreams resonated with each new pattern she created, its ancient power recognizing something fundamental in her work. Dark energy that had once served only to control now began to stabilize the connections between worlds, providing structure where before there had been only chaos. Draven's fingers spasmed around the artifact as it responded to her call rather than his commands.

Below, thousands of minds touched by her power watched in awe as reality shifted around them. Dreams no longer pressed against the physical world like invaders seeking entry - instead, they flowed naturally through the patterns she created, enriching rather than overwhelming.

The dreamscape itself seemed to sigh with relief as she continued her work, ancient tensions finally finding resolution in her weaving. Where Draven had tried to force the worlds to submit to his will, she invited them to dance together, each strengthening the other through their connection. The very air shimmered with new possibilities as the pattern grew more complex.

The power flowing through Liora transcended worlds, touching lives far beyond Somnus's borders. She felt the moment the young man's yearning crystallized into something tangible. His gasp of wonder echoed across realities as ethereal wings of pure aether sprouted from his shoulders, lifting him toward the crystalline city that had haunted his dreams.

In the temple of light, the priestess's prayers transformed into streams of radiance. Liora witnessed doubt melt away as divine power answered the woman's deepest questions. Tears of joy streamed down the priestess's face, catching the light like diamonds as she finally understood her true purpose - not to serve blindly, but to bridge the gap between mortal and divine.

Near the molten lake, the lonely girl's eyes widened as flame danced to life in her palm. Through their connection, Liora felt the moment isolation turned to wonder. The volcanic ash swirling around the girl responded to her awakening power, forming patterns that spoke of belonging rather than exile. A smile broke across her ash-stained face as she realized she was no longer alone in her uniqueness.

Each awakening resonated through the Veilstone, strengthening the new pattern Liora wove between worlds. These sparks of magic weren't just power awakening - they were barriers breaking down, ancient divisions healing as magic flowed more freely between realms. Every new connection added another thread to her weaving, creating something stronger and more beautiful than mere control could ever achieve.

The Ark of Dreams pulsed in response to these changes, its dark energy transforming as it encountered each new awakening. Draven's grip on the artifact weakened further as he witnessed his carefully constructed walls between worlds dissolve. His shout of rage cut through multiple realities, but Liora barely heard him. Her focus remained on the pattern growing between worlds, on the joy of each person discovering their true connection to magic. Through it all, her mother's presence grew stronger, no longer a whisper but a song of approval that echoed across every realm she touched.

Sweat beaded on Liora's forehead as she maintained her concentration, feeling the weight of both artifacts and the power flowing through them. Each new connection required precise control, every pattern had to be perfect or risk creating new tears in the fabric of existence. But her hands moved with certainty, guided by something deeper than conscious thought.

The palace roof trembled beneath them as another wave of power flowed through the connecting artifacts. Liora's weaving picked up speed, golden light flowing from her fingers like water as she worked to complete the pattern before the strain became too much. Through their link, she felt Draven's growing desperation as he realized he was witnessing the end of everything he had built - and the beginning of something he had never imagined possible.

***

The pressure in Gemini's skull eased, like a vice loosening its cruel grip. She gasped, sweet air filling her lungs as the fog of Draven's control lifted. Jayne's arms were still wrapped around her, trembling but strong, and Gemini squeezed her hand in silent acknowledgment that they had survived.

Blood trickled down Gemini's chin where she'd bitten her lip during the mental assault. The metallic taste brought her instincts rushing back, but something else demanded her attention. The soldiers - Draven's elite guard - stood frozen, their weapons slack in their grip as if waking from a deep slumber.

"Jayne," Gemini whispered, her voice hoarse. "Look at them." The guards blinked in confusion, some dropping their weapons as awareness returned to their eyes. One young soldier fell to his knees, ripping off his helmet to reveal tears streaming down his face even as blood began to drip down the front of his armor.

Gemini's heart ached as she recognized the signs of trauma in their expressions - the same haunted look she'd seen in countless patients back in Eldara. These weren't monsters; they were victims, puppets whose strings had finally been cut. The dagger Jayne had given her felt heavier at her hip.

Releasing Jayne's hand, Gemini approached the kneeling soldier despite her friend's warning hiss. His shoulders shook with silent sobs as memories of actions committed under Draven's control crashed over him. Gemini knelt beside him, her healer's touch gentle on his armored shoulder.

The other soldiers watched, their own horror and guilt evident in their stunned silence. Some removed their helmets, revealing faces young and old, all marked by the weight of unwilling service. Gemini felt Liora's presence in this miracle, her friend's power touching them all with mercy rather than destruction.

"It wasn't your fault," Gemini said, loud enough for all to hear. Her words carried the weight of truth, learned from years of helping others heal. "Draven controlled you, but that control is broken now. You have a choice." The soldier under her hand shuddered, hope warring with shame in his tear-filled eyes.

Gemini's hands moved with practiced efficiency as she examined the soldier's wound, a deep gash across his shoulder where armor had given way. His eyes held a desperate plea that went beyond physical pain - the need for absolution that she couldn't truly give. The familiar motions of healing grounded her as chaos still echoed through Somnara's streets.

"Please," he whispered, gripping her sleeve with his good hand. "I remember everything I did. The villages we-" His voice cracked, and Gemini pressed gentle fingers against the wound, channeling her focus into the injury rather than the weight of his confession. Blood seeped between her fingers as she worked, but the soldier's grip remained steady, as if her touch anchored him to reality.

A sharp whistle cut through the air, making Gemini's head snap up. Jayne stood rigid, her eyes fixed on something above them. Golden light rippled across the palace roof like waves breaking against stone, and darkness writhed against it in an impossible dance. The very air seemed to pulse with each clash of power.

"Gem!" Jayne's voice carried an urgency that made her blood run cold. "We need to move. Now." The soldier under her hands tried to rise, but Gemini pressed him back down, tying off the bandage with quick, practiced movements. Whatever was happening above them, she wouldn't leave this man half-healed.

Gemini's fingers trembled as she secured the final knot on the soldier's bandage, her mind racing to comprehend the impossible scene unfolding above them. The palace roof blazed like a second sun, each pulse of energy sending ripples through the air that Gemini felt in her bones.

Memories of the quiet girl who used to weave flower crowns in Eldara's meadows flooded Gemini's thoughts. That same gentle soul now stood against tyranny, wielding power that could mend broken minds and shattered spirits. Pride swelled in Gemini's chest, mixing with fear for her friend who carried such an enormous burden.

"It's her, isn't it?" Jayne's voice carried a note of awe that Gemini had never heard before. Around them, more of Draven's soldiers stirred from their mental prisons, each awakening marked by gasps of horror or quiet sobs as they confronted their restored memories. The healing had begun, but at what cost to the healer?

Jayne's calloused fingers found Gemini's, intertwining with surprising gentleness. Together they watched as darkness and light danced above Somnara, neither willing to voice their shared fear that Liora might lose herself in this final confrontation. The dagger at Gemini's hip seemed to burn with the weight of everything they'd sacrificed to reach this moment.

The air crackled with tension as another wave of golden energy pulsed outward from the palace. This time, Gemini felt something different in its touch - not just power, but purpose. Love. Hope. Everything that made Liora who she was, amplified through the Veilstone but unchanged in its essence. Gemini squeezed Jayne's hand harder, tears streaming down her face as she witnessed her friend's true strength manifest not in destruction, but in healing.

# A New World

The world spun as Rafe's eyes fluttered open, each heartbeat a hammer strike against his skull. Stone steps dug into his back, and the taste of copper lingered on his tongue. How long had he been out? His fingers scraped against rough stone as he pushed himself up, fighting the urge to vomit.

Liora. Her name burned through the fog in his mind. The last thing he remembered was Varden, their fight, then... nothing. Just darkness and pain, like someone had tried to tear his thoughts apart. He had to find her.

His legs trembled as he stood, using the palace wall for support. The world tilted, but he forced himself to focus on the roof where he'd last seen her golden light piercing the sky. Was she still alive? The thought of losing her made his chest constrict.

Around him, soldiers and rebels alike were stirring, looking as dazed as he felt. But something was different. The hatred and fury that had fueled their combat moments ago had vanished, replaced by confusion and... recognition? He watched as a rebel helped a former enemy to his feet.

The air itself felt changed, lighter somehow, as if a great weight had been lifted from the world. Rafe's headache began to fade, replaced by an unfamiliar sense of peace. Whatever Liora had done, it had transformed more than just the battlefield.

Two soldiers who'd been trying to kill each other moments ago now shared a waterskin, their weapons forgotten in the dust. Rafe's heart clenched as he recognized one as Marcus's brother - the same Marcus who'd died protecting Liora. Yet there was no vengeance in the man's eyes now, only understanding.

People emerged from their homes, blinking in the strange light that seemed to bridge the gap between dream and reality. His gaze caught on Varden, slumped against a pillar at the top of the stairs. The man's face was wet with tears as he stared at his family crest, the symbol of everything he'd betrayed. For the first time, Rafe felt something other than hatred for his former commander - perhaps even pity.

The sound of running feet drew his attention. Through the crowd, he spotted Gemini and Jayne holding hands as they raced toward the palace steps. The look of desperate hope on their faces mirrored what he felt in his heart. Blood pounded in his ears as he forced himself up the remaining stairs. His body screamed in protest, but he ignored it. Whatever had happened, whatever miracle Liora had worked, he had to reach her. The fate of two worlds hung in the balance, but all he could think about was making sure she was still alive.

Rafe's muscles tensed as he caught the movement - Kael dragging himself across the blood-stained stones, fingers clawing at the ground with desperate purpose. His former general's leg twisted at an unnatural angle, leaving a trail of crimson smears in his wake. The sword lay just beyond his reach, its polished surface reflecting the strange light that still filled the sky.

The sight stirred something in Rafe's gut. How many times had he followed Kael into battle, trusted him with his life? His betrayal had shattered that trust, cost them lives, nearly destroyed everything they'd fought for. Yet watching him now, broken and crawling like a wounded animal, Rafe felt his hatred crack.

A grunt of pain escaped Kael's lips as he stretched toward the weapon. His fingers brushed the hilt, then slipped away. Blood matted his hair where he'd struck the steps during their fight, but still he pressed on. The same determination that had once inspired armies now reduced to this desperate scramble.

The sword lay between them, an invitation to finish what they'd started. Rafe's hand settled on his own blade, the familiar grip offering no comfort. Kael's betrayal deserved justice, demanded it even. But was this justice, or just another act of violence in a cycle that had already claimed too many lives?

Rafe's heart lurched as he saw Kael's fingers close around the sword hilt. Time seemed to slow as his former commander twisted the blade toward his own chest, a look of grim determination etched across his blood-streaked face. Without thinking, Rafe lunged forward.

His boot connected with the weapon, sending it skittering across the stones. In the same motion, he drove his shoulder into Kael's chest, both men crashing to the ground. Pain shot through Rafe's already battered body as they landed hard, but he maintained his grip on Kael's wrists, pinning them to the ground.

"You're free now, Kael," Rafe growled through gritted teeth, feeling the man struggle beneath him. "You get to choose who you are now. I won't let you take the easy way out." The words tasted strange in his mouth - defending the man who'd betrayed them all. Yet something in him couldn't watch another death today.

Kael's laugh was bitter, hollow. "I chose this. Draven didn't control me." His eyes burned with a hatred Rafe recognized - not for others, but for himself. The same look he'd seen in his own reflection after failing to save his village.

"Then stand trial," Rafe shot back, tightening his grip as Kael tried to twist free. "Face the consequences as your father did." The words struck home - he felt Kael go still beneath him, the fight draining from his body like blood from a wound.

For a moment, they stayed frozen like that, both men breathing heavily. Rafe searched his former general's face, looking for any trace of the man he'd once followed into battle. All he found was exhaustion and defeat.

A rebel soldier approached cautiously, drawn by the commotion. Rafe nodded toward Kael's prone form. "Restrain him. Make sure he lives to face justice." The words came out harder than he'd intended, but the soldier understood, moving quickly to bind Kael's hands.

As they hauled Kael to his feet, Rafe caught a glimpse of something in the man's eyes - not gratitude exactly, but perhaps understanding. The same understanding that had spread through the streets below as Liora's power transformed the world.

Liora. The thought of her hit him like a physical blow. Rafe's head snapped up, scanning the palace roof where he'd last seen that brilliant golden light. Smoke or mist - he couldn't tell which - still curled around the highest towers, obscuring his view.

His heart pounded against his ribs as he stared upward, silently praying to whatever powers might be listening. She had to be alive. After everything they'd been through, after what she'd just accomplished, she had to survive. The alternative was unthinkable.

\*\*\*

Golden threads of power flowed from Liora's hands, weaving reality and dreams into an intricate tapestry. The Veilstone pulsed against her palm, its energy harmonizing with the Ark of Dreams as she merged the two realms that had been torn apart for so long.

Draven staggered backward, his face contorting as the connection to his power source severed. The dark energy that had sustained him for decades began to slip away, leaving hollow spaces where corrupted dreams had once festered. His skin grew ashen, cracking like ancient parchment left too long in the sun.

"What have you done?" His voice rasped, barely above a whisper. The imposing figure who had terrorized Somnus now seemed small, diminished. His hands, once crackling with dark energy, trembled as he reached for power that no longer answered his call.

The Ark of Dreams hummed with renewed purpose, its crystalline surface reflecting the golden light of Liora's weaving. Where Draven had forced the artifact to bend reality to his will, she guided it to heal the tears between worlds, creating something entirely new.

Watching him crumble, Liora felt no satisfaction - only a profound sadness for the man who had sacrificed his humanity for power. His eyes, once burning with malevolent purpose, now held only fear as he witnessed his empire dissolving around him.

"Your power was never yours to keep," Liora said softly, continuing her work as reality shifted and merged around them. The very air seemed to shimmer with possibility as dreams and truth found their natural balance.

Draven fell to his knees, his elaborate robes pooling around him like spilled ink. Decades of stolen dreams, of stolen life force, drained from his body, leaving behind the hollow shell of a man who had spent too long playing god. His fingers clawed at his chest as if trying to hold onto the last remnants of his power.

The tyrant's breath came in ragged gasps as he watched his perfectly controlled world unravel. The dreams he had stolen, the minds he had broken - all of it slipped through his fingers like sand. His eyes, wild with desperation, locked onto Liora's face.

"You cannot understand what you're destroying," he wheezed, reaching toward her with a trembling hand. "The order I brought... the peace through control..." But his words held no power now, just as his magic had abandoned him.

Golden light continued to pour from Liora's hands as she completed the weaving, each thread finding its proper place in the new fabric of reality. Through it all, she watched as Emperor Draven, the nightmare of Somnus, withered before her - not with a roar of defiance, but with the quiet whimper of a man facing his own mortality at last.

Golden threads tightened around Draven's withering form as Liora channeled the Veilstone's power. His physical decay continued, but she sensed something deeper - his consciousness, a writhing mass of corrupted dreams and stolen power, still fighting against her hold.

The air crackled with ancient magic as Liora extended her awareness beyond the physical realm. The Veilstone pulsed against her palm, its energy intertwining with her own as she prepared for what needed to be done.

Through the merging of realms, Liora glimpsed the thousands of minds Draven had violated over the years. Their fractured dreams called out for justice, their pain echoing through the newly woven fabric of reality.

"You sought to use the dreamscape to rule Somnus," she said, her voice carrying the weight of all those he had wronged. "Now you'll pay for those crimes."

Power surged through her as she reached into the core of Draven's being. His eyes widened in terror as he felt her grip on his very essence, realizing too late the true extent of her abilities. Kael Varden had just been the beginning of what she could do.

With a single, decisive pull, Liora tore Draven's consciousness from his decaying body. His physical form collapsed like empty cloth while his essence thrashed in her magical grasp, a dark storm of corrupted dreams and twisted ambitions.

She wove his consciousness into the dreamscape itself, binding him to the realm he had so long abused. His silent screams echoed through both worlds as the binding took hold, securing him in an eternal prison of his own making.

Through their shared connection to the dreamscape, Liora felt her mother's presence materialize. Lyra's form shimmered with quiet power as she faced Draven's trapped consciousness, her smile radiant with pride for her daughter.

Draven's essence recoiled from Lyra's light, but there was nowhere for him to flee. The tyrant who had tormented so many would now face an eternity with those he had wronged, beginning with the last Dreamweaver.

The newly merged realms hummed with possibility as Liora held the weaving steady, watching as her mother stepped forward to deliver Draven's final judgment. His fate was sealed, but the work of healing Somnus had only just begun.

Golden light spiraled from her fingers as she reached for the Ark, feeling its desperate pull to corrupt and control. The Veilstone's power surged through her, not to dominate but to cleanse. Cracks appeared across the Ark's surface, spreading like lightning through glass.

A high-pitched whine filled the air as the Ark resisted destruction. Memories of its victims flashed through Liora's mind - the blank faces of villagers, the tortured screams of rebels, Bennet's broken form. Her resolve hardened, and she pushed harder.

The Ark's crystal structure began to splinter, dark energy leaking from the fissures like poison from a wound. Liora wove her power through each crack, each break, unmaking the artifact that had allowed one man to enslave thousands.

With a sound like shattering stars, the Ark of Dreams exploded. Fragments rained down around her, each shard dissolving into nothing before it hit the ground. The artificial magic that had sustained Draven's reign dissipated into the newly merged realms.

Exhaustion crashed over Liora as the last echoes of the Ark's power faded. The Veilstone dimmed in her grip, its work complete for now. She stumbled, catching herself against a fallen pillar as the world spun around her.

A weak groan cut through her dizziness. Bennet lay crumpled nearby, his weathered face lined with pain from Draven's torture. The sight of her surrogate father pushed away her fatigue, and Liora rushed to his side.

Her hands shook as she helped him sit up, noting the burns across his shoulders and the haunted look in his eyes. "I've got you," she whispered, supporting his weight as he struggled to find his balance.

Bennet's calloused fingers gripped her arm, his touch as familiar as the mill's worn stones. "My girl," he rasped, managing a ghost of his old smile despite his injuries. "You did it. You really did it."

Blood trickled from a cut above his eye as he tried to stand. Liora steadied him, feeling the tremors running through his body. They needed to get him to Gemini quickly - but first, they had to make it down from this cursed rooftop where so many nightmares had finally ended.

Liora supported Bennet's weight as they made their way across the debris-strewn rooftop. His steps faltered, but his grip remained steady on her arm, anchoring her to this moment as reality settled into its new pattern around them.

The first rays of dawn painted the horizon in shades of rose and gold, so different from the sickly light that had bathed Somnara during Draven's reign. Below, the city stirred with newfound freedom, its people emerging from shadows both literal and spiritual.

Each step felt like an eternity as they approached the palace's edge. Bennet's breathing came heavy, but he refused to stop, determined to witness this sunrise. Liora adjusted her grip on his waist, remembering countless mornings at the mill when he'd taught her the value of perseverance.

The wind caught his gray hair, carrying away the acrid smell of battle that clung to them both. In its place came the scent of fresh bread from the bakeries below, a reminder that life continued, that simple pleasures could return even after the darkest nights.

Bennet's shoulders straightened as they reached the parapet, his weathered hands gripping the stone railing. Despite his injuries, his eyes sparkled with that familiar warmth that had guided Liora through so many difficult days.

"Well," he said, his voice rough but carrying that hint of humor she'd missed so desperately, "this is a bit more impressive than adjusting the mill's sails." His attempt at lightness cracked something inside her.

Tears spilled down Liora's cheeks as she turned and buried her face against his shoulder, careful of his wounds. The fabric of his shirt grew damp with her relief, her grief, her joy - all the emotions she'd held at bay during the battle.

Bennet's arms wrapped around her, strong despite everything he'd endured. His chest rumbled with a soft chuckle that held its own share of tears. "Though I must say, the view's better here than from the mill roof."

Liora's laugh came out more like a sob as she held him tighter, breathing in the familiar scent of grain dust that somehow still clung to him. After everything - the battles, the nightmares, the weaving of worlds - he was still here, still making jokes as if they were just facing another day at the mill.

The sun climbed higher, warming their faces as they stood wrapped in an embrace that spoke of survival, of family found and kept despite all odds. Below them, Somnara awakened to its first true morning in decades, but Liora barely noticed, lost in the profound gratitude of having her only father returned to her.

***

The roosters' crows pierced the dawn air as Rafe helped a wounded soldier to his feet. Strange, seeing the man's uniform - just moments ago they'd been trying to kill each other. Now the soldier gripped Rafe's arm in gratitude, tears streaming down his dirt-stained face.

All around the market square, similar scenes unfolded. Former enemies bound each other's wounds, shared water, exchanged names. The hatred and fear that had divided them melted away like morning frost. Rafe's chest tightened at the sight - how many lives could have been saved if they'd found this common ground sooner?

His gaze drifted up toward the palace spires, searching for any sign of Liora. The last he'd seen her, she'd vanished into the chaos of battle. Now an eerie calm had settled over Somnara, but his heart wouldn't rest until he knew she was safe.

Gemini appeared at his side, her satchel nearly empty from tending the wounded. "Have you seen her?" she asked, following his upward gaze. Rafe shook his head, unable to voice the fear gnawing at his gut.

A group of children ran past, laughing as they helped distribute bread from a nearby baker's cart. The sound startled him - when was the last time he'd heard children laugh in Somnara's streets? The city felt different now, as if a heavy shroud had been lifted.

The weight of his sword at his hip felt strange now, almost shameful. Rafe unbuckled the belt, letting the weapon clatter to the cobblestones. Around him, others did the same, armor and blades abandoned like shed snake skins in the growing light.

He thought of all the battles, all the losses that had led to this moment. Marcus, fallen defending a power he didn't understand. Nero's final sacrifice. The countless unnamed faces that haunted his dreams. Had it all been worth it for this single peaceful dawn?

Two palace guards approached, and Rafe tensed instinctively before noticing their weapons were sheathed. They nodded respectfully as they passed, heading to help clear debris from a collapsed market stall. The simple gesture nearly brought him to his knees - peace, actual peace.

But where was Liora? His heart wouldn't truly believe in this miracle until he saw her again, held her, knew she'd survived whatever confrontation had occurred atop the palace. The last time he'd kissed her felt like years ago now, though barely hours had passed.

Rafe watched Jayne's deft hands tie off a bandage around a soldier's arm. The man wore Draven's colors, yet Jayne treated him with the same care she showed their own wounded. Her usually stern expression had softened, replaced by something closer to peace. Beside her, Gemini moved from patient to patient, her gentle touch and kind words drawing grateful smiles from friend and former foe alike.

The sight stirred something in Rafe's chest - a mix of pride and lingering disbelief. These same soldiers had tried to kill them mere hours ago. Now they accepted help with quiet gratitude, their eyes clear of the shadow that had clouded them under Draven's control. One of them even clasped Gemini's hand, tears streaming down his face as he spoke of the horrors he'd committed while enslaved.

A commotion near the palace steps drew Rafe's attention. Two rebels escorted another wounded soldier past Kael Varden, who sat chained to a marble pillar. The former general's head hung low, but his posture lacked the tension that had defined him for so long. Even in chains, Varden seemed unburdened, as if Liora's victory had freed something within him too.

Rafe's hand instinctively moved to where his sword usually hung, finding only empty air. Old habits died hard. But watching Jayne share her waterskin with a former enemy, he realized those instincts might not serve him in this new world. Whatever Liora had done atop the palace had changed everything - had changed them all.

Rafe traced a finger along the rough stone of a fallen column, each scratch and nick reminding him of those who'd fallen. Marcus, charging headlong into danger to save others, his smile etched forever in Rafe's memory. Nero, whose wisdom and sacrifice had guided Liora when she needed it most. Even those whose names he never learned - rebels who'd given everything for a dream of freedom they wouldn't live to see.

The faces of the dead haunted him, their voices echoing in his mind. How many had died under his command? How many families had he failed to protect? The weight of command pressed down on his shoulders, heavier now in victory than it had ever felt in battle. Yet looking at the peaceful streets before him, at former enemies breaking bread together, perhaps their sacrifices had finally bought something worthwhile.

His thoughts drifted to the villagers who'd risked everything to shelter rebels, knowing discovery meant death. To Kael's father, who'd chosen execution over compromise. Each loss had been a stone in the foundation of this moment, their courage and defiance paving the way for Liora's victory.

A child's laughter pulled at his attention - the daughter of a baker who'd died in last month's raids. She played with a palace guard's helmet, her mother watching with tears in her eyes as the same guards who'd once terrorized them now protected their streets. The sight knocked the breath from Rafe's lungs. This was what they'd died for - not just peace, but the chance for joy to return to Somnus.

"All hail Liora!" The cry shattered his reverie, rippling through the crowd like lightning. Rafe's head snapped up toward the palace steps, his heart hammering against his ribs. The growing roar of voices drowned out his thoughts as people rushed forward, pushing past him toward whatever had caught their attention.

Rafe's heart lurched at the sight of Liora descending the palace steps, her slight frame supporting Bennet's weathered bulk. Her hair caught the morning light, gleaming like spun gold despite the grime and blood that streaked her face. She was alive. She was safe. The crushing weight that had settled in his chest since their separation finally lifted.

# Beyond the Veil

Golden light spilled across the palace steps as Liora guided Bennet down, her muscles trembling from exhaustion. The sight below made her heart swell - former enemies binding each other's wounds, children passing water to the injured, rebels embracing soldiers who had moments ago been their foes.

Her own body ached from channeling such immense power, but watching the people of Somnara come together filled her with a warmth that eased the pain. A merchant woman tore strips from her festival dress to bandage a rebel's arm while a palace guard held him steady. Two children - one from the city, one from the rebellion - shared a loaf of bread.

Bennet's weight grew heavier against her shoulder, his breaths coming in ragged gasps. Though he tried to hide it, she felt him stumbling more with each step. The torture he'd endured at Draven's hands had taken its toll, yet still he pressed on, determined to witness this moment of unity.

Movement caught her eye as Rafe sprinted up the steps toward them, his face streaked with blood and grime from battle. Her heart leaped at the sight of him, but instead of sweeping her into his arms as she'd imagined, Rafe immediately moved to Bennet's other side.

"Here, let me help," Rafe murmured, sliding his shoulder under Bennet's arm. The gentleness in his voice, the careful way he supported her mentor's weight - it made Liora's chest tighten with emotion. This was why she loved him - his instinct to care for others before himself.

Bennet tried to protest, but his legs buckled slightly. "I can manage," he insisted, though he leaned heavily on them both. Liora exchanged a knowing look with Rafe over Bennet's bowed head. Some things never changed - her stubborn mentor would always try to stand on his own.

Together they guided him down the remaining steps, their progress slow but steady. Each time Bennet stumbled, Rafe adjusted his grip without comment, preserving the older man's dignity while ensuring his safety. The simple kindness of it brought tears to Liora's eyes.

The crowd below had begun to notice their descent. Whispers rippled through the gathered people, faces turning upward. Liora heard whispers - "the Dreamweaver" - passed from person to person in tones of awe. She wanted to tell them she was just Liora, just the miller's apprentice, but she knew that girl was gone forever.

Someone started chanting her name, others quickly joining in. The sound swelled, echoing off the palace walls. Beside her, Bennet squeezed her shoulder. "They need their hero," he whispered. But when she looked at Rafe, she saw in his eyes what she needed most - not worship, but understanding.

Liora's legs trembled as she and Rafe finally reached the bottom of the palace steps. Her muscles screamed from supporting Bennet's weight, but she refused to let go until she knew he was safe.

A flash of familiar green fabric caught her eye as Gemini rushed forward, her satchel already open. Despite the exhaustion etched on her friend's face, Gemini's hands remained steady as she reached for Bennet.

"Let me see him," Gemini commanded, her voice carrying a new authority. The transformation in her friend - from gentle flower-crown weaver to battle-hardened healer - struck Liora deeply.

Relief flooded through Liora's body as Gemini guided Bennet to sit on a nearby crate, other healers quickly gathering around him. The weight of responsibility for her mentor lifted slightly, allowing her to focus on the man still standing beside her.

Rafe's hand found hers, his calloused fingers intertwining with her own. The simple touch grounded her, pulling her back from the edge of exhaustion that threatened to overwhelm her. His eyes searched her face, concern evident in the furrow of his brow.

"What happened up there?" Rafe asked softly, his thumb tracing circles on her palm. "Is Draven..." He trailed off, unable to finish the question that hung heavy in the air between them.

"He's gone," she whispered, the words tasting strange on her tongue. "Consumed by the very power he tried to control."

The memory of Draven's final moments flashed through her mind - his body crumbling as the corrupted magic ate away at him, his consciousness ripped from the mortal realm and bound to the dreamscape. She shuddered, and Rafe pulled her closer.

"The Ark?" he asked, his voice barely audible above the bustling crowd around them. His grip on her hand tightened slightly, as if afraid she might disappear.

"Destroyed," Liora replied, feeling the echo of its shattering still reverberating through her bones. She left out the part about Draven's eternal imprisonment in the dreamscape - some horrors were better left unspoken.

Liora's fingers trembled against Rafe's palm as the weight of what she'd done settled over her. The morning sun caught the remaining wisps of dream energy still floating through the air, golden threads that reminded her of her mother's presence in those final moments.

"The old Dreamweavers thought they needed to protect the dreamscape," she explained, watching a shimmer of power dance between their joined hands. "The Custodians believed they had to guard it. Even Draven..." Her voice caught on his name. "He wanted to use it as a weapon to control everyone else."

The memory of power coursing through her veins still burned, but it felt different now - not the raw, destructive force she'd feared, but something more natural, like breathing. Liora watched as a young girl nearby dozed against her mother's shoulder, a small smile playing on the child's lips as she dreamed freely for the first time.

"They were all wrong," Liora continued, her voice growing stronger. "The dreamscape was never meant to be separate, controlled, or guarded. It's part of us - all of us." She gestured to the people around them, former enemies now helping each other rebuild. "Dreams don't belong to the powerful. They belong to everyone."

Rafe's eyes widened as understanding dawned. "The Veilstone - you used it to-"

"To weave it all back together," Liora finished, remembering how it had felt to pull the fragments of reality and dreams into a single tapestry. "The way it was always meant to be. No more barriers, no more manipulation. Not just for Somnus, but for the whole world."

The enormity of the change she'd wrought hit her then - not just ending Draven's reign, but fundamentally altering how magic worked in their world. Some would call it blasphemy, others revolution. But watching the peace settle over Somnara, Liora knew it had been right.

"That's why the soldiers stopped fighting," Rafe realized, glancing at a group of Draven's former elite guard sharing water with rebels. "They're free to dream their own dreams now, not his."

A wave of exhaustion swept through Liora, making her sway slightly on her feet. Rafe steadied her, concern etching lines around his eyes. But she wasn't finished explaining - he needed to understand what this meant for their future.

"The power's still there," she murmured, feeling the gentle pulse of dream energy flowing through everything around them. "But now it's part of the natural order, the way it should be. No more masters, no more slaves to magic. Just people, free to dream and wake and live as they choose."

Liora's legs trembled with exhaustion as she leaned into Rafe's solid warmth, her face pressed against his chest. The familiar scent of leather and sweat mingled with the metallic tang of battle still clinging to his skin.

"I'm so proud of you," Rafe murmured into her hair, his voice rough with emotion. The simple words broke something inside her, releasing the tension she'd been holding since she first touched the Veilstone. She couldn't form a response, could only tighten her arms around him as tears threatened to spill.

The world narrowed to the steady beat of his heart against her cheek, the gentle rise and fall of his chest. After everything - the battles, the losses, the impossible choices - this moment felt like coming home. His hands traced soothing circles on her back, grounding her in the present.

A familiar squeal of joy pierced the air seconds before another body crashed into them. Gemini's arms wrapped around them both, her embrace fierce despite her smaller frame. Warmth bloomed in Liora's chest as she felt Gem's tears dampen her shoulder. The love radiating from her best friend - pure and unconditional - washed over her like sunlight. This was what she'd fought for, what she'd risked everything to protect.

"Get over here," Gem called out, her voice thick with emotion. Liora lifted her head to see Jayne hovering nearby, looking uncharacteristically uncertain. The spy's usual mask of cool detachment had cracked, revealing a vulnerability that made her seem younger.

For a heartbeat, Jayne hesitated, her body tense as if preparing to flee. Then Gem reached out and grabbed her hand, pulling her into their embrace. Liora felt Jayne's initial stiffness melt away as they enveloped her in their circle of arms and tears and laughter.

The four of them stood there, clinging to each other as the morning sun painted Somnara in shades of gold. Liora's heart felt too full, overflowing with love for these people who had become her family. Rafe's strength, Gem's unwavering faith, Jayne's hard-won trust - each had helped shape her into who she was meant to be.

Dream energy still shimmered in the air around them, responding to the intensity of emotion flowing between them. It danced like starlight, weaving them closer together. Liora could feel their individual dreams brushing against her consciousness - hopes for peace, for healing, for a future worth fighting for.

Through her tears, Liora caught glimpses of others watching their reunion - former enemies and allies alike, drawn to this moment of pure joy amid the aftermath of battle. Some were smiling, others wiping away their own tears. In that instant, she knew that this was what would truly heal Somnus - not magic or power, but love freely given and received.

***

The smell of smoke still clung to the air as Liora picked her way through the debris-strewn streets, supporting Bennet's weight against her shoulder. His familiar presence steadied her racing thoughts, grounding her in the simple task of putting one foot in front of the other. The morning sun cast long shadows across broken cobblestones and fallen weapons, painting the aftermath in shades of gold and grey.

Her heart clenched at the sight of a young boy helping an injured soldier - one of Draven's men - to his feet. The soldier's armor was stained with blood, but his eyes were clear now, free from the fog of magical control. The boy offered him water from a cracked flask, and something inside Liora shifted at their simple exchange of kindness.

"You did this," Bennet murmured, his voice rough from the torture he'd endured. "Not with magic, but with choice." His words carried the weight of pride, reminding her of countless hours in the mill when he'd taught her that the simplest actions often held the most meaning. Liora squeezed his arm gently, unable to speak past the lump in her throat.

A group of rebels emerged from a side street, carrying makeshift stretchers laden with the wounded. Among them, she recognized faces from both sides of the conflict - former enemies working together to save lives. The dream energy still flowing through the air responded to their unified purpose, shimmer like morning dew around their determined forms.

The sound of hammers rang out as others began clearing rubble, already starting the work of rebuilding. A woman's voice rose in song - an old lullaby Liora remembered from her childhood - and others joined in, the melody weaving through the ruins like a promise of renewal. Bennet hummed along softly, and Liora felt tears prick her eyes as she realized that this was true victory: not conquest or power, but people coming together to create something new from the ashes of the old.

The weight of countless sacrifices pressed against Liora's heart as she watched the people of Somnara working together. Her fingers traced the smooth surface of the Veilstone, feeling echoes of Nero's patient guidance in its warmth. The morning light caught the crystalline facets, reminding her of how his eyes had sparkled when she'd first managed to control her powers.

*They gave everything for this moment... it's now my duty to protect it.*

Memories of her mother's spirit flooded through her - Lyra's ethereal presence during the battle, her unwavering faith even as Draven's darkness had threatened to consume everything. The dream energy still flowing through the air carried whispers of her mother's last stand in the Ashen Dunes, of her choice to sacrifice herself rather than let Draven corrupt her power. Liora felt that same resolve burning in her chest now, a torch passed down through generations of Dreamweavers.

Marcus's face appeared in her mind - his initial distrust transformed into loyal friendship, cut short by Varden's betrayal. She remembered his final moments, how he'd believed in her even as his life slipped away. The memory of his sacrifice twisted like a knife, but it had helped forge her into someone strong enough to face Draven. Someone worthy of the trust these people now placed in her.

Beyond the physical reconstruction happening around her, Liora sensed the deeper mending taking place in the dreamscape she'd woven back into reality. Each act of kindness, each moment of forgiveness between former enemies, strengthened the fabric of this new world. Nero had taught her that power came with responsibility - not to control, but to nurture and protect. She felt the truth of his words now more than ever as she watched her people healing together.

Energy pulsed gently through her veins as she gazed across the awakening city. In every face she saw reflected the cost of this victory - the lives given, the sacrifices made, the faith kept through darkest nights. Bennet's steady presence beside her, Rafe's unwavering support, Gemini's loyal friendship - they were all threads in the tapestry she now had to preserve. The power within her settled into quiet resolve as she accepted this new role, not as a ruler, but as a guardian of the peace they'd all fought so hard to achieve.

Liora's steps faltered as they approached Kael Varden's hunched form. The former general slumped against his chains, dried blood caking the side of his face where he'd struck the ground during his fall. His once-proud bearing had crumbled, leaving only bitter defeat in its wake.

Bennet's leg shot out, aiming a kick at Varden's side, but Liora caught his arm. "No," she murmured, easing her mentor back. The dream energy still coursing through her veins heightened her awareness of Kael's turbulent emotions - fear, shame, and underneath it all, a desperate need to understand his own choices.

Kneeling before him, Liora reached out, her fingers gentle as she wiped away some of the blood from his temple. The contact sent a jolt through her - fragments of his memories, sharp with pain and regret, flickered at the edges of her consciousness.

"This peace you've created," Kael rasped, his voice barely above a whisper, "it's poisoned. Like everything touched by dream magic." His eyes, bloodshot but lucid, locked onto hers. "You have the Veilstone now. You've tasted what it can do. Are you here to take the rest of my mind?"

The accusation in Kael's voice cut deeper than any blade, stirring memories of that terrible night in the Ember Ruins. Liora's fingers trembled against his temple as she recalled how her power had exploded outward, fueled by grief and rage after Marcus's death. She'd torn through Kael's mental defenses like paper, leaving him screaming in the dust.

The dream energy rippled around them now, responding to her shame. Shadows of what she'd done flickered at the edges of her vision - the way she'd ripped through his memories, tearing them out root and stem. The Veilstone hummed against her chest, offering the power to do it again, to simply reach in and reshape his mind like clay.

"Please," Kael whispered, his proud bearing crumbling further. "Take it all away. The things I did for him, the people I..." His voice cracked. "I can still hear their screams. Every night, I hear them."

Liora withdrew her hand as if burned, fighting back the instinct to ease his pain. It would be so easy - just a gentle push with her power, smoothing away the rough edges of memory until peace remained. The temptation coiled through her like smoke.

"You have the power," Kael pressed, desperation bleeding into his tone. "You could give me peace. Isn't that what you fought for? What makes you better than him if you leave me like this?"

The words struck like physical blows, each one finding purchase in her deepest fears. Liora's power flared reflexively, golden light dancing around her fingers. For a heartbeat, she saw herself as Kael did - another wielder of dream magic, deciding the fate of others' minds.

But then she remembered Nero's lessons about choice and consequence. She thought of the villagers in Arcadia, their minds twisted by Draven's control. The horror she'd felt at seeing people reduced to puppets, their free will stripped away.

"The difference," Liora said softly, "is that I'm giving you a choice. Your memories - even the painful ones - they're yours. I won't take that from you, not even if you beg me."

"You'll face justice for what you've done," she continued, her voice growing stronger. "But you'll face it as yourself, with all your choices intact. That's the difference between Draven and me - I won't remake you into something else, no matter how much easier it might be."

The dream energy settled around them like falling snow as she rose to her feet. In its light, she could see the tears tracking down Kael's face, cutting clean lines through the blood and grime.

"I'm sorry," she whispered, the words catching in her throat. The admission felt small against the weight of her actions, but she forced herself to continue. "What I did to you - violating your mind like that - it was wrong."

His eyes widened slightly, confusion replacing the despair that had dominated his features. Liora felt his emotions shift through the dream energy - surprise, disbelief, and underneath it all, a flicker of something that might have been understanding. She resisted the urge to reach out with her power, to confirm what she sensed. That impulse itself proved how far she still had to go.

"I had no right," she continued, her voice stronger now despite the shame burning in her chest. The dream energy swirled around them, responding to her emotions, but she kept it firmly in check. "Whatever your crimes, whatever justice you face - it should never have included that. I became what I was fighting against, and for that, I truly am sorry." Movement caught her eye as more rebels approached with stretchers, and she knew this moment of truth between them would soon end.

Liora's boots scraped against broken cobblestones as she guided Bennet away from Kael's haunted gaze. The Veilstone pulsed against her hip with each step, its energy a constant reminder of the power she now carried. Her mind kept circling back to Kael's words, finding uncomfortable truth in his bitter warnings.

"You can't honestly believe what he said." Bennet's voice carried that familiar tone - the one he'd used when teaching her to work the mill, patient but firm. "About the magic being poison?" He stumbled slightly, and Liora tightened her grip on his arm, steadying him.

The weight of the Veilstone drew her eyes downward. Its crystalline surface caught the morning light, fracturing it into a thousand golden shards. Within its depths, she glimpsed echoes of what she'd done - the way she'd torn apart the barrier between dreams and reality, reshaped the very fabric of their world. Power like that could so easily corrupt, no matter how pure the intention.

Memories of the battle flashed through her mind - the rush of energy as she'd connected to both the Veilstone and the Ark, the heady sensation of holding two worlds in her grasp. She'd felt invincible in that moment, capable of anything. And wasn't that exactly how Draven's descent had begun? With the belief that his power gave him the right to reshape the world as he saw fit?

A child's laughter rang out nearby, pulling Liora from her dark thoughts. She watched as a young girl helped her father clear rubble from their doorstep, their movements in perfect sync despite their exhaustion. The sight stirred something in her chest - a reminder that true power lay not in control, but in connection. Yet still the Veilstone's energy thrummed against her palm, whispering of possibilities that both thrilled and terrified her.

Liora looked down at the Veilstone, hearing it's call. But did she have to answer?

# A New Beginning

The Veilstone hummed against Liora's palm as she gazed up at the temple's weathered façade. Memories of her first journey here flooded back - the fear, the uncertainty, the desperate need to claim this power before Draven could use it against them all. Now she returned with a different purpose, the weight of months spent rebuilding Somnus heavy on her shoulders.

Serra's latest report lay fresh in her mind. The scout captain had returned yesterday, speaking of other realms beyond Somnus's borders, realms where people were awaking to magic, where children woke with gifts beyond measure. The world was awakening, one soul at a time.

Not all the news brought joy. Some feared this resurgence of power, seeing echoes of Draven's tyranny in every unexplained occurrence. Others sought to control it, to bend this raw magic to their will just as the Emperor had done. But for each story of fear or greed, there were two more of wonder - of healing hands and protected homes, of crops coaxed from barren earth and storms turned aside from vulnerable villages.

Ancient stone steps stretched before her, worn smooth by centuries of forgotten footsteps. Behind her, she sensed more than heard her companions shifting restlessly - Rafe's protective tension, Gemini's quiet concern, Jayne's analytical assessment of possible threats, and Bennet's steady presence grounding them all. They'd argued against this decision, each in their own way, but had ultimately chosen to stand with her.

The temple's entrance seemed to breathe, wisps of ethereal energy dancing along carved symbols that now held new meaning for her. In the months since Draven's fall, she'd studied every scrap of lore about the Dreamweavers and the Custodians of the Veil she could find, understanding at last the true purpose of their power - not to control, but to connect.

Autumn leaves skittered across the threshold as Liora took her first step forward. The Veilstone's energy surged in response, as if recognizing its home. She'd felt its pull growing stronger with each passing day, its whispers of power becoming harder to ignore. Kael Varden's words still haunted her, and she'd seen the way some people watched her now - with the same fearful reverence they'd once reserved for Draven.

Golden light spilled from the Veilstone, illuminating the temple's interior in ways she hadn't noticed during her first visit. The walls told stories now - tales of Dreamweavers who'd walked this path before her, some rising to protect, others falling to the temptation of control. Her mother's presence seemed strongest here, as if Lyra's sacrifice had left an indelible mark on this sacred space.

A cool breeze whispered through the chamber, carrying the scent of ancient magic and newer possibilities. Liora's fingers traced the familiar contours of the Veilstone, remembering how it had felt to weave dreams and reality together. The power had been intoxicating, but she understood now that it wasn't meant to be wielded by any single person, no matter how pure their intentions.

Each step deeper into the temple felt like moving through layers of time itself. Liora sensed the echoes of past Dreamweavers, their triumphs and failures etched into the very stones. Some had sought to protect, others to rule, but none had truly understood what she'd learned in these past months - that the greatest power lay in letting go.

The chamber where she'd first claimed the Veilstone lay ahead, its crystalline altar catching the light that streamed through ancient windows. This time, however, she didn't feel the pull of destiny or the weight of prophecy. Instead, she felt something lighter, clearer - the certainty of choice rather than the burden of fate.

The Veilstone pulsed in her hands, as if acknowledging what was to come. She'd made her decision months ago, really - had known it since that moment with Varden in the courtyard. Now it was simply time to act.

Tears pricked at Liora's eyes as she traced the ancient symbols carved into the altar. Each marking told a story of choice - Dreamweavers who had stood where she stood now, facing the same temptation. Some had chosen power, others protection, but none had seen what she now understood with crystal clarity.

"The Veilstone was never meant to rule," Liora declared, her voice steady despite the emotion threatening to overwhelm her. "It's a guardian, a promise to protect, and that's what I'll honor." The words rang true through the chamber, seeming to resonate with the very stones themselves.

Golden light spilled from between her fingers as she lifted the Veilstone one final time. Its power called to her, sweet and seductive, promising everything she could ever want. But Liora saw past the temptation now, to the deeper truth that lay beneath.

With trembling hands, she placed the Veilstone back upon its ancient pedestal. "Until another needs you, I let you rest," Liora whispered, her fingers lingering for just a moment on the stone's smooth
surface. The power that had been a constant presence in her mind
these past months began to recede, leaving behind a profound sense
of peace.

The Veilstone's glow dimmed as Liora stepped back, leaving behind
not just an artifact but a part of herself she'd grown accustomed to
carrying. The power that had hummed beneath her skin these past
months ebbed away like a retreating tide, leaving her feeling both
lighter and strangely hollow. Her fingers tingled with phantom energy,
muscle memory searching for a connection that no longer existed.

The familiar warmth of her mother's presence bloomed beside her,
and Liora's breath caught in her throat. Lyra's ethereal form shimmered in the temple's filtered light, more solid than she'd appeared
since that final battle. The proud smile on her mother's face made
Liora's heart ache with a peculiar mixture of loss and triumph.

They stood together in companionable silence, watching the Veilstone settle into its ancient home. The crystal's surface caught stray
beams of sunlight, throwing rainbow patterns across the chamber
walls that danced like dreams taking flight. How strange that something so beautiful could hold such terrible potential for destruction.

Liora flexed her empty hands, remembering the weight of responsibility she'd carried. The choice to let go hadn't been easy, but it felt
right - like waking from a long dream into a clearer morning. Without
the constant hum of the Veilstone's power, she could hear her own
thoughts more clearly, feel her own heart beating steady and sure.

The temple air shifted around them, carrying whispers of ancient
magic that felt different now - less demanding, more like the gentle
reminder of a promise kept. Lyra's presence beside her anchored Liora

in this moment of transition, this space between who she had been and who she would become. The power might be gone, but something else remained - something stronger than magic, more enduring than stone.

Together they remained in the sacred space, daughter and mother motionless as time slipped past, both treasuring these final precious minutes they would share in each other's presence.

*** 

Liora emerged from the temple's shadow into piercing sunlight, her steps lighter than they'd been in months. The ancient stones behind her held secrets again, mysteries she no longer needed to understand. A laugh bubbled up from somewhere deep inside her, surprising even herself with its unfettered joy.

"Just normal Liora Solari again," she called out to her waiting friends, spreading her empty hands wide. The gesture felt strange without the familiar pulse of the Veilstone's power thrumming beneath her skin. Her fingers tingled with its absence, like a phantom limb she'd have to learn to live without.

Bennet's weathered face crinkled with understanding as he leaned on his walking stick, while Gemini beamed at her with tears gathering in the corners of her eyes. Even Jayne's usual stern expression had softened into something approaching a smile. But it was Rafe's gaze that caught and held her attention - the pride and love there made her heart skip.

The forest around them whispered with ordinary magic now - sunlight filtering through leaves, birds calling to their mates, the subtle shift of shadows as clouds passed overhead. Liora breathed it all in, savoring how different everything felt without the constant weight of power pressing against her consciousness. The world seemed both smaller and larger at the same time, more immediate and real.

"Normal was never the word I'd use for you," Rafe murmured as she reached the group, his hand finding hers with familiar warmth. Liora squeezed his fingers, noting how the simple touch held more magic than all the power she'd just surrendered.

Liora's boots crunched against the transformed landscape of what had once been the Ashen Dunes. Where desolate sands had stretched endlessly just months ago, patches of grass now pushed through the earth like stubborn hopes refusing to die. The sight of children playing among newly restored homes in Dunrow made her chest tighten with an emotion she couldn't quite name.

A merchant's cart rattled past, the owner calling out prices for fresh bread and vegetables. The scent of baking made Liora's stomach growl, reminding her of mornings at Bennet's mill. Behind her, she heard Gemini haggling with the merchant, probably ensuring the new settlers had enough to eat. Some habits died hard, even after everything they'd been through.

The statue appeared around a bend in the road, and Liora's steps faltered. Sunlight caught the carved stone features of her mother's face, softening them in a way that made her heart ache. The artist had captured Lyra's determination, the set of her jaw that Liora sometimes glimpsed in her own reflection. But they'd missed the laugh lines around her eyes, the gentle curve of her smile that Liora remembered from her dreams.

Her companions fell silent as she approached the memorial. Even the wind seemed to still, as if holding its breath. Liora's knees met the packed earth before the statue's base, her head bowing under the weight of memory and gratitude. The stone was cool against her forehead as she pressed it to the inscription: "Lyra Solari - Who Gave All For Somnus."

The words felt inadequate. They spoke nothing of her mother's laughter, or how she'd sing while working in their small garden. They couldn't capture the fierce love that had driven her to face Draven, knowing she might not return. Liora's fingers traced the carved letters, remembering the ghostly touch of her mother's hand on her cheek in the dreamscape.

A child's laughter pierced the solemn moment, and Liora looked up to see a young girl throwing seeds to ground-birds nearby. The sight brought a fresh wave of emotion - this was what her mother had died protecting. What she herself had almost sacrificed everything to safeguard. The simple joy of a child at play, unafraid and free to dream.

The sun warmed her back as she remained kneeling, aware of Rafe's steady presence behind her left shoulder, of Gemini's quiet sniffles, of Jayne's respectful distance. Bennet's walking stick scraped against the ground as he shifted his weight, reminding her that some survived to see this peace. Her mother would have liked that thought.

Something brushed against her consciousness - not the overwhelming power of the Veilstone, but a gentler awareness. The dreamscape might be woven into the world now, but some connections remained. For just a moment, Liora felt her mother's presence, as real as the stone beneath her fingers.

"Thank you," she whispered, the words carrying more than simple gratitude. Thank you for showing me the way. For teaching me that power isn't meant for control. For loving me enough to let me find my own path. The breeze caught her hair, carrying the scent of wildflowers - her mother's favorite.

Standing took more effort than she'd expected, her legs stiff from kneeling. But as she rose, Liora felt lighter somehow. The statue would remain here, marking not just what was lost, but what had been gained. New life sprouting from the ashes of sacrifice, just as her mother would have wanted. She turned back to her friends, ready to continue their journey home.

Liora's fingers traced the familiar calluses on Bennet's hands as they walked away from her mother's memorial, remembering countless hours of work at the mill. The roughness spoke of years of dedication, of early mornings and late nights spent teaching her everything he knew. Those hands had guided her through more than just the craft of milling - they'd steadied her when her world threatened to spin apart.

"Not sure what I'm supposed to do without my apprentice now," Bennet sighed, though his eyes crinkled with the hint of a smile. "Who's going to sort the winter wheat from the spring?"

"Don't worry," Liora laughed, the sound catching in her throat. "I'm coming back to help rebuild the mill. All of Eldara, actually." The words felt right as they left her lips, like puzzle pieces clicking into place. Her gaze drifted to where wildflowers had begun pushing through the scorched earth - nature's own rebellion against destruction.

"And after that?" Bennet's question drew her eyes to Rafe, who stood a respectful distance away, deep in conversation with Jayne. Heat crept up her neck as Bennet followed her gaze, his knowing smile making her feel like a girl with her first crush rather than a woman who'd faced down an emperor. His gentle chuckle told her he'd caught the direction of her thoughts.

Bennet's arms enveloped her in a familiar embrace that smelled of flour and sawdust. "I'm so proud of the woman you've become, Li," he whispered against her hair. "Not the power, symbol, or any of that - the woman." Liora buried her face in his shoulder, breathing in the scent of home as tears pricked at her eyes.

Liora stepped back from Bennet's embrace, her heart full and aching. The familiar scent of flour still lingered, but her attention shifted as she caught Rafe's gaze across the weathered stone path. He nodded to Jayne, already moving toward Liora with that familiar determined stride that had first drawn her eye in Eldara.

The warmth of Rafe's calloused palm against hers sent a flutter through Liora's chest as they fell into step together. His touch felt different now - more immediate, more real without the constant hum of dream magic between them. The afternoon sun painted long shadows across their path as they walked away from her mother's memorial, leaving the weight of prophecies and power behind.

"After we rebuild Eldara," Rafe's voice held a note of hesitation she rarely heard from him, "what then?" His thumb traced circles on her skin, each movement sparking tiny shivers that had nothing to do with magic and everything to do with being purely, wonderfully human.

Liora's heart jumped as she realized she could answer honestly, without the burden of destiny shaping her choices. "I want to see your home," she said, watching his expression shift from surprise to something deeper. "Help you rebuild your village, the way you helped save mine." The words tumbled out easier than she'd expected, carrying dreams of a future she'd never dared imagine during the war.

A familiar hand slipped into her free one, and Liora turned to find Gemini's bright eyes and determined smile. "Well, you're not leaving me behind this time," Gem declared, squeezing Liora's fingers. "Someone has to keep you two from getting into trouble."

Laughter bubbled up from somewhere deep inside Liora, pure and unfettered by fear or responsibility. It rang out across the transformed landscape, drawing curious glances from passing travelers. But for once, she didn't care who stared - she was just a girl, holding hands with the people she loved most, dreaming of tomorrow without the weight of prophecy on her shoulders. The sound of her joy mingled with Gemini's giggles and Rafe's deep chuckle, weaving together in a harmony sweeter than any magic she'd ever wielded.

Liora's cheeks warmed as Rafe leaned close, his breath tickling her ear. The familiar scent of leather and sword oil wrapped around her, making her heart skip. "I'd love for Gem to join us," he murmured, eyes twinkling with mischief, "but maybe she can find a new bunk-mate." His playful tone sent a shiver down her spine that had nothing to do with the cool breeze.

The words died in her throat as she caught sight of Jayne's fingers sliding between Gemini's. The usually stoic spy's expression had softened, her sharp edges melting away under Gem's radiant smile. Something clicked into place in Liora's mind - all those shared moments, the lingering glances, the way Jayne had slowly opened up to them both.

"I don't think that will be a problem," Liora whispered back to Rafe, unable to keep the grin from spreading across her face. She squeezed his hand, remembering how her own love had bloomed amid chaos and destruction. Perhaps it was fitting that peace would bring more such connections, weaving their lives together in ways that needed no magic to sustain them.

The afternoon sun caught the silver threads in Jayne's dark hair, highlighting the gentle way she tucked a stray curl behind Gem's ear. The gesture was so tender, so unlike the hardened warrior who'd first challenged Liora's control over her powers. Gem's resulting blush reminded Liora of sunrise over Eldara's hills - soft, warm, and full of promise.

A memory surfaced - Gem telling her that being human meant finding love in unexpected places. Back then, Liora had been too consumed by fear and power to truly understand. Now, watching her dearest friend find happiness with someone who'd once doubted them both, she felt the truth of those words deep in her bones. The world might have changed, but some magic existed without need of stones or prophecies.

The evening shadows lengthened as Liora watched her friends walk ahead, their silhouettes merging with the golden light of sunset. Her fingers still tingled where the Veilstone's power had once pulsed, but the absence felt right now - like setting down a heavy burden she'd carried for too long. A breeze caught her hair, carrying the scent of autumn leaves and woodsmoke from distant homes.

Her gaze drifted to Rafe's broad shoulders, to the way Gemini's hand remained intertwined with Jayne's, and her heart swelled with a different kind of magic. These people had stood beside her through darkness and light, through moments when her power had threatened to consume everything. They'd believed in her humanity when she'd doubted it herself. The thought brought a smile to her lips - they'd helped her become something entirely new.

What she'd told Draven in those final moments hadn't just been defiance. The truth of it resonated deeper with each passing day. Her mother had been the last of the old ways, the last Dreamweaver, carrying the burden of separation between dreams and reality. But Liora had chosen a different path, weaving the worlds together instead of trying to control them. The power didn't need to be contained or guarded - it needed to be shared, understood, embraced as part of the whole.

A child's laughter rang out from a nearby settlement, and Liora caught glimpses of dream magic dancing in the air around the playing children - visible now to anyone who chose to see it. No more barriers, no more secrets. The dreamscape belonged to everyone, just as it always should have. Her role wasn't to be its keeper but its teacher, helping others understand the magic that had always been part of them.

"Coming?" Rafe called back to her, his voice carrying traces of concern. Liora quickened her steps to catch up, her boots crunching against the transformed earth of what had once been the Ashen Dunes. She was no longer the last or the first of anything - she was simply Liora Solari, walking toward tomorrow with the people she loved. The rest would unfold as it should, one dream at a time.

# *Afterword*

Thank you.

If you've made it to this page, that means you've journeyed through *The Last Dreamweaver*—through dreams and nightmares, through struggles and revelations, through every moment that brought these characters to life. And for that, I am endlessly grateful.

Writing this story has been an adventure, one that I hope resonated with you in some way. Stories have a way of connecting us across time, space, and experience, weaving unseen threads between the storyteller and the reader. If even one moment in this book lingered with you, then this journey was worth every word.

If you'd like to dive deeper into the world of *The Last Dreamweaver*, I invite you to visit my website: www.emlucas.com. There, you'll find additional insights into the world, behind-the-scenes thoughts, and updates on upcoming projects. More importantly, by joining my newsletter, you'll gain access to *The Tavern*, a short story that unveils the fate of Rafe's family—a tale that carries its own weight of tragedy and resilience.

And this is just the beginning.

Stay tuned for the next adventure in the Dreamer Saga, *The Fallen Elyssian*. In this new tale, you'll meet a princess who leaves her floating city to discover a world she never expected to find, truths that will rock her to her core, and romance in the most unlikely of places. I can't wait to share the next chapter with you.

Until then, dream boldly, live fiercely, and never stop seeking the stories that move you.

With gratitude, E.M. Lucas.

.